Digging For Nightmares

Digging For Nightmares

"The Deeper You Read The Darker It Gets"

Steven R. General

As each page turns darkness creeps ever closer. (The cut version.) Adult 18+ only please.

Cover and design by SelfPubBookCovers.com/SongandSerenity

Please report any errors in text for corrections to the author at: blueauthor.15@gmail.com

Thank you.

Electronic Book ISBN: 978-1-988103-00-6

Book ISBN: 9781988103020
ISBN-10: 1988103029

TABLE OF CONTENTS

"Our hearts are wild creatures, that's why our ribs are cages."
— ELALUSZ

"When the lion kills, don't hate him. He's only being a lion. For he was once a cub --- cute and cuddly, playful and smiling but then one day the lion roars and he has lost his innocence forever. His world shall never be the same."

LUCAS

PROLOGUE

*Lost. Have you ever been truly lost? Not just in the physical sense
but lost in every sense of fibre that is your life and being. When
the mental, the physical, the spiritual, and the emotional become
forever lost in the fires of Hell. And even within the fires of Hell
there is no light --- only the darkness of the night now in days.
When you lose your way --- lose your soul --- there is only the abyss
of nothingness. Existence is non-existence and the heart becomes
an empty vessel of heart beating echoes without sound. You doubt
everything you thought you knew. When that dark door opens and
seizes your soul --- you lose the right to be called "Human."*

KYLE

She lay screaming on the ground as he stood above her --- looking down at her pleading eyes. He had just taken off her blindfold and gag and there was the look of utter terror on her face. She was a young girl --- barely eighteen years old and she now knew what was going to happen to her. Before that she was afraid but now she was terrified. The kind of terrified where one's heart feels like it is leaving the living chest. No one to hear her screams --- no one to help her. There would be no escape --- no rescue --- no hero on a white horse for her. She was alone in the wilderness looking up at a strange young man who had no heart. He didn't care. She had some marks on her young supple body. Some cuts and bruises and some burns but he kept her face unmarked. The girl was only marked a bit --- this time. She tried talking to him --- telling him he didn't have to do this --- that she wouldn't tell anyone --- that she had family and friends that loved her and that she was a good girl. "Just let me go," she pleaded, "I won't tell anyone." He just smiled at her as he started digging with the shovel. This time he was going to bury the girl --- alive --- not like those other times yet to come. He needed to experiment --- after all he was just learning how to do this. He was the young Zenith just beginning to rise to it's powerful apex. He had played those scenes over and over again in his head and now was the beginning. He relished and cherished the moment. He wanted to take a few pictures so he could enjoy them later but he knew that would be too dangerous if the police found them. He saved the pictures in his mind. He wondered how deep he should dig her grave? What would be a good depth? He didn't want to overwork or over do it --- the depth that is. Then again he wanted to make sure she would remain hidden --- so no person or animal could discover her. He had measured her so he dug the grave only a bit longer and wider than she was. He wanted a snug fit --- like a nice leathered Gucci glove that needed to be tugged on --- and he took his time digging. He wanted her to think about it as long as possible. It was a contradiction because he was on a time frame as well. He kept looking down at her as she kept pleading --- crying --- trying to get him to talk more. He didn't feel like talking though. He wanted to listen --- listen to her.

He noticed some crows nearby --- looking down at him from above. In his mind they were crowing to him saying --- "That's it … bury her alive! Bury all of them." That's what the crows seemed to be saying to him. He paused many times just to stare at her --- and to smile. He looked up at the crows and they stared down at him --- and her. The crows were hopping on the branches above and off to the side --- their heads tilting every now and then to survey the scene below and to get a better view he surmised. They seemed to be enjoying it. Perhaps they were waiting for food --- or to be entertained as well? He imagined they were smiling down at him. When the grave was ready he purposely lay down beside her and asked her to convince him to let her go.

"Why should I let you go?" He asked as he studied her face more closely. It was so youthful looking --- the skin baby like. He looked into her emerald greenish eyes. "You have a chance to stop me from doing this you know. Now is your chance. Go ahead --- talk to me --- convince me."

She asked him why? "Why are you doing this to me? Please don't." She sobbed some more.

He just smirked a smile --- paused and then answered her. "Because I can Darling."

She lay there crying --- blubbering --- telling him what she thought he wanted to hear. "I'll be your girlfriend --- the best girlfriend you could ever want. I'll do anything for you --- anything --- whenever you want. I could be your partner and help you get other girls."

That last remark surprised him --- about her helping him get other girls. "But I don't need a girlfriend --- or a partner and I can get other girls just fine. Nice of you to offer though." He knew she would do or say anything to try and get away from the inevitable. A short pause and then he added, "Anything else you want to say to try and change my mind?" Her eyes were looking deep into his greyish steely cold eyes. She just knew.

"Tell my Mom and Dad and little Sister that I love them please," she sobbed as tears rolled down the sides of her pitiful face.

"No," he said looking at her as he half smiled. "I don't work for the fucking post office."

He stared at her --- watching her helplessness --- enjoying every second of it. There was a strange kind of silence for the next few moments. He looked up and the crows were just looking down --- waiting. They seemed to know. He stroked her soft hair and he told her that she would have been a beautiful woman. "You would have been a beautiful woman," he gently whispered in her ear. She started to cry again --- this time louder. Then he lifted her up and she started screaming and struggling as he delicately placed her into the grave --- like some fragile piece of precious ancient pottery. He put her on her back so she could stare up at the trees for a few minutes --- and at him. The grave was a perfect fit. He stood there admiring it --- admiring her --- admiring his work. He took his time putting the dirt on her --- saving her face for last. No face covering for her --- she didn't deserve it. He wanted her to look into his eyes as long as possible. She struggled violently for those last few moments but she couldn't stop the dirt from covering her. She was really screaming now. "I don't want to die --- I want to live." She tried spitting up at him as he began to throw the dirt down upon her face. She was swearing at him --- calling him every name in the book. *He was right. He knew she was a bad girl.* He smiled at her feeble attempts. He took his time --- like a good meal --- this was the dessert.

After --- he sat by the grave staring at it for a few minutes. He could hear her struggling beneath the dirt and trying to move. He could hear her muffled coughing sounds under the dirt until it became less and less. Then there was a peaceful silence at first --- but then the crows. Their approbation seemed to be so much louder than before as they hopped branch-to-branch, shouting down to him in their excitement. He looked up at them as they stared down at him in admiration. He smiled.

He wanted the moment to last. He decided he would put some rocks on top of the dirt --- on top of her --- for an extra measure of entrapment. They would serve as her tombstones --- her markers for eternity. Then again he didn't want it to look like a grave so he did his best to disguise them as just a bunch of rocks like any other rocks in the forest. He put his ear down on the grave before he left forever and just listened --- but he heard nothing --- only the slight breeze rustling the leaves as the crows now were watching in silence. Suddenly a picture flashed in his head of maggots. He sighed and smiled. He wanted to remember this moment forever. There would be many more. He was just beginning to find his destiny. It was at that moment when he realized for the first time in his life that he felt truly alive --- and happy.

CHAPTER 2

September 28

And then I woke up. I'm absolutely drenched in a cold sweat realizing it was just another dream --- another terrible nightmare. I've had that particular dream twice now. My nightmares continue to punish me. My name is Kyle --- Kyle Krycanta and I'm going to Hell. They're buried out there. They're buried all over the place. All of them --- twenty-six that I know of and it is a total shock to me. And I'm starting to believe there could be even more girls waiting to come to me in my dreams? I had no idea that I did it --- that I was responsible. That's the truth. All those girls under the dirt --- under the rocks and sticks --- in the muck and the quagmire scattered in the forests and fields across the country like some unwanted seeds deposited in the darkness of the soil. Buried like one buries the garbage or refuse with the bugs crawling all over them feasting and laying their filthy eggs. The girls --- their eyes open --- at least for a while until they decompose. That is what I imagined. I guess I didn't close their eyes like in the movies. I still have trouble believing I did it though? It can't be true but it is? It must be --- I proved it! I shook the drowsiness from my head and started the car. Really I was nothing but a kid when the first one was taken and here I am driving to another possible grave. Driving down some back-country road that looks only semi-familiar to me. It is like a déjà vu to me that suddenly appears from another lifetime. That comes to me out of the dark shadows of my hideous secret nightmares. They come to me in bits and pieces you know --- the memories that is --- like some rotten jigsaw puzzle in my mind asking to be put together --- demanding to be put together --- relentless that they be put together and there is no order to them. No rhyme or reason in the order. They don't stop until I go to prove them. I liked it better before when no one knew --- when I didn't know the truth --- the horrible truth of what I really was or what I really am --- what I have become. *I liked it better when I felt like I deserved to go to Heaven.* When I had a chance to go to Heaven. When I had no conscience. When I didn't know. How I wish I could return to those not knowing times. I was happier then. Life seemed more valuable and worth living. When I could feel the sun shining on my face and feel it's warmth and welcome. Now when I see or feel the sun I just think of Hell. I wish I didn't have a conscience. I wish I didn't feel the smothering blanket of guilt. It sucks for me. How I wish I could go back in time and make it better. Will I ever get used to it? Will I ever be able to become normal again and not think about it every day and every night? I hope so because if I can't somehow figure out how I'm going to live with it --- with this horrible truth --- how am I ever going to survive with such terrible memories haunting me day and night? If I can't, that is going to be a very big problem for me.

Everything is different for me now. My life is different. I sleep different --- I think different --- food taste different --- the air I breathe smells like the stench of rotting bodies. It's like I am suddenly someone else --- someone I don't know or trust. Someone I didn't know existed in me. I'm afraid of myself. I don't trust myself to be around people anymore.

I have to wonder about the Police? Where were the Police? Why couldn't they stop me all those years ago? All those times? I must have left clues? I mean I was really an amateur back then. Will the Police come for me one day? It's been so many years? I don't think they're ever coming to get me. Unless I confess or get caught digging up a grave as I check for yet another buried nightmare --- another buried truth. It's risky going back to dig up these graves but I can't help myself. I'm driven to prove to myself that maybe this time it was just a dream. And I'm wondering if anyone else went to prison for doing something that I was responsible for? Someone who was really innocent --- that would really suck for them. I don't think I deserve to live.

I started to think about all those families out there, not knowing where their daughters or sisters are, their nieces or their aunts or their mothers, their wives. Not knowing if they are alive or dead --- not knowing where they are or what happened to them or having closure. They don't want to know what happened! I know that! Yet I can't tell them now that I know. There is turmoil in me of knowing the great evil I keep and that I continue to keep --- the terrible secret in my soul --- if I have one --- a soul that is? I really don't think I have one? I mean how could I now? I know if I do have a soul I am damned. Many would call me a monster --- a demon. I couldn't blame them for thinking like that. Maybe I am a monster but I don't feel like one. I don't feel like a murderer --- like a wild ruthless animal --- like a human predator. It is a strange situation. I do and I don't feel like a wild animal. Can I even explain what I'm feeling? Finding out something that isn't just a dream but has metamorphosed into the new reality. Even after a year of finding out it is still shocking to me. It's still hard to believe that I did those horrible things. Yet I have found many of them in the last year and those memories that are now haunting me are now my ugly reality. I don't like it and I no longer like what I am --- but the reality is I must face it --- that I can't ever take it back. I can't kiss it and make it go away. I can't make it all better. I want to be forgiven --- but I am a walking unhallowed soul --- or I am soulless? I don't deserve to be forgiven.

I grew up different than everyone else that I knew. At least I think so. As a kid I grew up in a family with three sisters and a brother and a mom and dad --- nothing abnormal about that. I was the youngest child. We weren't all that close. I used to be close to my brother. Funny thing was I was real close to mom. That is what I don't understand? Mom was the one that taught me ethics and morality. She taught me what was right and wrong. Sometimes it is her voice in my head telling me to be good. I guess it didn't work though? That's what I don't understand? Dad --- well --- he would just beat the shit out of me if I did anything he didn't like. Sorry, I don't usually swear. I try not to swear.

I got weights for Christmas when I was twelve years old and started exercising to become stronger. And I was a good athlete and played a number of different sports. By the time I was fifteen, Dad could no longer beat me up. I had become too strong for him. But I still have to question how I could do all these terrible things for all those years and not even know? I had no clue. That's the truth.

When I say I grew up different I mean I didn't feel things like most other kids. At least that is what I think now? I know it may be hard to believe but I just didn't think of them like people back then. Not really. Trying to think how to explain it? I didn't feel love is how I can explain it. It was like it didn't really exist to me. Like it was a shallow emotion and all fake. I'm not making excuses but I am trying to explain not just to you but also to me how this is even possible? I don't think my mom and dad had a true, real loving relationship. Correct that. I know they didn't. Maybe that's part of it? I'm not sure. This self-analyzing isn't working very well for me. I had few real friends. Oh, I played with other kids but it was different for me. I wasn't anti-social by any means. I could be quite social and charming when I needed to be --- when it was required --- when it was necessary. That is how I got some of the girls ... not all were taken like that. Some were just opportunistic snatches. They were in the wrong place at the wrong time with the wrong --- predator. You have to be aware of your surroundings you know. There is not just the physical camouflage to worry about. You have to worry about the spiritual camouflage --- if I can refer to it that way. Things are not always what they seem. That is what is so obvious to me but not to those girls that are now buried in their unmarked graves. They made mistakes and it cost them their lives --- their families --- and their futures. We are all animals when you think of it. Sounds asinine to even say it but it is so true. *Some just have that extra wilderness in them and are more dangerous to their prey.* Some animals in the wild kingdom seem so pretty and innocent and safe but are really the most dangerous forms of life there can be. I guess that is my category. I look safe but obviously I'm not. That is what I've discovered about myself. What all those girls discovered too late.

I've only had a couple of girlfriends through all those years --- in my life that is --- at least so far. Sounds strange to say at least so far. The relationships were short, usually only a few weeks or a few months. I did have one that lasted a couple of years when I was younger. That was just sex though --- at least for me it was. She wanted more --- I could tell but the truth is I grow tired of the same old sex with the same old person and the same old conversations. I get bored very quickly. Still I give her credit for lasting that long. In the end we decided to go our separate ways.

I have to turn right on this next gravel road. Not too much further to go. I always look behind me --- to make sure I'm not being followed. And I look up to the sky in case there is a helicopter or a plane. Always have a full tank of gas and make sure the car is tuned and in good shape. I carry tools for the car --- always have. You definitely don't want your car to breakdown at the wrong time --- in the wrong place. I never had to do these types of things before the memories came to me. Then again I was probably doing it all along but not remembering doing it?

This one will be number twenty-seven if she's there. I think it's a safe bet that I'm going to find her there. God I hope she isn't. Just once I'd like to be wrong. I didn't bury them too deep but they are all buried out of the way in some off beaten piece of earth. By the way, I guess I made certain not to kill any girls that I knew or was personally connected to that might lead back to me. I was a stranger to every one of my girls. I read where most girls killed are killed by someone they know --- an acquaintance or family member. Not me though. And now that I remember a bit more I know there were a few acquaintances or family that I felt like killing. I was daydreaming though. I would never do it --- I think? It would have been so easy but there was more risk and risk like that I don't need. I'm learning as I go you know. Or am I relearning how to kill? My mind is a total mess.

It is late September now and the leaves are changing colours. I remember as a kid I used to like playing in the leaves. Now the leaves hold a different meaning for me. They look nice and so very pretty with all those colours cascading down the roadside in the wind as my car drives by. Some leaves are on the ground with the reds, the yellows, the browns, and the oranges. Like a colourful blanket of rainbow leaves covering all my graves --- the truth --- and so much more. I can appreciate the good things in life --- the beauty that surrounds me in nature and the sunrises and sunsets. The red leaves remind me of blood, and the other coloured leaves of the rotting dead flesh of the girls. Yet, even with that I can't help but think how grand nature is ... how beautiful they look like that. Much better than if they were green again. *The leaves look better and prettier dead than alive.* I've heard people say that looking at their relative in the casket --- *"Oh look at Aunt Marie --- she looks so peaceful and happy lying there."* What a strange thing to say at a funeral?

There are no cars out here on the back road. I haven't seen anyone or a car for the last few miles. Still I must be careful. I'm pretty sure this particular grave is only a few yards off the road to the right. In the beginning I guess I mostly buried the girls further back in the bush? Not always though? I call it the bush but it is really just the forest where the trees are. That was the beginning though. I've discovered that later I would bury them just off the roadway and spent less time covering them up. Hell, why should I work up a sweat carrying some dead soulless weight? And I was in a hurry I guess. It is still a little fuzzy to me. I wish the nightmares would stop. I wish they would just go away --- and the memories. *GOD --- I could use a little help here!*

As I get closer I find that I'm starting to breath heavier now. My heart rate has increased. It always does that when I get close. It won't be long now until I discover another terrible truth. I brought my trusty shovel so I can check. *I hate my shovel.* I even have a story if I'm stopped and they ask why I have this steel shovel. You see I have an interest in rocks. I collect them --- fossils to be more specific. I make sure I have some samples in my car to you know --- back up the story if I need to. To give my story more credence and substance so the cops would believe it. I never had to use it though --- my back-up story. I have never been questioned or stopped by the cops about the shovel or anything much. At least I don't think so? And I always travel the speed limit and obey the laws. Oh wait --- I was stopped once when I had a girl in the trunk. I remember one of my dreams now.

She was unconscious and not quite dead yet. The cop never even knew. He was just checking for seatbelts. What an ass! You have to be cool no matter what. I would have been a great poker player. From what I can remember I'm pretty sure I would have had to kill that cop if he was any better at his job. Lucky for him he was more interested in making sure my seatbelt was buckled. What am I talking about --- killing somebody like it is nothing? Killing a cop! I am messed up.

I know I have something wrong with me? Like an amnesia or a sickness or a virus or something? But I don't remember bumping my head. Or I have some kind of split personality disorder I don't know about? Kind of like that scene from the Boston Strangler movie. Yea --- that might be a good example? Or maybe I'm like that Sybil character with Multiple Personality Disorder? That is what the psychiatrists call it. I have no idea though? Otherwise how could I not know or remember all those girls through all those years?

The nightmares are so vivid and real. I would see a girl's face --- her eyes and hear her screams. Sometimes I would see their hands or feet. Little bits and pieces of the past I guess. These dreams are devouring my soul if I can put it that way, releasing the awful truth. Oh, I said I don't think I have a soul like regular people. Maybe all predators don't have a soul? Fuck --- my life sucks right now! I swore again. I don't like to swear. What is happening to me? It's like I have lost control.

Little bits of information were released to me about what happened, where they were and so that is when I started to go looking --- to go digging. I just had to know. The nightmares are forever harassing me. And after finding more and more of them --- the girls I mean --- well --- I just couldn't stop looking. I'm trapped --- trapped in Hell. *I'm digging up my nightmares.* Perhaps I should have just stopped but this may be difficult to believe but I actually worry about something. I've been wondering if there are any girls that are recent? If I'm still doing it and not knowing I'm doing it? I wonder if I will have new nightmares with new faces? I think I stopped collecting girls eight years ago but I can't be sure? I call it collecting --- like one collects butterflies or rocks --- kind a like a hobby or something.

They are part of my collection. It's not like a hobby though --- not really. I can't be sure if more memories are going to come to me. And like I said, they don't come in any order. There is no timeline to them. I don't mean to ramble but my mind is pretty screwed up right now.

I do cry at night you know. You don't believe me do you? I even cry sometimes during the day when I'm by myself --- especially if I happen to see a girl that looks like part of my broken collection. I've cried so hard and long my eyes ache. Then I started to think that perhaps I'm like an art collector who keeps his valuable paintings downstairs in some locked vault that no one can see --- except him? Kept away from the eyes of the world to see. Buried in the dirt. That's bloody sick and I wonder if I have gone insane. *Does an insane person know they are insane?* I think I'm starting to see more and more of them in public that are looking like my girls from my past. I call them my girls since I don't quite know what else to call them? Oh --- I think I said that before. I was the last thing they saw before --- you know --- I took them --- their bodies and souls I mean. How the hell did I ever become such a sadist --- such a killer of life?

Yet here I am two decades after the first one and then I start getting these crap dreams. They sneak up on me like a cancer. It's like they are trying to ruin my life. I have a lot to think about these days and nights. Here is my story of how I got here --- to this moment in time. Then I realized something --- the danger of releasing secrets --- especially dark secrets. The kinds of secrets that should stay buried forever. Secrets that should stay buried in the dark earth with the sticks and the rocks and the rotting flesh and bones. The maggots will do their work. I've just been feeding the maggots.

And then another dream comes to haunt me so now I remember the first one. I'm pretty sure she was the first one? Her name was Marianne and she was from a long time ago --- when I was just sixteen years old. I was nothing but a kid back then but as I now know I was a kid that killed for the thrill and the excitement. I had just got my driver's licence and borrowed the family car for a few hours. That's how it started. Just going for a drive and sipping on a coke and enjoying my new found freedom.

CHAPTER 3

To Marianne – "Cry all you want. No one will hear you!"

Hi. Let me introduce myself. I had to name myself so I chose Lucifer but I actually go by many different names. I hardly ever call myself by that name though --- and never in public. Lucifer would just freak out too many people. I think you know why? Besides --- who in the hell would name their kid Lucifer? And I don't want a pussy name like Kyle. I prefer to say my name is Luc --- and I tell them it's short for Lucas. It's just easier that way. And I love to come out and play. I play rough though. Kyle doesn't even know I exist. I have some very big surprises for Kyle in the near future. He doesn't have a clue. I'm going to tell him later --- in his dreams. He's going to shit his pants when I tell him. What a dumb ass he is! It's so easy to manipulate and control him. He doesn't have a clue what really happened so I started showing him in his dreams --- our dreams that is --- just little pieces at a time though. It's like a jigsaw puzzle. I love to fuck with him. Fuck him up good! That is almost as much fun as killing. Naw --- it's not! The moments just before the kill are the most fun. And I love the nature of the chase and planning it out. That moment of capture just before my girls even know it is happening to them --- before it's too late. When they realize what's happening they're always surprised -- like it can't be happening to them.

That Kyle is a pathetic puss. I don't even like the shithead. Sometimes I wish he would just leave. Get the fuck out of here and let a real man live your shitty life. I just wish I could kill the fucking son of a bitch wimp but it is what it is. Someday though --- there is always a someday to look forward to. To take over and Luc can play 24-7. There are so many girls and possibilities out there. I see them in the warm weather all dolled up and showing their skin. I get wet just thinking about them --- a world full of candy. Life is good and it is going to get even better!

In the beginning I would get Kyle to get the parent's car after school, or sometimes on a Saturday or a Sunday. I always made sure to hide myself and not come out until the time was right. I'm not dumb you know --- not like Kyle. He is so easy to fool --- to lead --- to manipulate. I also have some fetishes that I don't necessarily want to disclose to someone close to me. They're very dark. So I save that part of me for my girls --- when we have our private moments. I call them my girls because once I have them --- I own them body and soul. I would hop in the car with Kyle and go for leisurely drives and I remember a feeling of being free, *of being released from my cage,* escaping the smothering fog. Driving down that long lonesome highway of tears --- although I would eventually end up on those backcountry roads in the company of a young girl --- or a woman. I started off with only the young girls --- eighteen or a bit older I imagine. Just about to finish high school and move onto college or university --- or get married. I don't want them too young. I'm not that fucked up ya know! I would take over Kyle cause he would never do anything like this. He wanted to --- I know that for sure. He was just too much of a chicken shit to do anything about it. I'm not like him. He's a fucking pussy! He'll never be a real man like me. I got no problem doing it. I just love to think about it 24/7. It is all I think about. How I would do it to the girls but especially who would be next. There will always be a next as long as I breath and my heart beats I will collect my girls. That's another thing Kyle doesn't have a clue about. You have to be careful keeping trophies though. That is how assholes get caught. My trophies --- well --- I have one hell of a surprise for my boy Kyle.

I don't talk in my sleep. I've tape recorded myself just to make sure. When I'm old --- too old for all this I guess I will look back and ask myself that shit everyone asks at the end of his or her life? Any regrets? I'll only have one regret. That I didn't kill enough girls --- I could have collected more. I could have killed way more. Good thing is I still have more time to do what needs to be done. What I was born to do! I have a particular talent and skill set with the girls. I would have made a terrible doctor but a great executioner.

One afternoon we ended up near this rural school. I use the "we" phrase just cause Kyle was physically in the car. I had never been there before but I go where opportunity knocks. Sometimes it knocks real loud --- like a thunderbolt and I always answer the door! This one was more like an accident of opportunity. I'm not from Heaven by any means --- not by a long shot. *I'm the walking evil everyone wants to talk about but nobody wants to meet.* Real life can be a bitch huh?

Kyle and I are pretty good looking. Well, we should be since we are the same physically. Lots of girls would say we are handsome. Being handsome and cute helps but being able to talk with them and make them feel at ease and to trust us --- well --- that is number one. Fat guys get pretty girls. Always wondered about that but if you have personality and humour and can get the girls to trust you that's what counts the most --- and I'm good at that. And for some having confidence and money is what counts.

The sun was out and it was nice afternoon. Good day to go looking or as I like to say go hunting. I remember that day not only because it was our first but I actually ran over a couple of geese on the road that afternoon. I think they were geese? We were going down this two-lane back road and there were some houses off to the side with these ponds on the front lawns. Quite a few houses with ponds actually. What the hell are these people doing with little bitty ponds out in the country? If you want water live on a lake or river for crying out loud. Anyway, next thing I know these two geese --- they might have been swans, came waddling out trying to cross the road. We ran over them and Kyle slammed on the brakes and they both got wedged under the burning rubber on the road. We skidded about seventy feet or so. We got out of the vehicle and looked for them but nothing but feathers scattered down the road for seventy plus feet. Those swans got cooked under the right front tire. Stupid birds! I didn't care and thought it was pretty neat. I couldn't even find those bird's bodies --- not a trace. Like they were cremated right on the roadway under the tires. No one in the houses even knew about it. Our screeching tires and still they were oblivious to what had just happened right in front of their houses. People can be so bloody stupid and naïve. I never honked the horn. Ah, the smell of burning rubber and flesh in the afternoon. Made me salivate for more! I love it!

I used to hunt as a kid. Dad would take me out with his .22 and a pellet gun. Sometimes I would have the pellet gun and sometimes I would have the .22. I remember when I was about seven or eight years old and being in some farmer's field full of tall corn stalks. No corn or anything cause it was winter. A bit of snow on the ground and it was cold. I remember seeing my breath like a fire was coming out of my mouth. I pretended I was a fire-breathing dragon. Not much luck hunting that day. The animals weren't cooperating. So we did some target practice on some old tin cans and old bottles that we found. We would set up the cans or bottles and pick them off with the .22. I pretended the cans and bottles were regular people but Kyle would always pretend he was the police shooting bad people --- or the military killing the enemy. I preferred killing the regular people. Everyone is guilty of something --- even the regular people. Once you're born I figure we all have sins of some sort.

Anyway, I have to be careful when I show myself. Always had to be in control around others. Better get back to that cornfield story. I remember we were walking along the outer edge of the cornfield. To my left it was open and in front of me about 200 feet away was some bush. We were heading to the bush area where the trees were. Thought we might get some rabbits or pheasants. I remember being about four or five years old and going hunting with Dad. This one is a different story. I get side tracked a lot. If you don't like it you can fuck off. I bounce around back and forth telling my stories. I don't remember much but I remember Dad shot a rabbit and he ordered me to carry it. He shot it with his .22. I followed Dad and Kyle was carrying it up this hill when the rabbit started to twitch and go a little crazy on him. Kyle screamed and dropped the rabbit thinking it was still alive. Dad gave Kyle hell for dropping the rabbit when it twitched. Dad said it was just the nerves twitching on the rabbit and that the rabbit was stone dead. I would have never dropped that rabbit. I like it better when they twitch and cry. When we got home Dad cut off the rabbit's foot and gave it to Kyle and told him to keep it. Dad said it was supposed to bring good luck. What a fucked up belief? Kyle kept it in our old dresser drawer in our bedroom for a couple of days --- until it started to smell. Mom traced the smell and found the dead rabbit's foot and freaked out and threw it away. She was yelling at Kyle and Dad. What the hell? It's only a dead foot? Better get back to that cornfield hunt. As we were walking along the corn line there was this one chickadee sitting at the very top of this one cornstalk. The bird was chirping like crazy. I remember the bird was singing, "Chickadee-Dee-Dee, chickadee-Dee-Dee," or something like that when Dad said, "Go ahead and bang him kid." So Kyle aimed the gun and banged the Chickadee. Kyle got the bird good cause he was gone in a puff of feathers. Dad and Kyle went over to look for him but we couldn't find him --- the little chickadee. Kyle asked Dad where he went and Dad just laughed and said, "You blew him to smithereens kid." Kyle felt bad but I didn't. Served the little bastard right. It was as if he was asking for it when he was singing, *Go ahead … I dare your … take your best shot.* When I think of that bird I can't help but think of the girls. In a real sense they were and are like that bird. Daring me to do something. I'm good at taking dares though --- especially those kinds of dares. Those girls should know better. Well, I should get back to my swan story. Like I said I bounce around a lot sometimes. It was after those swans getting squished and cooked --- yea --- they had to be swans cause I don't think geese are all white like that? Not unless they are albino or something. I switched places with Kyle and it was about fifteen minutes after those swans that I drove by this school and saw this girl walking beside the road all by her lonesome. Kyle was gone. Elvis has left the building you could say. In this case Kyle is Elvis --- as if I have to explain it. The girl was in a dress and was looking good. She was wearing these soft bluish shoes. Her hair was dark brown like the colour of chestnut and it wasn't short but it wasn't long either. It was kind of in-between if you know what I mean.

I watched her for about a minute just to check things out. She had a black backpack with her --- not a big one but a smaller one and she was walking alone. I sat in my car watching her --- waiting --- just to make sure. I was after all a fledgling back then --- and I wanted her so bad so I made sure I didn't make any mistakes. I kept my cool. It wasn't easy but I had planned everything and her time had come. My first girl --- GOD I loved it! When I saw my chance I went in like a snake waiting to pounce or rather strike --- at the perfect moment. I wasn't nervous like Kyle would have been. She turned and was looking back at me as I slowed the car beside her. I already had the window rolled down on her side. I crept up slowly to her and I made sure the music was not too loud but had good tunes on. And I always made sure to smile at them. I remember her looking over at me first with a worried look on her face but I made sure not to frighten her --- at first that is.

"Hi," I called out the window in a friendly tone. "My name is Lucas --- Luc for short. You're pretty. What's your name?"

"Marianne," was her only response as she turned her head to look at me.

I remember her eyes looking at me. She had nice eyes and they seemed to invite me in. She was dressed nice too! She had a good figure. Really more like a young woman than a girl. She grabbed her backpack as she adjusted it on her back. She was just eighteen years old. At least that is what she told me later.

"Well, whatcha doing pretty Marianne? Where ya headed?" I asked in my safe, sexy voice as I flashed my pearly white smile at her.

"I'm not doing anything much? Just heading home." She said as she shot me a small smile back.

She eyed my car and me for a second and then replied, "What are you doing? You're not from around here." She touched her hair ever so slightly with her right hand. Girls do that when they like ya.

"Me? Well, I'm just driving around in my wheels looking for a pretty girl to go for a short ride and enjoy some good tunes with me. Know anybody like that?"

I flashed another big smile at her. There was a slight hesitation on her part as she looked around. I quickly added, "Ah come on. I'm safe and it sure would be nice to go for a short ride with you. We could get an ice-cream or something?"

She came a little closer to the window and leaned in ever so slightly. She turned briefly and looked up and down the road as if asking herself if it was all right. "I don't have much time for a ride."

"I don't have much time myself. I gotta get home soon too so we have that in common Marianne. Hop in. I only have about twenty or thirty minutes tops. I'll drop you off wherever you want after --- I promise."

She smiled and felt a little safer and said, "Oh, all right then," and she opened the door and hoped in. "But only for twenty minutes or so like you said."

"That sounds great!" I replied.

And at that she put her backpack on the floor and asked, "Where are we going Luc? Where do you go to school?"

"Where ever you want to go pretty girl. I'm your co-pilot and you're the pilot. I'll just drive around a bit and we can get to know each other better. I go to Robinson High School but I just moved here with my folks. First you better buckle up so you are safe. I want you to feel safe ya know." I smiled and she smiled back --- her lovely eyes looking my way.

We got talking about stuff --- about each other. All the stuff I told her about me was nothing but bullshit though but she ate it up like chocolate syrup on a vanilla ice-cream cone. We never did stop for ice cream. It didn't take long to get out of that small town and once out of town I looked for a good place to get her. I found it and I stopped on this gravel road in the middle of nowhere.

"Why are you stopping here?" she asked looking at me.

I turned the radio down. "Just so we can talk and get to know each other better. I like talking and being with you Marianne. Do you always hop into cars with handsome boys?

She smiled when she heard that but quickly added, "Well, no, not usually but I do have to get back soon so we can stop for only a few minutes. Okay?"

"Yea, I have to be quick too and get home and make sure I'm not late for supper. It sure is quiet out here isn't it? Except for the radio and us that is."

"You have a girlfriend?" She asked as she had a little smirk on her face. She asked me kind of shyly --- which was cute in a way.

"I don't know? You tell me?" I gave my head a little shake and smirked back at her.

She smiled and that's when I suddenly grabbed her. She was quite startled. She got mad after I grabbed her.

"Hey!" She yelled out. "That's a bit too fast! Take your hands off me Lucas!"

I was too strong for her. She struggled more as fear came to her face when I wouldn't let go. I just smiled at her as I held her. She started kicking and screaming so I put my hands across her mouth --- she tried to bite me but it wasn't long until she struggled no more. I made sure not to kill her but just enough pressure so she would pass out. After she passed out I quickly tied her up and got out of the car. I looked up and down the road to make sure it was safe and then carried her off into the bush. I carried my shovel in one hand and her over my shoulder in the other. I was a bit nervous and wanted to be quick --- to get her off the road and out of sight. I carried her back into the bush but she woke up while I was still carrying her. She was only out for a few minutes. It was perfect because now the fear and screaming could begin and no one could hear her --- except me. My plan was working perfectly.

You want me to tell you about some of the girls don't you. I would start by torturing their minds --- telling them what I wanted to do to them --- how I would do it --- that I was going to do it. I can be so creative. I really should work for the government. I'm an expert. And I love my handy work! And I experimented with different girls. I'm a curious sort of fellow. I wanted to try different ways that would lead to their deaths. I can get pretty graphic but believe me --- the words fall far short of the reality. They say a picture is worth a thousand words and they are right. I'm a curious fuck. Thank GOD for the Internet. It gave me some great ideas on methods that were used in various cultures and through history but I'm also very creative. I don't mind blood. Some people are squeamish. I'm not. I bet you have never had a nice drink of warm human blood. Sometimes I would drink their blood right in front of them --- savouring the taste like a good bottle of wine --- telling them how good they taste. Lifting the cup to my lips --- smacking my lips at the taste. It freaks them out even more. I like telling them I'm going to cook them for my supper. It will be a romantic supper --- and she will be the guest of honour. That puts real fear into their eyes. Maybe some day I'll tell you about some of it. The chainsaw I only used a couple of times although I did like starting it up and threatening the girls. I liked watching them freak out. Kyle doesn't know that stuff yet. He's too much of a wimp. I really don't think he could handle the imagery of it. It can get pretty messy. He has enough trouble with just the idea of dead bodies. He's the type of guy that would faint at the sight of blood. What a fucking big suck that guy is.

For the first girl I just held a short knife to Marianne's throat and told her to keep quiet if she wanted to live --- that I would let her go after. It worked and she kept fairly quiet. There was some whimpering but I must admit she did a good job. I didn't mark her up too bad for this first one. I was after all in a bit of a hurry. I wish I wasn't. I didn't mark her face at all. Not for this first girl anyway. When I think about it most times I didn't mark the girl's faces up. Later I hardly marked them at all. I guess you could say it was my reward to them --- not to mark their face. Kind of like a sign of respect. I know --- you think that is strange? Marianne was still tied up so I put the gag back on her after I started. She was just too loud otherwise when I was starting my real pleasures. I've given up trying to analyze why I like this kind of stuff. You do realize that is what serial killers tend to do --- right? People have a fascination with serial killers or the bizarre. Even I'm fascinating by what I do. I don't fully understand it --- I just accept it.

CHAPTER 4

September 28 – 1:21 P.M. - Kyle

I'm getting closer to the spot. Funny how I can remember where to go even though I'm pretty sure I only know this place from my dream. I can't trust my memory --- especially because of what happened in the past. Maybe I have been here more than once? I don't know what to think now?

I remember a blonde girl in my high school. I knew her just a bit because one of my friends knew her. She was so good-looking. What a body on that young girl. It should be illegal for a young girl to have a body like that. It's like teasing a wild hungry tiger with red meat. That's how I look at it. So many girls like that. What was God thinking? I don't mind though. I like to look. Just never thought it would go beyond that. I mean I went to Church for Christ sake? Sorry --- I don't usually swear but this is all so shocking. I never asked that pretty blonde out even though I was pretty sure she liked me. I regret that. Then again it was probably better that I didn't ask her out or get too close. Now that I know I can be dangerous. I should come with a warning message like a package of cigarettes --- or on a bottle of poison. That I'm very dangerous and there are possible side effects --- that I'm a danger to your health --- to your life. I'm like a cigarette in the old days before people knew they were dangerous to smoke. Hell, I'm way more dangerous than any cigarette. Yet even today people, young people are still smoking. And I should know since my aunt and my mom both died of lung cancer from smoking. I'm more dangerous than cancer though and I'm a hell of a lot quicker. Dad died a few years after mom died. The coroner determined he had a heart attack.

The question I keep asking myself is how am I going to go on now that I know what I've done? I don't have any answers yet but I have to find a way --- or my life will be over. Either I would get locked up like an animal or I would have to kill myself. I still might kill myself. Maybe I could leave a letter to let all those families know where their girls are? I'm not there yet --- you know --- not ready to kill myself or leave any letters. And here I always thought I was a good boy? Boy, was I ever wrong about that! Mom was wrong too! Anybody that thinks they know me is wrong about that too! *It just goes to prove you can never ever really truly know a person --- or even yourself.*

The wind is staring to blow just a bit, a nice soft breeze. I have my windows down and the air is cool. There's the stream up ahead so I know I'm real close to where she is resting. It's kind of strange that some wild animals haven't dug up all those other graves? I would have thought wild animals would smell the human flesh and go digging for a meal. I hear human flesh doesn't taste all that bad. GOD I just thought of something! I hope I never ate any of them.

The thing is the other twenty-six were all buried in the same exact spots as in my dreams, or I should say my nightmares. I found their bones and bit and pieces of their clothing. I spent a long time staring at their skulls, their hands, and their feet. It was weird touching them for what seemed to me to be the first time. It wasn't the first time though. I'm actually hoping this one isn't there. Even if she had been moved or taken away by some animals that would be more comforting to me. I get no real satisfaction realizing here is another one. Except more proof that I'm a monster. Mom seems to always make me feel guilty even though she's been dead for years. I still hear her voice in my head, *"You remember to always be good Kyle and make good choices. You're a good boy."*

I was the good child according to her. I need a psychiatrist but I can't even go see one to talk about it. I'm going to have to figure out how I'm going to deal with all this crap. For now I just take it one day at a time and one night at a time. The nights are getting longer though. I have trouble sleeping.

I'm stopping the car now as this looks like this is the spot. Here is the part I dread. I'm taking deep breaths but that doesn't help. I close my eyes and try to use imagery. I imagine lying on a sandy beach as the waves gently lap the white sand at my feet. That doesn't help either. I take a quick look around to make sure no one is in the area. I haven't seen anyone for a while. Well, here goes. I open the trunk; take another quick look around before I get the shovel. It is a good, short steel shovel. It's easy to carry and good for digging. I made sure to park about 50 yards from where I need to go into the bush. Just in case a car comes, the driver wondering what am I doing parked there and comes into the bush looking for someone. I begin walking back along the roadway. I walk quickly as I don't want to spend too much time here. I hear some birds singing, songbirds and I notice some sparrows and a few blackbirds in the trees. They seem to be watching me. A slight cool breeze is rustling the leaves along with the crunching sound of my shoes on the gravel road. I come to the spot and one last look down the roadway both ways and then into the bush I go. I don't think I have to go far --- maybe a minute or two. I come to a two-foot vertical rise in the rocks like a small cliff. I see a rock at the base and use it, like I used it last time I suspect. The rocks are a bit slippery, there's wetness on them even though it didn't rain. It is just the dew on the ground or perhaps water seeping up from an underground spring. I grab a couple of small saplings to steady myself. I don't remember it being slippery like this in my nightmare. Then I see the spot where she is buried --- where Marianne is buried. I try to remember to use her name and I find myself whispering her name in the forest. I imagine I hear her name echoing off the trees. I read somewhere that true serial killers don't call their victims by their names. They do that to dehumanize their victims --- or so the theory goes. So I guess because I use their names I'm trying to deny being a true serial killer. I'm failing that test miserably though. The area looks slightly different after all those passing years but this is definitely the spot.

I would expect it to look different; after all it was a long time ago when it happened. The ground is level now and easy to walk on --- or I suspect drag or carry a body across. As I approach the spot I start to remember more as I look around. Some things still look familiar. When I look at the grave with the rocks on top I know I'm in the right spot. I look up to the trees half expecting to see crows --- they aren't there. So I take a big breath and then remove the rocks that are on top of the gravesite. I count the rocks. There are nine of them and they each weigh around ten to twenty pounds I'm guessing. I should have brought gloves. What an idiot I am! My hands are getting dirty and I might cut my hands from the rocks. I'm so stupid not to bring gloves. I brought them the other times I was digging up the graves. How could I forget them? They are in the trunk of my car. Well, I sure as hell am not going back to get them now. I want to hurry so I begin digging down where I figure her waist is? I keep stopping and to look around every few seconds. Listening for any sounds. I'm spooked and need to be careful. I thought about doing this in the night but that would be even spookier. Besides I'm off in the bush --- alone. I dig down and I must be deep enough by now but I'm not seeing anything yet? I start digging faster and following the silhouette of the grave. I'm sweating and breathing harder now but all I'm seeing is dirt. Then the earth in the grave gets much harder --- like it has never been touched before. I keep digging and after three feet down I realize something for the first time. There is no body there? No bones --- no clothes --- no shoes --- nothing! There is no Marianne in the grave? *What the hell! Did I move her? Did someone find her? Someone must have found her. I don't like this. She's gone! This is spooky!* She's supposed to be there. She's the first one that's not in the grave. I look around for any signs of tampering but nothing. I quickly put everything back the way it was before I started to dig her up. I work fast and it doesn't take me long to get everything back the way it was. I rush out of there as fast as I can. I run back to the car and start it up and drive off. *What the Hell is going on? She's supposed to be there?* Shit! I don't even turn on the radio while I drive away.

Lucas

So Kyle found out the first bitch isn't buried there. GOD I love fucking with that guy. I figured it out long ago when after a few days I hadn't heard anything about a missing girl --- about Marianne. I thought what the fuck! Why isn't this all over the news? *"Young Girl Missing,"* should have been in the newspaper headlines and on the television but not a sound or even a whisper in the news about what I did --- nothing about her. So I waited a bit. At first I thought maybe her parents didn't give a fuck but then I thought Marianne would be missed at school --- missed by her friends and I came to one conclusion. She wasn't missing? Did they find her and keep things quiet for a reason? I mean she had to be dead. But I wondered why no police or media? It wasn't easy but I waiting six months and then I went back to check the grave. Winter was over and it was March and the temperatures were warmer --- so the dirt was no longer frozen and I could dig her up. So I went back to the grave to dig her up and check. I found the same thing Kyle just found out. Marianne wasn't there but the grave looked the same as when I put her in? After I dug it up I put it all back just the way it was before. It really confused me for a few days. So then I began to look for her but I had to be very careful about it. I needed to know what the fuck happened?

Marianne

It was dark --- so very dark --- and cold. And the feeling on her skin was a damp type of cold --- like dirty loam or sphagnum moss. And then there was the weight. Slowly she woke up unsure at first where the hell she was. Then she remembered. There was just enough room around her head for a small pocket of air. When she struggled those last moments her head moved about violently as she tried to escape the falling dirt from the shovel. She couldn't open her eyes now and she knew she shouldn't even try. She began struggling with the restraints on her wrists. It was extremely difficult but after a brief violent struggle she realized she had one hand free --- and that meant the other hand was free as well. It was so difficult to move even a little bit from the weight of the dirt on top of her. She wouldn't give up though. She was a fighter and she wanted to survive! She wanted to live! She thought of her sister --- her mother --- and began digging with her fingers --- digging ever so slowly up towards that blue sky she remembered seeing before being buried. That beautiful blue sky was her freedom. And then she remembered his face --- the one sick bastard responsible for all this --- the look of sick joy on his face as he covered her with the dirt. Her heart was racing so she tried slowing it down --- trying to conserve her little pocket of air. *Claustrophobia --- the fear of tight enclosed spaces is a fear many people have but there are degrees of claustrophobia. Buried alive is one of the more extreme measures.* And here was this innocent teenage girl just walking home from school a couple of hours ago and now she was fighting for her very life. She thought of her death out in the forest alone and no one ever finding her. Her fingers digging the dirt like a mole burrowing tiny tunnels in the darkness. She started to think about worms eating her body --- the beetles eating her and her fingers worked faster at a more desperate, frantic pace. She almost passed out a few times but she fought it with all her spirit. She thought of GOD. She didn't usually think about GOD but she did now. *"GOD --- please don't let me die like this --- I want to live."* And then as if it was a miracle she felt her first fingers break the surface of that grave. It was only her left hand but a sudden surge of hope rushed through her body. She might live yet. Her hand felt like it was taking a first breath of fresh air. She frantically started throwing small handfuls of dirt away as best she could. Then her right hand reached out like some plant striving up to reach the sunlight in the heavens --- to live. Less than a minute later her hands worked in a frenzy uncovering the dirt from her face area. She was so lucky the grave was not deeper because she was as close to death as anyone had ever been before. She had to move those rocks piled on top of her. The sick bastard had even put a rock right on top of her head. She managed to push the rocks away. She was shivering and trembling as she continued to become unburied.

When her hands finally reached her face she took her first small breath of fresh air and she felt happier than she had ever felt in her short life. The dirt was still around her mouth and she began spitting that filthy dirt out of her mouth. She coughed but was careful about making any noises --- as she feared HE might still be around. She incessantly wiped the dirt from around her eyes so she could see again --- *oh to see the light again --- her eyes blinking as they began to adjust. It was so good to see and breathe again.* It was still daylight out. Nothing was going to stop her now. Once she got her upper torso free she sat up. It was a matter of moving the remaining rocks and dirt from her legs and then she managed to stand up. She trembled and shivered --- and was afraid. She looked around and noticed the crows above her. They were still there but they were quiet now and seemed to be staring down at her --- watching her and what she was doing. She shook the dirt from her hair and wiped the dirt from her as best she could and began walking --- walking out to freedom --- to a new chance in life. As she walked away the crows began crowing wildly. She turned one last time to look at them. Strangely her stare silenced them. She turned and walked to the gravel road always looking --- always listening for HIM. When she reached the road there was still no sight of HIM. His car was gone. She trembled and felt faint. She couldn't remember the licence plate or the make of the car. She couldn't even remember the colour. She was still terrified but SHE was free --- and SHE was ALIVE! Thank GOD!

Lucas

Kyle is a big shit fuck but he did two things right. First he won a huge amount in the lottery. He bought a single lottery ticket when he was twenty years old and the fucking ticket won. What a lucky break! I was ecstatic cause now unless the fuck took a job I would have more time to do my collecting and nothing is more important to me than that. The second thing Kyle did was become interested in taxidermy. It was a new hobby of his. Kyle does fish and he is pretty good at it. I'll talk more about that later.

What I discovered in my so-called detective work was that I found out Marianne's family moved within a few days of her escape. Further Detective work on my part and I discovered they moved about eight hundred miles away. I'm smarter than any Detective. Hell, I think when the police do solve a crime that nine times out of ten they have the wrong guy and convict the wrong fucker. Kyle doesn't know about Marianne so his mind is pretty fucked up right now. But there's another thing Kyle doesn't know. I've kept track of her through the years --- *the one that got away*. She's grown up now --- thirty-eight years old and living in the same town her family moved to twenty or so years ago. And I've got a surprise for both of them --- Marianne and Kyle that is. He still thinks it's been a few years since the last girl for fuck sake. *What a doofus!* Like I said --- he's fun to fuck with. That's why I made him go all the way out to the spot where he thought he was going to find Marianne. Now he's panicking --- wondering where the hell the body is? I'll have to watch him to make sure he doesn't do anything stupid. When a person is in a panic they can do some pretty stupid things.

Kyle doesn't know but I started using laundry soap and lye with the next few girls. It was my idea as I read it breaks down the body and bones quicker. Gets rid of the evidence. Later --- many years later when the world started to learn more about D.N.A. it was a great decision by me to use the lye. Like I said, I'm real smart sometimes and I learn from my mistakes. I don't make many mistakes. Not when it comes to collecting. In the beginning I didn't collect the girls for long. It was usually just for an hour or two before I disposed them. But what I really wanted was to prolong the capture and enjoy myself --- to be able to take my time with each girl and make each second count. Later I kept the girls for much longer. When I had honed my skills more and really knew what I was doing. That's when I kept them longer. I was more confident. I was becoming an expert. Like a wild tiger that sometimes makes a fast kill but at other times will play with the prey first --- truly enjoying those moments. And I only collected one girl at a time. No need to complicate things or get greedy. You see Kyle and I bought this farm with some of the lottery money. It was a place off the beaten path and very, very private. Kyle would do his taxidermy on the fish in one room downstairs. Kyle doesn't' have a clue but after my first girl, that Marianne that got away, I decided that would never happen again.

Okay, so I guess you want to hear about the first girl? I love telling these stories because they help me relive those treasured moments. Think of it like a scary movie. For you it is not real. Didn't happen to you --- not yet anyway. Scary movies are fun to watch but we know they are only actors following a script. They may look real but they are all nothing but a big fake scene. That's why I like my stories better. They're not bogus. I'm not going to talk about everything. Just the good stuff --- the stuff that gets me excited remembering it. The stuff that gets me wet --- that gets my dick dripping. I love my work. Nothing makes me happier when I'm doing my thing --- working on my girls.

CHAPTER 5

September 28 – 2:32 P.M. – Kyle

I run back to my car, my head in a swirl. Even though I hoped she wouldn't be there I really did expect her to be there. I'm so confused? I guess it's good she isn't there but what the hell --- I need to know where she is and what happened? I'm sure she was real and it is really screwed up to go to the grave and then find nothing there? Damn this is really going to mess my mind up even more! I'd better pay more attention to my surroundings. I can think more about this later. I need to focus on the moment and get the hell out of here. I need to try and remember. That might help me think why she isn't buried there? Did I move her to a different spot? But then why is the gravesite and stones still there as if untouched? God I find that I'm really breathing hard … not from the run but from the shock of the empty grave? I quickly put the shovel in the trunk and get into the car. I start the car and take one last look around my surroundings. I'm alone --- in more ways than one. *"Okay Kyle,"* I say to myself, *"take it easy and don't panic."* Easier said than done though. I put the car in drive and take off. My mind is racing now. I better try and focus on the driving or I might end up crashing the car into some ditch or tree. I have to go and find some place and think about this. I know --- I will go down to the water. Running water like a set of rapids or a waterfall seems to soothe me for some reason. I'll find a nice quiet spot near a river and think for a while and try to relax. Shit man --- I did not expect that. What the fuck is going on? Was she just a nightmare this time? But the grave is there? No, she is real and so is that dream. Fuck --- now what?

Lucas

Kyle is bloody freaking out! Shit I love it! I get a kick out of seeing him suffer mentally. Not as much as the girls but fuck man --- what a shithead he is. I'm going to have to tell him eventually. I know he's going to have trouble handling it. Tell him about Marianne and what happened. Hell --- he's going to have a hard time trying to deal with the other secrets I have in store for him. He doesn't even know I exist. What a true fuck up he is! He doesn't even know that I haven't stopped collecting girls. He's hoping there are no more girls but there are other girls. Heck, I've been a busy guy. Kyle has more nightmares coming his way courtesy of me. And we are going on a little trip. You see I have plans. He doesn't know it yet but I have a special someone I want to meet. I want to have a little get-together with an old friend of mine. That's right. We are going to visit Marianne again --- you know --- for another one-on-one meeting. I have some unfinished business to attend to. Won't she be surprised? The one girl that thinks she got away for good. Well --- I'm going back and this time she won't be so lucky. Oh --- there's one other little thing I should mention. You see Marianne has two kids --- two girls and they are just the right age --- the age range I love --- teenage girls. I'm going to meet her two young daughters --- a nice one-on-one meeting with Marianne's daughters. Yea --- that's right --- the daughters are first. I wish Marianne had more daughters but hey ... two will work just fine. They are like ripe, juicy fruit ready for the picking. I like em at that tender age when they might still be a virgin. I really don't care if the girls are virgins or not. It's not a deal breaker for me. That's just an added bonus. I've already planned it down to every last detail. I have a hell of an introduction planned for them. I'm thinking that I just might show them my very own special surprise. *Isn't that a sick twist?* I love being sick and twisted. It's just so much --- how can I say it? Fun! Won't Marianne be surprised --- and the girls? GOD I love being me --- what guy wouldn't want to be me? I've been dripping just thinking about it. *Don't ya just love family reunions?*

Kyle will have a fucking heart attack when I tell him. I'm going to wait until springtime to collect them. Winter's coming and I don't work too much in the winter. So sometimes I travel where there is no snow --- no frozen ground. I've got it all planned out. I'll collect one girl before winter comes here --- and one or two more when we go south for a bit of a vacation. Then we'll go and see how Marianne and her daughters are doing in early spring. I'm not going to tell Kyle until after though. When the dirty deeds are done.

I want to mention how I have evolved over time. One has to adapt in nature if one is to survive and make no doubt about it --- I'm a survivor. It was different back when I first started doing this collecting thing. As I mentioned, there was no real DNA analysis yet that one like me had to be worry about. It wasn't even around. Sure there were some forensic techniques but they were rudimentary. Blood types, fingerprints, footprints, bits of clothing, tire tracks --- stuff pretty much like that. Forensic evidence has changed over the years. It is more of a science now and if you aren't careful you can get caught making a mistake. And there are more cameras in society these days not just on street corners or in stores either. There are lots of cameras or civil surveillance in many urban areas. Everyone pretty much has a cell phone and can take pictures quite easily and quickly. Someone can track your cell phone even if it is off. Or they can trace your location using cell towers if you take or receive a call. I don't even have a cell phone most times. The odd time I have used burner phones that you can just throw away when you are done. And even then it is rare that I use or carry a phone. If I do have a phone I always use a Jammer pouch that blocks the RFID, the GPS and Wi-Fi signals among other things. It's the same with a laptop or tablet. There are snoops around and well --- you better know what kind of breadcrumbs you are leaving for someone else. One can't be too careful about things these days. The vehicles I drive don't have GPS or Bluetooth in them, or any type of electronics that could be used for tracking me or where I go. I get a bit paranoid about it sometimes if I think about it too much. The good thing about it is that I think I have some natural abilities for my kind of work and I learn real fast. I read quite a lot. I seldom use credit or bankcards and only when I'm off the grid --- never around the trapping area. I carry cash --- lots and lots of cash. And I sometimes wear disguises. I have even had some dialect coaching so I can talk with different accents --- not just straight English. For example, if I meet a Russian girl or French girl or Irish or Scottish or Australian girl or whatever --- well --- I just use that dialect to help gain an even higher level of trust and familiarity. And if for some reason the girl turned out to be a witness to the police later she would say I spoke with such and such an accent. I studied and speak a few languages and that has helped me with the girls. Like I said. I'm a smart shit. I'm not bragging. I just take my work seriously. The girls don't get away now. I'm too proficient in the capture --- in the killings. I'm still in my prime you know. Like I said --- I don't make mistakes. Not anymore. I like to think of myself just like that movie --- I kind of laugh when I think that. You know the one that says, "I can't be bargained with or reasoned with --- I don't feel pity or remorse or fear or pain --- and I absolutely will not stop --- ever --- until you are dead." *That's me --- except I do like to see them suffer.*

Samantha and Stephanie

Samantha and Stephanie Wynne were laughing and having a ball. They were happy girls and had not a care in the world. Life has been good to them. They love school, all their friends, their mom and everything about their life. They only see their Dad occasionally since the divorce many years ago. They love Dad and miss him and there were only two things about their lives that they wished was different. That Mom and Dad were still married and together and that Mom could enjoy life more and not have those terrible nightmares from her past. But right now the girls were laughing and having a great time at the centre. Being a twin and an identical twin at that has its benefits. The least of which was the very close bond the two girls had together. They did everything together. They even slept together sometimes, right down to reading the same types of books. They were well --- like one person in two bodies. They were totally different than the predator when you think about it --- two people in one body. The girls were the most identical twins there could be. Although one had to realize identical twins are different than other people --- even other twins --- the fraternal kind. And people had trouble telling them apart. Not just their looks were the same but their voices and their personalities seemed to be cloned in the psyche of each other if one can put it that way. They looked a lot like their mother at that age except they were blondes. The facial similarities were apparent and being so young and having the whole world in front of them for the taking. Life was good. They loved their small town and this is where they had lived their entire lives so far. The small town, called Nookville, was the only home they had ever known. Sure they travelled a bit with Mom but they didn't travel very far --- nothing abroad and all within a few hours of their home. They were for all intents and purposes small town girls. The twins had been enrolled in a variety of physical activities through the years like yoga, gymnastics, and dance. They had been practicing it since they were very young. And the girls had years and years of the Mixed Martial Arts training. They had training in Tai Kwan Do and Jiu-Jitsu classes for a number of years. Marianne took classes with her two girls for years and although not as proficient as her daughters --- Marianne was still very good in the Martial Arts. The twins were good enough to enter some MMA tournaments and sometimes they trained against full-grown men. They could fight and grapple with the men quite well and they were beating most of their opponents.

Marianne loved her daughters more than anything. Life had been difficult for her. That guy had really messed her up for a long, long time and she was still messed up --- but she found a way to survive. After escaping from that damp dark grave she wandered the back roads until it began to get dark. She was in shock and she was so lost and afraid and cold. She just wanted to get home and feel the loving arms of her Mom and Sister--- and to soak in a nice hot bath. She barely knew her Dad as he took off and left her life when she was only six years old. That hurt her a lot. Her Mom and younger Sister found her walking the back road in the dark. They went looking for her when she didn't return from school. They had been looking for two hours and were about to turn around and get some friends to help them search. The Mother just thought Marianne was at a friend's house at first. Then she got a bad feeling about it. When they found Marianne walking in the dark on that back road she was so filthy. Marianne told her Mom what happened and for some reason the Mom decided the best course of action was to just leave town and leave quickly. Marianne wanted to call the police but Marianne's Mom didn't trust the police for reasons she never divulged to anyone. And so within two days the family uprooted and moved many miles away to the small town of Nookville. It was a beautiful place and the three of them tried to start a new life there. There was just one problem for Marianne though and that was no matter how far she moved away she couldn't get away from herself or the memories. Marianne understandably had a lot of emotional baggage with her. It should be no surprise that the trauma Marianne experienced was quite devastating to her. She saw a shrink or rather a psychiatrist at her Mom's insistence and it helped but there was always the nagging worry HE would find her. That He was looking for her. And there were nightmares pretty much every night in the beginning. That was really the main reason why Marianne's marriage broke down so quickly. She married young but found love hard but even more difficult was the trust part. Marianne's Mom had a few relationships with men but they were not easy relationships either.

Marianne's sister Sandra seemed to adapt better to male-female relations in life. When Sandra was older she moved about an hour away from her sister. That is where she met Joe, who became her husband. They had no children although they tried for years. Then Joe and Sandra got tested and Joe was diagnosed as sterile. He had a low sperm count and could not have children. Sandra was fertile but the problem was with Joe. So Sandra

was looking at various agencies --- and hoping to adopt. She had been trying for a few years to find a child and in the meantime was doing some
foster care support. Joe was a truck driver and so was away for much of
the month. Off driving with his load leaving Sandra alone. She was lonely
but she loved Joe. They had talked many times about him finding another
profession, something that would allow him to be home more often, especially at night. The separation was putting a strain on the marriage --- and
Sandra wanting desperately to have a child. He was looking but not having
luck with a job that paid enough for him to quit his truck driver position.
He didn't mind being a truck driver and he was oblivious to the actual strain
all this was having on his marriage. Sandra loved Samantha and Stephanie
dearly. Now that she was an hour away she only saw the girls every other
weekend. That was good but it wasn't enough. There was an emptiness that
Sandra felt and the girls helped fill that emptiness in her. Now the twins
were getting older though and were more into teen things --- including an
interest in boys. Her nieces were drifting away from her.

When Marianne had her twins all those years ago she was so happy.
It was a joyous time for her. It was the happiest time she could ever remember. The two little girls kept her busy and as you can imagine she was
overly protective of her little treasures. Can you blame her? Her past was
a constant reminder to protect herself and especially her children. When
the girls were barely five years old Marianne told her daughters for the
very first time what happened to her so many years ago. That awful truth
and how she met the face of death on that day. That it was to be kept a big
secret. She thought the twins might be too young to understand and so she
saved the gory details for later years but it did help set the mindset of the
two girls --- and Marianne. Marianne thought about what happened a lot
but even more she couldn't help but wonder if she should have reported it?
If that animal she met that day had done it before --- or if he did it to more
girls after? That is what bothered her the most. *Were there more girls --- was
HE still doing it? Was HE still alive?* It was too late to report it now. Marianne
wasn't even sure she could remember his face. All she remembered was
that he was handsome and how his face turned to pure evil. Her mom

had made the decision all those years ago to say nothing --- and to just move away --- to flee like a wounded animal. Marianne distanced herself from her Mom after that. She allowed her daughters to visit Grandma but Marianne partially blamed her Mom for how her life turned out. Marianne and her family were preparing for the future --- whatever that might hold for them. They had no idea a great storm was coming their way. That HE would be coming for them. That He would be there soon and that there would be nothing they could do to stop Him.

CHAPTER 6

Lucas:

I know what you are thinking. You're thinking I'm a bad person. I got over that a long, long time ago. I hate it when people judge me. Don't judge me when you are not perfect yourself because that is really how I justify what I do. I'm kind of like that Stanford Prison Experiment gone wild but way worse. Besides I don't give two shits what you think. Those girls think they are better than me --- that they are too good for me but the reality is that I'm too good for them. They're here for me --- for my pleasure --- all of them.

Kyle won't have any idea until after when it is too late. Like I mentioned I feel like hunting again so we are off to a different town --- a different hunting place. They're all over the place --- the girls I mean. I seldom go back to the same area unless a fairly long time has passed by. I call them girls although I do collect older women too. I'm not prejudice. I don't want old hags though. And the girls have to look pretty. Not into ugly bitches but come to think of it there was that one fat bitch. She had a mouth on her. I shut her up good in the end. I do prefer my girls around a certain age. What I do like is when I get a woman who thinks she can control me or lecture me. They think they can control the situation. I love when they think that. It's time for Kyle to take a day or two off. I'm dripping for a little playtime.

I have the van now. We have several vehicles and depending on my needs I decide what vehicle is best. I like to use the van mostly. It has more room than a car. The van has a rotating licence plate. It's like a triangle. Saw it once on a movie --- a James Bond movie I believe. So I thought, I can rig something like that up. I have an electrical switch and can rotate the licence plate to three positions --- all with different plates. And I put in a bed but underneath I have a secret hiding spot --- where the girls can go. Other times I like to take the car. This time I'm going to a town about two hours away. Nothing too far away as I expect it to be a day trip but I might extend it out for two days. It all just depends on the situation. I've got all the stuff ready that I will need, zip ties --- I use zip ties now. I used to use rope but the zip ties are fast and strong. And sometimes I use a cloth rather than a blindfold. If I'm stopped I have to be able to explain why I carry this stuff. The shovel of course and my special knife that I use for when I go hunting. I hunt animals too! I have a few guns. I used to hunt more for animals but well --- nothing compares to my style of hunting. And I carry blankets to cover the girl when she is lying in the back. And of course my handgun --- just in case I need it --- if I have any problem with a cop. I use hollow point but I also use the M855 green tips for armour piercing. Haven't had to use it yet but like I said, I come prepared. I bring chloroform --- just in case. And I do have a Taser that I use sometimes --- or I use the needle. I travel light for the main part and stay under the radar.

It's 11:00 A.M. Saturday morning and seventeen-year old Amanda Noones is staring at the music CD she holds in her hand at the local Walmart Store. She checks the list of songs on the newest Taylor Swift music CD but has already decided to buy it. Amanda heard that the CD had just been released and so came to the store to buy it. It was her lucky day but there are eyes upon her. Amanda is unaware eyes are studying her --- that these particular eyes have an interest in her. Amanda is with her friend in the music section at the Walmart as they both focus on the

C.D. These eyes are not interested in the other girl though. They watch Amanda from a short distance away and had already begun to plan a series of events. The eyes are wearing a camouflage cap with a black hood pulled over top so the cameras in the store would have difficulty identifying the owner of the eyes. The eyes knew she would be the next one. Amanda may have been just seventeen-years old but to guys she looked as good as any woman ever could. She wore black leggings that showed off her great legs. The eyes were drawn closer to her sexiness. She had a white top that reminded the eyes of the flavour of vanilla. Her hair was a gorgeous blonde with sunglasses nestled on top of her head. She looked like the kind of girl with model potential oozing out of her waiting to be discovered. She would never be discovered though. The eyes didn't like the idea that the girl of interest was with a friend. That didn't matter though. It might complicate things but the eyes didn't care. They had decided.

"Lynne --- I'm buying this Taylor Swift CD for sure." Amanda smiled at her friend as they giggled at the treasure.

"I'm buying it too!" Lynne looked over at her good friend. "Let's head back to your place so we can hear it and dance the afternoon away in your bedroom."

"I thought that was the plan all along?" Amanda smiled at Lynne. They both laughed oblivious to the danger facing them.

The eyes had been watching them secretly for the last ten minutes. These eyes had been searching the store for the last thirty minutes when the one young girl came to their attention. The eyes only really wanted the one but if need be the two girls would do. The eyes would follow and wait --- wait for an opportunity --- to take.

The two girls moved to the express checkout at the Walmart. The eyes went outside and waited --- glancing at the front exit doors --- turning back looking at the girls. Just in case they decided to exit another way. The eyes wanted to make sure the girl didn't get out of sight. If they went to the washrooms HE wanted to know. The eyes wanted to see if they came in one car --- who they came with --- and where they were going.

Amanda called her Mom on the cell phone. "Mom, where are you? We're at the front cash waiting. Are you ready to go?" Lynne was examining her CD while Amanda talked to her Mom.

"Okay darling --- I'll be right there. I'm back at the running shoe section. I'm leaving now."

"Okay --- we'll wait for you at the front door Mom."

Amanda and Lynne walked to the front door but stopped just inside the double front doors. The eyes watched from outside. The eyes didn't stare but pretended to be waiting for someone. It was all a ploy. The eyes had made a small purchase and paid cash --- as they always did. The eyes bought some chewing gum --- the sugarless kind. The eyes waited for them. Then a lady showed up and the eyes figured she must be one of the kid's mothers.

"Shit!" The eyes whispered under his breathe. *It must be the mother of one of the girls --- and their ride.* The eyes were hoping they were taking a bus --- which would mean the girls would have to walk. Now that seemed unlikely to happen.

The mother and two girls walked out past the eyes --- oblivious to their surroundings as they gabbed away. The eyes waited and then followed them keeping a short distance behind --- wanting to know where the girl's car was parked. Perhaps there was still some hope for the eyes. The eyes noticed the cameras up on the poles in the parking lot. HE hated cameras. *What has society come to with all the snooping devices that are now everywhere? On the highways --- the sidewalks --- the stores --- everywhere it seems --- fucking electronic snoops. Even the damn satellites had cameras.* The eyes were always aware of cameras and surroundings. It is how the eyes survived not being caught all these years.

The lady and girls walked to a white Hyundai but before they reached the car the lady clicked the FOB and the car's lights lit up. The eyes now knew and luckily the van was not very far away from the car. It would be easy to follow. The eyes hurry back to the van and start it up. The white Hyundai hasn't moved yet. They were all too busy talking. Then the Hyundai begins to back out and starts heading out of the Walmart parking lot. The eyes put the van in gear and start to follow --- about three cars behind. The eyes watch the inside of the Hyundai. The preys are busy talking. *They really should watch where they are going. They could have an accident. It's just as bad as texting and driving.* The eyes smile --- the hunt had begun.

The eyes follow the Hyundai down the main street for a half a mile and then the girls pull into a small shopping plaza and park. The Mother and girls walk into the mall to do a bit of shopping. The eyes follow them in --- staying far back --- looking for the cameras. They go into a fashion boutique and twenty-five minutes later come out carrying several bags. The eyes think what a shitty way to spend a day --- for him. Following the girls waiting for an opportunity to collect. The eyes know it is all part of the game. That's just how it is. *If you want the prize you have to go through the wrapping paper.*

Back to the car the Mother and girls go --- laughing --- giggling without a care in the world. The eyes are waiting patiently in the van. The Hyundai starts up and the girls are on the road again --- the eyes following again. The Hyundai heads out to the highway with the eyes following. *"Where the fuck are they going now?"* the eyes think out loud. Six minutes later they turn off and after a few more turns end up on a little street with a Cul-de-sac. The Hyundai travels to the very end and parks in a driveway. *So this is where the girls live.* The eyes park well before the house and watch the Mother and the two girls go into the house. As the eyes watch --- deciding what to do, HE notices a Police Officer come out of the house next door to the girl's house. The cop kisses the woman and heads towards his car. *Shit! A cop lives next door to the girl's house.* The eyes quickly decide to leave but they remember the house --- the location --- for future reference. Or as the eyes put it --- it goes into the bank for now. There is a time and a place for everything. This is not the time, nor the place. The eyes are disappointed --- for now. The van leaves but the eyes are hungry --- hungry for a girl --- a woman --- something. The van travels back the same way --- back to that little Shopping Centre the girls were at. The eyes had noticed the place has no cameras in the parking lot.

On the way the eyes notice a lady at a bus stop --- probably in her late twenties. She is standing waiting for the bus. She's very pretty --- she would do and she was by herself. She was dressed real nice --- great high heel shoes --- great legs --- the whole package. She was about as close to a ten as one could get. A quick scan and the eyes notice there are no cameras. The eyes get the road map ready --- they always carry a road map to use to ask for directions. It is a great distraction. At the last minute the eyes decide to forgo the map and just ask how to get to the Walmart. *Everyone knows how to get to Walmart.* The van stops in front of the bus stop. This won't take long. The eyes exit the van leaving it running and calls out to the lady as the eyes walks towards her.

"Hi there! Do you know how to get to the Walmart? I think I'm close."

She smiles back and begins giving directions. "Yea --- just continue straight for about five or so lights." She points down the road as she talks.

The eyes come closer feigning interest. "Just go straight?"

"Well --- go about five or so lights. You'll see a Shell gas station on the left. Turn left there and that road will take you directly to the Walmart. Only a short distance --- it's on the right side after you turn left."

The eyes quickly scan the road --- no cars in sight. Not a very busy road right now. This is great. Just as the eyes are about to grab the lady it hears voices. The eyes turn and behind him walking on the grass to the sidewalk are three teenagers coming to the bus stop --- two girls and a boy. They're talking on their phones --- all three of them. The teens look ahead and see the man and lady. The eyes thank the lady and get back into the van and start driving.

"Shit! Shit! Shit! Those fucking teenagers! Fucking bastards!" The eyes are pissed and fists begin pounding the steering wheel. *"So close --- so fucking close! Shit! Rrrrrrrrrbhh! I should have just shot those fucking kids and grabbed that lady. She was sweet.* Then the eyes thought --- *no --- ya can't shoot the kids. It has to be a clean get away. Fuck!*

The eyes drive back to that small Shopping Centre they were at earlier. Maybe a girl would be there. This had been a shitty day for the eyes. Not every hunt resulted in a capture but he was zero for two and that sucked.

Missing two sweets in a row. Fuck. He thought about following the bus and seeing if there was an opportunity to grab that lady. No --- better to find a new one. Those kids saw him.

Ten minutes later the eyes were at the small Shopping Centre. The eyes parked the van and just watched. Watching the girls going in and girls coming out. It was a slow day and didn't look promising. Nothing the eyes saw really stood out or caught his fancy. Then a lady arrived in a light blue mini-van. She looked promising but the eyes would wait until she got out to see how she looked. The eyes were looking for a certain type today. When she got out the eyes knew this was the one. She was gorgeous and must have been in her early thirties. She went around to the passenger side and pulled out a small young child. She put the child in her baby carrier in the front of her chest and walked into the mall carrying her purse. The eyes watched her. The parking lot wasn't busy. The eyes positioned the van beside her van. This would need to be a quick one. Twenty-five minutes later the lady was walking back to her van with the child. She carried two bags in her left hand. When she was closer she used the FOB to unlock the doors and opened the side sliding door and she put the two bags of groceries and her purse on the floor of her van. Then she delicately put her infant in the second row of seats, carefully strapping the child into the safety seat. She closed the door and then opened the driver's door. The eyes were hiding behind his van --- looking around one last time and it was perfect. No one would see. As the lady turned to enter her van the eyes snuck up behind her and pricked her on the back of her neck with the needle. Almost instantly she was unconscious and as she slumped over the eyes caught her preventing her fall. Quickly the eyes opened the side door and transferred the lady into his van --- the zip ties and gag were on her in a matter of seconds. The eyes had lots of practice doing this type of thing. The eyes closed the door and the white van drove off and out of sight. The infant in the lady's van began crying for Mommy but no one heard those cries. The eyes were happy now. It was a going to be a good day after all!

CHAPTER 7

I found a spot and pulled over a few blocks away from the Shopping Centre and scooted in the back --- quickly checking on the lady. She was still unconscious. I checked her vital signs and breathing. She would recover nicely. I unhitched the secret latch and lifted the mattress to the upright position, picked up the lady and gently laid her into the hiding spot. Once there I looked more closely at her. She was absolutely stunning --- one of my all-time best captures. I decided this one would make the journey back to the farm. No forest for her. I wanted to spend time with this one. My heart was racing --- anticipating the fun ahead --- for me at least. I just had to remember to travel the speed limit and not do anything to draw attention to me. I was soon on the highway and driving back to the farm. I loved these times --- the anticipation. I thought of Christmas when I was a young child and how fun it was seeing all those presents wrapped under the Christmas tree. I would check the presents to see which ones had Kyle's name on them. Then I would put all Kyle's presents into one pile to see how many were all for him. They looked so nice --- just laying there --- waiting to be opened. The girls are just like those Christmas presents --- waiting to be torn apart and ravished --- to be destroyed. My mind continued to wander and I smiled as I found myself thinking about the time I was given my first gun. That gun provided hours of fun. All the target practice hours, that eventually led to shooting birds and squirrels. Hell ... if it moved I wanted to shoot it. At first I would shoot just to kill it but I soon discovered that if I shot the animal and just wounded it --- well --- that was much more fun and entertaining to watch. I don't really understand why that is? I can't wait to get home.

I put the van on cruise control for the main part making sure it was right at the speed limit. The police had radar traps. I saw a few cops hiding near the overpass bridges. The dirty bastard cops. Radar should not be permitted. It isn't fair --- not a level playing field. I hate cops --- always have. They have a job to do but there are too many that use their authority to cause shit. I counted four cops in their hiding spots along the way. I knew these were the most dangerous times. Once back at the farm I would feel more at ease but even with this anxiousness it still makes me feel more alive. I would always look at the cop as I passed but made sure to keep my head pointing straight ahead. The eyes though would look off to the side to make sure the cop stayed where he was. My mind began to wander again. I looked at the other vehicles on the highway. There was a divider on the highway. Two lanes in one direction and then a wide strip of grass, perhaps seventy feet separating the other two lanes going in the opposite direction. It was safer and the rationale for its construction was it helped prevent the head-on crashes and thus the mortality rates. The data supported that. The times I would be driving with my girls, and there were many, I was especially careful of the other drivers. I didn't want some asshole not paying attention on a lane change or whatever and involving me in an accident. Keeping a nice, safe distance from other drivers was a requirement of the job. Yet on the way home I couldn't help but let my mind wander some more. I thought about that lady in the back and wondered about her. *Did she have just the one kid? What was her name? Did she have a job? What about her family?* There were so many questions that I wanted answers to. I really liked learning all I could about my girls. It makes me feel closer to them in a way. It helps me remember them later --- after they are gone. I like to remember them. I especially like to remember the way they suffered --- the way they faced death and the way they died. I wondered about this lady. I hoped she would be tough. I liked the tough ones better. The ones that think they're tough. In the end they all broke down just because well --- they were human. I thought about what I might do to her but at the same time tried focussing on the road. It wasn't easy. As I got closer and closer to the farm my excitement grew. I preferred taking them to the farm. When I carried them into the forest there was always the time constraints --- usually a couple of hours at best. It was like voyeurism in the forest. *Would someone just happen to blunder into my privacy?* I had to be more aware of my surroundings no matter how secluded the surroundings. At the farm though there was time, time to do really good work. Time to prolong the screaming and the fear. For some reason I thought about this one girl I had years ago. Her name used to be Michelle. I hadn't thought of her in a while yet for some odd reason she came into my head. I could picture her perfectly. I even remembered what she was wearing when I snagged her. She was twenty years old and had long wavy light brown hair with slight dark streaks in it. She was just ever so slightly freckled. Even her legs and back had these soft, ever so slightly brown freckles on her skin. The skin was like smooth, warm satin. She would have been a dermatologist's dream. Someone the dermatologist could use as a poster child for advertising. What great skin she had. She wore black shorts that day and white running shoes with pink laces. On her right ankle she had sported an ankle bracelet of a tiny dolphin. She had a tank top on, bare arms just past the shoulders and a tiny, tiny necklace with four tiny pendants on it. There were three little crystal puppy dogs and one yin and yang pendant. I still remember. Michelle had said the little puppy dogs represented her two best friends and her. They had called themselves the "Three Musketeers" and according to Michelle they did everything together. Homework, parties, swimming, shopping, lunches at the school --- everything. I knew all about her friends --- not just the "Three Musketeers" but also some of her other girlfriends. And I knew about her boyfriends. The girls always talk --- eventually. I don't know a lot about other serial killers --- not really. I read about them but like most things I figured what someone read in the newspapers, in books, or on-line was a lot of bullshit. Not the real truth. I figured most serial killers didn't give two shits about the victim's particulars. I'm different though. I considered myself a new breed --- a better breed. I want to know my girls or at least some things about them. For

Michelle she had spent three days visiting the farm. I laugh when I used the term visiting the farm. Then I thought of that song Hotel California. The one where you check in but you don't check out. I smirked as I drove. The leaves were changing colours and the drive along the highway was a thing of beauty. Especially when passing the hills where one could admire the cascading shifting of colours. The trees getting ready for winter --- the leaves dying yet at their greatest moment of beauty --- the leaves sacrificing themselves so that the trees could continue to survive. Nature is nothing but a cycle of life and death. I thought about my own life. It is a puzzling journey really. I'm already thirty-six years old. It is hard for me to believe. *Where had all the time gone? It seemed to just disappear so suddenly?* It used to be easier to get young girls. I could use my youth and good looks to talk to them - to seduce them --- to get them to trust me. Now I was just a dirty old man talking to the girls. Things were changing. Now I had to use different tactics mostly. The girls were more reluctant to just get into the car for a drive. Times were changing too! Kids these days are much more streetwise than twenty years ago. But the reality is that kids can still be easily tricked. Parents need to realize even though you talk to them they can be tricked. It's so easy to hide one's identity over the web or social media. I did it but I was also very careful. I knew the police also pretend to be teenage girls to try and capture predators. So I now stick to the opportunistic snagging method. Make sure you have a good plan and be aware. And be a good boy scout. Always be prepared just in case something goes wrong.

I thought back to that one lady that just got away at the bus stop. I shook my head. I was still upset those teenagers showed up. I was happy I had another girl but like many people, you pine at the one that got away. It is silly really but she was dressed to the nines and looked like she would be worthy of my attentions.

I notice a cut-off ramp that leads to a gas station. I signal and pull over to the ramp to exit. I want to make a quick stop to check on my new lady friend. That's when I notice a cruiser behind me pulling off too! I check my speed and eyed the cop in the side mirror. I signal again to pull into the gas station and the cop is following me. I decide I should get gas rather than just pull over and then leave so I drove to one of the pumps. I get out and see the cop pull up to the pump beside me. I lift the nozzle and clear the lever and start to pump gas in my van. The cop did the same to his cruiser. There were two cops. I put in twenty dollars and then slid the nozzle back into the pump. I was well aware where and what those two cops were doing the whole time. The cop pumping gas was looking at me --- or so it seemed. I fake a small smile the cop's way --- then turn away. I went into the store to pay for my gas. I had the cap and hood pulled over my head. There were cameras as usual. I was paying by cash when I heard the door chime. I looked back and two cops were entering the cashier area. I put my hand to my side where my handgun was under my jacket. I was ready. Both cops stood behind me while I got my receipt and said thanks to the cashier. The one cop reached for some sugarless gum and then walked over to the soft drinks and pulled out two cokes. I watched them secretly like a great cat --- ready for a kill. My face showed no emotion. I turned to walk back to the door and the other cop stepped forward.

I heard the clerk say "Afternoon Officer. Just the gas today?"

The cop answered, "No --- add the two cokes and the gum thanks."

I walk briskly to the van --- got in and start it up and drive away. I would have to check on my girl later --- when it was safer. Now I was constantly looking in my rear mirror as I drove to the ramp to get back on the highway. I breathed a sigh of relief and muttered under my breath.

"Dirty cops! Fuck you!"

My breathing became more normal after a minute or two but within four minutes that cop car was behind me again. I eyed my side mirror. *They were running my plate* --- that's what I was thinking. Suddenly the cruiser's lights began flashing and the siren began blasting.

I grabbed my handgun and muttered, "You're going to die Pigs! Fuck you," but the cruiser just as suddenly pulled out in the left lane and passed my van and sped off in front of me. They were going somewhere else.

"You're lucky you fucking bastards! You got no idea how lucky you are!"

I figured I was only about thirty minutes from the farm. After that I started to play over and over the gun battle I would have had with those cops. I was loaded for bear and had no doubt I would have killed both of those officers but the problem would have been their radio. They would have called for backup and given my plates, van and other information out to the other officers. I thought it all out as I drove and imagined a great gun battle and roadblock scenario. I was very smart and cunning but I had one hell of an imagination. I remembered how I would practice my quick draw back on the farm. I was fast, very fast and accurate --- a true expert and marksman with firearms whether with a handgun or the various rifles. I was even an expert with both the bow and crossbow. I had so much potential. I would have been a great sniper for the police or military. Problem was I liked killing a bit too much. And I was very athletic and nimble. Since the very beginnings I was a fan of the Ultimate Fighting Championships, known as the U.F.C. My Martial Arts background would be a problem for most people. I'm like a shark --- if one could put it that way. I'm a perfect predator --- a perfect killing machine --- a miracle of evolution. I feel no pity.

CHAPTER 8

I continued to check my mirrors as I turned onto the ramp leading off the highway. I made sure to signal all my turns. I was still upset but I hadn't seen any cops for the last thirty minutes. I made a quick stop on the shoulder of the road and scanned the sky. No helicopter and no planes. I waited a minute to make sure I wasn't being followed. I can't wait to get home. It has been quite the day but it is about to get better. I travelled the road for just over two miles then signalled my right turn. Three quarters of a mile later I signalled a left turn. The area now is mainly farmland with the odd patches of woodlots. It is flat land mostly with grazing areas for livestock or working the hay. I travelled the road that leads to the farm. It is a gravel road and is usually nothing but a cloud of dust when travelled on but it had rained hard and now the road threw no dust. Three miles later I signalled and pull into my driveway --- the whole time watching my rear view mirror. An old mailbox at the front entrance stood and looked like a slight breeze might knock it over. The little red wooden flag was up so there was mail in the box. I stopped and got out of the van. I left it running. I stretched my legs and arms as I scanned the familiar surroundings. It is a desolate place --- just like a farm should be --- private.

I climbed back in the van and put the mask on that covered only my eyes. Standing at the bed I pushed the release to the latch and slowly opened the lid. I peered inside as the light entered the box and there looking up at me is the lady.

She tried to talk --- tried to scream as I looked down at her. I smile. She was alert and I was thinking she was ready --- ready for the games to begin. I closed the lid and latched it, took off the mask and opened the sliding door. Before closing the door I turned to once again look at the mattress. She would be one of the fortunate ones. She would be going in the house --- down to the basement. I got out of the van and closed the door and walked to the mailbox. I opened the mailbox and removed the five pieces of mail inside. I briefly looked at the envelopes but I was much more interested in the other package that was in the van. I drove up the driveway until I reached the gate. I walked in front of the van and unlocked the front gate. I had fashioned a heavy-duty steel front gate that would deny entry to unwanted visitors. I got back in the van, put it in drive and once past the gate relocked the gate and drove to the farmhouse. It was a long driveway --- about one hundred and fifty yards that had a gradual dip at about the halfway point. Then it was only a matter of a slight uphill drive to the farmhouse. There were small trees and shrubs for the first hundred yards of the driveway but it cleared nicely as it approached the house. It was only at that point that the farmhouse was visible. The driveway snaked its way to the back of the house. I backed the van up to the bottom of the stairs and shut the van off and just sat there for one minute. I savoured the feeling as the excitement grew.

I live alone and by all accounts would fit the profile of a typical serial killer --- if there were such a thing. Lonely, few friends, and a very quiet sort of fellow and never caused any trouble. Neighbours might say I was the type of guy that kept to himself but seemed so normal at the same time. The neighbours seldom talked with me. I was a private person.

Kyle had bought the farm when he was but twenty years old. His parents were both dead and he had been on his own since he was eighteen years old. The two years following the death of his parents had been a rough transition for him. But luck changed its ugly destiny as it sometimes does without explanation. Kyle won the lottery --- a few million dollars and his direction in life would change forever. He gave a bit of the winnings to his siblings --- more out of a feeling of obligation than deserving. He wasn't close to them and it was his way of saying good-bye and good riddance. He had always wanted to buy some place for himself and with the lottery win it was now possible. He had finished high school and after winning the lottery he found the farmhouse that would become his home. The farmhouse was really an accident. He just happened to see an advertisement for a farm and the remote location appealed to him for some odd reason. He phoned to inquire about it. The farm had been abandoned after the previous owners had died. They had both committed suicide in the farmhouse. The couple had lived there for decades but the wife had developed cancer and was on her deathbed or so the story goes. So one night the man and wife lay down together for the last time and swallowed some strychnine that was always kept around the farm for the poisoning of rodents or birds. It is a deadly type of poison that results in muscular convulsions and eventual asphyxiation --- a terrible way to die when you think of it. You would think they would have found a more humane way to end it. They were not discovered for several weeks and were found lying in the bed in the upstairs bedroom. They looked so peaceful. Few people wanted to buy such a property when they learned the sorted details of the couple's passing. Kyle found it interesting though and Lucas especially loved the story. Lucas prodded Kyle like he does and Kyle quickly bought the property.

The farm itself was old. The real estate agent was not sure how old the property actually was. The historical records were spotty. What was known was that at one time it was a dairy farm with Holstein cows providing the milk and dairy products. There had been chickens there and quite possibly other livestock. The land was just over two hundred acres with a small stream cutting through the northeast corner of the property. There were three ponds on the property. Sixty acres were cleared for the cows and livestock and one hundred and forty-six acres were woodlots - mainly hardwoods with just a sprinkle of softwoods. There had been no livestock on the farm for a number of years. There was an old barn that was still in pretty good shape considering its advanced age. The barn itself was big and chock-full of the remnants of old farming apparatus everywhere. Three old tractors long past their shelf life with old rubber tires cracked all to hell. Parts missing from each machine and from a time when the owners would salvage parts from one machine to another to keep them running --- to keep the farming functioning. Kyle had bought a new tractor, used for the plowing and such. Strewn everywhere from the floor to the rafters was an array of materials from hay to old farm implements that most people had no idea what they were used for. There were a number of stalls for the cows with old milking pails hanging on old rusty nails at each stall. Kyle had discovered some very old carriages at another outbuilding and wondered about the horses of the time. Likely they would be kept separate from the cows. A person could enter the barn and just stare in amazement, there was just so much to look at. It was a like staring through a looking glass back to a different time, when life was much tougher. Most windows in the barn were broken and in bad shape from falling sticks and debris when the winds would come. There must have been a lot of storms in this area. Strangely there seemed to be no manure anywhere on the farm that one could see. Yet the one thing that was truly bothersome was there were so many flies around the farm. Maybe they sensed this is where they belonged --- a place of shit and dead animals --- a place where flies could feed and breed. The place still had the smell of livestock. It smelled like one would expect a farm to smell. The roof of the barn was in fairly good shape. There was only one tear in the southwest corner where a large tree branch had fallen through eons ago. The tree branch long removed by someone unknown but the gap to the sky ignored and remaining.

There was an old chicken coup off from the barn some eighty feet away. Two concrete walls lined the sides as it was dug down about five feet from the ground level. Old wooden posts lined both sides, each post about six feet apart. The posts were in rough shape and supported an old tin roof. Old hay was everywhere along the floor of the coup. The parts where the chickens would have been housed were no longer there. The coup reminded Kyle of some long lost tunnel like an ancient apparition. It was long, perhaps one hundred and fifty feet or more. The concrete walls had weathered fairly well and Kyle imagined a time long past when chickens would spend their lives roosting there. He imagined them laying their eggs for the farmer --- or to be sold at the market. He also imagined at times the chickens getting their heads cut off to be fare for the dinner table. He would cringe thinking about that but Lucas just thought how he would have loved doing that. Lucas would imagine himself as the executioner and carrying out the beheadings at the old guillotines during the French Revolution. Cutting off the heads of chickens sounded like fun. He remember stories his dad would tell him about cutting off the heads of chickens and how they would run around the yard for a minute without any head attached. Lucas thought he would like to see that. If only his girls could do that. He tried that a couple of times but they didn't cooperate. Oh, how he would have loved to see one of his girls running around the yard --- with no head.

The farmhouse itself was very, very old. Constructed of old concrete and various stones and old wood. The roof had been modernized and shingled properly. The wiring had been updated to two hundred amp circuit breakers. The outside of the house had wooden type shingles from the roof to the concrete base of the house. Kyle found out quite by accident one evening that those shingles were the home to hundreds of bats when they exited the house just at sundown. It sent a shiver down his spine when he happened to be sitting on the porch one evening having a tea when he noticed that the wall beside him seemed to start to move. Then as if at recess time on some school yard when kids swarm the playground hundreds upon hundreds of bats climbed out, hanging upside down for a second and then letting go and dropping down only to start flying into the evening sky to search for food. It was a hell of a scary sight to suddenly be surrounded by bats flying in every direction only inches from your head and face. The bats never touched him but Kyle panicked and moved off the porch and ran about fifty feet away from the house. He turned to see the house come alive, like some evil scene from an old Frankenstein movie --- the walls seemed infested by the bats. In a minute or so the bats had left the farmhouse and were gone, flying into the semi-darkness and out of sight. That really shook Kyle up. He asked neighbours about the bats and they said it was a common thing on many farms and actually they were good at keeping the insect population down. He worried and imagined the bats coming into the house --- while he was sleeping --- crawling across his bed and towards his neck and jugular --- going for the warm nectar of his body fluids. He never saw one bat in the house though and although it took a while he eventually got used to the idea of swarms of bats filling the air. What he found out was that the bats returned to their shingles before the sun began to rise. It was like some Dracula movie that the bats would die if touched by the rays of sunlight.

Kyle was advised when he first moved in that it would be a good idea to keep some cats around --- for the mice. Being on a farm meant lots of mice and critters might find their way into the house. With cats the mice were reluctant to enter the old dwelling. So he picked up three cats for this purpose. He gave the cats all the same name --- Jasper. They were all males. He didn't want females and he sure as hell didn't want kittens. Through the years he replaced the cats when they died and his mouse problem was pretty much none existent. The farmhouse had a front porch that rose about four feet off the ground. The porch at the back was about twelve feet off the ground with thirteen steps leading up to the house. The back porch was large and screened so several people could sit and enjoy the view without being bothered by the mosquitos, deer flies, horse flies, or black flies eating you alive. Kyle had expanded the back porch with screens after witnessing all those bats so he could have a feeling of protection from them. At first some bats would fly into and hang on the screen, their sharp claws at the end of their wings clinging as they prepared to leave. After all the bats were there first. It was their home really. There were several windows at the front and back of the house but only two at each side of the house. Some windows had been modernized with proper screens and some were left in their original ancient design. Kyle bought the house, lock, stock, and barrel, meaning it came fully furnished from everything in the house to the barn and all the outbuildings. He got rid of all the soft furniture and especially the bed and frame where the suicide had occurred all those years ago. It was strange that it was still in the house but everyone was afraid to touch it. There were some very cool, antique furniture pieces throughout the property. The daughter who had inherited the property after the suicide basically put a lock on the property and had someone else gather all the pictures and personal belongings. The house was unoccupied and had been abandoned for a few years.

Kyle found that there was nothing especially outstanding about the place on the middle or upper levels. The floors creaked and groaned when walked on, especially the set of old wooden stairs leading downstairs. The entire aura of the place would have made for a great horror movie location. Downstairs was the true gem. It was a large area with an old set of stairs leading down to a very dark place. No windows here and natural stone and rocks walls gave the place a dampness that one could describe only as grave like. Kyle put two de-humidifiers down there and did a lot of work to make a nice, comfy living area where he could work. It became a self-contained basement apartment in a way. He had put in a kitchen and one room off to the side became his taxidermy area. He worked on fish for a few years but recently had done less taxidermy work. He had more customers years ago but as he scaled back he accepted less and less fish to work on. He had all the tools though and he had several fish up on the walls for display. He had been a very good taxidermist and the fish looked just like they should --- alive. He had specialized in trout but could do any fish. He stayed away from mammals or birds. For some reason he didn't mind fish though. He was completely unaware of the four rooms that were hidden behind the secret passageway towards the front of the house. Lucas found the hidden entrances quite by accident one morning a few years later and he was amazed at their existence. Really ingeniously hidden by someone from another era. It wasn't a secret bookcase that would pull out or a secret rising staircase but something totally unexpected. Lucas just happened to be around the old oil tank and he did three things at the same time when suddenly the oil tank shifted just a fraction of an inch. Lucas stood looking at the discovery and quickly tried to remember what he had done to trigger the release of the old oil tank. It was a functioning oil tank and from the looks of it, the release hadn't been used in a very, very long time. Lucas used both hands and it took a few seconds when he realized the tank could be moved out just enough for a person to squeeze through. There was some kind of opening there and it was dark. Lucas was excited discovering this and wondered where did it lead? *What was back there but especially who built it and why?* He went to the workbench and got a flashlight and returned to the entrance. He proceeded to squeeze by the sticky spider webs that brushed his face and body. He blocked the tank so it wouldn't suddenly close trapping him for eternity. He wasn't sure what to expect? It was both exciting and scary and a bit disturbing. As he entered he saw a very old light switch just inside and to the right. He flicked the switch expecting it not to work. It worked and two very dim lights came on in a short, narrow hallway. Lucas kept the flashlight on just in case. This place was the kind of spooky no movie could even come close to. The walls of the hall were natural rock, cold and dripping wet. The hallway itself was only about seven feet long and at the end was an old wooden green door with blotches of red on it. There was a very old lock on the door. A skeleton key hung down to the left of the door on the rock wall. He almost didn't see the key, as it was the same colour grey as the rock wall. *Would it fit the old lock?* He noticed beside the skeleton key something scratched on the face of the wall. It was some kind of message in an old ancient type of font. Lucas used his left hand to wipe away the dust and then blew away the remaining debris that was still clinging to it. The other hand tightly grasped the flashlight. He was actually afraid. He had never been afraid of anything before. He was not the afraid type but this was something else. He smiled nervously with eyes staring at the scripture like message. He wiped the message like one might swipe an old blackboard --- so he could read it. He held the light up and read the six words. The message read, *"DEATH COMES TO ALL THAT ENTER!"* Lucas couldn't resist. He was in awe --- what a fucking adventure this place was turning out to be. He reached for the skeleton key and lifted it off the hook. He looked at the key. It was obviously very old. He placed the key to the old lock and tried to put the key inside. It slid in only part way and the key wouldn't turn at all. *"Shit!"* Lucas muttered under his breath. He put the key back and turned around and began to exit the chamber. He squeezed by the oil tank and went to the workbench in the main room and put the flashlight down. He began frantically searching for something. He needed to get past that lock and that green and red door. *Where did it lead and especially what did the inscription mean?* He found what he was looking for. Lucas found a can of WD-40 and shook the can --- it still had pressure in it. He sprayed a bit into the air and it worked. *Good --- the nozzle was clear.* He hastily picked up the flashlight, turned, and headed back, squeezing into the secret chamber once again. It made him think of some ancient tomb --- like the Egyptians might build. He started to wonder about the inscription. *Was the place booby-trapped?* He didn't care. He needed to see what was back there hidden for so long. He grabbed the lock and generously sprayed the lubricant into the lock. Then he grabbed the key once again and sprayed it as well. He waited a few seconds and then ever so slowly put the skeleton key back into the lock. This time the skeleton key fully inserted and he began to try and turn it. At first it didn't work but slowly the lock seemed to be cooperating. He took the key out and sprayed again into the lock. This time he tried spraying the outside of the lock as well. He waited for a few seconds and then re-inserted the skeleton key. This time the key turned more and as he turned the key back and forth careful not to force it the lock suddenly snapped open. It was a heavy lock and had to be centuries old --- maybe older. Lucas smiled. "Yes!" he exclaimed quietly but excitedly. For some reason he felt the need to whisper. He removed the skeleton key and rehung it on the wall. He again looked at the inscription. His breathing was rapid. The ancient lock had two settings to open fully. He opened it and it emitted a loud squeaking scream like sound at the final opening. He noticed a tiny ledge on the wall that could only have one purpose --- a resting place for the lock. He delicately put the lock on the narrow, small ledge. He noticed his hands were actually shaking as he did this. He transferred the flashlight to his left hand and with his right hand he touched the lever to the door. He imagined this lever had not felt human hands for hundreds of years. It was made out of some kind of metal and had a curvature to it that was unknown. He pulled the lever first up, then down but it didn't fully move. He put his shoulder on the door trying to push but the door wouldn't budge. He kept trying but something was definitely stopping the door. *"Shit! So close! What the fuck!"* Lucas muttered louder. He stepped back thinking what could he do? Break the door down if need be but then he looked up. The ceiling was only a couple inches above his head but something was up there right above the door. He shone the flashlight up to see better and saw it. It was really barely noticeable. It was some kind of little door like thing? He stared at it trying to figure out what it was? He reached up to it --- to touch it --- to feel it --- and it moved as it brushed his hand. He pulled his hand away --- it felt like it was alive!

CHAPTER 9

Lucas quickly pulled his hand away like one would flinch upon discovering a spider on one's arm. He moved the light closer to try and get a better look. It was covered in a thick like spider web --- the type of web that looked like a matted blanket --- and there was a huge, dark spider looking down at him with four black eyes. Lucas wasn't normally afraid of spiders but this one was huge and he had touched it --- or it had touched him. Slowly the spider backed up and then disappeared into some hidden crack --- or rather crevice near the mini-door. He reached to his sheath and took out his knife. He scrapped away the spider's web careful should the spider suddenly re-appear. He definitely didn't want the spider suddenly falling down on him. He sprayed some WD-40 thinking that would drive the spider further back --- wherever it had gone. He noticed on the sliding door there was the symbol of an arrow. He used his fingers to push the sliding door and it slid about six inches back revealing a small handle. He gripped the handle and pulled downwards and heard a loud clicking noise behind him. He quickly turned back but saw nothing different. He pushed the handle back to its original position and heard the definite click again. It was coming from the green door. He pulled the handle down again to hear the click --- then turned his attention to the door. He grabbed the lever on the door and pulled upward and pushed on the door. This time the door opened ever so slightly --- creaking at it's every movement. He had to give the door an extra push every couple of inches. He was about to enter an area when he thought about that warning. He couldn't help himself --- he had to see. When the door was half way open it suddenly started opening all by itself --- making a screeching sound as the hinges ever so slowly released --- until it was finally open. It sounded like the door was breathing. He shone the flashlight inside and what he saw was astonishing. It was difficult to see clearly as there seemed to be a mist and musk in the air and there were a number of spider webs everywhere. The room was alive with spiders as they tried to scurry away from the entering light. He shone the flashlight to the left of the door's entrance and there was light switch there. He turned it on and suddenly there was flickering light at first but the light seemed to be getting brighter. He stood staring for a minute not believing what his eyes were seeing. There were three tables --- more like old operating tables --- and there was lots of medical equipment. He found an old broom and swept away most of the spider webs as he entered the room attempting to look everywhere at once. *Why would an operating room be down here --- and so hidden?* He walked about the room, which seemed a good size --- about forty by forty feet. The ceiling was higher here --- about seven and a half feet tall. Here too the walls were natural rock. There was a ventilation system to try to keep the room fresh. He turned it on. It still worked. He noticed something. He noticed that the tables --- all three of them had restraints on them. He noticed something else. When looking back at the green door it had closed slightly and was beginning to close on its own. He ran to the door to stop it from closing. He grabbed the door just in time and that is when he noticed scratch marks on the inside of the door. He stared at the scratch marks --- they were human claw marks --- from someone who had tried to get out. He grabbed a wooden stool and placed it so the door would not close. He checked the door to make sure it wouldn't close on him and then went back to inspecting the room more fully. The room was full of medical supplies and although rudimentary compared to todays standards --- they sufficed for the time. There were bottles of ether and chloroform for anaesthetics --- and the room was well stocked with supplies. Off in the corner to the right of the green door there was a large chest that really looked rather like a pirate's treasure chest. It looked out of place sitting there. It was covered with an old, grey wool blanket. He was drawn to it and removed the blanket. The chest was made of wood and wrapped in metal. It was some kind of storage box. He saw there was a lock on the front of it. *"Shit --- another lock,"* he whispered. He still felt the need to whisper in this tomb like room. He looked around but could find no key. *"Fuck --- I'm going to have to break in."* He hurried out of the room --- back to the hallway that would lead out to the oil tank. As he moved he kept an eye out for the giant spider and he wondered if there was more than one giant arachnoid hiding somewhere waiting to pounce. *"Shit that thing was big,"* he muttered to himself. He squeezed by the oil tank and hurried to the workbench. He found an old hammer and chisel and hurried back to the special room. This time when he entered the room he smiled. *This was fucking neat.* It was the coolest place Lucas had every seen --- and it was real. He knelt down at the chest and grabbed the lock but when he grabbed it he noticed it wasn't even locked. *Quite puzzling? Why have the lock if the owner wasn't going to lock it? Did the owner forget or did something happen that he couldn't lock it?* So much was unknown. The lock barely turned so he sprayed a generous amount of lubricant on it and removed the lock. He placed the lock on the dusty floor --- then picked it up and thought it better to put it on a small table beside the chest. He flipped the latch and lifted the lid --- slowly. For some reason he was thinking of giant spiders. He peered inside as he ever so slowly lifted the lid. He noticed the chest was half full of various items. When the lid was high enough to stay up on its own --- he looked down and saw jewellery, lots of jewellery and identification pieces. He picked up and examined some of the jewellery but was quickly drawn to the identification pieces. He started reading each one and noticed they were all women --- and he counted thirteen in all. *Did the guy who once lived here --- was he a Coroner --- or an Embalmer or something else?* Then he noticed something else in the old chest. Inside and tucked in a side sleeve was a black book with the words in gold like print on the front cover that said *"JOURNAL – PRIVATE."* He immediately reached for the book --- his eyes wide in excitement.

The cover of the journal was black with a hint of grey and its dimensions were small. The journal was about five inches by nine inches or so. Kyle dusted it off and opened the first page:

"This is the private property of Karl Garrick and is not to be read by any human living or dead."

Lucas' eyes looked about the room after reading that. He couldn't stop reading now. He turned the pages and began to read the first entries.

July 14 1821

I am Karl Garrick of Mishing Township and this is my journal. My beloved fourth wife Mary had borne me with my daughter, Patricia, and my son, Paul. My first wife Sally died at the age of seventeen years two months after sixteen months of marriage. I married my second wife Elizabeth six months after the passing of my beloved Sally. Elizabeth died at the age of nineteen years and two months after nine months of marriage. My third wife Rose I married eight months after Elizabeth died. Rose died at the age of twenty years and three months after twelve months of marriage. Sally died at labour with child that would have been a son. Elizabeth and Rose died of the disease. They bore no sons or daughters. I married my beloved Mary eleven months after Rose died. My beloved daughter Patricia from Mary died at fourteen years and seven months of age of sickness. My beloved wife Mary died at thirty-one years of age in the year of our lord 1802. My son Paul it seems will survive me. He married Debbie Connelly but lost his wife to disease after fifteen months of marriage. She bore no children.

I am near the end of my life as I have a sickness that does not look promising and so this is a confession of sorts not to Church or God but to any daring enough to read these journal entries. I am and have been the Doctor here since my arrival in 1783. And although I have served many members I must confess that I have acted as a Satan in cloak of darkness. For not only have I permitted many to die that I could have likely saved I have in fact nurtured their deaths and well I realize this is wrong in the eyes of God I continued to do so. Further to this confession I have also taken those girls in the Townships surrounding that were healthy for my own pleasures and purposes. These girls I confess to twelve as the Number. Some are in the back three hidden rooms from here and some their bones and ashes remain no more.

At that revelation Lucas looked about the room --- mesmerized at his finding for if true that meant that a serial killer once lived here and that these were his hidden chambers of death and torture. He had found one that was like him and perhaps left his legacy to be fulfilled and passed on from here. He was torn to get up and look for the other three rooms or to continue reading. He chose to continue reading:

Since this is my confession as I am near the bed of death I confess to you reader sometime in the future where these rooms are hidden and their entry and since you found this lair you are without doubts the type that likes a good riddle and so from my pen I tell you there is but one entry to the other three and beyond is the cavern of escape should need be. This also is hidden as I have spent my life developing the intricacies of said devices. And so herein lies the Riddle.

Be warned that all mortals that try to enter the world of my own you must do so carefully and with thought. For if you make a false step there can be no doubt but of certain death to those that error in the entry. So if your curiosity is greater than your fear of death I avow the following:

You can squeeze to the left you can squeeze to the right Trying to get by for they both are so tight but only One is the way tho they are both out of sight one is of death And one is of life But who do you visit remember Thy name one is of darkness and one is of flame Always travel this way and safe ye shall be Whether room two three or four I decree.

Lucas would later check the history of the oil tanks and he came to the realization that someone else and most likely a few people over time must have carried out some of these modifications. Oil was not available for heat in the early 1800's. That meant that someone changed the entry system to the front chamber --- and more than once perhaps.

He stopped reading and got up and looked about the room. *What could it mean and where were these other secret passages?* It took a long time for Lucas to solve the riddles but he eventually found the correct passages and managed to enter the other rooms. He figured out which entries were safe. He used the same answer to the riddle to travel further to the depths of despair --- better known as the long darkness.

When he entered the second room for the first time he noticed this room was set up as a medieval type of torture chamber. This room was about the same size in dimensions as the first room. There were many devices in this second room and many items looked very menacing. He had to look up and research the many contraptions to see what and how they were used. He smiled when he realized he was not so alone in his way of thinking --- nor his deeds. He was in awe not only with the rooms but that there was another like him that lived all those years ago. He wondered what was it like back then and how different it would have been? The thought excited him. The third room had old barrels along two sides of the rock walls. After checking he realized the barrels were full of acid --- strong acid that had been used for the disposal of bones and flesh and such he imagined. There were even instructions on how certain apparatus should be used for their greatest effect. *What struck him as puzzling and strange though was how did all this stuff get down here? And who built these elaborate secret chambers?* Many of the things in these back rooms would not have been able to fit through the downstairs doorways. The way he had entered it just wasn't possible. There must be a way --- another way the acid drums and such were here? For a long time it was a puzzle to him. It was when he entered the fourth room a month later that he was truly shocked. It took him a month to solve the entry and he was cautious and always remembered the warning of the scripture to a terrible death to those that do not proceed cautiously. He stood in the fourth room ---- mesmerized. He wasn't sure if he was still breathing or if his breathing and heart had just stopped. *"Hooolllly Shit!"* he kept saying slowly over and over again. *"This was one fucked up guy. He's my hero --- a true master --- and my mentor. Thank you so much Mr. Garrick."* Whenever he needed inspiration he would go to this room and just stare for hours at what was before his eyes. Lucas had a name for this new place. He named it *"The Palace of Pain."*

CHAPTER 10

I sat at the steering wheel thinking. I thought about how lucky I was to have Kyle stumble upon this farm. I opened the van door and slid out of the van and walked to the backdoor of the farmhouse. I unlocked the door and opened all the doors leading to the basement. What I had discovered was that the oil tank when further lubricated opened even wider. Still not wide enough to get those vats or barrels downstairs but wide enough for human bodies and such. I was not yet ready for the back rooms. That would come later. I hurried back to the van. I opened the back van doors and climbed inside. I put the same mask on that I used earlier --- the one that covered my eyes. I then undid the latch and lifted the lid of the bed fully. There lying looking up at me in fear was the lady. She looked exquisite even with her hair messed up. I spoke to her in a soft voice. I used a heavy Russian accent as I spoke to disguise my voice.

"I know you are afraid. I'm going to untie your legs so you can walk but if you struggle I will carry you into the house. It would be safer if you didn't struggle --- in case I drop you and you get hurt. I know you will be thinking of escape but know that I have done this many times before. It would be better for you if you did not try to escape. No one has ever been successful. And I know you are wondering about your young son left in the van. I will tell you he is all right --- he is not hurt. Nod your head yes if you understand."

The lady tried talking with the gag on.

"I know you want to talk and you will be able to in a few minutes. I will try to make you more comfortable and then we can talk and I will tell you why this is happening. As you can see I'm wearing the mask and keeping my identity a secret because I do want to let you go sometime in the near future --- in a few days. That is why I'm wearing the mask --- so you won't be able to identify me later. You no longer have your cell phone as that was disposed of before you were put in my vehicle. I'm going to blindfold you before we walk into the house. This is for your own protection so you can't see your surroundings and tell the police later about the place or me. Nod you head yes if you understand."

The lady nodded her head yes but her eyes could not disguise her fear.

"Would you rather walk or be carried? Nod your head if you are agreeing to walk."

The lady gave a slight hesitation and then nodded her head.

"Okay --- you agree to walk without a struggle. I will put a blindfold on you now so you won't see your surroundings. Then I will help you stand up. I will guide you and hold your arms. Listen to my voice and follow my instructions exactly. I will keep you safe. Do you understand? Nod your head if you understand." The lady nodded her head again.

I placed my hand behind the lady's head and put the blindfold on her. She was breathing very hard and trembling. I cut the zip ties at her ankles. Luckily she was wearing black leggings that protected her skin slightly when she had struggled. There wasn't a lot of room in the box so she wouldn't have been able to move around much. I wanted her skin to remain --- virgin like --- smooth like a baby's ass.

"I'm going to help you stand up now." I helped her stand up.

The first thing the lady noticed was that he must be very strong because she tried to help him as least as she could but he had no problem lifting her up. Once she stood up she felt better but still very much afraid. He held her by her left elbow and his voice was soft and gentle.

"I'm going to lead you forward --- take small steps and stop when I say stop."

They began walking forward for about five feet. She was counting in her head. Her husband had told her about the importance of every little detail if by chance anything should happen to her. She was a beautiful woman. And her own training she relied on as well. She tried smelling her surroundings --- anything that might help her later.

"Stop!" I commanded. "There's a drop. I'm going to help you sit down --- bend your knees so you can sit." The lady did as asked. I jumped out of the back of the van to the ground and turned around.

"I'm going to help you down to the ground now."

I stood in front of her with arms outstretched and pulled her forward and lifted at the same time. I lifted her easily and then gently touched her to the ground. She was on dirt --- the place had the smell of a farm.

"Walk with me as I guide you."

We began walking. The lady was counting the steps in her head and then after eight steps the man told her to stop.

"There are some stairs in front of you that go up. Each step is about six inches high. Feel for the first step."

She found it and began going up the stairs slowly but it was difficult as she felt her way with her feet. He steadied her but she almost tripped once and it was taking far too long.

"Don't be afraid but I'm going to carry you."

Suddenly I picked her up and began going up the stairs. She was airborne as she tried to talk through the gag, *Wait --- I want to walk,* but it was too late. She had counted seven steps but since he picked her up there was no way for her to count the remaining steps accurately. She did notice the stench of a farm and animals. That was quite evident. She felt herself being carried up the stairs and tried to count --- estimating about how many steps there might be. Then she felt herself turning left and right and soon she was very disorientated. Then she felt herself going down. She was being carried down some stairs now. That was evident to her. A few seconds later he took her off his shoulder and planted her feet on the floor. He removed her blindfold and she saw the man standing slightly to the left in front of her --- smiling. He had straight teeth that were white and she imagined he was probably quite handsome by the features she could see. She tried not to stare. He had very sexy grey eyes behind the mask. She didn't want to let him know she was trying to remember his features. She quickly glanced around the room and noticed it was large. One side of the room was setup as a living area and the far side was setup as a work area it seemed.

"I'm going to put this around your ankle --- for your own safety. It's padded so it shouldn't cause you too much discomfort."

It was an ankle shackle that was attached to a wire. She followed the wire and saw it was attached to a large steel ring on the nearest wall about four feet off the floor. *She was to be leashed like a dog!* He attached the ankle shackle securely to her left ankle. It was secure but not too tight. Her hands were still zip locked behind her back. He removed her gag and for a second there was a silence.

"What about my hands? They are very uncomfortable." She looked directly at him, and then lowered her eyes in submission. She was still very afraid but wanted to remain calm. Her husband had told her that a victim should always try to remain calm. There were advantages most times to staying calm.

I nodded and went behind her but before cutting the zip locks with a small cutter I held in my hand I reminded her, "Remember that you are never to try and remove my mask. Think of it is as your insurance policy. If you see my face I will have no choice but to kill you. The mask is so you won't be able to truly identify me later when I let you go. I do plan to let you go. I have no desire to kill you. Do you understand?"

She nodded and answered, "Yes, I understand. I won't touch your mask."

I cut the zip ties and her hands were free. She massaged her wrists where the ties had been.

"My son! My son! You mentioned my son. I want to know more about my son. What can you tell me about him? Jeremy is only five months old and he was left in the van alone. Oh GOD, my poor son!" She started to panic thinking about her baby.

In a calm voice I replied, "As I mentioned, your son is fine. I heard it announced on the radio that they found the boy in the van within a few minutes of him being alone. Your son is fine and unharmed. The authorities have him. They are looking for you. They won't find you though."

I judged her response. I noticed more clearly that her facial features were exquisite. As I stared at her I thought her to be of Mediterranean descent --- or perhaps Mexican. Her slight accent confused me. She was simply gorgeous --- even with little make-up. She wore a wisteria coloured top with a sleeve length mid forearm. It wasn't tight and showed her fit body nicely. Her breasts were full and hanging like ripe fruit. Around her neck she wore a necklace with a trinket. She wore pure white running shoes with soft purple laces. I noticed the ring on her left finger.

"I'm leaving you for just a minute. I have some things to take care of but it won't take but a minute. Think of any questions you may want to ask me and when I come back you can ask me. I will answer as best I can. I also have some questions for you."

I turned and charged up the stairs and closed the door behind me. I went out to the van and took a quick look inside and then locked the doors. I looked about to make sure nothing was out of the ordinary. Then I went back in the farmhouse. I went to the windows and peered through the curtains for one last look outside before heading back downstairs to the lady. I descended the stairs --- almost out of breath in my excitement. The lady was still standing and had surveyed the room as best she could in those short, few moments.

"I know you have many questions and so perhaps now is the time to ask me if you want answers. Why don't you sit? Are you thirsty? Would you like some water or a drink perhaps or something to eat? Please sit."

The lady sat and I sat down beside her on the brown chesterfield. She moved away from me. I waited for questions.

"I could use a water sir," she stated.

I got up and walked across the room to a small refrigerator. I opened it and pulled out two small, bottled waters and returned and handed one to her. I kept the other one for myself. She accepted --- eyeing me closely.

She thought about the wire attached to the ankle shackle. Perhaps if she somehow got behind him she could use it around his neck to choke him so she could escape. Then she thought he probably has the key to the shackle on him but what if he doesn't? She would have to make sure he had the key first before even considering an escape. Then again she would somehow have to get behind him or he would have to have his back turned to her. She knew he was strong. That was clear by the ease that he carried her. She thought about kicking him but that wouldn't help her. It would not be easy --- and very dangerous to attempt an escape. She needed to know more.

"You said my son was okay and safe --- that you heard it on the radio. What else can you tell me what you heard on the radio? What did they say?"

"Only that you were missing and the child was in the vehicle --- a light blue van parked at the Sander's Shopping Centre. The child was safe and police were seeking witnesses. Anyone that was at the Centre to come forward no matter if they thought they knew anything or not. That is all that was said. Oh --- and a description of what they thought you were wearing at the time. That's about it."

The lady nodded her head. She felt relief that her son was okay. "I want to know why am I here?" She dreaded the possible answers but she wanted to know. She needed to know.

I nodded back. "Fair enough but first I want to know your name. Tell me your name." *I already knew her name as I had her purse with all her identifications. And it was mentioned on the radio. I was just testing her --- to see if she would be honest with me.*

"My name is Giacinta."

"Nice to meet you Giacinta." *She was telling the truth so far.* "You can call me Victor. Obviously that isn't my real name. If I told you my real name well --- then why would I insist on a mask for myself? You understand right?"

She nodded that she understood. She had thought about giving him a fake name but then she thought that he probably has her purse and was testing her. She was right.

"You are here because I want you here. That is the simple explanation. I mentioned that I have done this sort of thing before. I kidnap women --- pretty women and bring them back here for a time. I get to know them a bit and --- okay --- I'm not going to bullshit you but I have sex with them. And I'm going to have sex with you. Whether you agree to it or not doesn't really matter to me. It is going to happen. It would be better if you don't fight it too much but that is entirely up to you."

She stared at him and gulped and her eyes got very big at his candour. She started breathing heavily and found herself begin to panic more.

Lucas expected this type of reaction. It wasn't his first rodeo.

"Calm down. It won't help you. You really need to remember that if my mask were to come off --- all bets are off. I would have to kill you quickly. That is something you should not forget."

She stared at him and knew he wasn't kidding. She could just tell he was all business. His voice was very calm though. She was trying to grapple with the idea of him letting her go. *Why would he do that?* So she asked him.

"Why should I believe you would let me go?"

"Well --- because I mean it and I am telling you the truth. I've done this before and the girls are now back living their own lives. The girls are not from here so you probably haven't heard about them. Two of the girls were so afraid they refused to cooperate with the police and two girls did cooperate but didn't have enough information to help the police. I plan to keep you for a few days --- a week at most and then if you cooperate and I feel safe --- I will set you free at some location far away. You will be back with your husband and son after that."

She measured his every word and tried to determine if there was any truth to what this strange man was saying. Then without thinking she blurted out,

"You had better let me go right now. My husband is a police officer --- a Detective and he won't stop looking for me. He'll find me and when he does he'll find you. Let me go right now for your own safety."

The man suddenly jumped up and stood in front of Giacinta. His facial features had changed. He bent forward facing her --- his face inches away from hers --- his grey eyes looking right into her blue eyes. She instantly regretted saying what she said. *GOD if only she could take back what she had said.* So now the man knew her husband was a police officer --- a

Detective. But he didn't know she was a police officer as well. She was off on Maternity Leave along with an extended leave. Thank GOD her police ID was in her van. She just hoped the radio wouldn't mention it --- that she was a police officer. The man continued to glare into her eyes for a few seconds.

"So your husband is a police officer. Well --- isn't that interesting." Then the man said something in a foreign language to her. She thought it sounded Russian or Croatian or something. It sounded angry.

Giacinta gulped and swallowed. She was very afraid now but she then said, "Yes --- so you'd better let me go immediately." She tried staring back. *His eyes made her think this is how it must be looking into the eyes of a great white shark --- cold and lifeless.*

Then the man still looking into her eyes said, "This changes everything." The man turned and stormed upstairs and slammed the door.

There was silence all around her now and Giacinta thought, *"Shit --- why the fuck did I have to mention that? Fuck!"*

CHAPTER 11

Giacinta was alone downstairs and now she was even more worried. At first she heard him walking around upstairs. The floor was squeaky but now she heard nothing but her own breathing --- and her heart beating. She wondered what would happen now? She should not have mentioned that her husband was a police officer but thought it might scare him. It didn't work. He didn't look scared at all. He looked really pissed off. She thought about it and decided it might be better to try and apologize to him --- if she got the chance. She would just have to wait and see if that would be in her favour.

I sat on the sofa upstairs and turned on the television with the remote. I turned to the news station. Within a few minutes the local news was talking about the missing lady. I listened carefully. She was a mother of one and was twenty-nine years old and was the wife of Detective Martin Bello. Her name was Giacinta Bello but what caught my attention even more was that she was a police officer and currently on a paid leave for the baby. Giacinta was a Staff Sergeant with the local detachment.

I smiled when I heard that. "Well --- sheeeiiit! How about that fuck face? My first police officer and her husband is a Detective to boot. The shit is going to hit the fan over this one. Seems like I have some planning to do."

I watched the rest of the news and every ten minutes the news would loop --- the news station doing their best to hype up the story. How the police were on full alert and they mentioned other police departments would be helping in the investigation. It had been five hours since her disappearance. The police were calling on the public's assistance and looking for witnesses. I thought good luck finding witnesses. I was pretty sure there weren't any.

An hour later Giacinta heard the door at the top of the stairs being unlocked. She couldn't see the door, as her range of motion was quite limited because of the wire. She had looked for something --- anything that she might use as a weapon --- or something to cut the wire and free herself but there was nothing. That hour was a difficult one for Giacinta. Her mind was racing a mile a minute imagining all kinds of things that this man might do or be thinking. Even with her training she was terrified. She knew this guy was dangerous --- she could sense it and her instincts were rarely wrong. Then she saw the man's boots coming down the stairs ever so slowly.

The man came down and when fully in view flashed a very delectable smile at her. It was strange? She tried to smile back but it was so contrived --- so fake --- and he could tell. She decided to speak first --- even before he was at the bottom of the stairs.

"Victor --- um --- I want to apologize for what I said early. I shouldn't have threatened you by telling you my husband was a police officer. I was just trying to convince you to let me go immediately so I could be with my child. Mothers can be like that --- I just want to be with my son Jeremy." She made sure to mention the son by name. It was an old psychology trick to personalize one's identity to the attacker. So he would think of her as a person rather than objects to be abused.

"Oh, that's okay Giacinta. I shouldn't have lost my cool but it did throw me for a bit of a loop. You know what a loop is right Staff Sergeant Giacinta Bello?" I stared at Giacinta, enjoying her agony.

She stared back, her eyes beginning to slightly water. *Shit --- he knew. It must have been mentioned on the news.*

"Okay --- so you know. I surmise the news mentioned that. So now what happens Victor?"

"Well --- I did think about it for the last hour and I've decided it doesn't change anything. You don't know who I am or anything about me --- you don't know where you are. You have no idea how far we have travelled since you were unconscious. And I don't want to kill a police officer --- especially if I don't need to. I mean I would rather not. I don't want a life sentence or quite possibly the death penalty. However, same rules apply. If I feel the need to kill you rest assured that I would do so without hesitation. I've served time in several Russian prisons and they are a lot tougher than your prisons here. And I'm not afraid to die like most people. And I do accept your apology. Thank you for giving it."

"Okay then. I'm not going to cause you any trouble and again --- I'm sorry for what I said. In the end though remember that you would have known this information anyway since it was on the television. I just gave you some of it a little bit earlier."

She noticed the contradiction that he didn't want a life sentence or death penalty --- then mentioned the Russian prisons and that he would kill her without hesitation. That he was not afraid of death. Giacinta was trying to judge him but he was a hard one to figure out. She knew he was probably very smart --- with intelligence on the high scale. He also seemed well educated judging by the way he talked. He had a heavy Russian accent and now she knew he was probably Russian because he mentioned the prison. For some reason she imagined that he may have been a person of high ranking in the Russian Mafia or Crime Syndicate or even the KGB. He seemed like he might even have been military at some time.

"I won't hurt you unless you make me. I'm going to make some supper. Do you have any food preferences? Are you a vegetarian or vegan or something? Any allergies? I was going to make a salad and perhaps some spaghetti and meatballs but I can make something else."

Giacinta looked at him. She couldn't believe he mentioned hurting her and making supper in the same conversation. Finally she answered, "And would I eat upstairs or down here?"

"You would eat down here and I would eat with you if that's all right. Or you could eat alone. I will leave it up to you."

Giacinta thought about it. She really didn't want to eat with him but she felt she was on shaky ground and maybe eating with him would help her in the end. "Okay --- we could eat down her --- at the table."

"Okay then, it's settled. I will go up and prepare the dinner. It won't take long ---maybe thirty minutes or so."

Giacinta watched Victor go back up the stairs and heard the door close and then lock. She sighed. She spent the next twenty-five minutes looking around the downstairs as best she could --- just in case she missed something. She was fairly sure he lived alone as it was highly unlikely he had a partner in crime. She then wondered if Victor ever had visitors. She sincerely doubted he would. He seemed like a loner to her. She noticed that all the stuff that could help her was on the other side of the room --- far out of her reach. The workbench especially caught her interest --- with the tools clearly in plain sight. She could see vice-grips and wire cutters and a hammer. The workbench was full of tools she could use but all were out of reach. She sighed looking at the power tools. Even when the wire that was attached to her ankle was stretched to its furthest she was still twenty feet away from reaching the workbench. She wondered if there was something on her side that she could use as a tool to reach the workbench. She looked about for a long pole --- a piece of rope --- something to reach the bench and drag a cutter over. She couldn't find anything but kept looking --- thinking. *"Come on Giacinta --- use your brain and your training. You can get out of this situation."* She also wondered if he ever left the farm. *He must leave to go shopping or to run errands.* Then she thought about his statement that he would have sex with her tomorrow. That thought made her feel sick --- like a pit was in her stomach eating away. She decided she would do what she had to do to survive. Then she changed her mind and decided to fight and not have sex. She thought of her son Jeremy, and her husband. She would not be a docile captive. She would cooperate but not when it came to sex. She just needed that one chance to get away --- even if she had to kill him.

I was making the salad. The Spaghetti was boiling, the meatballs were cooking, the sauce was steaming but all I could think about was the woman downstairs waiting for me and at my disposal. I had much to think about. This was the first time one of my girls was married to a police officer but her being a police officer complicated the situation even more. I was pretty much on autopilot when cooking dinner. I decided fairly quickly what I would do. I didn't trust the police --- in fact I hate and despise them. I understand they have a job to do. I was rational in that regard but I didn't want to socialize with them at all. The lady downstairs was different though. To me she was a beautiful lady first --- almost perfect it seems. Her physical beauty --- hell --- the Pope would notice the curves on this lady. Her hair seemed like silk and her skin. GOD her skin was glowing and youthful. She was a mother and that meant she gave birth. I thought about the sex and wondered if her vagina had stretched back. *Would it be a nice fit or would it be like the Grand Canyon?* I had taken many girls these last two decades. I lost my virginity when I was very young to a neighbour, Tina White, a married lady of twenty-four and ever since then my screw count had grown. I had sex with Mrs. White about ten times before she broke it off. She just got too nervous about her marriage and about the legalities. So she ended it just like that. I was pissed but didn't tell anyone.

Mrs. White never knew she fucked Lucas --- she thought it was Kyle she was fucking. Kyle still thought he lost his virginity when he was twenty-two. I shook my head side to side slowly in a *"What a fucking idiot"* motion as I thought about it. Then suddenly I was back to reality. Dinner was ready. I got a large tray and put a small amount of spaghetti and salad in two bowls, along with two paper plates and two plastic forks. No metal utensils for her. I had some napkins and two plastic cups to drink from. I decided that later I would burn everything in the open fire pit that was at the back of the farmhouse. I had a few open pit fireplaces on the farm. There was also a commercial incinerator that a previous owner had bought and used at the farm. It must have been used to dispose of livestock at one time. I had used it to dispose of other things when the need arose. I would never turn my back on Giacinta unless I was well out of her reach. The furniture was bolted to the floor downstairs and there was little that could be thrown. It was not the first time a girl had visited my palace. I opened the basement door. I was ready.

Giacinta heard it open and gulped. She stared at the stairs like a deer might look at the deep brown grass blowing in the wind --- waiting for a predator to pounce. Then she heard him coming and a second later saw his boots coming down the stairs. She completely lost her appetite and wasn't hungry anymore. She hadn't seen any clocks downstairs. She had no idea how long she was unconscious in the vehicle. It could have been fifteen minutes or it could have been twenty hours or more. She felt disoriented and wished her mind wasn't so foggy.

I came down the stairs and when I saw her I smiled and said, "I hope you like it. I made it from scratch." I then placed it on a table that had only two chairs. "Come --- sit please."

Giacinta stood a distance away. She felt like that deer at the water hole suddenly trapped as a lion approached. "I'm not very hungry," she managed to say.

"Well --- try to eat just a little but please join me and sit."

Giacinta felt compelled to sit even though she regretted agreeing to have dinner with him. She didn't want to upset him though and so she sat at the chair nearest her side of the room. Her wire just barely reaching the chair, she only had about one more foot of length that she could move. She noticed the paper plates, the plastic fork, and the plastic glasses. Giacinta looked at him and knew he was playing it safe. There was nothing that could be used effectively as a weapon or threat by her.

"I see you used your best China and silverware for our dinner." Giacinta forced a smile as she said it.

"Oh --- I think you can understand why. Less dishes to wash." I grinned back at her. "Would you like a glass of this nice red Chianti I brought down for this special occasion?

Giacinta immediately red flagged the comment and thought of that famous movie. "No thanks --- I'll just have the water." *What the hell --- Chianti?* Her heart rate suddenly seemed to increase four hundred times.

"Suit yourself. I'll have a glass though." I poured myself a glass and then added, "I'll just let that sit and breath for a minute."

I set out two small servings of the spaghetti, and two small bowls of salad. It looked good but she was unsure about eating any of it. I served her first --- like any good host should. Then I served myself.

"Go ahead --- eat --- before it gets cold." I said as I looked at her.

She felt very uneasy --- looking at the food --- then at him.

"Giacinta --- look --- I promise I didn't put any drugs in the food or drinks. You have my word. Would you like to switch plates with me?"

Giacinta looked back at him not sure what to think but trusting him was not one of her options. "If you wouldn't mind," she suddenly blurted out as their eyes met briefly.

He nodded his head --- smirked and then switched the plates. He proceeded to eat. "Ummmm --- tastes great if I do say so myself."

Giacinta still wasn't eating. Now she was wondering if he anticipated her saying that and wondered if the drugs or even poison was now in front of her? He suddenly reached over with his fork and took a small bit of her spaghetti from her plate and ate it --- then the same for her salad.

"See --- no drugs or poison." I grinned at her but really I was pissed off at her distrust. *The nerve of this fucking bitch, agreeing to supper and then acting like this.*

Giacinta managed a small bite of spaghetti in front of her but then switched to the salad. It was obvious she didn't feel like eating with him.

I finished my supper and when it was obvious Giacinta wasn't going to eat any more I got up. I looked at her for just a second and then asked, "Would you like a fruit salad for dessert. Would you eat that?"

"No thanks Victor. Thank you for dinner. Sorry I wasn't more hungry."

"That's okay. I'll leave some fruit down here in case you get hungry later --- and some oatmeal cookies with some tea."

He moved off to the side and pretended like he was about to pick up her plate and take it away. He didn't though. He suddenly poked her in the back of the neck with something. Giacinta grabbed at the back of her neck and looked up at him and noticed he was staring down at her --- smiling.

She tried to stand up but she started to feel funny. It was too late. The man was behind Giacinta before she could move as she tried to fight back. She struggled briefly--- kicking at the table and chair. She used her nails to try and claw at his grip but had trouble reaching him. She started to scream in panic. Then she felt herself getting dizzy and her eyes blurred and then there was the darkness. Her body went limp in his powerful arms.

CHAPTER 12

I laid her gently on the floor and reached in my pocket for the key. I released her from the ankle shackle and tossed her limp body onto my shoulder and carried her back towards the oil tank. I opened the entrance and entered the dankness of the hallway. I turned the light on --- walked to the green door with the red blotches and grabbed the skeleton key unlocking the lock. Then I reached up above --- slid the small door and pulled the latch. I reached over and turned the lever and the green door opened. I entered --- turned the lights on and lay Giacinta on her back on the closest table. The table was slightly padded with restraints at the feet, wrists, head and waist. First though I quickly undressed her until she was completely naked. Then I walked over and opened a drawer and pulled out a pair red satin panties and bra trimmed in black. I put them on Giacinta and then attached the restraints. I left her head and hips free. I checked her vitals and she was breathing normally. I wanted her alive and conscious when I began to have my fun. I went over and sat in a chair --- looking at her --- watching her heaving breasts rise and fall with each breathe. I got up and got a brush and proceeded to brush her soft hair. I noticed her perfectly manicured hands as well as her feet. It was obvious she recently had a professional manicure and pedicure. A soft pink hue on her fingernails and a bright red polish was on her toenails. I manipulated her hands --- closely examining each one. Then I examined her feet --- they were soft and perfect. I smelled every inch of her --- even her feet. It was heavenly. For twenty-five minutes I examined every inch of her. I checked her entire body --- her skin and not one imperfection. Not one freckle --- not one mark. She was a perfect physical specimen. This one would be one of the chosen few. She would get the special treatment. Then I went to the drawer and took out a small bottle of perfume and sprayed a bit on her --- then stepped back and admired my work. I thought of one more thing I could do. Back to the drawer I went and took out a lipstick --- bright blood red and gingerly applied it to her soft succulent lips. I had done this before. The lipstick went on perfectly. I put the lipstick back in the drawer and keeping my eyes on Giacinta I went over to her and ever so gently began touching her skin again --- while she slept. Her skin was so soft. It seemed softer than any of my previous girls.

I kept glancing at my watch. It was 11:48 p.m. when she first started to move --- barely a stir. I still had the mask on. I had checked on her several times as I waited --- to make sure she was breathing and her vital signs were okay. I could have given her the antidote and I thought about it but decided I liked the waiting. Besides it wasn't quite time. I wanted this feeling to last. It gave me time to think --- what I was going to do. Giacinta stirred several times and then finally her eyes began to open --- to focus better. She was still slightly groggy as she raised her head and looked about this new room with a new terror across her face. She realized where she was now --- that she was strapped to a table barely able to move her arms and legs and that she was almost nude and that I was staring at her --- with a smile. She tried talking to me but her words were slightly slurred at first --- like she was drunk. She wasn't. She looked at her restraints and struggled some more. She struggled violently for a minute and then laid her head back staring at the ceiling. That is when she noticed the big mirror above and she saw herself --- totally exposed --- legs spread. She saw she was wearing some sexy red panties and bra --- not her own undergarments. Giacinta kept trying to talk to me but she had trouble speaking. After five more minutes her speech returned to almost normal.

"Let me go!" Giacinta demanded as she raised her head to look at me. "You don't have to tie me up. I told you I wouldn't fight you. It's not too late."

I sat smiling for a second and then got up and walked ever so slowly towards her. "Welcome back Giacinta. Did you have a nice sleep?"

She stared at me and realized I'm not what she thought I was. She now regretted not trying to escape earlier when she was tethered to the wire.

"You drugged me!" She screamed back at me.

"Yes --- I did --- and you disrespected me Giacinta. I'm very, very disappointed in you."

"How did I disrespect you Victor?" She used his name this time --- hoping to connect with him.

"You accused me of trying to drug you at dinner. You thought I put some drugs in your food and drink. I had to eat some of your food just to prove to you that I didn't put drugs in it. I told you I didn't but you still didn't believe me --- you just as much called me a liar. That's how!"

"I'm sorry about that Victor but you have to know that would be a normal reaction considering the circumstances. I meant no disrespect to you." Giacinta thought if she could talk to him nicely he might change his mind. She doubted it. She tried to think back to her training. She tried using psychology on him.

"Yes --- I suspect that could be true but I didn't like it. None the less the damage is done." I glanced at my watch ---then took it off and placed the watch on a small table beside the restraint table. I rarely wore a watch. "Almost time Giacinta."

Giacinta strained her head to see what time it was. There weren't any clocks in the room. "What do you mean it's almost time? Let me go. I want to go back to the other room."

This room was scary. She noticed some other stuff --- medical stuff near the table she was on. She looked at it trying to figure out what it was for?

"Why it's 11:57 --- almost midnight Giacinta."

She looked at him questioningly. "What --- what's that mean?" She asked fearing the answer.

"Well --- I promised I wouldn't touch you until tomorrow and its almost tomorrow. Just three more minutes --- one hundred and eighty or so seconds and I always try to keep my promises Giacinta." I smirked as I stood beside her.

She started to struggle again but she was totally trapped and helpless.

"Struggle all you want. I will tell you many other girls before you struggled just as you are struggling now and not one has ever escaped. Now I'm not saying it couldn't happen but it isn't likely."

"You let me the fuck up you sick bastard. My husband and the police are going to find you. Let me go before it's too late." She screamed at him at the top of her lungs.

"Go ahead --- scream all you want Giacinta. There is no one around to hear you. The nearest person is miles away and this room is soundproof."

I walked near her face and stood there looking down at her. She closed her eyes as she felt my hand touching and stroking her soft hair. She moved her head about trying to avoid my touch. Then I leaned my head down and whispered, "I told you that you are here for the night Giacinta."

I walked over to her left side and took hold of her left hand. I looked down at her wedding ring and smiled. I had her fingers straight and examined the ring.

"That's a nice wedding ring. I'll just take this for now --- you won't be needing it." I proceeded to remove the ring from her finger. She protested and tried to curl her fingers. The ring came off.

"Leave my wedding ring alone --- don't touch my wedding ring --- please put it back."

Then I removed her pretty necklace and her ankle bracelet as well. "I'll just take these as well while I'm at it." I walked over and opened a small drawer and placed them inside. She watched me all the time.

"Why did you take them? I want them back."

"Well --- first things first Giacinta." I walked to her other side where the equipment was. She turned watching me all the time. I pushed the equipment that was on little wheels closer to her and then stuck an intra-venous needle into her right arm where the vein was.

"Uh --- what's this? What are you doing?"

She looked at me questioningly. She was terrified and it showed in her eyes.

"I have a confession to make. When I found out you were a cop --- well --- I hate cops --- have for a long time. They used to come and visit us at the school when I was just a kid but I soon realized cops lie and can't be trusted. I guess I should introduce you to my little friend here." I paused as I pointed to the machine. "I call it Mr. Dracula. I'm really sorry Giacinta --- I really am but this machine is what coroners use to flush blood from the body --- from the cadavers." The man smirked as he pointed to the machine.

Instantly Giacinta began to cry and plead for her life. "NO! NO! You don't have to do this. I give you my word I won't give out any information. Just let me go like the original plan," she sobbed.

"I can't let you go Giacinta. You know too much. You could give my description to a police artist --- you would do that if I let you go. You know you would. Sorry Giacinta but this is the only way." I was smiling as I said it --- I was enjoying her reaction.

"But I don't even know what you look like --- you have the mask --- I haven't seen you."

I turned my back to her, as she pleaded some more. When I turned back I had taken off the mask. "Oops --- the mask is off --- too late now Giacinta. You've seen me."

She closed her eyes --- turned away and screamed, "NO! I haven't seen you! I did not see you."

I moved my face closer and she felt my breath on her face. She kept her eyes closed and then I softly whispered into her right ear.

"Oh --- one last thing I should tell you --- your little son --- Jeremy --- well --- he didn't make it. He died in your van from heatstroke in that parking lot. When they found him it was already too late. If only you had parked the van in the shade Giacinta. If only you had left some windows down. Poor Jeremy."

She turned to look at me. She began to sob. I started the pump and turned back to look at her. When she heard the pump she screamed out, "You fucking bastard! My son Jeremy --- my poor baby --- you tell me it isn't true." Her eyes full of tears --- "You're lying!" she screamed.

She stared at me trembling and fighting but I just smiled. "If only you had parked in the shade --- imagine how much your son suffered Giacinta. You left your son in the van to cook."

Giacinta saw the dark, red blood start leaving her arm in the tube and screamed out to silent echoes, "NO! NO! NO! STOP! Her head started to feel light-headed.

"Don't worry --- it won't take long ---your just going to feel a little dizzy and a chill for just a few seconds. Sweet dreams Darling --- bye-bye now. Sleep tight."

Giacinta heard pounding on the doors and men calling out her name as she faded out --- many men shouting her name to her but then there was only the darkness.

CHAPTER 13

Lucas:

I felt satisfied but somewhat dissatisfied if that makes sense. It was a mixed feeling. I really wanted a true session with Giacinta but I didn't want to mark her. I wanted her to be a chosen one. She was like a cherished prize. Giacinta not only was married to a police officer --- she was an officer. There was no one to save her. That brought great satisfaction to me. I knew the police would have a massive hunt for her leaving no stones unturned. Cops play favourites when it comes to their own brotherhood. I am sure there were no witnesses as I was very careful in the capture. Usually I collect girls in more secluded areas but there was almost a type of desperation in me. And Saturday morning had frustrated me when I lost that gorgeous lady at the bus stop and that pretty teen girl at Walmart. I just lucked out with Giacinta --- with her gorgeousness and being a cop. So I began planning for another one --- or perhaps two before paying a visit to Marianne.

Kyle:

I sat on the couch Sunday morning watching the television. It was all over the news --- the disappearance of a female cop. The problem was I couldn't really remember much of Saturday. I had another blackout --- a lapse in memory like when someone drinks too much alcohol, except I wasn't drinking. The loss of memory more than just bothered me. I was pretty sure I had gone to the local town for gas on Saturday but that was about all I could remember and I wasn't even sure about that. It was not the same town as the lady cop. I haven't been to that town for quite some time. It bothering me though --- the lady cop and the baby left in the car. It would be highly unlikely that the mother would leave a baby like that. Something must have happened. The police arrived at the scene shortly after the 9-1-1 call was received and after a check the owner of the van was identified as another police officer. Staff Sergeant Giacinta Bello was missing. The hunt for her was only just beginning.

I couldn't stop thinking about it and decided to go outside and check the van. I just had this feeling I couldn't shake. I opened the back door and went down the steps. It had rained quite a bit the last several hours. *Okay --- that was good --- at least I remembered the rain.* At the bottom of the steps I looked for footprints but there were none. Then again that rain had been heavy at times. I opened the van, inserted the key and turned the key. The fuel was almost full. *Okay --- that was good because I remembered filling it up.* I looked around the van but found nothing amiss.

I looked at the bed. It was just a simple bed to use when I went camping or if I needed a place to sleep. I started to feel stupid. Still --- my past dreams and the realization I had done terrible things without even knowing made me panic. I got out of the van and closed the doors. I went back in the house and decided to go downstairs. I opened the door to the basement --- turned on the light and went down the steps. I stopped at the bottom looking about hoping not to find anything --- expecting not to find anything. A quick look and nothing looked different. The table was cleared --- I walked around stopping to look more closely at everything around me. It all seemed in order. *That big ring on the wall must have been a cosmetic piece --- like a big doorknocker --- although it was not on any door.* I turned and walked to the other part of the room with the workbench. I looked about searching --- trying to remember if I came down here yesterday. I spent ten minutes downstairs looking about --- searching for something to jog my memory. When I was satisfied I turned and went up the stairs --- turned the lights off and shut the door. I went back into the living room and felt a bit better. I still had this eerie feeling though. Something wasn't right but I couldn't quite put my finger on it. I decided to go upstairs to look but found nothing strange or out of place. I decided to go for a ride around the property on the all-terrain vehicle. *That usually relaxes me and besides --- it was fun to drive the 4x4.* I put on my rain suit, as it was wet out. *There were a few mud holes that I liked to play in.* I slid on a pair of riding gloves and boots and walked out the back door. I went into the barn where the all-terrain vehicle was parked. I had mud tires on it and a winch. When I entered the barn I looked around to make sure everything was in its place. It was. I mounted the all-terrain --- put the key in --- pulled the choke and it started right up. I let it idle for about twenty seconds and then slowly slid the choke off. I put it in drive and slowly drove out of the barn. I turned right out of the barn --- the lot was mostly mud now. When it was dry it was a dust driveway. Off to the sides some forty or so feet there was tall grass. I hadn't cut the grass in a while. I thought I should cut it before winter but hadn't got around to it. I proceeded down the farm road for a way and started to pick up speed. Driving the ATV was fun --- even with the cool air blowing in my face. It seemed to wake me up more. I looked to the left and decided to head over to the next outbuilding. I hadn't been there in a while and thought I'd better check it out. I turned off the road and slowed my speed to about ten miles per hour, as it was bumpier than the roadway. My all-terrain had good suspension and handled the bumps with ease. Soon I was approaching the first outbuilding on the property. There were seven outbuildings in all --- four smaller ones like this one and three larger ones. As I approached I noticed some branches on the ground that had recently fallen. They must have fallen during the recent rainstorm. I did a once around the building in slow gear inspecting the old structure. I believed it was likely the first outbuilding on the property. It was approximately twenty by twenty and about twenty feet high. The wooden building had a few broken pieces but nothing a few boards and nails couldn't fix. I just always found an excuse not to fix it and I wanted to find old wood that would match the age of the wood of the building so it would look the same. I stopped the all-terrain in front of the doors. They consisted of two rather large swing doors that would latch and lock in the middle. When I first bought the property there were no locks on the outbuildings. After moving in I decided I would put proper locks on every outbuilding and keep them locked at all times. I was originally from a town and was used to having to lock things up. Out here on the farm there really wasn't a need to but I still felt the need to. I've lived here a number of years but never had anyone come onto the property. I think I might have had my sisters come twice in all those years. They didn't like the farm. It smelled too much like a farm to them. I had my brother over about four times in all those years but not recently. The outbuilding was right on the fringe of the trees --- or "bush" as I call it. I noticed two of the trees nearest this outbuilding were about as close to dead as a tree could get. They must have got a sickness. They really should be cut down and used for firewood. Then again those dead trees gave the place a type of old country character. I took out my big set of keys. I had a lot of keys and I initially had trouble remembering what all these keys were for. I found the key that unlocked the front doors. I tried to remember the last time I even looked inside. I couldn't. I opened the doors fully and put two sticks up to brace the doors open --- otherwise they would just swing back closed again. I walked inside a few feet and stopped to look. It was chock-full of junk. Junk I didn't even know --- junk from another lifetime long ago. It was like going back in a time capsule. I scanned up to the rafters and it was full up there. I got up there once many years ago but it was hard to climb around. One day I really should just come out to the outbuildings and take a good, long hard look. I turned and walked out and closed the swing doors and locked it up again. Then jumped on the all-terrain and started it up. It didn't need the choke this time. I turned and travelled back to the main farm road and continued on. Soon the road forked and I decided to go left --- for now. The road curved hard left and there were a few puddles that the all-terrain splashed through. I saw the next outbuilding --- this one about twenty-five feet by twenty feet. They were all old buildings really but this one was also an early one. Over a hundred years I thought --- or a bit over a hundred. I turned left again and headed for it. I slowed my speed as I approached. I couldn't circle the outbuilding, as it was build part way in the trees --- at the back end of the building. Or the trees had grown around it? I wasn't sure which came first --- the trees or the building? I stopped in front and sat on the machine just looking. It sure was quiet out here when I shut the machine off. I got off and the grass was tall --- about a foot tall --- and very wet. I walked all around the building and this building was in better shape than the first outbuilding. Sure there were some slits open between the planks of wood but they were small. I noticed some knots in some of the wood showing small holes. At the back of the building there were two knots of wood and to me they kind of looked like a couple of eyes were watching me. The trees were thick at the back and I had to fight my way through. I found myself moving sticks out of the way so I could get through.

"I'll have to come back here and clear some of this out."

I continued through circling the building --- inspecting it. Standing at the front I took out the big ring of keys again and unlocked the front door off to the left. I found the key quicker this time. This building had a door that was regular size and two large swinging doors off to the right. I remembered this building had two old wagons in it --- one was really more a buggy. They were no longer in very good shape and the one buggy needed a new wooden wheel. I imagined horses pulling the wagon long ago and people long since dead riding in them. I swung open the old door. You had to step over a board at the bottom that was about eight inches up from ground level. Otherwise you would trip. I looked inside and this outbuilding was not as full as the other one. Still there were lots of things inside. Hanging on the wall were old horse bridles --- stirrups --- reins --- collars and stuff I didn't even know. There was an old rusted plow piled behind the buggies. I slowly walked around and looked up. Up in the rafters hung lots of interesting things. I spent ten minutes looking --- touching some of the items --- and then decided time to leave. I walked out and relocked the door. I climbed back on the all-terrain and started it up. I looked up and the skies were getting darker. I decided I might have time for one more outbuilding to check out. I didn't mind the rain so much but the wind was beginning to pick up. There was a storm coming and it looked like it was going to be a good one. I had generators at the house in case the power went off. I drove back out to the farm road and headed back in the same direction I came. When I got to the junction I turned left --- heading away from the farmhouse and to the next outbuilding. I travelled for two minutes and the rain started to drizzle down. I saw the next outbuilding ahead on the right. This was a larger outbuilding about thirty feet by twenty-five feet. It wasn't the largest outbuilding on the property but it was the largest one that was fairly close to the farmhouse. I drove up to it and noticed the wet grass had recent track marks heading towards the building. I followed the tracks wondering what the hell is this? I hadn't been out here in quite some time. I followed the tracks and stopped at the side of the outbuilding where a door was. It was another single doorway. At the front of the building there was one very large swing door that would open to about eight feet wide. This was an old building as well but not as old as the first two outbuildings. I knew that because of two reasons. One was the wood and the second reason was the construction. This building might have been only seventy or eighty years old. I sat on the all-terrain letting it idle as I looked around. I noticed the tracks turned around and headed back in the same tracks I came in on. I shut off the ATV and dismounted. I walked to the door and unlocked it and opened the door. This door got stuck half way but I pushed through forcing it to open. I entered the building. I walked around but everything seemed in order. Suddenly I heard the door slam behind me. I ran to the door and swung it open. I looked about but decided it was just the wind catching it and slamming it shut. I was alone and my imagination was getting the better of me. Since I saw those tracks I decided to walk around the outbuilding just as I had the others. *Whose tracks were those? I'm sure I hadn't been out here in quite some time.* I walked around --- this time in the other direction --- a clockwise rotation. This building was away from any trees. It was a good sixty feet from the tree line. When I reached the back of the outbuilding I just stopped and stared. I saw a set of tracks --- footprints --- where someone had walked and crushed the wet grass down. I took a deep breath and followed the footprints. As I got closer I saw what I dreaded. There --- just at the tree line was a freshly dug grave --- and there were some rocks on it. I stared at the grave and started to tremble. Just then a bolt of lightening flashed and in the same instant thunder roared. I jumped back quite startled. The lightening bolt hit a tree about three hundred feet to my right. In lightning terms that was pretty close. The rain began to really pelt down as I turned back to stare at the grave. I looked up to the sky as the hard, cold rain fell upon my face. The wind started howling and I could barely keep my eyes open as the rain pelted down on me, and the fresh grave. I didn't have a shovel with me. I would have to go back to the farmhouse and get it and then return to dig up this fresh grave.

"GOD help me," I managed to whisper under my breath as I stared in fear at the dirt and the rocks in front of me. It was as if they were teasing me and calling my name over and over again.

CHAPTER 14

I started to walk back in the direction of the all-terrain --- the way I had come. I stopped half way to turn and look back at the new grave hoping it wasn't there. As if it would magically disappear. It didn't. The rain continued to assault me from above. I climbed on the ATV and sat down in shock. I leaned forward, put my face into my cold, wet hands and began to cry. Five minute of crying and hearing the thunder rumbling above me left me feeling empty. I started the machine and raced back to the farmhouse. I don't even remember driving to the farmhouse. All I could think about was that grave. At the farmhouse I remembered I had to get the shovel. I stopped at the entrance to the barn and left the ATV to idle. I hopped off and ran inside to get the shovel. I saw it just inside the door --- where it usually was and grabbed it --- inspecting it for fresh dirt. I didn't see any. I turned back to the idling all-terrain and put the shovel on the rear racks. I used the bungee cords I always carried on the all-terrain to secure the shovel. Then I turned the machine spinning the tires but this time I headed out down the driveway. I drove to the gate and noticed it was still locked. I checked and saw no tracks that anyone had tried to go around it. No one had entered that way. I was just hoping some tracks were there --- that an intruder --- a trespasser had come onto my property. I didn't want to believe I was responsible for the grave. I suspected I had dug it though, especially after all my nightmares --- and finding all those poor girls. I turned and started racing back to the gravesite. The rain continued pelting down on me and it was fell so hard it actually hurt when it hit me in the face. The rain felt like hail. I soon arrived and slowed down. This time I drove the all-terrain all the way to the back of the outbuilding almost right up to the fresh grave. I stopped the machine and just stared at the grave. My breaths were deep and my eyes watered but not so much from the rain. I shut the machine off, dismounted and walked to the back and just stared at the shovel. It was like it was my enemy. I listened to the rain falling upon my rain gear and it reminded me of tears from heaven. I unfastened the three bungee cords that secured the shovel and lifted the shovel off and then looked at the shovel --- and then the grave. I started walking those last few feet to the grave and the rain suddenly began to slow down. It was now no more than a drizzle. I heard one long growl of thunder from the heavens above. I pushed the rocks off the grave and to the side. Then I dug the shovel into the dirt. I removed the first shovel of dirt from the grave and stopped. I looked up at the dark skies as the mist fell upon my face.

"Please GOD! Please Mom! Give me strength to face this."

Then I looked down to the grave and began to dig faster. It was cold and windy out but I still found myself sweating. I began to shiver and tremble as I got closer to whatever or whoever was buried there. I thought of the missing police officer. I piled the fresh dirt to the side and when I was about three feet down I noticed the dirt wasn't fresh anymore. It was hard --- like it had never been touched. I continued digging but discovered the entire grave was like that. No one was buried there? It was much like Marianne's gravesite. I breathed a sigh of relief. *There was no body --- no girl buried there but what the fuck was going on? Was this a grave for someone yet to come?* No matter what question I asked I had no answer. I was happy it was empty but just like Marianne's grave it was a total mystery to me. I went back and sat on my all-terrain thinking about it for about ten minutes but could think of no explanation. Finally I returned to reality and noticed the thunder had stopped. The rain was still mist like. I picked up the shovel again and began to put the dirt back into the grave. I was faster now and was finished in no time. I packed the wet dirt down to try and make it level. Then I thought about covering it with grass but it was already late September and winter was coming so I just left the bare dirt on top. I placed the shovel on the back rack of the ATV and secured it with the bungee cords. Then I walked back inspecting the site more closely to see if there were any signs that someone had walked anywhere else. I checked but found only those tracks near the grave. *I began to wonder if I dug the grave? I had that blackout yesterday and how I couldn't remember all those girls that came to me in the darkness of night. I proved the dreams were more than just dreams. They were real. I found all those girls after all. I kept thinking about that police officer I saw over and over again on the television and wondered if I had anything to do with it? I don't want any more dreams --- no more nightmares GOD.*

I went over to sit on ATV and although I was cold, wet and shivering I sat there trying to think. *I would have to do a total search of the farm --- just to prove to myself that she wasn't here on the farm--- and that there weren't any more girls.* That was going to take time but I wasn't going to do that now. I had to get back to the farmhouse and think some more --- and search the farmhouse thoroughly. I would search the property later --- when the weather was better. I turned the key and started the ATV up. I let it idle --- not to warm up but to think some more. *My mind is a mess again.* I looked up to the dark clouds and shook my head and sighed. *I had much to think about and it wasn't going to be an easy thing.* I put the ATV in drive and drove back to the farmhouse at a fairly slow speed. There were many puddles on the road now and I just splashed through them. My gloves were soaking wet and my hands were freezing. The wind was still blowing and gusting. The storm was not over --- that was obvious. I arrived at the barn and drove the all-terrain inside and parked it and shut it off. I left the shovel on the back rack just in case I needed it later --- when inspecting the property. I stepped off the machine and glanced about the barn. Now everywhere I looked I wondered --- wondered if there would be more dark secrets staring back at me. I turned and walked out of the barn past the white van --- looking at it as I passed. Then I went up the back stairs and entered the house. I took off my boots and wet rain gear and hung it up on the standing wooden coat rack just inside the doorway. I stood there for a second --- looking --- trying my best to remember yesterday but nothing came to me. I was an empty vessel. All I heard was the silence --- except for the ticking of the giant clock, as each second seemed to pound in my ears.

As I stood at the doorway for some reason I began to think of the commercial incinerator that was on my property --- and the empty grave. The incinerator from years past must have been used to burn dead livestock on the farm. I had never had livestock on the farm. I was not a farmer. No animals or crops during my stay. Still I couldn't stop thinking about the discovery of that recent grave. I started to panic and then put my rain gear back on and my boots. I just had to check out the incinerator to see if it had been used recently. I hurried down the stairs and over to the barn. I hopped on the ATV and started it up. Then I took off spinning the tires as I accelerated out of the barn. I turned right and then right again onto the road that led to the other roads on my farm. There were a few trails that I used the all-terrain on. In the winter when the snow came I used the skidoo. The farm had a couple of hills near the back that I sometimes used the ATV on. The rain had stopped now and soon --- in about thirty minutes night would come. I came to a road on the right and splashed through the many puddles at a good clip. I was in a rush to get to the incinerator. My heart was racing as my gloves strangled the handles of the ATV. A minute later I saw the incinerator up ahead and started to slow down. I was checking for tire tracks or some sign that someone had been here recently. I knew I hadn't been out here for a few months --- since early summer or so I thought. Around June or July --- I wasn't sure. I stood up on the all-terrain, scouring the ground for any clues. I saw none. It had after all rained very hard that previous night and day. I stopped in front of the incinerator and sat there for a second looking around. I turned the ATV off. I didn't know how old the incinerator was but it was fairly big. I didn't even know if it worked or when the last time it was even used. There was an old holding pen nearby --- off the front of the incinerator. That must have been where the animals were housed --- until they were burned. I didn't even know how it worked --- although it seemed simple. Put something in --- close door --- push button and come back later. There were no trees around. The incinerator was in the open. On the top were two giant smoke stacks.

I dismounted the ATV and didn't even take off my wet gloves. I walked to the front of the incinerator and stopped, staring at its ugly grey front door. I slowly raised my right hand and reached out testing the air for heat. My right glove touched the incinerator but if felt cool. I took off my gloves and used my bare hands to touch the exterior. It still felt cool. I breathed a sigh of relief at its coolness. I pulled the handle and opened the large door at its entrance. Inside I saw white powdered ashes. I stared at the ashes and wondered what they once were? Whatever they were they were no more.

"Thank GOD."

I closed the door and in my mind it almost sounded like the echo of some prison jail cell slamming shut. The noise from the door closing disturbed the quietness of the farm. I slid my cold, clammy gloves back on and looked around. I better get back before darkness came. The problem wasn't the ATV. It had great lights and lit up the darkness very nicely. I was pretty sure I didn't leave the back porch light on before I left. If I came back too late it would be very dark back there. That might be a slight problem. I needed to remember to replace the motion sensor light for the back porch. It had stopped working recently. I then mumbled to myself to write it down so I wouldn't keep forgetting. I hopped on my trusty all-terrain. I found myself staring at the incinerator. I hated it. I was thankful the incinerator was cool. I was beginning to doubt myself again and that wasn't good. If the incinerator had been warm --- or hot --- well --- that would mean another girl. Now I would go back to the farmhouse and think --- and try to relax. Try to do the impossible. Tomorrow was going to be a busy day searching the rest of the farm. I started up the ATV and drove back to the barn. I turned the lights on as I drove and looked around at the coming darkness. The farm could be a scary place in the dark. I got back to the farmhouse just at dark. I noticed the inside lights were on in the kitchen and inside the barn. I didn't remember turning on the barn lights. I must have left them on though. I hadn't' turned on the outside lights to the back porch. I parked the ATV in the barn and shut it off. I covered the machine with the ATV cover and couldn't wait to get inside the farmhouse and get out of these cold, wet clothes. First though I walked over to turn off the barn lights. Before I turned them off I paused and turned for a quick visual scan of the barn's interior. Noticing nothing unusual I turned off the lights and walked out of the barn into the semi-darkness. When I got to the bottom of the stairs I heard my cats calling me. I turned around to see three cats running towards me at racing speed. I called to them.

"Okay --- come on Jasper. You all look a little wet. Guess you wanna come in and spend the night huh? Did any of you catch any mice today?"

The cats surrounded me --- purring and rubbing my legs like cats do. I went up the stairs, the cats in my way and I opened the door and three wet cats scurried inside. They wanted to be in a dry place for the night too! I opened three cans of cat food while they purred down below at my feet and I fed my Jaspers. That night I couldn't stop thinking about that freshly dug grave. I had covered it back up after finding it empty but it got me to thinking. If it was covered up that meant that now someone could put a body in it and I would be none the wiser. I decided that tomorrow I would go back to that empty grave and dig half of it up to leave half the grave open. That way if anyone --- even my amnesiac self decide to put a body in it I would know. That grave was really bugging me. I just hoped someone found that missing cop real soon. The storm wasn't finished yet and more rain, thunder and lightning were coming. I heard the long, deep, lonely rumble of the thunder as I stared at the ceiling in the darkness. I felt exhausted. It would be another long, lonely night for me.

CHAPTER 15

I had a restless night and didn't sleep well. I woke up early --- around 6 A.M. and lay in bed for another thirty minutes but I couldn't sleep. I got out of bed, got dressed and was in a hurry to go out and search the rest of the farm. The sun wasn't even up yet. I made coffee and a toasted multi-grain bagel with raspberry jam. I sat at the kitchen table and all three cats were meowing at the back door. They wanted to go out. I got up and walked to the door and opened it. The three cats looked outside but didn't go out.

"What --- you don't want to go out now? It does look like rotten weather out there. It's cold and wet. Well --- are you going out or not?"

The cats just stood at the door. Finally I used my foot and shooed them out the door.

"You can go in the barn to keep dry if it rains. Go and catch some mice. Do your job."

As soon as the cats were out I quickly closed the door. I've often wondered why people talk to their pets? Those cats didn't have a clue what I was saying. And why do people --- including me ask them questions? As if someday they are going to answer me for Christ sakes. I laughed at that thought. Still I liked having the cats around. I would have rather had a dog but they require more maintenance. Cats you could just forget about. They're survivors. Cats give owners more freedom.

"I really should get a dog," and then I laughed because here I am talking to myself again. People do that a lot --- talking to themselves. It is strange really when you try to rationalize certain human behaviours. The only thing rational about humans is that they can be quite irrational.

I went back to the kitchen table, sat down and gulped down my coffee before it got cold. I hate cold coffee. I finished what was left of my multi-grain. Then I put the dishes in the sink and quickly rinsed and washed them. Most times I didn't even use dishwashing soap. I rinsed them and put both the mug and plate on the drying rack. I didn't bother drying them. I just let them air dry. Then I went to the bathroom and brushed my teeth. I looked at my messy hair and combed it. I went to the living room and sat down for a few minutes in front of the television and on the news the big story was that female police officer that was still missing. There wasn't any breaking news except that additional officers had been assigned to the case and that the police were still asking for any witnesses who had been in the area who had seen anything or anyone suspicious. There were twenty-two police officers assigned to the case and there was going to be a press conference at 11 A.M. this morning. I checked the time on the television --- it was not quite 7 A.M. I shook my head while watching the news and then thought I'd better start searching the farm. I wondered what would I do if I found something? Was I willing to go to the police and turn myself in? I decided I would cross that bridge when and if I came to it. I got up and shut off the television and walked to the back door. I put the rain gear on and picked up my gloves but discovered they were still damp. I found another pair of gloves from the shelf beside the door. I laid the wet gloves on the heater just off the door where I should have put them the night before. I opened the back door and looked up to the sky and saw nothing but clouds. There was no sign of any sunshine so far. The clouds were dark ominous looking and were packed full of rain. They looked like they were harbouring an ocean that could be released at any moment.

I went outside but saw no sign of the cats. I walked over to the barn --- my boots seemed to slurp in the mud and water that covered the entire lot. I removed the tarp covering the all-terrain and climbed on but noticed the key wasn't in the machine like it should have been.

"What the Hell? Where the Hell is the key?"

Reaching in I checked the pockets of my rain suit. No keys. I reached inside and checked my pants pocket but nope --- nothing there. I searched all my pockets but no freaking key.

"Shit!" I yelled out as I frantically searched.

I trudged back into the farmhouse --- kicked off my boots but kept the rain suit on. I remembered I wasn't wearing the same pants as yesterday. I hurried over to the laundry basket and saw the pants on top, picked them up and searched the pockets. I was relieved when I found the ATV key in the pocket.

"I'm an idiot."

I had an extra key for the all-terrain but didn't want to lose this one. The key had a bright red string tied to it so it would be easier to find. The kind of attachment that many people use for sunglasses so they can hang the glasses around their neck. I put my boots back on and hurried back to the barn hopping on the ATV and pulled the choke and started the machine. Thirty seconds later I pushed the choke slowly in and let the machine idle for fifteen more seconds. Then I put it in gear and started to drive out of the barn. I saw one of my cats --- Jasper number one with a mouse in his jaws. I smiled. I didn't see the other cats.

I drove out and was soon on the road that would lead to the many side roads on my property. I knew them all from the many times I would drive around the property. I even made a few roadways myself over the years. I decided last night that I would remove half the dirt from the grave first and then continue searching the rest of the property in a clockwise like direction. I would search the west arm of the farm first. It was going to take a long time to search so many acres.

It had rained heavily last night and the winds had come full force. There were many downed branches and I noticed the trees had been fully stripped of whatever leaves had been left. In no time I was back at the gravesite and drove right up to it. I quickly dismounted --- unhooked the shovel and began digging. I dug what I thought might be the front of the grave but then realized there really was no difference. A body would be able to be laid in any direction. None the less I dug out half the grave and piled the dirt to the side. It didn't take long as the dirt was soft and I worked very fast. When I was done I rested on the shovel --- my head looking down at the gravesite. I tried to think --- tried my hardest to remember making this grave but couldn't. I thought of my blackout times and some of the girls from my dreams that I buried.

"Shit man," I said in disdain. "Maybe I should just end it and kill myself?"

I couldn't help thinking that it was highly likely I had something to do with that lady cop missing. I wondered if I would get a new dream --- with her face lying with the maggots --- her eyes staring up at me. Her face splattered on the news stations did nothing to jog my memory though. I thought that was good --- maybe it wasn't me. Maybe she ran away but leaving her kid in the van? That didn't make sense. Maybe someone else took her? Maybe she was having an affair? A mother wouldn't leave her kid though. After five minutes of daydreaming and my imagination getting the better of me I decided I'd better continue the search. Right now I was doing what I refer to as a perimeter check --- with an odd interior check. I wanted to check the three ponds and the stream area as well.

I bungeed the shovel on the back racks of the ATV, as I glanced around it was eerily quiet. There was no rain --- no wind --- not even a bird. It was well --- strange. It was damp --- the kind of dampness that goes down deep to the bones. I started the machine up. As I drove out to the main trail I stood on the foot rests and pegs for better viewing. I was going slow trying to get a better look. Once out of the tall grass I turned left and picked up my speed slightly. I stood there --- splashing through the puddles as I searched. These farm roads were more like pathways and were better suited to all-terrain vehicles, tractors, or 4 x 4 pickup trucks with a good set of mud tires. It could get quite muddy in spots. A car might be okay in mid summer when the trails were hard and dusty. I didn't see any more graves and started to enjoy the ride a bit more. Being on the ATV was fun but I had a nasty job to do now. I was looking for a body or some evidence of a body. About ten minutes later the trail started to enter a swath of trees. This is where the trail would cross the stream. I slowed down as I entered --- looking left to right as I descended the hill that had a few turns up ahead. I approached the stream --- which was bloated from the recent heavy rains. I knew although it was deep the ATV would easily cross it. The stream was about ten feet wide and this section was slow. It was about two feet deep as the ATV crossed splashing into the river just above idle speed. I had a locking feature on the ATV that would lock all four wheels into true four-wheel drive. I engaged it just in case it was needed. Better to have it on than off. I lifted my feet onto the front racks so they wouldn't get wet as I crossed. Everything looked fine so I continued on. Soon I would be at the first pond. The ATV started going up the slight hill ---I stood on the ATV leaning slightly forward. This section of the trail was slightly steeper. I exited the trees and the trail turned right. Within a few minutes I approached the first pond. It was the smallest pond of the three. I hadn't been out in this area in quite some time. Not since the springtime but I wasn't sure. There was a small off shoot trail that led to the pond some thirty feet in. I eased in, standing on the foot pegs looking for any signs if anyone had been there recently. I stopped the ATV and shut it off. I started walking on foot through the tall grass surrounding the pond. This was a standing pond meaning it was fed only by the ground water. I walked around the perimeter looking for tracks but saw none. I feared the ponds --- not because I couldn't swim because I swam quite well but because this could be a spot a body could be weighed down and thrown in and be virtually undetectable. When I was satisfied there were no tracks I got back on the ATV to continue searching. It wasn't until I got to the third pond that something didn't seem right. The third pond was the biggest pond --- and the deepest. The pond itself was rectangular shaped. It was fed not only from ground water but also from a small outlet linking it to the stream. The mini stream entered the pond and exited the pond only to link again with the main stream. The stream ran through the wooded area, then through the open areas of the farm, finally going once again back into the woods on the other side of the property. This third pond had a trail all the way around it with two small wooden bridges built to allow a person on foot --- or an ATV to cross them. I idled the ATV slowly across the first bridge as I stood searching the ground for tracks. Then I noticed near the second bridge some tracks near the pond. The grass had been recently flattened and was different than the surrounding grasses. I stopped the ATV and shut it off. I dismounted and walked slowly towards the pond not taking my eyes off the tracks. I looked for footprints but was unable to find anything conclusive. I stood at the water's edge staring at the muddy, stained water --- wondering if anything was at the bottom. I gulped. If I wanted to check --- to be sure --- I would have to find a way to go in. The water at this time of year was extremely cold. I bent down and dipped my hand in the water to check temperature and felt its coldness.

"Man that's cold," I said as I took my hand out and shook it. "Shit!"

I thought about getting my scuba gear from the farmhouse. I hadn't used the scuba gear for about two years --- when I went scuba diving in the Philippines two winters ago. I hoped I didn't have to dive but I would have to be sure the pond was free of bodies. As I was looking at the shore I noticed a few deer tracks right at the water's edge. I walked over inspecting the ground more closely and then realized it was two deer that must have come to the pond for a drink. The tracks were recent. I looked more closely at the flattened grass and saw that it was indeed the deer that had made those tracks. No human footprints.

"Whew! Thank GOD it was the fucking deer. These guys are giving me a heart attack."

I continued inspecting the rest of the perimeter of the farm --- not finishing until it was almost dark. I was relieved that I didn't find any other tracks or signs. I was also starving. I didn't bring any food except for one granola bar and a bottle of water. I wished I had brought a hot thermos of coffee with me. It would be dark soon so I headed back to the farmhouse. As luck would have it I would pass by the incinerator again but since I had already checked it the other day I sped by at forty plus mile per hour. I glanced off to my right as I passed and suddenly hit the brakes. The incinerator door was open. I turned the machine around and drove up the door. I stared at the door. I was certain I had closed it the other day because it made such a loud clanging noise when I closed it. I was sure I latched it. I got off the machine and walked over to the incinerator. The door was fully open --- like someone had opened it to look inside. I was hesitant to approach and stood facing the furnace --- breathing heavily. I walked up and peered inside --- not knowing what I might find. I looked inside and saw the same white ashes I had seen yesterday. I found a long stick and used it to poke inside checking the ashes for remnants of bones or teeth. Nothing. I looked about for footprints. I was looking for new footprints. I saw no footprints except my own boot prints. I kind of wished I saw someone else's footprints. Then I would know it was someone else doing these things. I extended my gloved right hand near the open door to feel for any heat. I felt none. Then I felt the exterior of the incinerator again. It was stone cold. I took my glove off just to make sure. I felt no warmth. I slammed the door shut and made sure it was shut this time. I pulled on the door to make sure it was latched solid. A shiver ran down my spine. I stood there looking around like a lost child --- afraid of the unknown. Tears were beginning to form in my eyes. I was so unsure.

I walked over to the ATV and sat down on it. I took off my gloves and then it happened. I broke down and started bawling real tears. The kind of tears I cried when mom and dad died. I covered my face with my hands while leaning forward on the handlebars.

"I can't go on like this --- it's too much. I need answers." My lips quivered.

CHAPTER 16

I cried for ten minutes before realizing that it was dark out. When I noticed how dark it was I looked around half expecting to see someone but I was alone. My wet eyes squinted trying to see but I could barely see the incinerator now, and that was only a few feet away. I wiped my eyes and face. I started the ATV up, turned on the lights and headed back to the farmhouse.

As I was walking up the steps I heard my cats. They were meowing --- all three of them. In the dim light coming from the kitchen I could see the three cats looking at me waiting at the door. It was like they were saying, "Where they hell have you been? Hurry up and let us inside." The door barely opened wide enough when the cats squeezed and scurried inside. Then they stood at the doorway. It was like they were demanding to be fed.

"Oh all right. At least wait until I get my stuff off for Christ's sake." I realized I used the Lord's name in vain and immediately apologized. "Forgive me Lord. Didn't mean to say that."

After feeding the cats, the cats took off to the living room, all three climbed up on the couch. I turned the television on and was listening to the news while I was in the kitchen making supper. Nothing fancy --- as usual. Mostly my meals were either frozen dinners or sandwiches or soups of some kind. I heated up a can of vegetable beef soup with two toasts --- and a hot tea. When it was ready I got a tray and walked into the living room I went to sit on the couch right where Jasper number three was and Jasper wasn't moving. It was like he was saying, "Go ahead --- sit on me. I dare you." I sat down slowly and the cat reluctantly moved to the floor in a flash. From what I heard on the news the lady cop was still missing and there were no new leads. The police were expanding their search areas and lots of volunteers were searching ravines, alleyways, and fields. They were going house to house asking if anyone noticed anything. I got tired watching the same old news and so grabbed the remote looking for something else to watch. I went to the movie channel and saw that "Silence of the Lambs" was on.

"Shit! I'm not watching that ever again." It was just too close to me.

I finally found a show more suitable and watched "Pawn Stars." I found it interesting and for a short while I forgot about my troubles. I ate supper and during the next commercial break got up to get another hot tea. As I got up all three cats lifted their heads from their slumber to watch me walk to the kitchen. Then the three heads went back to sleep. I washed the dishes --- no soap --- like a true bachelor. This time I dried them and put them away. I got my tea and went back to watch the television. I felt tired --- after all I hadn't slept much at all last night. I checked the time and it was just before 8:00 P.M. I finished my tea and walked to the bathroom. This time not one cat raised a head. I brushed my teeth --- rinsed --- and then turned most of the lights off. I was so tired I walked back to the living room and lay down on the couch --- scattering the cats. I fluffed the pillow --- trying to get comfortable. Sometimes I slept on the couch. It was a good couch --- nice and comfy. I lay there thinking that I needed a bit of a vacation from this place --- to get away and forget about stuff. I decided I should go away for a few days. Perhaps go south a bit. Take a vacation although I was always on vacation in a sense but to try and get away from the place --- especially now. I decided I would leave tomorrow. Then I fell into a deep sleep and slept great.

The cats woke me up in the morning just as the sun was rising. I saw it shining through the kitchen windows with the red and white curtains. I sat up and noticed I was fully dressed. I was so tired I didn't even take my clothes off to sleep. I sat up --- said good-morning to the Jaspers and rubbed my hands across my eyes to get the sleep out. I got up and walked to the back door and opened it. All three Jaspers made a mad dash to escape the house. I watched them race down the stairs and bolt into the barn. Except Jasper number three. He raced off to the front of the house. After all mice were everywhere on the farm. It was a good hunting place. Even the odd squirrels and birds were fair game. I looked up and it looked like it was going to be a gorgeous day.

I closed the door and decided to have breakfast first. I would change clothes and get dressed after. I cooked bacon and eggs --- rye toast and butter --- and hot coffee. When it was ready I decided not to eat at the table but to eat in front of the television as usual. I carried breakfast to the couch and sat down. I grabbed the remote and turned on the television and turned to the news. Just as I was about to take my first bite the news announced,

"There have been some new developments in the case of missing Police Officer Giacinta Bello. Early this morning her cell phone was locating using GPS technology. We were informed the police now have the phone and are examining it. This could be a huge break in the case but police are releasing few details regarding the phone."

I stared at the television listening intensely. For some reason I felt an uneasiness hearing the news. I switched the news off and turned to my favourite music station. I continued eating breakfast --- trying to relax but kept thinking of that missing police officer.

"That must mean she was kidnapped --- or abducted if they found her phone," I whispered to myself. "I hope they find her soon --- and find her safe and alive," I added.

After breakfast I washed and dried the dishes --- brushed my teeth and then got changed. I packed some clothes in a small suitcase and was soon ready to go. I put some timer lights on and looked about the house to make sure I didn't forget anything. I made sure the place was locked --- although it was unlikely anyone would come onto the property. I decided to take the car this time and put my suitcase in the back. I then turned and yelled out to his cats.

"You're on your own for a few days boys."

There I go again --- talking to my cats like they have a clue what I am saying. I didn't see any of my cats. I got in the car and started it up, letting it idle for a minute or two. As I exited the driveway I noticed my two "Beware of Dog" signs and chuckled. Soon I was on the main highway driving south --- not even sure how far I would go or what town I would go to. All I knew was I would drive until I felt like it. I put my favourite Sirius XM radio station on and felt better. I was more relaxed. It felt good to be away from the farmhouse. After two hours I stopped at a Starbucks drive thru for a coffee. I drove for seven hours stopping for gas just once. I pulled over to look at the map to see what towns were around. I continued driving and an hour later I noticed a little motel and decided to stay there for one night. I paid cash and asked where is a good place to eat.

"What do you like to eat?" The young girl at the front desk asked.

"Steak, spaghetti, hamburgers --- I don't care right now. I'm just hungry," I answered back.

"Well --- there's a pretty good steak house just down the road about half a mile. It's a bit pricey but the food and service is really, really good. It's called Jerry's Steak House. There is a big sign in front on the left. And they open for breakfast at 5:30 A.M. if you want a good breakfast tomorrow morning."

"That sounds great. I'll try it out. Thanks?"

I found the steakhouse no problem and she was right. The food was great. I was used to eating alone and the place wasn't that packed. I noticed a table of three very pretty ladies looking over at me. One girl in particular --- a brunette with wavy hair seemed to be secretly looking my way. I caught her looking at me more than once --- she smiled and then quickly turned away. I finished my supper --- no dessert and then returned directly to the motel. The motel was nothing fancy --- that's for sure but it was clean --- and convenient. I had money and I decided that for at least one of these nights I would find a high-end motel or hotel to stay in. I also liked to camp and thought that maybe I would spend one night out under the stars --- depending on the weather and temperature. Once in the room I turned on the television to watch the news. I decided I wasn't going to but couldn't resist. There was nothing new on the missing police officer's case but the news channel was really playing up the finding of the missing cell phone. There wasn't as much news about the officer in this area. Then again I was further away. I watched television for a bit but then decided to read. I started reading a sci-fi novel. After an hour of reading in bed I put the book down and turned off the lights. Then I remembered to phone the front desk and request a 6:30 A.M. wake-up. I didn't sleep well. I woke up before the wake-up. I had a strange dream just before waking up. I dreamt about my incinerator for some reason. In the dream it was burning red hot and there was a lady inside --- a lady I didn't know. I sat up in bed and noticed I was soaked. I looked about the room trying to remember where I was. I was angry that I had the dream but I couldn't remember all of it. That got me even more worried. I tried to remember more --- I just couldn't. After several minutes of pacing around the room I decided to get the hell out of here. I had a quick shower, which only made me feel slightly better. I packed up and checked out of the motel and then went to Jerry's Steak House and had breakfast and coffee. I tried to settle my nerves. It wasn't working. I chewed on the multi-grain bagel with cream cheese and sipped coffee down. It seemed to have little taste to it. There were a few people there --- most were truckers. After breakfast I walked to the car and took out the map and put it on the hood of the car. I decided today I wouldn't drive as far as yesterday before deciding on a place. Some vacation. I decided shopping might help I didn't really have any idea what I might buy. I took out my toothbrush and walked back to the Steak House to use the washroom. I walked to the washroom and once inside gave my teeth a good brushing and rinse. Like most people I rinsed my toothbrush first, put the toothpaste on it, rinsed it again under the sink, then brushed my teeth and then rinsed the toothbrush again. I rinsed my mouth bending over the faucet. These types of washrooms were after all not the cleanest. Then I walked to the car and started it up and drove south. I looked at the clock on the dashboard and it was just before 8:00. My mind wasn't right though --- it was drifting. Discovering that fresh grave on my property and now the incinerator dream was messing me up.

"I need to find a waterfall or running water --- rapids or something so I can sit down and think properly."

My brain felt numb --- like some doctor just shot it full of novocaine. Ironically, a short time later I noticed a bridge off to the right with a dam and some rapids. I didn't even remember driving the last couple of hours. I decided to pull over and see if this might be a good spot to sit and watch the water and listen to the rapids. I pulled off the highway onto a small road that came to a "T" junction. I stopped and saw the sign with the symbol of a picnic and washroom area. I turned right and in a few seconds the road curved to the right and before I knew it I saw the parking lot. There were two other vehicles parked there --- one a Chevy pick-up truck and the other a car that I didn't know the make. I parked the car and still in a daze somehow ended up near the dam. I glanced at the clock and it was 10:20. I saw a picnic bench that looked like a good place to sit and think. I walked to it and sat down facing the dam and rapids. I could hear the power of the dam as I watched the water rush over the dam. It was hypnotic to me. I needed to unwind. I just stared trance like at the water. The sky was both cloudy and sunny but at the moment the sun shone down on the picnic table and for once the sun felt good. I felt its warmth caress my wounded body. I couldn't' stop thinking about my recent dream. Why would I dream about the incinerator? I could think of only one reason and I didn't like the answer. Or could it just be my imagination since I was shocked to find the door open the other day? After all, the incinerator was cold when I touched it --- and those things take a long time to cool down after being used. At least that is what I thought. So it couldn't have been used. Then I thought about the fresh grave. I thought to myself, "*Kyle --- you need to relax and forget about all this shit. This is supposed to be a trip away from those thoughts.*" Then I heard a voice --- a female voice. I turned to my left and there standing looking at me was a pretty young girl. The sun was behind her and partially blinding my view. Her hair looked golden in the sun and her eyes seemed the colour of honey. She noticed that I put my hand up to try and block the sun as I squinted looking at her. She moved a bit off to the side so I wouldn't have to look into the sun to see her. She looked to be in her early twenties. These days it's hard to tell a girl's age sometimes.

"Hi --- my name's Gail. Can I share your picnic bench with you? It has the best view out of all of them and I want to take some pictures of it. Do you mind?"

Before I could answer she plunked herself down and sat smiling at me. I noticed her hair was slightly wavy and she looked like a Disney princess as the sun reflected off her.

"Well --- I --- ah --- was hoping for some alone time --- just to think about some things."

"Sorry for invading your space. I won't be long. Truth is when I pulled in here there weren't any cars here. Then just after I pulled in some guy pulled in --- the guy in the pickup truck and well --- I kind a get the feeling he is following me. He came over and tried to talk to me --- telling me how pretty I was. I told him to leave me alone. He gives me the creeps. So I'm kind of here to be rescued --- if you don't mind. I don't want to be alone with him. When you drove in it was a relief. I'll keep quiet and let you think but if I pretend I know you I am hoping he just leaves me alone." She waited for my response.

I looked back over my shoulder and saw some guy with long hair watching us as he stood beside the pickup truck. She was right --- he did look creepy. When the guy saw he was being watched he got into his truck and drove off.

"Well --- he's leaving. Looks like you've been rescued." I gave a half smile.

She smiled back. "Thanks so much. You did rescue me. You are like my prince in shining armour." She gave a soft smile while looking at me. "Can I sit here just a short while? I'll be quiet. I promise."

"I guess that'll be okay. Where are you going after this?

She turned more so she was facing me. "I'm going to Basille to visit my girlfriend. Going to visit her for a couple of days. I won't be able to see her until she gets off work though --- that isn't till 5:00. I haven't seen her forever --- since she moved."

I shook my head and said, "Ah'" to confirm what she said.

I turned and was now staring at the waterfalls. I was just thinking about stuff. Gail was looking at me --- I could feel her eyes trying not to stare through a slightly awkward silence --- except for the sound of the dam. The sound of the rushing water seemed to lessen the awkwardness.

"You said you wanted to think about some things. Don't mean to pry but can I help? Do you need someone to talk to? Maybe an outside perspective might help? Is it financial problems?"

I stared straight ahead. "No, it isn't financial problems."

"Family?"

"No --- not family."

"Girl or relationship problems?" She had noticed he wore no ring.

I didn't answer this time.

"Oh --- girl problems. It'll be okay." She wanted to help him.

"We probably shouldn't talk about it." I continued to stare ahead.

"Okay --- we don't need to but if you need an ear --- someone to just listen and not judge, just know I can be a good listener. Hey --- you never told me your name?"

"Oh --- sorry. My name is," there was a very long pause --- "Luc." She noticed a bigger smile cross his face now --- and those lovely grey eyes were looking at her.

"Well --- glad to meet you Luc." She extended her hand and Lucas shook her hand --- it felt so warm and alive.

CHAPTER 17

Kyle:

I've been driving for quite some time now. It is dark. My mind feels more refreshed. Going for a drive does that --- it relaxes me. That waterfall stop helped. I'm not sure where I am at the moment --- and there is a slight rain starting to fall. Up ahead there is a lighted neon sign just ahead for a hotel. I don't want to spend the night in the car. This hotel looks better. The kind of hotel that could would have a nice bed --- and a restaurant. I pull in the front entrance and there is a terrace that would shelter any guests from the rain upon entry. I walk in and there are three receptionists there.

"Good evening Sir. May I help you?" One of the girls said with a smile.

"Yes --- good evening. I'd like a room please."

"Do you have a reservation Sir?"

"No I don't. I was just driving and got tired. I hope you have a room available?"

"I'll just look Sir." A few seconds later she said, "You are in luck Sir --- we have one room left. It's on the seventh floor."

"That'll be fine. I noticed you have a restaurant. Is it open?"

"Yes sir. It's open until 10:00 P.M. It is just down that hallway and to the right." She pointed to the hallway.

Kyle shook his head. "Great."

"I'll just need your credit card Sir."

"I'd prefer to pay cash."

"We are still going to need you credit card Sir."

"Well --- believe it or not I don't actually have a credit card. Don't believe in them."

"Really? Well, I will need some kind of I.D. How about your driver's licence Sir?"

"Could I just leave a large deposit of cash? I'm kind of a private person."

She stared at me like I was some kind of freak. I didn't want to stand out --- to be remembered.

"Very well Sir. We would need a five hundred dollar deposit plus the room is two hundred and twelve dollars. So we would require seven hundred and twelve dollars in cash. You would get the five hundred dollars back in the morning. Is that all right Sir?"

"Yes --- yes --- that would be fine." I took out a wad of hundred dollar bills and counted out eight of them and handed them to her.

"Are you a member Sir? There is a discount if you are a member."

"No --- I'm not a member."

"Would you like to be a member Sir?"

"Thanks anyway but no."

She hands me the change --- a receipt for both the room and the deposit and then the key to the room along with a brochure explaining the amenities at the hotel.

I turn and walk directly down the hallway to the restaurant. I want some dinner. I could get my bags later.

"He didn't have a credit card?" One of the reception ladies asked the other receptionist.

"I guess not. It doesn't' happen often but some people do just pay the cash. Most customers don't care about giving their driver's licence or I.D. but I do understand their thinking. Sometimes I like to be anonymous too!"

I slept great last night. I'm not sure why but it was the best sleep I've had in quite some time. I had asked for an 8:00 A.M. wakeup call. I needed the call to wake up. That's unusual. I sat up in bed and felt pretty good. I was a long way from home and this was just what I needed. To get away from all my problems and forget about them --- and a good nights sleep. I showered and shaved --- packed my suitcase and carried it out to the car. Then I went to the restaurant and ordered breakfast. I had pancakes --- which I hadn't had in months. I paid the bill and then went to the restroom. I pulled the toothbrush out of my pocket and brushed my teeth --- without the toothpaste this time. Then I went to the front desk and handed in the room key.

"Was everything all right Sir?" A bright eyed lady at reception asked.

"Yes thank you. The room was great and I slept great."

"Can I make any other reservations for you Sir?"

"No --- that's quite all right."

"Very well Sir. Have a great day and thank you for staying with Starlight."

It was 9:35 A.M. when I was back on the road. I checked the map for the best way to get back home. I was ready to get back to the farm. I felt so much better. I hadn't thought about the grave or the incinerator or the missing cop since yesterday. After checking the map and deciding the route I headed out. I turned on the radio and chose to listen to some blues music for the first part of the drive. I chose a different route to go home that might save me a couple of hours. I drove pretty much straight through only stopping for gas and at the drive thru for coffee and snacks on the go. It was just after 9:00 P.M. when I got home. As I pulled in the headlights pointed at the mailbox. I grabbed the mail and then drove the long, eerie driveway to the locked gate. I unlocked the gate and swung it open. Then re-locked it behind me. As I drove further up the driveway I started to get that feeling again --- of not knowing. I hadn't watched the news for a couple of days. I parked the car near the back steps and got out --- still no motion detector light. Tomorrow I'm going out and buy one. I grabbed my small suitcase and before I was to the top of the steps three cats rushed by me.

"Did you miss me Jasper?" I said it to all three cats.

The cats were meowing. They wanted to get inside to their favourite sleeping place on the couch. I opened the door and the cats went directly in --- meowing and purring all the time. I turned on the main light and put my suitcase on the table. The first thing I did was feed the cats. I opened three cans of cat food --- the cats making figure eights at my feet. I put the food down and bent down to stroke them but they were too busy eating. I decided on some tea so I put the kettle on for a tea and made two whole-wheat cheese sandwiches. When everything was ready I got a tray and went into the living room and turned on the television. Try as I might to stay away from the news I couldn't. I turned to the news but had to wait until 10:00 P.M. In the meantime I flicked through with the remote but didn't really find anything that caught my fancy. One hundred and sixty-three stations and nothing to really watch --- go figure. I was finished my snack by the time the news came on. The cats were now on the couch and all three were rubbing up against me --- purring. I stroked them for a few minutes and then they curled up and went to sleep. Then the news came on.

"Police are not releasing any new information on missing police officer Giacinta Bello. She has been missing since last Saturday. Police have not released any information on the cell phone that was found a few hours after her reported missing. Police are asking the public for any information. Someone out there has some information on the officer's disappearance."

There was a loop on Officer Bello --- where she went to school --- her family. Then the news mentioned something that caught my attention. Officer Bello was eleven weeks pregnant with her second child.

"Shit! She was pregnant and she had a young child." I stared at the television. "Wow! That's so sad. I hope they find her soon and catch the guy or guys who did this."

I tried to reassure myself that I was not involved --- that I had nothing to do with it. That it wasn't me. The last girl was eight years ago. I had stopped now. I was a good guy again.

I should make an appointment with the psychiatrist but I worried what the psychiatrist might do if I told him or her that I was somehow involved in the deaths of so many girls. I certainly didn't want to end up in some loony bin --- locked up in some psychiatric ward. Guilty by reason of insanity they call it. Not legally responsible for my actions. Or end up in jail. Who the hell cares? I'd still be locked up.

"Fuck that idea. I've been clean eight years now."

I started to think collecting girls was like being an alcoholic. Like if I just didn't drink I would be cured --- that I would be okay. I wasn't sure if I believed it though. I dreaded sleeping at times --- because of the nightmares. I wish I could just go on a long sleep without any dreams. I hadn't had a nice dream since --- well --- I can't even remember. I was tired from the long drive and I was getting sleepy. I had felt rejuvenated earlier in the day but that drive was a long one. In bed that night I had trouble falling asleep. My mind kept thinking of that grave --- and that this was the room the old couple committed suicide in so many years ago. I decided tomorrow I would go for a drive around the farm again. This time, checking some of the other areas that I hadn't been to. Finally I drifted off to sleep. I dreamt I was travelling but to where I didn't know. It felt like it was far, far away.

When I woke up in the morning I felt better. I had slept right through and the cats that usually woke me up early to go outside let me sleep this morning. Maybe they knew I needed to sleep? Once I was awake the cats wandered up to meet me.

"Come on sleepy head," They seemed to be meowing at me. "We want to go outside now. Move your ass." So I moved my ass and let the Jaspers out.

"What a life those cats have," I mused to myself. "Sleep, eat, explore --- hunt. No worries in the world. What would a cat have to worry about?" I envied them.

After a light breakfast I drove all around the farm but saw nothing strange. Everything was as it should be. I drove back to the fresh grave --- just in case --- to check it out. When I got there it was as I had left it. Half buried and half open.

"Good!" I said out loud. "Make sure you stay like that!"

I stared at the grave and knelt down and picked up a handful of the dirt. Cool and damp as the dirt sifted through my fingers back down to the grave. I thought of my own mortality and how time was rushing by. I had money --- was still fairly young. Why wasn't my life better? Why wasn't it more fun? I should have more friends but I was always worried that someone might get close to me. Better to stay at a distance.

I thought about the saying "No Man Is An Island." Then I spoke to the grave, "I may not be an island but I definitely feel like one." I felt like I was a peninsula --- with a tenuous narrow strip connected to the mainland.

I thought about my family --- my bloodline --- my sisters and brother. It was different now. Life was changing. I remembered when I was young. Oh, I had problems but they were miniscule compared to what I was facing now. I had been thinking of my own mortality and my own death. I thought about GOD. Would GOD forgive me? I really didn't mean to do those things. Would GOD know it wasn't my fault?

"I'm going to read the bible more." I muttered to the grave.

I looked up to the sky as I said it. Like that would save me. There's a bible somewhere at the farmhouse. I didn't believe in much of the bible. Sounded like bullshit to me really. Written by men --- too far fetched. But I believe in GOD --- just not the religion parts too much --- same for the church. I hadn't been to church in forever. I thought about all the religious wars past and present in the world. How stupid is that? They believe in GOD but bomb and kill fellow human beings. I thought of my own situation. I believed in GOD but this was different. People going to war knew what they were doing. They were killing on purpose --- with intent. They believed GOD was on their side. As if GOD takes sides. I didn't know what I was doing. Like stepping on an ant under the shoe. You don't even know you stepped on it and why is it that it seems the most religious people sometimes turn out to be the most hateful against those not in their faith?

"GOD --- I'm just a man trying to be good --- to do good things. It's just so hard sometimes. If you could just give me a sign or something?"

I looked up to the sky and waited --- nothing. Then I heard a voice in my head.

"You need to go away --- far away --- on a vacation." I wondered if it might be GOD speaking to me? I wiped the dirt off my hands and then used the wet grass to wash them. For some reason the image crossed my mind of being baptized.

CHAPTER 18

I decided I would go away but not until January when winter would likely be in full force. I thought about going somewhere warm where there would be no snow or ice. I thought of the tropics --- or even Australia. That would be their summer time. I wasn't quite sure. I could decide later where to go. Maybe I would just drive far away. I like driving. I had the television on while I was thinking when something on the television caught my attention. I turned the volume up. The news report came on about yet another missing girl.

"The Palmer Police Force is asking the public for assistance in the disappearance of twenty-three year old Brianna Cawthorne who has been reported as missing. The Police have located Ms. Cawthorne's car at the Palmer Conservation Parking Lot about twenty minutes south of the town of Palmer. The car is a blue late model Ford Focus --- licence plate number 2YN 46B. Ms. Cawthorne was on her way to visit friends but never arrived. Ms. Cawthorne is described as five foot four inches in height and approximately one hundred and twenty pounds. Her hair colour is strawberry blonde. Police are asking anyone remembering this car or Ms. Cawthorne to contact them at the police number below."

Then the news station moved on to something else. I was sure that Palmer was one of the towns I drove through? Then I thought of that girl in the parking lot at the dam and rapids but her name was Gail. Yea --- her name was Gail. And she was taller than five foot four inches. She was about five foot seven --- I think? I tried my best to remember. Well --- at least this couldn't be one of mine. She had the wrong name --- and she was taller. I couldn't remember the colour of the car though. I remembered the black pickup truck and the creepy guy. I shrugged it off after coming to the conclusion it wasn't me. I thought that the Brianna girl probably shacked up with some guy. When she sees or hears her name on the television she will probably call in that everything is okay. Then again why would her car be left abandoned like that --- and her cell phone? People --- especially girls always have their cell phones by their side. Maybe her cell battery was dead. Yea --- that must be it. Girls should be more careful.

There wasn't any new news on the missing officer and girl the next three months. As for the missing girl in Palmer they never found her as far as I know. It was as if both girls disappeared off the face of the Earth. I decided it best to not think about it. I was sure it couldn't be me. I haven't been having any more dreams about any new girls --- that's a good sign. It made me feel better. I am more certain than ever that I wouldn't be dreaming about any new girls. The nightmares had stopped. I felt much more at ease. I had been thinking about flying to Hawaii for a two-week vacation. I had been to Maui in my mid-twenties and had liked the island. Ten days in Hawaii would be a nice break from the winter doldrums. I just wished I had a mate to travel with me. I thought about joining a dating agency. That is what I did --- I thought about it. Never seemed to happen though. I started thinking how society views people who are alone. Going out for dinner alone --- people looking at me eating by myself --- like I'm a misfit or I have leprosy or some kind of highly contagious disease. Same for the movies --- sitting alone in a movie theatre while everyone else is there with friends or family. I remember how people would stare at me in Hawaii. I tried not to picture it. I used to tell people that I just recently lost my wife and family in a terrible car accident and that I was trying to recover. Getting people to feel sorry for me --- to stop their questions --- and their stares. I thought the only people travelling by themselves were businessmen who had to be there. They didn't have a choice. Mixing business with pleasure was an added bonus. The idea to travel to Hawaii didn't take long to trash. I decided on a round-a-bout southerly drive instead. That would allow me to travel at my leisure with no real time frame --- and to sightsee and enjoy myself. Besides --- my last driving trip was very relaxing.

Lucas

Kyle thought the idea for the round-a-bout trip was his own but in truth it came from somewhere else. It came from the back of Kyle's mind where I lurk. It would be a safer way to collect girls. Hawaii had lots of tourists and they generally travelled as couples or in groups --- not that it couldn't be done but it had more risk to it. On the islands they would have a record that I had visited them. Not that it mattered greatly since there were lots of tourists but it was a numbers game. I had collected a few girls abroad in the past --- not just Hawaii but other countries as well but travelling abroad is a different kind of animal that requires different considerations. So I put it in Kyle's mind to postpone that Hawaiian trip. We could go another time. The southerly round-a-bout drive would still be in January. I was satisfied for now. I thought I could wait until then to --- you know --- fulfill my very unique needs.

Kyle:

Have you ever noticed how time seems to stand still when you watch the clock? It doesn't really because time is time but it all comes down to a matter of perspectives. I watched the clock and crossed off the days on the calendar for my trip south. Funny thing was it really didn't matter so much when I left since I could pretty much go anytime I wanted. I'm not tied down to anything in particular. No real job or obligations to attend to.

Yet I had January 10th as the date of departure. The return date was set as tentative with a target of three weeks.

The night before the trip I went through my checklist for the trip. I am really an organized soul and believe on being prepared. I packed two suitcases and stared down at them the night before.

"I'm going to make sure not to forget to bring some good clothes --- in case I want to go to an event or something,"

Jasper number one and two were with me --- watching me. They had seen it before and so knew I was planning to be away for a while. They would have the place to themselves. *I'd better remember to fill up the cat food dispenser before I leave --- and the water dispenser. And I'll leave the bathtub filled with some water --- just in case.* Putting the Jaspers outside wasn't an option. January could be a cold month and these days when the cats went outside depended entirely on the weather. Sometimes I would choose and sometimes the cats would try and decide whether to go outside. They could probably survive in the barn --- lots of hay as an insulator but it wouldn't be very comfortable --- especially if a cold snap reared its ugly face. I love my cats --- although I wouldn't admit it. They are after all the main relationships in my life. They give me some comfort and someone to talk to. I remembered the time I bought two walkie-talkies. They were on sale and it was a good price. They had a range of forty-seven miles. After buying them though I thought about it. *Why the hell did I buy them? It's not like I have another person to call.* I kept the walkie-talkies anyway. It was the same for the telephone. Telemarketers and wrong numbers mainly. Oh, I would use the phone to call out --- to make appointments or phone stores to see if they carried such and such. The phone might as well have been unplugged until I needed to use it. When I was done I closed the suitcases and carried them down near the front door. Then I made sure the cats had their food dispensers ready. Now all three cats were watching me in the kitchen. I fed them but they didn't leave my side all night.

Lucas:

Meanwhile I've been filling up my little secret cache of goodies into the van's secret hiding places. *This is going to be a good trip. I get excited planning --- anticipating all those possibilities.* I seem to be salivating when thinking about it. It was like Christmas --- only better --- much better. For some reason I thought about that movie Predator and how the alien squealed in delight admiring the trophies he collected. *For me this isn't a sightseeing tour. It's all business --- and pleasure of course. This trip is my practice trip --- my appetizer so to speak. I haven't forgotten about Marianne and her two daughters. I'm saving the main course for Break. That family is going to have one hell of a memorable Spring Break.* I smiled when I thought about them. That would be my crowning moment. I have already planned much of it in my head many times. It would be difficult but not impossible. For now I concentrated on what was at hand.

Kyle:

In the morning I got up and noticed a fresh coat of snow on the ground. Only about five inches of the white powder and it glistened like thousands of little stars in the morning sunshine. I put the timers on for the lights and set the thermostat down to a low sixty degrees Fahrenheit. That would keep the pipes from freezing and the cats would be warm enough. They had fur after all. The cats were following me around like they were on a leash. They didn't want me to go. It was like they could sense something and they needed to protect their master. I sat down on the couch with my morning tea and all three cats were up on my lap --- purring as I stroked them.

What's wrong? Oh --- you know I'm going away huh. You're not stupid are you? You'll be all right. Just keep the place mouse free. Do your job now.

I finished my tea and walked into the kitchen ---the cats on my heels. I washed and rinsed the cup and dried it and put it away. Then I gave the place a quick final once over, even going downstairs. The cats followed me, meowing like they were pissed off. I was ready and so I went outside locking the door behind me. Jasper number one jumped up on the kitchen windowsill to watch me. Then the other two Jaspers were up on the windowsill watching as I drove away --- out of sight.

CHAPTER 19

Kyle:

I needed four-wheel drive with the drifting snow in the driveway. It wasn't a problem though. Soon I wouldn't be seeing snow but green instead. I like green much more than the white. Spring would be coming in a few months and that's my favourite time of year. It was a time when the leaves would be budding --- birds returning --- and a time for babies to be born in nature. And it was a time before the bugs came out. It wasn't spring yet but I was heading where it would be spring like --- to me anyway.

The hours whizzed by as well as the miles and soon there was no more snow --- only occasional small pockets of white --- and then no snow at all. It was late when I decided to stop at a motel. I glanced at the dash clock --- it was almost 10:00 P.M. *Wow! I drove a lot today. I made good time.* I wondered why I wasn't fatigued after all those hours. I had stopped for coffee and gas but other than that drove right through. That motel wasn't the nicest place. I mean it was clean but it was also dark. The motel itself was small and only one level. It was really an emergency stop kind of place. It had the look and feel of a Norman Bates kind of motel. I'm not even sure what town I'm in. I register and go quickly to the room. I brought a sub with me and although not a proper dinner it would do. Once in the room I notice the wood panel-ing on the walls and even the ceiling. I don't like wood paneling as to me it makes the room seem darker. I don't want to feel like I'm staying at some log cabin. *Okay --- I'm here tonight and it will have to do but from now on I am going to arrive earlier and check the place out. It's the kind of place that a person would only stay one night in. The price is good --- or rather cheap. You get what you pay for though. I don't have to worry about prices. Life is too short. Hopefully the bed is comfortable.* I check the bed out and it seems firm enough but the comforter is pretty ragged. I lift the sheets and think, *the sheets are --- well --- let's put it this way. No way I'm sleeping in them.* I trudge out to the van to get my own blanket --- a nice comfy blanket with three wolves on it and a waterfall. Many times I sleep between this particular blanket and it is warm and cozy. I fold it and climb between the folds like I was in a cocoon. I read a chapter from my book and then turned the lights out. Tomorrow I would ask the receptionist if there were any places around here worth sightseeing. Or I would drive until I saw the next roadside Information Centre. I tossed and turned and woke up a few times --- staring at the red digital clock in the room. I couldn't wait for morning.

I woke up early. I stretch and look about the room. *It's not the kind of place I usually stay at. I know I already said that. Tonight will be different.* I walk into the bathroom and ugh --- it reminds me of a gas station washroom. The bathtub has rust stains. I turn the tap on and let it run. At least the water is starting to get hot. I rinse my face with water and stop to stare at my reflection in the mirror. I see a couple of wrinkles and shake my head. *I'm going to have to see what girls use to hide their wrinkles.* I grab my shaving cream and lather the one-day old beard and shave it clean. *Well at least that feels better. Now to get the hell out of this dump and find a good place for breakfast.*

At checkout --- the clerk --- an old lady that would have looked much better in the dark told me about a diner down the road.

"Lots of truckers stop there. The place serves breakfast to 11:00 A.M. and they serve a great breakfast. Their coffee is to die for." The lady that needed a mask blurted out as she chewed gum. It might have been chewing tobacco.

"Uh --- okay --- thanks." I tried to minimize eye contact. I exited at about the same time she smiled and showed her crooked, yellow stained teeth from decades of cigarette smoking. *For some reason I imagined her serving me breakfast. I was losing my appetite quickly.*

Twenty minutes later I was at the diner. It was early and the sun was barely out --- or rather it was trying to sneak a peak. The place was fairly busy --- a good sign that the place might have good food. No one to seat patrons so I just stood there. Some lady yelled out,

"Just find a place to sit. Someone will be with you shortly."

So I walked over to an empty booth and slid my ass in across the seat. I looked around the place and it looked inviting enough. Most patrons were sitting at the tables. They must have been truckers. There were about twelve transports parked out in the parking lot. Must be regulars --- or just travelling through and stop here every trip. And then I saw a young redhead walking towards me smiling. She had a great smile and she looked way too classy for this place. I mean it wasn't a dump by any measure but this girl looked like centrefold material. I know people exaggerate sometimes but I'm not kidding. Her gaze caught me in deep thought and soon she was at my table.

"Morning --- hi --- my name is Tabitha and I will be your waitress. Would you like a coffee to start?" Her eyes seemed to peer through me --- waiting for my answer. Finally I answered when I returned to Earth.

"Morning --- sorry --- yea --- a coffee would be great to start. Do you have any honey?" *I felt like I was blushing.* She looked at me --- smirking. *Then I wondered did she just think I called her honey?* "I meant honey for the coffee." I added with stupor in my voice. The pause in dialogue seemed deafening. *What's wrong with me today? It has to be that cuteness factor I decided.* Her smile size just doubled.

"Most people don't have honey with coffee but with tea instead. You're like me though. I like honey in my coffee too! Yes --- I'll bring you some honey with your coffee. Here's the menu. I'll give you a few minutes to look it over." She handed me the green menu thingy. She was still smiling those pearly whites. "Be right back with the coffee."

I watched her walk away. I tried not to stare but the view --- it looked pretty nice. She turned and caught me looking. She sent me a small smile special delivery back over her shoulder. *Shit! I didn't want to look like a dirty old man*. I turned away pretending I didn't notice. She came back with my coffee within a minute. She put it down in front of me --- along with four packets of golden honey and the milk and cream. She was smiling ever so slightly --- and she had her tongue just out to the side of her mouth. *She must be doing that subconsciously.*

"Are you ready to order or do you need a few more minutes? The breakfast special is offered before 8:00 A.M. and you are in time for the special. It includes two eggs anyway you like, bacon, sausage, hash browns and your choice of toast. Free coffee fill-ups all for $5.99. It will fill you up." She paused while I looked at her. "Or you can order from the menu. We have fruit dishes as well as well as cereal, oatmeal and well --- you can see on the menu for yourself." She tilted her head waiting for my response. Her eyes blinked three times at me.

"No --- I don't need more time. I'm ready to order. That breakfast special sounds good thank you."

She stared at me. *I think I just gulped*. "And how would you like your eggs? Scrambled, sunny side up, over easy, poached?"

"If I could get them sunny side up please?" *I feel like a teenager again. I think this must be a teenager girl serving me? Why isn't she in school?*

"Sure --- sunny side up --- and the toast?"

The toast? I repeated. *She's looking at me with the deepest clear blue eyes in the universe.*

"Yea --- the toast. Do you want white, whole-wheat, rye, or multi-grain toast?" She waited.

"Oh," I tried a fake laugh as I shook my head. "Of course. I would like rye toast please --- with butter."

"Sure thing. By the way what's your name? You're not a regular customer. You must be passing through --- or you just moved here?" She stood waiting for an answer.

I looked up at her. It was easy looking up at her --- until her piercing eyes looked upon me. "My name is Kyle and yea --- I'm passing through. I'm on a kind of vacation exploration trip."

"Glad to meet you Kyle." She seemed satisfied with my answer. "I'll be right back with your breakfast."

She turned and walked away. *I was watching her leave again --- feeling guilty --- and old --- a dirty kind of old. I should know better. I could swear she added a little extra wiggle to her walk away this time. I don't usually feel so undone --- not since I was about 22 and lost my virginity have I ever felt so rattled --- and that was a long time ago.*

I quickly scanned the restaurant to see if anyone was watching me. I had a vision that everyone in the place was staring at me --- shaking their head and pursing their lips at me.

"Dirty old man. She could be your daughter." I checked and no one was looking my way. I was being ignored. Whew!

I settled down and started normal breathing again. I looked out the window. I had a view of the parking lot. Not much of a scenic view. The seats were comfortable and the noise in the place wasn't too bad. I started thinking where I might like to explore today. Whether I wanted to stay in this area for a day or two or to continue on. The lady at the motel had mentioned that there was an old train station --- a museum of old trains just up the road on this highway. I wasn't really into old trains though. If you've seen a few old trains you've pretty much seen them all. I wasn't interested in the railroad. Exotic, expensive cars --- now I would be interested in that. But they wouldn't be in this type of place. I don't mean that as an insult. Just that it is an out of the way kind of place that likely had the local strip mall as the centrepiece of attraction. Yea --- probably best to move on --- although there might be some neat wildlife around here? Then I heard a noise that brought me back to reality.

"Here's your breakfast Kyle." Tabitha was standing at my side smiling down at me --- waiting for me to move my elbows so she could put the food down on the table in front of me. Her teeth had to be the whitest, straightest teeth I have ever seen.

"Oh --- that was quick." I moved my elbows away. She put the food down. Her proximity to me caused my breathing to stop for a second. This girl really had to get into modelling --- or movies in Hollywood. GOD was generous to her.

She slowly rose up --- like a movie in slow motion mode. She turned her head looking at me --- smiling all the time. *Her scent was intoxicating and caused me to think of warm, hot honey as it sifted through my ole factory senses. Was that vanilla and cinnamon that I smelled coming off her?*

"I noticed you've already downed half your coffee Kyle. I'll be right back to top it up. Enjoy your breakfast and if you need me --- just look."

I think one of her eyelids just blinked at me or rather winked at me? She turned and seemed to float away like she was on a cloud. I watched like a kid in the candy store for the first time. That wiggle --- well --- it should be illegal --- or come with a for adults only sign. She quickly returned and bent over and ever so slowly poured the hot coffee into my half-cup. It made me want to drink my coffee faster --- so she could keep pouring it. I glanced at her breasts as she bent over but quickly glanced away. *They're just mammary glands --- just mammary glands I tried to tell myself. No there not --- they were made for sex. I felt slightly dizzy.*

"How's the breakfast?" She asked. "Is everything okay." Her eyes always seemed to find mine.

"It's very delicious. Thank you." I said as manlike as I could. *It might have sounded sheepish?*

She turned and walked away. *Was she even serving the other customers? I couldn't remember. Okay --- she was. I saw her doing the fill-ups on the coffee. I'm just imagining things.*

I probably took twice as long as usual to finish my breakfast. I managed five cups of fill-ups along the way. *I'm going to be pissing all morning.* Finally when I was done she brought me my bill except this time she sat down right opposite me --- facing me. She didn't hand me the bill right away but was clutching it in her right hand --- looking at me. She turned to look around to make sure no one was staring --- then turned back to face me.

"So Kyle --- are you in town for a while?" She didn't wait for my answer. "I hope so. I hope your not just passing through town and leaving us." She stared into my eyes and her lips pressed ever so slightly together. *Her lips look like they were made for clamping things. I was starting to get aroused --- again.*

"Well --- I'm not sure yet. I don't know if this town or area has any good things for a tourist to visit? So I just don't know. Anything worth seeing around here?" *I attempted to stare out the window and not at her beauty. I wasn't all that successful.*

She leaned forward and whispered, "There are some very good things to see here Kyle. Just give our little town a chance."

I felt my face begin to blush. I wasn't sure she meant what I heard. Then I found myself blurting out quite by accident. "How old are you?" *There was a silence as I regretted asking the question.* Then I added, "How long have you worked here?"

"I'm older than I look Kyle. I'm 22 years old and I've worked here for just a few months." She smiled and handed me the bill. She didn't put it down on the table but held it out for me to take out of her hand. Even her hands looked good. I reached for it and I'm sure I had a stupid smile on my face. I grabbed the bill and our hands touched just ever so slightly. She smiled at me more as our hands touched.

"22 --- you don't look 22. You look much younger." I gulped.

"Yea --- I know but I could show you my driver's licence. *A slight pause --- was I actually starting to sweat?* Then she added, "And I am definitely attracted to older men." Another pause as time seemed to stand still. Well --- I better get back to work. I hope you stay here Kyle --- nice meeting you. Hope we meet again --- soon." *And then she slinked out of the seat as graceful as any ballerina might and she walked away. I watched --- in shock. She turned to look back. Damn --- caught again! This place needs more oxygen.*

I sat there sipping the last drops of my coffee trying to recover. Then I looked at the bill and noticed she had slipped in a separate piece of paper. I read it ---

Kyle, here's my phone number. Please call me. I'll be waiting.
If you can't call I get off at 4 P.M. Pick me up. I could definitely
show you what this town has to offer. You won't regret my offer.
I'll be waiting for you.

Tabitha – 863-951-8874

I stared at the note for a second not believing it. *This kind of stuff just doesn't happen to me.* I looked up and saw her looking at me from across the room as she stood serving another customer. She smiled at me and snuck in a quick wave. Then she went back to serving the other customer. I put the note deep into my pocket. That's when I noticed I trembled. *I'd better get out of here as I felt I might possibly faint.* I paid my bill at the cashier and she said something about coming again to Mandy's. *Coming again? My mind is in the gutter. Did I leave a $14.00 tip for Tabitha on a $6.00 bill? I don't really remember.* For some reason I thought that I should try to act like James Bond --- whatever that means? In other words try to look cool. *I suck at looking cool --- at least around her.*

As I walked out to the car my legs felt like warm mush. I sat in the car for a minute and pulled out the note --- reading it again. As I read it I thought maybe she was trying to get a bigger tip. Maybe she flirted with others. It didn't seem that way though. She handed me that note with her phone number. She seemed like she meant it. Especially when she said she was really 22 years old and liked older men. Then I remembered I still had to brush my teeth. Normally I would go back into the restaurant to use the washroom to brush but instead I got a water bottle in the car and brushed them in the parking lot. I looked and no one was around. After I brushed I rinsed and checked to see if anyone was watching me. No one was taking pictures. I started the car and began to drive --- not really knowing where

I was going. I had to take a leak --- five cups of coffee will do that to you. Then I thought what do I want to see in this town. I realized something. *I've already seen what I want to see in this town — I want to see those wonderful eyes and ass again. I hadn't felt so wonderful since ---well --- I've never felt like this before.*

CHAPTER 20

I don't remember where I went that day. It's all a blur. I do know I watched the clock very closely. I didn't have a phone but I decided I was going to be at that restaurant parking lot well before 4:00 P.M. It might all be for naught --- I might feel a fool but come hell or high water I was going to be there. I practiced my dialogue --- what we might talk about --- like I was reading from some script. I didn't know anything about her, or she anything about me. All I knew was the encounter in the morning at the restaurant with her was electric. Then I thought it was silly really. Our age difference of fifteen years --- the distance in miles between us --- and the fact we were complete strangers. None the less I would be there. There was no way I was going to spend another night at the same motel so I drove around in the day finding a more suitable motel or hotel just in case. My mind thought all kinds of things. Especially the fact that I was extremely rusty in this type of thing --- whatever it could be called. It wasn't really a date --- or was it? I tried not to think about it too much but it was the only thing I thought of. My so-called vacation just got a new twist to it. I don't even think I had lunch?

I was at the restaurant parking lot --- waiting outside at 3:30 P.M. hoping I wasn't being played for a fool. I parked the van facing the doors and far enough away to be unnoticed but close enough to be noticed --- if that makes any sense. It was still cloudy and overcast out. Seconds seemed like hours and the more I thought about it the more I thought I really should just drive away --- but I didn't. I just couldn't.

Then at 4:00 P.M. a few girls were starting to leave the restaurant. At 4:02 still no Tabitha. Oh well --- that's how the cookie crumbles came to my mind. And then she walked out with another girl. They stopped in front of the door and I could see her looking about the lot. *Was she looking for me?* I got out of the van and then she saw me. I saw her smile --- even from that distance. She waved at me and I gave a half wave back. Then she said good-bye to the other girl and started walking towards me. A little smirk was on her face all the way as she wiggled towards me --- her heels clicking on the pavement like a countdown towards NASA doing a space launch.

"Hi Kyle. Are you here for me? I hope so," she called out when she was half way to me.

"Hi Tabitha. Well --- I did get your note so here I am." I gulped while trying to look cool. I don't think it was actually working.

"Great --- I'll just signal my friend Amy that she can leave. That I have a ride --- okay?"

I nodded my head okay --- trying my best not to stare at her. It was like trying not to breath. It only worked for so long --- only even shorter. I was no Tarzan when it came to holding my breath.

She turned back to wave at Amy and she waved back --- got into her car and sat there for a minute before leaving. She wanted to make sure everything was okay I guess.

Truthfully I started thinking that perhaps this wasn't such a good idea. I mean she was something special but I briefly started to wonder about my dreams again. They flared up and I started to wonder. *Is this how it happened with those other girls. I started to get more nervous. But there hadn't been any girls in 8 years. I started to think maybe I was cured. Still --- was I putting this girl at risk?*

Then she was suddenly at my van. She walked right up to me and hugged me. She whispered in my ear, "I'm so happy you're here --- that you showed up? Then she kissed my cheek. I was a goner. *This girl not only had me at hello but she had me at that first smile this morning. I just set a world record for falling in love I think?*

"Me too!" I gurgled back like a frog waking up after hibernation. Then I said it again --- more clearly --- "Me too!"

"You drive a van huh?" She smiled as she looked at me.

"Well --- I brought the van with me this time. I have other vehicles though."

She seemed to be staring right through me. Like she already knew me.

"Let's say we get out of here Kyle. I need to unwind after work." She walked over and got into the van. *Shit! I should have walked over and opened the door for her. How could I be so dumb? She didn't seem to notice though --- or care --- I think?*

Once in the van and buckled in she looked about the van. *What was she looking for?* She saw the bed and turned to look at me. Her eyes asked the question.

"Ah --- sometimes when I'm travelling I may not be around a motel or hotel so I sleep in the van." I tried to explain. *I was sure my face flushed red.*

She nodded her head and said, "Oh, I guess the bed comes in handy, huh?" She had a half crooked smile --- her sexiest smile yet. It felt like I had just been KO'd by the heavy weight champ of the world.

"Where should we go Tabitha?"

"Anywhere but here --- okay --- turn right on the road. You're new in town. I know where we can go."

I started the van and proceeded to drive. She laid her head back on the headrest and then said, "Kyle --- tell me a bit about you. Where are you from? What do you do for work? Just tell me something."

Well --- I'm from Dotroy. That's a small town about eleven hours drive north from here. There's snow up there right now. I'm actually retired --- I don't have a job per say. I decided to travel to get away from the snow."

"You're retired? Already? How old are you? Aren't you too young to be retired? Must be nice."

"Well --- I am lucky to have some money that permits me to retire. I keep busy. I have a farm up there. No livestock or crops but a nice place. Lots of space and air and nature." There was a pause.

"I love nature --- and animals. How old are you?" She asked me again.

"I'm" --- there was a long pause --- "I'm 37." *I looked at her waiting for the hammer to drop. What --- you're 37 --- you're old enough to be my father. Good GOD you are a pervert.* It didn't happen though.

"37 huh? That's not too old at all. Like I said I like older men. There's something mysterious about them. Unless they're bald and fat." She laughed and I laughed along with her.

"Thankfully I'm not bald or fat." I added as we laughed. *It felt good to be with her. I really like her not only because she's gorgeous --- she's too good for this place but her personality made her easy to talk to. She's the total package. She's the type of girl that no matter what boy she was with everybody else would say she's too good for that guy.*

A slight hesitation and then, "So --- are you married --- in a relation-ship?" She half turned to look at me.

"No --- I'm not marri --- I don't have a girlfr --- I'm single. Otherwise I wouldn't be here right now."

"Okay --- good." *She seemed to like that answer.* Have you ever been mar-ried before?" *She was asking serious questions right away. Was that good --- or bad?*

"Ah --- well no. Never married before. Came close once though." *I lied. I've never really been close. Thinking about it was the closest I ever came to getting hitched.* I tried to redirect the questions towards her to avoid the subject.

"Tell me a bit about yourself Tabitha? Have you lived here all your life?"

"My parents moved here when I was five. Dad took off when I was ten. I don't see him but I am close to mom and sis. My brother is three years older than me. He's living pretty far away. I miss him. I graduated College at 19 and used to work at the Auto Parts Store in town but the owner was coming onto me and I didn't like him. I am ready to leave Wilstin for good." There was a pause and then, "Any idea on how long you might stay Kyle?" *Those blue eyes were like a whirlpool drawing me in. I was being sucked in --- and I didn't mind at all.*

I looked at her. *I really should be watching the road more.* "I'm not sure when I'll be leaving Wilstin? It all depends on things." Then I changed the subject. "You graduated College at 19? You must be pretty smart. What did you graduate in?"

"Graphics Design. I've been interested in it and I'm very good with computers. I'm not sure what I want to do though. I will need to leave this town for better job opportunities."

"You should be a model." *Did that just come out of my mouth?* She looked at me and touched my elbow. *Wow! It felt like a hot tidal wave just kissed my heart.*

"I get that all the time. I've been offered a couple of modelling jobs. Haven't taken anything yet. I'm more a down to earth girl rather than a jet setter traveller type." Then she added, "Thanks for the compliment. I'm not all dolled up right now. You should see me when I'm all dolled up with my make-up, hair, dress, and heels. Really I'd rather just wear jeans and a white T-shirt. I'm just more comfortable in those."

Suddenly I had an image of her in blue jeans and a tank top --- the jeans hugging and caressing her ass in my mind. "Well, you look pretty good with even a little bit of make-up I must say. You have a natural beauty Tabitha."

"Thanks but let's talk about something else --- not just my looks --- okay."

"Sure --- what kinds of things do you like to do in your spare time?"

"Well, I have years of dance classes and ballet and gymnastics but I also play piano. I like listening to music too --- and watching movies but I like nature best."

I stared at the road. I couldn't get her words out of my head about her being a dancer --- and a gymnast. *She must be pretty flexible.* I'm sure my face gave it away --- as much as I tried to suppress it.

"Yes Kyle --- I'm extremely flexible and can get into all kinds of positions." She was looking at me and had the tip of her tongue touching her front teeth --- slowly caressing the top of her lip. *She has to be reading my mind. Does this girl have any idea the effect she is having on me? Good GOD!* Then back to reality.

"Mmmmmnnnn --- I am bit flexible myself. I do some MMA training. That's Mixed Martial Arts so it helps to be flexible." I tried to diffuse the images of her in all the Kama Sutra positions I could think of. I didn't want her thinking I was a pervert or anything so I tried not to think of her being flexible.

"I know what MMA is. I watch it sometimes. I like the James Bond movies and action movies too!"

"You watch MMA?"

"Yea, if the fights are good. I even do a bit of MMA in my spare time. Have you had supper Kyle?"

"No, are you hungry? I could take you to a nice place if you want." *I'll do pretty much anything you want was at the tip of my tongue. I suppressed it. And she does a bit of MMA in her spare time. What an angel. No, correct that. What a Goddess!"*

"Do you want to go to a nice place? We don't have to. I'm not a Gold digger or anything." *She had a way of looking at me that made me feel like butter in the microwave.* "We could just go for hamburgers or something else if you want."

"Ya know --- I had a sub for supper last night and I'd like to have a nice supper tonight. Where's the nicest place in town." I smiled at her --- trying to read her responses.

"Okay --- turn left at the next light. About a quarter of a mile on the right is considered the best place in town to eat. Are you sure? I hope you're buying cause I can't afford to eat there. We don't have to go there."

"I'm fine with that. I could use a good meal tonight and money isn't a problem." I tried my best to convince here that it really was not a big deal. I hadn't been on a date in --- well --- years and I wasn't going to skimp on this girl.

"Okay, but just because you're buying me an expensive supper don't think you're going to get laid. Like I said, I'm not a Gold Digger." *She tilted her head downward and for the first time I saw a slight shyness in her eyes.*

"No --- of course not. I would never think that Tabitha --- honest I wouldn't." I tried my best to let her know that was not my intention at all.

She giggled at me trying to convince her otherwise. She reached out to touch my hand and again I felt that tropical electric tidal wave flush over me. "Don't worry --- I wasn't suggesting that you were expecting. One can never tell what the night will bring though."

The dinner was great, great food, great ambiance, and great conversation. *I felt closer to her than any girl I can remember. I feel like maybe this could be the one to help me break down my walls --- to come out of my prison so to speak --- to help exit my winter. I feel hope again --- hope that I wasn't lost and she could really help me --- rescue me so to speak. She made me feel human again --- and wanted --- and it felt good. And I felt like I might rescue here --- not that she needed my help. It reminded my when I was a child --- when the world felt safer --- and kinder --- and I was happier.*

After dinner we walked to the van --- laughing and we had our arms around each other. I knew it was fast but it didn't feel fast. It felt like the kind of wonderful some people never experience. I almost forgot about my terrible dreams --- my nightmares --- almost. I was a bit worried but it had been eight long years since the last one.

"I know this spot Kyle. It's a nice secret spot where we can talk, listen to music and I see the stars have come out. We could look at the stars. You drive and follow my directions. Would you like to go there?"

"Okay --- I'll be like your chauffeur." We both laughed and she held my one hand as I drove.

In fifteen minutes we were parked at this spot on a hill. It was only one lane in but it was paved. I turned the van off and suddenly she scooted over and sat in my lap. It surprised me. I had to move the steering wheel to make more room. I was harder than I had ever been.

"I hope you don't mind me sitting on your lap Kyle." Her eyes looking through my soul I imagined.

"Mind? Why would I mind? I don't mind at all." I had the biggest smile on my face.

We listened to the music in between our conversations about --- well --- pretty much everything. Then it happened. I couldn't resist it any longer. I kissed her lightly on her cheek --- her eyes looked at me and seemed to shine in the moonlight. Time seemed to stop and then she looked at my lips and I saw her lips part slightly and then we kissed. *GOD she's a good kisser.* I was breathing so heavily I thought I might cum just from her kisses. It had been a long time --- a very long time. Her tongue met my tongue and my mind was awash. We kissed and each kiss seemed to be getting longer --- and wetter. This was one hell of a good vacation. Then she turned to look back at the bed and looked at me. It was as if the bed was calling our names --- whispering our names to go back there.

"Why don't we go back there and lay down Kyle?" She seemed to say in a soft cooing voice.

"Okay." I gulped.

She got off my lap. I wanted her back on. *I'm sure I am dripping from pre-cum. This is it! This is really it! Shit! I don't have a condom. Fuck! Really? She is going to want a condom --- unless she just wants to make out some more?*

She walked back and sat on the bed --- looking at me --- waiting for me. "Well?" She looked at me like a true vixen patting the bed to sit beside her.

Kyle went over and sat on the bed beside her. But it wasn't Kyle anymore. It was Lucas.

CHAPTER 21

I woke up in the van in the morning --- smiled and reached over for Tabitha but she wasn't there. I quickly sat up looking for her but didn't see her. I got up and looked in the front seats but she wasn't there either.

"Tabitha?" I called and waited for a response. "Tabitha? I called out louder ---still nothing but quiet. "Tabitha? Tabitha? Tabitha?" Each call came louder.

I opened the door to the van and that is when I noticed the van wasn't in the same spot where I had parked with Tabitha. It was parked in a different area. An area I didn't know? It was unfamiliar. There was a river here --- and a forest?

"What the hell?" I yelled out. I looked all around and called for her. Then a cold wind went through me. I couldn't remember last night --- anything after the front seat when she was sitting on my lap. Try as I could my mind was a total blank. I started to panic --- really panic. I searched the area for any clues but it was just forest --- and river.

"What the fuck!" Shit! This is not good!" I've got to find out what happened. I hope nothing happened. Please GOD!"

I got in the van and starting driving ---not recognizing anything. I got onto a main road and twenty-five minutes later saw a gas station. I pulled in to ask for directions. I walked in and there were two attendants waiting.

"Good morning sir --- and how are you on this fine day."

"I'm fine. Look --- I think I am a bit lost. Am I still in Wilstin?"

"Wilstin? Naw --- Wilstin is about forty minutes drive back the way you just came. You gotta go back that way." The older guy pointed the direction out while standing at the big window, "and just keep straight. That'll take ya back. Ya want some gas?"

"No thanks --- I'm good for gas."

I was out the door in a flash and on my way. My mind was a mess and I was never so afraid in all my life. I started to imagine. *GOD --- what if I killed her? If I killed her I am turning myself in. I'll turn myself in to the authorities. I'd rather be in prison than live with killing Tabitha. This just can't be. I've had another fucking black out. Tabitha --- please be alive.*

I arrived in town and started recognizing familiar places. I drove to Mandy's ---Tabitha's place of work. I parked and shut the van off and just stared at the building. *GOD I hope she's inside.* I went inside but didn't see her so I asked one of the girls. The waitress Amy recognized me.

"Tabitha's not scheduled to work today. You're the guy she was talking about --- the guy who picked her up after work yesterday. I recognize you. How was your date? Did you guys get along?"

"It was good. You say she's not working today?"

"No --- she scheduled to work tomorrow though." The girl had a questioning look on her face. "Something wrong Mister?" Her eyes were looking at me. "You look worried or something?"

"No --- nothing wrong. Do you have a phone I can use? I don't have a phone. It's a local call."

"There's a pay phone over there." Amy pointed to an old phone on the wall. It was the type of phone that hasn't been around for years.

"Okay --- thanks." I walked over and dug for an old phone card. I found the piece of paper in my right pocket with Tabitha's phone number and dialled her number. It rang and rang until finally voice mail answered.

"Sorry but I can't come to the phone right now. Leave your name and number when you hear the beep and if you're lucky --- I'll call you back." And then the phone beeped.

I hung up. *Shit! I was hoping against all hope that she would answer. I didn't want to leave my name on the voice mail.*

As I was leaving the girl had noticed I didn't get to talk with Tabitha. Amy was the nosey type and Tabitha was her friend. "If you didn't get her sometimes she likes to sleep in on her day off until 10:00 or even 10:30."

I turned and flashed a fake smile her way as I walked out. I got in my van and looked at the clock. It was 9:35 A.M. I half expected the radio to announce a young girl was found murdered but all those other girls were never found. *It hasn't happened in 8 years. Try to remain calm. Maybe she's just sleeping in her bed like that girl said. I should just leave --- get the fuck out of here fast but that lady in the restaurant knows me, and my van. If Tabitha is even missing I'm fucked --- unless that Amy were to disappear? Fuck! What the hell are you thinking Kyle.*

I left the parking lot and drove through town. It was quite a small town with only a few stores or businesses. Mayberry was bigger than this place --- not that I really knew. I found another phone and called Tabitha's number. Same thing --- it went to voice mail. It was after 10 in the morning now. I called again at 10:55 and this time someone answered --- a girl.

"Hello," the girl seemed to almost whisper.

"Hello --- Tabitha?"

"Yea --- who's this?"

"It's Kyle. What happened last night? I don't remember."

"You've got some nerve calling me. You don't remember. Yea --- right! I told you not to call me. Don't ever call me again or I'm calling the police! You're one sick bastard. Leave me alone or else. And stay away from my workplace too! I don't ever want to see you again. If I even see you I'm calling the police!" Then Tabitha slammed the phone down.

I put the phone down and in a daze walked back to my van. Her voice ringing in my ears --- *"You're one sick bastard --- leave me alone --- I'm calling the police,"* over and over. I got in and sat there and began to cry. *Thank GOD she's alive! Thank you --- thank you --- thank you GOD!* My eyes welled up full of tears because she was alive. I was relieved. But for some reason she now hated me. *What the hell did I do --- or try to do? How did she get home? How did I end up wherever the hell I ended up? I wanted to talk with her --- and apologize although I didn't know what for? I just want to find out what happened?* In the end decided I should just leave. *It's too dangerous for her --- for my Tabitha --- even if she was mine for only a few short hours. It's a terrible thing for a man to lose all hope.* So I sat in my van confused --- trying to think what happened and what I should do? *She was special --- I really, really like her.* I want to know what happened but part of me didn't want to know. *What if I was mean to her? I must have done or said something bad. I blacked out and I had absolutely no memory after her asking me to go in the back of the van with her. There can be only once indisputable fact --- that I am still dangerous.* I sat in the van for fifteen minutes in a daze --- then put the van in gear and just started driving. Where to? I had no idea.

Lucas

You're all wondering what the hell happened last night aren't you? I know you are. That bitch is one lucky fuck. I have to consider all the variables when I collect my girls. The only reason I let that girl live was the circumstances and risks were too great. Like I said, I minimize my risks. There is no need for reckless, emotional decisions to guide me. Fact one --- I was at the restaurant and that girl served me. I didn't notice any cameras but there were lots of people there both inside and outside in the parking lot that could be a witness. Fact two – the bitch told someone at work she was going out with me --- I mean Kyle. Fact three --- what a stupid fuck Kyle is to use his real name. Fact four --- Kyle met the girl back at the restaurant and that Amy chick watched Kyle quite closely when that Tabitha girl came to the van. She may have even written down the van's licence plate. Fact five --- Kyle took that girl to that upscale expensive restaurant for dinner. Lots of people again ---- potential witnesses. Like I need her to turn up missing after she's out on a date with Kyle. Fact six --- I don't want Kyle getting no girlfriend. It fucks up my plans --- my time. A girlfriend just gets in the way. I put the idea in Kyle's head to go on this vacation for two reasons. First --- the main reason is I want another one --- the next one. I have needs and they aren't going away. I need a good solid torture session. The second reason, which isn't so important, is that wimp Kyle needs a vacation. He isn't as strong mentally as me. He's a goody two shoes fuck. He has way too much guilt about shit. Hey --- I don't mind him having a good time but he was getting way too serious with this girl way too fast. It was interfering with my plans and this trip. So I scared the shit out of that girl. She was surprised as shit when I showed up. I left the charm in the front seat. I got right down to my animal instincts with no regard for her feelings. What'd I do? Not much. I was actually pretty good considering. I just grabbed her real rough all of a sudden. I can turn my eyes into a wild beast on cue. It takes practice but when Lucas comes out to play --- like I said --- I play rough. So I grabbed her real rough and pulled her close. She actually fought back. It didn't do any good though. It was a short struggle only because I knew already I was going to let her go --- let her live. She started yelling to take her home right now. I let her go. I was still angry but I'm always in control of myself. So I let her go and said,

"I thought you wanted to suck and fuck bitch? Oh --- I get it --- you're one of those fucking tease bitches --- nothing but a waste of my time. Okay --- I'll take you home bitch. I'll take you back right now."

She tried to get out of the van. You know the "fight versus flight" reaction. I wouldn't let her though. It was hard but I actually started apologizing --- telling her I was just role-playing and didn't mean it. I knew she wouldn't buy it. So I drove her home --- or near her home. We talked on the way --- well --- it was mainly me doing the talking. She was really pissed at me but I wanted her to calm down. Didn't want her calling the police and saying I attempted to rape her. I could have raped her easy. I even offered her some money with my apology. I tried to act like Kyle --- it sure wasn't easy acting like that wimp. When we arrived and she got out, she turned and told me,

"Don't ever call me again --- fuck you!"

Then she stormed off and I drove out of town and found a place to sleep in the van. I thought to myself what a waste. She was so beautiful and I could have had a great time with that one. If only Kyle didn't fuck it up.

She left me dripping with a huge erection. I jacked off in the van thinking about her --- what could have been. Damn my hand. I need the real thing. It's time for a session. Oh well --- you know what they say --- there's plenty of fish in the ocean. And it's a big ocean too!

Kyle:

I started driving but to no place in particular. The rain is coming down now. Not hard but enough to make visibility a bit of a problem. I turned the wipers on. My mind is in a fog like state and every few minutes I have tears welling up in my eyes. Between the rain and my tears I better be careful. Part of me doesn't care and I start to think about just driving the van off the road --- into some tree or ditch. I don't though. I look at the clock and it is now just past noon hour. It's 12:07 --- lunchtime but I'm not hungry at all. I don't even feel like a coffee. Check my gas --- still have over half a tank. Better stop for gas soon and get my bearings. *I'm really depressed. That Tabitha incident has shaken me. I wanted it to work. I wanted it so badly. Even in the short time I knew her she made me realize what I've been missing. I sigh and begin to cry again. I realize I think I might actually love her. Never had the chance to love her more but when all your hopes are dashed in an instance --- well --- it's tough to take. I take solace in the fact that she's okay --- that she's alive. If she were dead I would either kill myself or turn myself in. I'm sure of that. I see a restaurant gas bar up ahead on the right. It's a big place. I'll stop here for gas and get my bearings. Figure out what to do next? Where to go? Maybe I should just turn around and go back home --- to the farm. I suddenly think I should have gone to Hawaii. I could be lying on a beach --- feeling the waves --- sipping a drink with one of those stupid umbrellas. Feeling the sun and relaxing. Shit!* I fill up the tank --- it's a self-serve station. I then park the van and go inside the restaurant. I decide on a coffee with a corned beef sandwich on toasted rye with mustard. Guess I am a bit hungry. I ask the guy what's the nearest town and in what direction? He looks at me funny --- like I'm lost. I am in more ways than one. I stare at my sandwich. I can't stop thinking about Tabitha. I wished I smoked. I don't though. It would have relaxed me. Sitting at the table I look around. I notice that I'm the only guy --- correct that --- the only person sitting at a table all alone. I shake my head ever so slightly and sigh. Sipping my coffee thinking how that is one strange combination. *I should have ordered a juice and taken the coffee for the road in my thermos. I left my thermos in the van. Stupid fuck. At least I ordered the large coffee. Maybe that will perk me up.*

I finish lunch then walk to the van while it's still raining. *What a piss poor weather day! It would be a good day to be inside cuddled up to someone nice and warm. I remember last night --- her on my lap --- her head on my shoulder --- those oceanic eyes looking at me like they were happy for the first time in a while --- her smell --- her hair. And I was happy in the moment --- full of hope of what might be.*

"Fuck!" I yell out too loud.

I look around to see if anyone heard me --- if any kids heard me. I'm the only idiot walking in the rain. At least no one heard me. Thank GOD for that. I get in the van and sit for a second watching each raindrop explode against the windshield. *I think I've cried more tears the last year than rain that has fallen from heaven the last century.* I reach for the map to see where I am. I look at the clock. It's 12:59. I decide I'll drive for another four or five hours. *Maybe I can drive out of this rainstorm. It seems to depress me more. I need some sunshine.* As I put the map on the passenger seat I notice something. It's near the back of the seat --- where the backrest meets the seat. *What is that?* I get up and walk over and reach for it. I pick it up. It's Tabitha's necklace. *It must have fallen off that beautiful neck last night. It looks like an expensive necklace. There's a locket with a clasp along with an angel and the words L-O-V-E joined together.* I hold the treasure in my hands. The necklace in my hand makes me feel close to her again. I opened the locket and inside I see a picture of some people. Not sure who they are but I think it is a picture of her mom and sister? The picture must be a few years old? The woman's an older woman --- around my age --- maybe a bit younger.

"Tabitha's going to want this," I whisper under my bated breath.

I swallow and look around. *What should I do? Keep it as a keepsake? Drive back and give it to her? She hates me now for whatever I did? She was really pissed off at me. I could mail it to her? Should I call her and tell her she left it in my van?* I sat in the van with the necklace in my hand --- watching the rain disintegrate against the windshield. *What do I do now?* I think about seeing her one more time and my heart starts to race. It's torture.

CHAPTER 22

For thirty minutes I sat there --- staring at the rain --- manipulating the necklace through my fingers. *I have to call her. She'd want the necklace and picture back. It would be the right thing to do.* I walk back into the restaurant. I let the rain soak me. I don't deserve to be dry. Some people are standing at the exit waiting for the rain to slow down. They stare at me walking in the rainstorm like I'm some kind of idiot. *Well --- I am an idiot.* I walk by them pretending I don't notice them staring at me. I enter the restaurant and ask inside about a phone.

"I have an important phone call I have to make," I told a lady. She points to two phones near the entrance. I walked right by them and didn't even notice them when I walked in.

"Thank you."

I walk to the phones and pull out Tabitha's phone number. I didn't throw it away. I use my phone card and dial the number --- my heart seems ready to explode. One ring --- two rings --- three rings --- four rings --- I think it is going to go to voice mail when a girl answers. I don't even remember if she lived at home with her mom or with a roommate or by herself.

"Hello?" I hear a soft voice.

"Tabitha?" There's a short pause but it seems long. "Before you hang up I found your necklace in the van --- in the front passenger's seat. Now I know I must have screwed up but truthfully I don't remember. I have a condition where I sometimes black out. It doesn't happen often so I really don't know what happened after the front seat. I'd like to send your necklace to you. I'm really a good guy --- really I am. I know you probably don't want to see me so I could send it to you. I'll send it express post or courier so you won't have to see me again." There was a long pause but I could hear her breathing. *At least she hadn't hung up on me yet.*

"You have no idea how sorry I am --- really I am." My voice quivered and I tried to whisper and hide my face from patrons in the restaurant walking by.

"I want the necklace back. I've been frantic looking for it. It has a picture inside." Tabitha finally spoke.

"I know --- I think it's your mom and older sister but that's a guess. Sorry for looking. I figured you'd want it back. It looked like it could be special. Where could I send it to make sure you got it?"

"Why are you whispering? She asked. "You seem to be whispering --- I can barely hear you."

"Sorry --- I'm in some restaurant on the phone and customers are walking by so I'm trying to be private. I could mail it to the restaurant where you work. Do you know the address? I have a pen ready?

"What restaurant are you at? I could pick it up --- bring someone --- but only in public. You scare me."

"I scare you? I'm so sorry Tabitha. I'm so sorry. I realize now that I need help." A huge sigh travelled over the phone. "I don't remember anything after the front seats. I woke up in some parking lot miles away. I freaked out wondering what happened? What happened to you? If you were all right." I emitted another long sigh. "You have no idea how tough this is for me."

"What restaurant are you at?" She asked me again.

"Ah --- I'm miles away Tabitha. I just started driving after you hung up on me this morning. The restaurant is --- hang on --- I'll ask --- Hey --- hey --- what's the name of this restaurant?" Gargle noises over the phone. "It's called the Millstone. I think it's about two or so hours away from you?"

"That's too far. You said you would mail it to me --- right?"

"Yes --- I can do that --- no problem. Where would you like me to send it Tabitha?"

There was a pause and then she spoke. "Send it to my work place --- the restaurant. I'll get it there. I don't want to give you my address."

"I understand. I have a pen. What the address? I'll send it in care of. Okay --- I'm ready."

"Send it to Mandy's Restaurant, 1569 Highway 17, P.O. Box 193, Wilstin, Texas, zip code 75978." Mandy's is spelled with a y --- did you get it? Read it back to me."

I read it back to her. It was correct.

"You are going to send it to me --- right Kyle?"

"Yes --- I promise I will send it. I'll send it today. I just need to find a courier service. I'll ask around and send it express. I'll put my return address on it --- just in case it doesn't get delivered. They always ask for a return address anyway. Thanks Tabitha and again --- I'm sorry."

There was a pause and then, "Thank you. That necklace has a special meaning for me."

"I thought it might. That is why I chanced calling you --- even though you said if I called again you would call the police. I've never been in trouble with the police before but since I don't know what happened --- well --- you can't imagine what it's been like for me. Bye Tabitha."

"Wait!"

I waited but there was nothing the next five seconds. "Is there something else Tabitha? Is there a problem with the address or something?" I waited.

"No --- the address is correct. I was just wondering about these blackouts you mentioned. How long have you had them and what did the doctor say?"

"I've had a few blackouts and it isn't because of drinking or anything. I just get them and I don't know when they are going to happen. I must be able to function and drive and stuff because I've had times --- the occasional times I have woken up in some strange place miles away --- like last night. It's very scary. I haven't been to a doctor. I guess I should huh? But I'm a bit afraid. I'm just hoping the blackouts stop and go away."

"You haven't been to a doctor? Kyle --- you have to see a doctor. Maybe they can help you --- with medication or surgery or something. You should see a doctor right away."

I know --- you're probably right --- and I will --- see a doctor."

"Promise me you will."

"Yes --- I promise I will."

"Right away --- no procrastinating."

When I get back I will make an appointment. I'm supposed to be on a bit of a break --- a vacation right now. Some vacation huh?"

"Where are you going?"

"Not sure --- just pointing the van and travelling and hoping to see some interesting sights along the way. I've scheduled myself to be back by the 20th. I have to get back to my three cats."

"You have three cats?"

"Yea --- they're back at the farm."

"Who's looking after them? What are their names?"

She wants to talk. Thank you GOD. "Their names are Jasper one, Jasper two, and Jasper three. I just call them all Jasper though. Kind of like the George Foreman thing. They are on their own right now. I left them food --- water --- and a few big litter boxes. They'll be okay. Done it before and they are okay."

"That's terrible that they're all alone. No one likes to be alone. And who is this George guy?"

"Uh ---he's a famous boxer who named all his kids George. Kind of crazy huh?"

"That is crazy." She laughed just a bit. "Okay --- I'd better go now. I'll be expecting that necklace now."

"Don't worry --- you'll have it soon. I promised after all. I keep my promises."

"Kyle."

"Yes Tabitha."

There was a pause. And then, "I guess you can --- call me from time to time. I want to make sure you make that appointment to see that doctor."

She said I could call her --- from time to time. That's a start. An opening --- a sliver of hope no matter how small.

"Thank you Tabitha. I'll call in a few days just to make sure you got the necklace." I couldn't help but sneak in the tiniest smile. I felt so much better. My eyes still hurt from all the tears but I felt better.

"Okay --- I've got to go now --- bye."

"Bye Tabitha. Talk soon." I waited and then she hung up. I listened to the deadness of the phone but now I was smiling.

After hanging up I looked in the yellow pages of the phone book for courier services. I then went over and asked a couple of waitresses where a courier service was so I could send a package fast. They had no idea, as they had never used a courier service but an old couple sitting at a table nearby spoke up. They had heard me talking.

"You can go to the local Post Office. They provide courier service."

They gave me the directions --- which were very good. Within fifteen minutes I was at a Post Office and had Tabitha's necklace packaged and ready for delivery. I paid for the fastest delivery and was told it should arrive tomorrow before noon. I was given a tracking number and receipt that I put in my wallet. It felt good to send it --- because it was going to Tabitha. I wanted to keep my word --- it was important.

Soon I was back on the road and the sun was trying it's best to come out. I drove further away from Wilstin --- although that was where I left my heart. I stopped at an out of the way motel and stayed the night. It was mid-range. I watched some television --- then tried reading but my mind had trouble focussing. I finally fell asleep after 11 but I think I woke up about ten times at least. When I finally got out of bed in the morning the first thing I did was open the door and look outside. Finally a sunny day was here. I was beginning to think I was destined to see nothing but rain for the rest of my life. I tried making a coffee but didn't trust the coffee maker. When I looked inside the coffee maker it looked like it hadn't been cleaned since the Jurassic period. I decided on a shower and then checked out. I found a little coffee shop and went in. I had a coffee and a multi-grain bagel with cream cheese. The bagel was still warm. I asked and they bake their own right there in the back so it was freshly baked. Man it was good. I thought about having a second one but didn't want to pig out. Their coffee was superb. It even smelled great. I bought a bag of that coffee and wondered if it would taste as good once home and back at the farm. When I was done I used their washroom to brush my teeth. I kept thinking about Tabitha and wondered if I should phone her. It was before noon though and the package was supposed to arrive sometime after noon hour --- although they weren't specific. I'd better wait until around 3:00 P.M. That should be enough time for her to get her necklace back. So I drove around looking for things to do --- things to see. I ended up on a hiking trail. Just happened upon it by accident. I like to explore so I went exploring. A few miles in I found an old building --- must have been a mill or something a long, long time ago. It was beside a stream and part of the stream had been diverted to run through --- or rather under the building. The roof was long gone as well as many of the walls. There really wasn't even a floor in it. No doors just openings where the doors used to be. The building itself was the colour of stained white plaque and some birds were inside. They must have claimed it as their home or sanctuary. I looked down in the stream and noticed a ton of minnows swimming around. I thought about them being in their own little world oblivious to the problems of the rest of the world. Much like people really. Only aware of what concerns their world. I wondered what it would be like to be one of those minnows --- or birds but only for a second. I looked up at the sun and it was still high in the sky so I decided to explore some more. I traversed some hills and the trail separated into five other trails. Nothing was marked --- no signs. I started to think I'd better be careful. I hadn't seen anyone and I didn't want to get lost out here. I took the left trail and in a short time came to a very narrow wooden walkway bridge --- only about three feet wide. I noticed off to the left barely visible an old house long abandoned. It barely resembled a house really. It was small and the base of the walls was all that was really left standing. Inside was a pile of junk. Old clothes --- a broken bathtub --- just junk really. The thing that caught my eye though was a very old tattered doll. I walked over and picked it up --- carefully. It was very fragile and looked like it would fall apart without delicate hands. It made me think of my girls --- I couldn't help it. I was breathing deeply and my eyes got wet. I tried not to think of my girls and started to wonder who this doll belonged to so long ago. *What was its history? Who was this little girl? What was her name? Who was her family? When did they live? Were they still alive? Why did they live way out here?* So many questions that I would never know the answers to. I brushed the doll off trying to clean it but it was too filthy. For a minute I thought the doll was looking at me with sadness in her eyes. It made me cry. I brushed off the doll as best as I could and laid her down on some clothes. I covered her like a little girl might do putting her doll to bed under the sheets. I don't know why I did this? I stepped back looking at the doll --- like she was sleeping comfortably. A long sigh snuck out of my lips. I looked up through the canopy of trees and it was getting later. The sun was lower now. I guess time flew by while exploring this house. I started heading back and it seemed in no time I was back at the van. When I got in the van I just sat there before starting the engine. I did a lot of thinking and soul searching today and I think it was good for me. I felt sadness but I felt a strange kind of peace. I started the van and then thought of Tabitha. I wondered if she got the necklace. I looked at the time and it was 5:00 P.M. *Wow! Today seemed to go by really fast. Where did all the hours go?* Soon I was on the road and as per my routine looking for a place to eat --- and thinking about a certain phone call. *Should I phone Tabitha and ask if she got the necklace? Or should I wait a couple of days?* I didn't want to seem anxious but I doubted if I could wait a day or two to call her. I decided I would call her.

I found a restaurant and outside in the van I wondered what would I say to Tabitha beyond the "Did you get your necklace back?" *What else could I say? Would she be willing to talk to me again?* So I practiced what I might say. I even took out a piece of paper and wrote things down. I didn't want to seem pushy or anxious though. The main thing was to make sure the package was delivered. That necklace was important to her. She said so. I got out of the van and as I walked into the restaurant I was trying to decide do I call her before supper or after? Better do it before supper as I would be too nervous eating supper and leaving it till after. I saw the phone and dug for my phone card. Good thing I had lots of dollars on it. I didn't need to look up Tabitha's phone number because now I knew it by memory. I half dialled the number --- then paused and hung up. I started to panic. *What was I going to say again?* I took a deep breath and dialled again but again I hung up after the first ring. I tried to convince myself that maybe it would be better to wait to call. *This is dumb --- just call her.* So I dialled again and this time the phone was ringing. My heart was beating faster at each ring --- half hoping she wouldn't answer. Just as I thought it would go to voice mail I hear her voice.

"Hello."

"Hi Tabitha? Is that you?"

"Yes Kyle --- it's me. Thank you for returning my necklace."

"Oh good. I wanted to make sure you got it --- that's why I'm calling. They told me it would arrive sometime this afternoon but I wanted to make sure."

"Well --- I got it. Thanks again."

Her conversation seemed shorter than the previous one. Now that she got her necklace back were we done? I wondered.

"That's good," a bit of a pause. "So how are you?"

"I better now that I have the necklace back. That was a big relief. I would have hated to lose it. Where are you now?"

Good --- she is wondering where I am? But is that because she wants to make sure I'm not in town or interested in where I am? "I'm even further away now --- at another restaurant. I went for a walk today --- on a forest trail --- to try and clear my mind --- and think about things."

"I do that sometimes --- walking on a wooded trail. It seems to help rejuvenate me --- to refresh me --- to clear my mind."

"Yea --- I enjoyed it. On the trail I found a really old abandoned house so I went exploring. It was very small but it made me think about who might have lived there --- and when?"

"Sounds pretty neat Kyle. As long as there weren't any ghosts around --- or the house wasn't haunted."

"No ghosts --- at least pretty sure there weren't any ghosts around. I wouldn't go there at night though."

She giggled ever so slightly. "Look Kyle --- I have to go. I have some people here. Thanks for sending my necklace back. And don't forget your promise."

"My promise?"

"Yea --- that you would see a doctor when you got back."

"Oh yea --- I promise I will. I didn't forget."

"Bye Kyle."

"Okay --- bye Tabitha. Nice talking to you." And then she hung up. *She had some people over. I wondered if there were any guys over at her place. I had no right to ask but it bothered me that that might be a possibility.* I sat down for supper. Tonight I had a hamburger and French fries and gravy. I did have a small salad to appease my healthy side that was bugging me. As I was eating I was happy because I had talked with Tabitha again --- and that she got her necklace. I decided while I ate that I would cut my trip short. Tomorrow I would drive back to the farm --- back to the snow and winter. My heart just wasn't in it anymore.

CHAPTER 23

In the morning I was up early as usual. I don't know if I mentioned it but I haven't really slept in since I was a teenager. I have this belief that as you get older --- you get up earlier in the morning --- and go to bed earlier as well. I slept better last night because of two reasons. One; Tabitha got her necklace back and two; Tabitha and I talked on the phone again. Granted it wasn't quite as long as our previous conversation but she did say she had company over. I felt in a better mood. Better than I had felt in a long, long time. I checked out of the motel and was soon on the road heading back. I knew the drive would take at least a couple of days but I felt energized. I was on the road by 7:30 A.M. and at 9:22 I had pulled into a restaurant for breakfast. I gobbled it down and this time filled my thermos with coffee for the road. I drove all day and finally after the sun had set I pulled into another motel to stay the night. I figured I would get back to the farm sometime late tomorrow if all went well. I had another good night of sleep --- wow --- two nights in a row. That's a record. Time seemed to fly by and before I knew it --- I was back in my familiar stomping grounds. The roads were cleared of snow and so were easy to travel. When I got to my driveway it was a mess though. The snow was piled deep with snow-drifts. There was no way I was getting through that. I had to park on the road and walk in --- which sucked. I unlocked the gate and walked to the house. I went inside and the cats were all over me. I spent a few minutes getting reacquainted with them. I opened the door to see if they wanted to go out. They didn't. They wanted to spend time with me inside but I had something to do first. I had to plow the driveway. I got the keys and went out to start the tractor. I pulled the choke and on the third try Old Nellie started up. Old Nellie was the name I gave the tractor. She was a good ole girl. I warmed her up good and then proceeded to clear the driveway. She was good, powerful, and dependable. It took two and a half hours but finally the driveway was cleared and I had a small patch to park the van at the back porch. I would finish plowing the lot in the morning when there was daylight. I drove in the barn and shut Ole Nellie off and covered her up. I walked the long walk back to the van parked at the road and admired how white and clean everything looked. The snow crunched under my boots and my breath left my lips like I was a heavy smoker. I never did smoke though. I've always been into fitness and athletics. And seeing my mom and dad smoke all those years turned me off smoking. I started the van and drove it slowly along the long driveway to the house. I unloaded the van --- which didn't take long and was soon in the house being mobbed by the Jaspers once again. I looked at the clock. It was now 11:30 P.M. It was time for a quick supper and bed. This time when I went to bed all three Jaspers were sharing the sheets with me. Soon I was asleep --- dreaming of Tabitha and what could have been --- or might still be.

I was awake early and looking down noticed the Jaspers were gone. They were probably downstairs languishing on the couch --- waiting patiently for me. I remembered I needed to plow the parking area and barn area but that shouldn't take too long. And I would have to brush all the snow off my other two vehicles. I got up and peered out the window. Snow! Lots of white snow on the ground, everywhere I looked. Even the tree branches were fully covered. The trees looked like they were pure --- and sleeping. It didn't look windy out but placid and calm. Sometimes in the coldest mornings you can hear the cold --- the odd cracking sounds of molecules collapsing or the sounds of my boots crunching on snow as I walked. I hope it is warm out --- warm as far as winter goes. The sun is rising and I see hopes of rays of sunshine. It might just be a nice day. I get dressed --- go downstairs and walk to the kitchen. That got the cats moving. They follow me into the kitchen eyeing my every move. It was like they are saying, *"Where the Hell did you go?"* or *"It's about time you got up and fed us! Hurry up --- we want to go outside and hunt some mice." Pretty sure the mice are tucked away all cosy and sleeping though. The cats will have to wait. Too much snow out there right now I think. It's too deep. I'll let them out after I plow the lot.* First I want a light breakfast though. I make toast --- whole wheat and sprinkle it with a touch of cinnamon. I make a coffee and then go to my usual roost --- in front of the television. It's only been the last little while that eating alone has started to bother me. I've been a bachelor for a long time and never thought much about eating alone at home. Then I saw a couple of movies that showed the guy --- alone like me eating at a table --- no one to talk to or smile at. Just eating alone looking at the four walls. It looked strange and well --- made me think of me. I eat mainly in front of the television because it takes my mind off thinking. I sit in front of the television putting my food in front of me on the small tray or coffee table. I don't particular want to watch the news --- especially since it is almost always bad news but I force myself. I eat and watch and thank GOD nothing about any missing girls. I'm always watching --- half expecting that some girl is going to be reported as missing. Fifteen minutes of news is enough and I search the TV menu to see what else is on. You would think with almost two hundred stations that something worthwhile would be on one of them. I shut the television off and just finish in silence. It's kind of spooky. My eyes look around the living room and start to wonder what life experiences have played out here. I hardly ever think about the old couple dying in the bedroom. No wonder I got the place at a good price. I do my regular chores meaning wash the dishes and brushing my teeth. Then I put on my coat, hats, scarf, gloves and boots and I'm out the door to plow. I shoo the cats away from the door and slip out. The place looks good. Snow banks were getting high but I used the front bucket on the tractor to level them down to more visible heights. After forty minutes the lot was plowed. I admire my work. I decide to see if the cats want out. I open the door calling the Jaspers and they come running --- stop at the door to survey the outside and then gingerly tiptoe out onto the porch and down the stairs --- all three head straight for the barn. I decide it would be a good idea to start the skidoo up and see how it runs. I forgot to get it ready for winter.

Usually I take it in to the dealer and have them check it out for a worry free winter. Forgot to do that this year. I find the keys and head out to the barn. I see two of the Jaspers slinking quietly around. They're in hunting mode. I smile. I uncover the skidoo and check the tank. Climb aboard and put the key in and it starts almost right away. That's a good sign. I lift the hood while it's idling. I was pretty sure the fluids were good and I was right. I slowly gas it and the sled moves out of the barn. The Jaspers are probably pissed that I disturbed their hunt. I turn my head to see Jasper three with a mouse in his jaws. I think one of the mice took off running when he heard the skidoo and exposed himself to the jaws of my cat.

"You're welcome," I rattle off in my mind to Jasper three.

I do three small loops around the parking lot and everything is in order. I go back in the barn and put the helmet on. Your face can get frostbit really quick on a skidoo so having the face shield is a no brainer. A quick look and off I go into the fields breaking trail. Snow depth varies from two to four feet in the drifts. I decide to go and check on that grave. I don't expect anything different but something is prodding me to check it out. On the skidoo I get there in no time and drive by the outbuilding and back to where the empty grave is. I know where it is but it is more difficult to find in the snow. I find the grave and shut the machine off. I use my boots to kick away some of the snow. I notice that there isn't any dip? I think there should be a dip where I left half the grave open but there isn't? Might just be the way the snow has blown? I kick away the snow and I can see I am at the right spot. There's the fresh dirt to the grave. Not sure which end I am at though. It looks like the dirt has been filled in? I work faster and start to sweat. I'm kicking and scooping the snow with my hands and then it sinks in. My worst fear stares back at my eyes. The grave has been filled in and I didn't do it. I start to panic. *Is there a girl down there? Did I do it again? Shit!* I stare at the grave with dagger eyes. Then I look around to see if anyone is watching me. I'm in the middle of nowhere and I'm looking to see if I am being watched --- pretty damn stupid when you think of it. I kick at the dirt with my boot to check how hard it is. It's pretty hard. Frozen solid. I decide to go back to the barn and get the steel shovel. I'm sweating profusely --- especially my upper half. *I'd better change when I get back to the house.* I jump on the skidoo, fire it up and speed back to the house. I'm going really fast.

After I change my shirt I head back to the barn. I get the shovel and bungee it to the skidoo and immediately speed back to the grave. This time the ride seems longer. It isn't --- it just seems that way. I arrive --- hop off and grab the shovel. I take off my jacket and jab the shovel into the dirt. It just deflects off. The grave is frozen. I begin to chip away and it is slow going. I'll only dig the top half of the grave I tell myself. The part I left open. I'm slamming the shovel into the grave but shit --- the dirt seems as hard as diamonds. After ten minutes of me swearing and cursing I come to the realization. This isn't working. I've made very little progress. Either I am going to have to wait for the dirt to thaw or I need another method. The not knowing is killing me. I wonder if I built a fire on top of it if that would help? Then as a last resort I try to think --- *did I fill it in before I left and forget that I did it?* I try to think but I realize no way. That's not a possibility. This is going to take some work. I put my jacket on --- look down at the grave in disdain and climb onto the skidoo and head back to the barn. I need the toboggan and some firewood and some supplies. My mind is a blur as I head back to the barn. I gather my supplies --- the axe --- the wood --- check for my lighter. Gathering the wood --- including the tinder took a couple of hours. I'd rather be relaxing in the house or driving to town but I need to know. By the time I get back to the grave it's late afternoon but now I'm ready. I haven't eaten since breakfast but I don't care. I clear the grave a bit more with the shovel and put the tinder down. I light it and it begins to burn --- slowly at first. As the flames begin to rise, I put the bigger pieces of firewood on top. Soon I have a good bonfire going. I move the skidoo away as I can feel the heat. I check the dirt with the shovel but it is still pretty frozen. Should I stay and wait --- watching the fire burn or should I let it burn most of the night and come back in the morning. I look at the sun as it disappears and decide it's best to let the fire do its work through the night and come back at first sunrise. I pile my stuff --- minus the bit of wood that's left into the sled and start the machine up. I drive back to the house in the dark. It's one of the eeriest drives I can remember. I'm hungry and then again I'm not. I'm very confused. The Jaspers are going to be waiting for me. They must be pissed off at me. *How am I going to sleep tonight?* I hope I can sleep but I believe it might be a very long night for me.

I park the skidoo in the barn but don't cover it. I want to be ready to go first thing in the morning. The Jaspers are waiting for me. Now you can't tell if a cat has expressions but I am pretty sure they are mad at me. All three are up on the porch waiting for me. *Sorry boys --- stuff to do. I might have a girl's body out there? Cats don't' care. They're all about me creatures. I love em and they all have their personalities.* Back to reality --- I open the door and in they go --- like teenage girls running to see some pop star. I'm hot and take off my layered clothing. They can wait. I put my gloves on the register so they'll be dry tomorrow and after I get my stuff off I feed the Jaspers. I have to shower before I eat. I just feel too yucky. In the shower it feels so good having the hot water caress my body --- the steam rising as I breath it all in. I shampoo and shave right in the shower. I call it a quick shave rather than using the shaving cream in front of the mirror routine. I dry off but truthfully I am thinking of nothing but tomorrow and the shovel and grave.

I microwave a frozen dinner. Well --- it's fast at least but I'm going to need more. I find some cold cuts and lettuce in the fridge. The lettuce I have to throw out --- no good. So I make a toasted sandwich with mustard. Actually pretty good --- and three baby dill pickles. I'm still hungry which surprises me so I have an apple. Funny thing was I sat at the table to eat all this. I thought about the grave as I chewed. I had no dishes --- just used paper towels --- and the one fork for the frozen dinner. After I lay down on the couch. The Jaspers seem to know to move just before I flop down. I watch television. No news though. I don't want any news. I just want to relax or try to. The vacation was pretty good --- except for that Tabitha incident. I start to think of her and think about calling her. She said I could but I decide my mind is in too much of a mess right now. I'll wait a few days or at least until I get this grave question answered. GOD I hope it's empty.

I see two girls but I only see them from behind. I can't see their faces for some reason? One has red hair and the other has wavy brown hair. They're in a forest or near a forest --- I'm not sure? There's also an open field and we are on the edge where the trees meet the forest. The girls seem to be talking and pointing to something. They seem unaware I'm standing behind them. Suddenly they're both on the ground and they're bound at the wrists and ankles. There are lying in some tall grass although some of the grass is flattened. They're still alive. One of the girls is covered in blood --- I mean covered --- head to toe. I look more closely at her and see she has patches of skin cut away and removed. The brown haired girl is in deep shock --- and she's crying. The red haired girl is beside her --- waiting for her turn. She's struggling but it doesn't do any good. I can hear them pleading with me but I don't answer. The de-skinned girl can barely talk. I just watch. The eyes look around and we are alone --- all alone. There is no one to hear the cries of pain except me --- and the cool breeze I now feel. I see the knife in my hand --- shiny and red. My hand is red --- there's red all the way up to my elbow. My heart is racing and I hear a voice telling the red head,

"You're next. You have beautiful skin."

I hear crying and then I see the knife cutting away skin. Big patches and she quickly spills her blood. Her white skin is white no longer. I see a propane torch move over her skin. Her skin begins to change and bubble. After, the knife cuts into their chests and removes something. It's their hearts. They aren't beating now. Hands hold up both hearts. They barely fit but I'm careful not to drop them. The girls are dead --- the ground covered in blood like a butchering place for pigs. Then the hand with the hearts come closer to the eyes --- I look at them careful not to mix them up. This one is the heart of the brunette and this one is the heart of the redhead. I compare their size --- they look identical. The hearts come closer yet and then suddenly I take a bite out of each heart --- human hearts that were pumping life seconds ago. I compare their tastes as I swallow. They are so very warm.

I suddenly bolt up from my nightmare. "What the fuck is that?" I'm in shock!

I am still on the couch --- the television going. I check the time on the satellite and it is 3:36 A.M. *Oh GOD --- that is the worst one yet. I'm doing terrible things --- the most terrible things one could even imagine in my dream. Is it true? Could it be true? This was just sick --- totally sick beyond. Skinning them alive--- burning them and my GOD --- eating their hearts.* I'm completely drenched in sweat. There were two girls in my dream. *I've never heard of two girls missing or being found like that --- two girls together. Fuck! I still have the graphic image in my mind. There were leaves --- I think. I can't remember. I don't want to remember. I try to remember. It was warm --- the weather --- I think. Where was this? It was near some tree line and a field or pasture. Could it be that fresh grave I found? Was it from a long time ago? Was it recent? Did I really do that or was it just a dream? Shit! I don't want any more nightmares like that. Tabitha's right. I'd better go and see about these blackouts. Maybe it was just a dream --- different from my other nightmares. Then again who the fuck has nightmares like that? Shit! There was a redhead. Was one of them Tabitha? Was Tabitha the redhead? No --- it can't be Tabitha? I think the redhead was taller in my dream. Crap --- I'm not sure?* I get up and wander around the living room --- then the kitchen. I go downstairs turning the lights on. I am shivering and feel sick. I start to vomit. No way I'm going to sleep now. In my previous nightmares I did terrible things to girls --- some more than others but this --- eating their hearts --- what the fuck? It was way more graphic. I go back upstairs and sit down on the couch again. I'm not going to sleep. That's for sure. I going to wait for sunrise --- and go and check that grave. Then I start crying like I've never cried before. The cats run away --- I'm scaring them. I feel so alone and feel like I don't belong anywhere --- that there is no place safe for me to go.

That was the longest night of my life. I'm going to need sleeping pills. But now sleep is becoming my worst enemy. That is when the nightmares lay waiting for

me. Where dark secrets lay waiting to ambush me. I sleep without the protection of a soul.

Light is beginning to filter in from outside. The sun is rising. I made it through the long night. The ticking of the clocks reminded me of those girl's heartbeats. I get up and still I don't see the Jaspers. *They must be hiding from me. Perhaps they now know who I really am?* I call them. They don't come. I walk to the door and peek my head outside. The fresh cold air feels good. It wakes me up. I'm sleepy but dare not sleep. I have to find the answers to that grave. The dirt should be thawed by now. I call the Jaspers again. Finally they come out. I see the three of them slinking out from their hiding spots. They were all hiding together in the cupboards --- trying to give each other solace I suspect. Slowly they approach me and stop ten feet away --- looking at the door --- then at me.

"Do you guys want to go out or not?" I ask them. *I don't expect an answer. It just gives me an excuse to talk to someone --- or something alive.* "Sorry bout last night. Didn't mean to scare you."

They walk towards me as I open the door and they flee outside straight to the barn. I know sometimes they travel to the outbuildings --- plenty of places to catch mice --- so many mice on the farm. It's a paradise for them. I close the door and get ready to go to the grave. I don't feel like breakfast. Not even a coffee or a tea. Then I think I'd better take a thermos with me at least. It's pretty cold out.

I'm ready in no time and on my way. I travel half speed --- thinking --- hoping nothing is there. *GOD --- there better not be anybody buried there.* I feel dizzy and nauseous. As my skidoo approaches the outbuilding it feels like my heart is about to burst. My breathing is heavy. I park and shutoff the skidoo beside the grave and just sit there for a second --- staring at the smoldering grave. The fire is almost out --- just embers and ashes burning now. I get off and grab the shovel and take a deep breath. I stick the shovel in and it goes in good. The fire has done its job and now I can dig. I start digging and each shovel full of dirt brings me more anxiety. I tell myself, "*Please be empty --- don't let anyone be there.*"

The deeper I dig the slower I go --- just in case there is girl there. I don't want to poke her if she is there --- or if there are two girls there. I'm very careful. I look around and see no one. *Didn't expect to but my mind is really wild. I start thinking the cops are watching me --- airplanes are watching me --- or even satellites are taking pictures. I have a stupid imagination.* And then I'm at the bottom of the grave. Nothing! It's empty! I drop the shovel and fall back to sit on my skidoo and almost miss the skidoo. Then I cry again. Not cries of pain or sadness but cries of relief. Then a thought comes to me. The incinerator? I'd better check that out. I leave the grave half open half full of dirt and then put my stuff into the sled. Before I start the skidoo I look up to the sky and decide to kneel down beside the skidoo. I pray for the first time in years.

"Dear GOD --- Please let there be no more girls for me to find. Dear GOD --- Please help me --- and give me strength. Please GOD!" Then I start to bawl again.

After a minute I try to stop crying and grab the thermos and take a swig of coffee. It's nice and hot. There is absolutely no wind. I wipe the frozen tears from my face. I put the thermos back and hop on the skidoo and start her up. For some reason I think why do guys always have girl names for their cars --- their skidoos --- their toys? I turn and start to go to the incinerator. I feel better knowing the grave is empty but why the hell was it covered again? I can't figure that out? Maybe I'll never know. I don't even remember driving to the incinerator but suddenly there it is. I drive right up to it and the door is closed. I stop and don't even turn the skidoo off. Opening the door I see the white ash and it looks the same as last time. *Good ---there's nothing strange or funny happening here.* I close the door and latch it and hurry back to the barn. Back at the barn I drive in slowly and see all three Jaspers in the one stall looking at me. I shut the machine off and see two of the Jaspers have a mouse in their jaws. The third Jasper is still looking. I'm too tired to collect my stuff. I trudge out of the barn and up the steps to the back door. Once inside I just stand at the door --- looking --- and listening. I hear nothing but my heart and my breathing. I want to go to town and get away from the house for a few hours but I am too tired. I'm wiped. I have to sleep but I'm afraid to sleep. I go upstairs to try sleep. I'm staying away from the couch for a while. I briefly think of Tabitha as I close my eyes. *What a fucking life I have.*

CHAPTER 24

Lucas

I love messing with Kyle's mind. I covered that grave back up before our little vacation trip down south. What a stupid fuck he is. Normally I don't get too graphic with the nightmares. He is going to have to get used to it. I'm even going easy on the guy for fuck sake. I could have shown him much worse. Those other dreams were mild compared to the one he had last night though. Even though I held back he is still freaking out. A little bit of blood and he can't sleep anymore. He saw Dances with Wolves. What the fuck is the difference except it's a human heart? No big deal. I'd better lay off the dreams for a bit though. He needs to recover. I don't want him to fall completely apart. Those two girls --- the brunette and the redhead --- well --- do I have a surprise for him. Our little vacation was just the thing I needed. I took a risk with the two girls instead of my regular one but they were together and alone and I didn't have to move them far. I kind of rushed it --- only a couple of hours of fun. I'm satisfied for now. I can't wait for Kyle to phone Tabitha --- that fucking redhead bitch. I know he will. Kyle has a big surprise waiting and it is special delivery especially for him. He's still stuck on her but she's gone baby. I made sure of that. Even better is that it is almost Spring Break. Kyle and I are going on a trip this Spring Break. Going to visit Marianne and invite her to my little party. She's going to be the guest of honour. And her two daughters are coming along as special guests too! They all invited. I have it all planned out and I drip just thinking about it. I can't wait. I'm not going to be kind to Marianne like before. No --- this time she's going to experience my good stuff. I like Spring Break. Always have. Don't ya just love Spring Break?

Kyle:

I wake up and am relieved I didn't dream last night. I don't remember dreaming --- that's good. I have no idea what time it is? I go downstairs feeling better and see the clock is 1:30 P.M. The sleep was good. I feel so much better and check outside. Weather looks good. I decide I will go to town and get something to eat. I need to shop for some groceries and re-plenish my supplies --- and the fridge. I throw some water on my face and get dressed. I remember I still have hot coffee in the thermos. Wonder if it is still hot? Where is the thermos? Shit! I left it out in the sled. I go out the door and stomp off to the barn. Don't even put my coat on. I see it in the toboggan and pick it up and take a swig. It still pretty warm but could be warmer. I decide it is good enough. I go back in the farmhouse and get my coat --- can't forget that. Then back outside to the car. I decide to take the car. Otherwise I would stare at the passenger seat and think of nothing but Tabitha. I start the car up. It took three engine turns but it starts and I let it warm up. I have a remote start. I should have used it to warm it up. The seats and interior are cold. I have a block heater too! I 'll have to remember to plug my vehicles in. It's better for them in the wintertime. I drive to town, which is about twenty-five minutes in the summer time. It takes me about forty-five minutes this time. Roads are good but snow packed. The drive feels good. And there are people. Now I don't feel so alone. It's not big as far as towns go but it is a nice way to spend part of the day. Two small malls and they do have a Walmart. I spend about thirty minutes farting around and fill up my thermos at the drive-thru coffee shop. I buy a light sensitive sensor for my back porch. I finally remembered. I decide to stop and get a little something to eat before leaving town. My appetite is back. I park at one of the town restaurants I sometime go to and have a chicken soup and ham sandwich and cold milk. It hits the spot. I leave a twenty percent tip and head back to the farm. I look at the clock and it's now 4:37 P.M. I wonder if the one Jasper finally caught his mouse in the barn. He probably did. I smile for the first time today. Driving back I'm sipping from my thermos and thinking of my Tabitha. I like calling her my Tabitha. I decide that I will call her tonight. After all, it's been a couple of days.

I get back to the house at 5:20 P.M. and the cats hear me drive in. They are up at the top of the porch and I'm not even out of the car yet. Talk about impatient. I get my groceries and carry them up the steps. It will take two trips. I open the door and let the cats in first then dump the first load on the kitchen table, then go back for the second load. The Jaspers are meowing. They want to be fed.

"Just wait boys. I'll be right back to feed you," I say as I head out the door. *There I go talking to the cats again --- like they understand what I am actually saying. My language to them probably sounds like their meowing to me. I don't understand their meowing.*

They watch me leave. Jasper number two is licking his front shoulder --- pretending he doesn't' care. I'm back in a jiffy and decide to give the Jasper's a treat. I pour some cream into three small bowls and put it on the floor. They rush over as if they know whose bowl belongs to whom and begin lapping it up --- loud purrs from three cats fill the room. I put the groceries away but I'm not hungry at all --- not yet anyway. I still have that soup and sandwich in my stomach. I make a tea and have two oatmeal cookies. I sit on the couch and I get a chill just sitting on there. I turn on the television and watch the news. So depressing. Maybe I should have bought a newspaper while in town. Sometimes I like to read the newspaper --- only certain parts of the paper --- the front section and the horoscope section. Bloody horoscope. What a stupid section. Like when my horoscope says romance is possible today. How stupid is that? Like that ever happens. There is nothing on the news about any girls missing. That's good. I really don't need to hear that another girl is missing --- especially right now. I sip my tea and eat my cookies. I don't like dunking them. Some people do but not me. I don't want any soggy cookies touching my lips. I start to think not about television but about Tabitha. I should call her but what time would be good. I decide I'll call after 7:00 P.M. That seems like a good time to call. I look at the clock --- 6:22 P.M. --- I have thirty-eight minutes to wait. I should call just after 7:00 P.M. --- Maybe 7:02 P.M. That way it won't look like I planned it. Yea --- I'll call at 7:02. I try not to watch the clock but man --- is the clock broken or something? It seems to be moving at a snail's pace. I decide to make another tea while I'm waiting. Drink it and at 7:00 P.M. decide I better pee. After I pee I come out and decide to call. I dig out the piece of paper with her phone number and dial. After the third ring I hear this:

> *"We're sorry you have reached a number that has been **disconnected or is no longer in service;** if you feel you have reached this recording in error please check the number or try your call again."*

What the hell is this? The phone number is no longer in service. I redial and call Tabitha's number and get the same message. I call it again and get the same stupid message. I stare at the phone in shock. Shit! I wanted --- I needed to talk with her. I decide to call the telephone company directly. I dial for assistance. Tell them my problem that I can't connect. The operator is no help.

"Sir --- I realize you think that phone number should work but I am telling you that phone number is no longer in service." The operator tells me.

"Do you know when it was disconnected or what happened?" I plead.

"No sir --- I don't have that information. Is there anything else I can help you with?" She's very polite.

"No --- I guess not," and I hang up.

I decide I'll call her work tomorrow and see what happened. Maybe it was just some glitch or there is a simple explanation. Shit! I wanted to talk with her. I feel so frustrated --- and afraid. I watch television and at

8:00 P.M. make a snack substituting for my supper. My heart just isn't in it. It's been a long time between girls for me and Tabitha was the first girl I felt like I could break the jinx. I'll call tomorrow. I just hope she's working. I'm wide-awake and finally decide at 12:30 I'd better go to bed. I go upstairs realizing no way I'm sleeping on the couch. It's my enemy for the time being. I trudge upstairs feeling down again and can't sleep. I read my book and actually read quite a few chapters. Finally my eyes get heavy and I look for the clock --- then remember I don't have one. Perhaps it's time to spring for a clock for the bedroom. I turn off the light and toss and turn a bit and finally sleep finds me.

Next thing I know I am awake and light is coming in from the window. It's morning and the cats didn't bother me again. Maybe they are learning to let me sleep? I get up and go downstairs and check the clock --- 8:00 A.M. on the button. I put on a coffee and feed the cats --- they must be full of mice as they just push it around. I splash some water on my face and shave. Too early to call I think so I decide on a shower and while in the shower I wonder what would be a proper time to call. They might be on breakfast rush hour about now at the restaurant. What was the name of the place again? Then I panic cause I can't remember it? Shit! I calm down and then I remember it ---oh yea --- it was Mandy's Restaurant in Wilstin. Whew! I get out of the shower and don't even dry off. I scamper off into the living room and find a paper and pen and write Mandy's Restaurant in Wilstin, Texas. Then I smile and tiptoe back to dry myself off. I throw the damp towel in the hamper and notice I'm going to have to do laundry soon. I walk to the kitchen and pour a coffee and then look outside. It's snowing and blowing again. I open the door --- the Jaspers look outside and decide on an inside day.

"Okay boys --- I don't blame ya."

I smile again but it all seems fake to me. I like smiling. I need to smile way more even if it is just for show. Good for my health I decide. I eat a light breakfast, as I don't want a lot of food in me. I'm too nervous about phoning Tabitha later --- at 11:00 A.M. I look at the clock and it is only 8:30 A.M. I decide I'm not watching the clock this time. I want the time to go fast. I actually sit at the table and put the radio on. I don't do that very often. It's a special day though. I avoid the clock like the plague. I force myself to look over --- what the fuck --- it's only 8:52 A.M. *Come on clock. Get moving!* I decide to go outside. Maybe that will help time go faster. I get dressed for the cold and go out to shovel the porch and steps. I even do the front porch and steps. Not the walkway though --- too deep. Better get the snow blower for that. It's in the barn with all my other stuff. I start it up and do the front walk and bits and pieces of the lot where the snow has drifted. I finish and decide I will do the driveway with the tractor but I'd better check what time it is. I put the snow blower back and go in the house. I look at the clock. It's 10:25 now. That's better. I decide I should have another shower to get me closer to 11:00 A.M. I remind myself that's a good time to call because it's after breakfast and before lunch. I undress and jump in the shower and it feels good. All I am thinking about though is the phone call I will make to Tabitha. I wonder if she thinks of me at all? I still don't understand or know what I did to piss her off so much. She got her necklace back so I am hopeful I am back in her good books. I took a long shower and after I dry off I get dressed and look at the clock. Still have ten minutes so I just sit in front of the phone --- waiting the last ten minutes. This time I'm not waiting till two minutes after. I'm calling right at 11:00. This it torture --- watching the clock and waiting. All it is doing is getting me more nervous. By the time 11 rolls around I will be such a mess I won't even be able to talk to her. I'll be like some babbling idiot having a breakdown. I get up and walk around trying to dissipate my anxiety attack. It works a bit. Finally I go and look and it's 11:00 A.M. on the clock. I sit down and dial the number --- or rather I try to. I get half the number and hang up. I take a deep breath and then try to phone again. Finally at 11:07 I manage the whole number and let it ring. My heart is in my throat. A girl picks up --- I gulp.

"Is Tabitha there?" Somehow I manage to get out those three short words.

"She doesn't work here anymore." My body and mind go into shock. "Hello --- is anyone there."

"Uh --- she doesn't work there anymore? She quit?" I ask still in shock.

"Ah --- I think she quit --- I'm not sure. All I know is that yesterday I show up and am told she doesn't' work here anymore."

"Oh --- do you know where she is? I'm a friend but haven't spoken to her in a few days."

"No --- sorry. I don't know anything."

"Okay." I'm about to hang up dejected when I call out, "Wait --- hello --- hello."

"Yes, I'm still here. Anything else."

"Yes --- I wonder if Amy is working?"

"Amy isn't scheduled to come in till noon hour."

"Okay --- thanks --- I'll call back at noon. Thank you."

"Okay," the girl's responds and then she hangs up.

So Tabitha isn't working there anymore? What happened? When did she quit? Wait --- did she quit? The girl on the phone wasn't sure. And her home phone number is no longer in service. I'm in torture. Then I thought about my recent nightmare --- that girl with red hair. *No fucking way! It can't be. It just can't be. I would never hurt her.* I'm so afraid as I wait for noon hour.

The minutes seem like days as I wait for noon hour. My mind is mush and I'm frozen in time. It's like I have passed into another dimension. GOD --- I hope she just moved away. She never mentioned moving away when I talked with her just a few days ago. All I can think of was the redhead in my nightmare might be her? I never saw her face in my nightmare. I try to remember everything about Tabitha, every detail about her physically and try to link it to my nightmare. Was the hair the same? The height? The weight? The skin? I get no satisfying answers. I pace and I pace some more. I open the door and try to breath the fresh cold air. It doesn't help. Finally the agonizing hour arrives and I pick up the phone and dial while filled with fear of what I might hear. I dial --- I can't breath. On the fifth ring I hear a voice.

"Mandy's Restaurant." It's a girl's voice.

"Hello, I wonder is Amy there?"

"Yea --- she's here. Just a second and I'll get her. Who's calling please?"

"It's Kyle." I swallow wondering if I should have given my name.

"One minute please." And then an excruciating wait that seems to take forever.

And finally she answered. "HELLO!" She seemed to say very loudly. Like she was angry.

"Hello --- Amy," I replied meekly. "This is Kyle. I was wondering did Tabitha move away or what happened? Where did she go? I called and." I never got to finish as she interrupted.

"Kyle --- Tabitha's gone. She's left town and did it rather suddenly. That phone call you made to her a couple of nights ago --- you're an asshole. She told me about it. She's gone and you won't ever see her again. You blew it. She really liked you."

"She liked me? Your saying I made a call to her a couple of nights ago? I don't ---"

"Don't play dumb with me Mister. You're just lucky she isn't calling the police on you. Don't ever call here again. And if I even see your face I'll call the police. Fuck Off! And stay the fuck away." And then she hung up on me.

I sat there on the couch with the phone in my hand stunned. *She liked me ringing in my ears. She moved away. What the hell happened? Did I blackout again and make a phone call to her and if so what did I say to her?* I put the phone down in its cradle and was numb. *She must be alive. Amy said she moved away but my dream. Did I really kill those two girls like that --- eating their young hearts? Was one of the girls Tabitha? But she moved away quite suddenly.* I tried to remember the hours of my trip. *Are there any blackouts beyond the time I had Tabitha in the van?* I remembered as best I could my entire trip trying to see if it was even possible. In the nightmare it was daytime? I decide no --- it can't be Tabitha. If that nightmare is true it can't be Tabitha. She's moved away. I'm relieved and troubled at the same time. I get up and start pacing like a wild tiger with nowhere to go. Like I'm trapped. I am trapped --- in the mazes of my own mind. My mind is in a cage. GOD --- I wish I never met Tabitha. And then it comes upon me like a nuclear blast --- more tears and a horrendous feeling of agony and guilt. I realize at that moment that I truly love her.

CHAPTER 25

Lucas:

I told you I was going to get rid of that Tabitha bitch. And all it took was a phone call. I'm a genius when you think about it. I wanted to kill her so badly but because fuck up Kyle took her out there's too much of a connection. Like I said, I don't kill acquaintances or girls I know. That's the first place the police look --- an old boyfriend --- a spouse --- a neighbour or friend --- someone at work. My girls are clean --- we meet and then they're gone. That's the way I like it. It's true I have killed a few girls that I met briefly in the past but I make sure it was long ago and long forgotten. You don't do this for decades without knowing what you're doing. I don't rely on luck but skill and planning and nerves of steel. And I realize that lately I have been taking more risks. I have to make a conscious effort to tone it down a bit. Don't want to get over confident. If I keep doing this right the girls and me could be doing this for even more decades. That's the plan.

I couldn't go on that Spring Break trip. Something came up which pissed me off so I'm going in June instead. I'm going to take a huge chance. Taking three girls at once is going to be tricky --- really tricky. But I've been planning this for a long time. Years in fact and believe me when I tell you I am a damn good planner. Marianne and her daughters are living their lives and have no clue that I'm coming for them. They have no idea the eyes are on them or will be very soon. This is going to be my greatest achievement. The one that thinks she got away --- that it's over --- that it's in the past and she's safe. Her guard is going to be down after all these years. She feels safe now. I get so excited just thinking about it and her two sweet innocent daughters. Identical twins and GOD I hope they're virgins. I'll find out soon enough. I get hard just thinking about it. I'm going to take over for a few days and we are going on another road trip. Kyle has no idea of course. First, I'm going to watch the girls --- observe their habits. That should take anywhere from three to five days of surveillance --- unless opportunity knocks early. It's going to be tricky but it's definitely doable. I've been getting the van ready for the girls. Making sure they'll be comfortable for their trip back. That makes me smile --- the comfortable remark. It's a long trip. The longest trip I have ever carried girls in the van. I'll be driving back non-stop.

I've waited so patiently and now the time is so close. Kyle knows about the trip. He thinks it is just another road trip. He's going to have some longer blackouts while I do my good work and soon it will just be me. That goodie two shoes has no place in my world. We'll be arriving just at their Summer Break. I've checked when their summer break is. Don't you just love vacations? I do. They can be so much fun and I'll be meeting new people. The twins haven't been properly introduced to me yet. Soon --- very soon and Marianne is going to witness it all.

The day has finally arrived. The day we leave. Fuck head Kyle is worried about the stupid cats. Jeez --- it's the longest he's ever left them alone and he actually thought about bringing them along. Fuck that! I convinced him the cats are fine. The weather is warmer and there are lots of mice and rodents and things on the farm for them. The cats have water and food and will be fine. He has no idea how long the trip will be. The van is packed and we are ready to rock and roll. Kyle starts the van and we are finally on our way. He looks back for the cats but they aren't there. Don't worry about them Kyle. They don't give a fuck about you. He locks the gate and off we go. I feel free and alive. Like I'm going to visit some old friends for a good time. Soon we are out of the rural area and on the main road heading towards the highway. We are hours away from our destination but are getting closer with each second. That's how I look at it. They say every journey begins with the first step. I don't know who they actually are but it makes sense. I have it planned. We are going to stop for that first night and sleep in the van. This particular trip, there are no hotels or motels for us. It's all van occupancy from here on in for us. We are like the Klingons with a cloaking device --- like the alien in the Predator movie. We are human chameleons from here on in. We even have some extra gas cans so we don't have to stop at gas stations near the town. Everything is cash and carry. I want to remain under the radar as much as possible. Too much is at risk.

Kyle is travelling the speed limit --- just like he should. Not so important now but on the way back it will be even more important. Like I mentioned I hate cops. I think most people get a pit in their stomach when a cop car flashes the lights for you to pull over even though you haven't done a damn thing wrong. That's because deep down in your gut you don't trust them. I know I don't. Sure --- there are good cops but I don't want any cops --- good cops or bad cops fucking with me. Stay the fuck away if you know what's good for you.

The first part of the trip is uneventful. There is a small fridge in the van that is there especially for these types of road trips. We just have to make sure we park in a spot that the cops won't visit in the night. Don't want them knocking on the window --- checking on us. Once, years ago I got tired and pulled off the road for a little shut eye. Thirty minutes into my snooze a cop was banging on the window with his flashlight. He was peering in and I figured he was just checking to see if I was all right. Really though he was up to no good. That was a long time ago when I was a teenager. The cop said he wanted to make sure I hadn't been drinking. I wasn't drinking. He was snooping. Fishing I call it --- not exactly legal either. He asked what was in the trunk of the car? I told him fishing gear. Then he asks me, mind if I have a look? What a fucking asshole! I open the trunk and he checks not just my fishing gear but looks everywhere. I watch him to make sure he doesn't plant anything. Nothing was there that shouldn't have been and then he says okay, you can go and he just leaves. He seemed pissed off he didn't find anything. He did an illegal U-turn right in front of me. Get the fuck out of here and go to a coffee shop fuck head. That is what was going through my head.

The bed in the van is actually really comfortable. I made it bigger and Kyle hasn't even noticed it is bigger. I did that to make more room underneath in the secret compartment for our --- you know --- extra luggage. I laugh when I say that. I love my mind --- the way it works. I'm so witty. We sleep great that first night. No nightmares for Kyle the last little while. I want him healthy for this trip. I love summer time cause the girls are wearing shorts and showing off their skin. I really love the fall too. The dying leaves --- the coolness of the air. Like I mentioned I love the changing colours of the leaves. Come to think of it I think I love the fall better. And I like spring just because bloody winter is over. Everybody is probably glad when winter is over --- especially if it is a long winter.

I decide it's time for Kyle to disappear for a while. I'm up early --- just after 6:30 A.M. I get dressed and I head off looking for a MacDonald's drive-thru for a breakfast and a coffee. I find one ---they seem to be everywhere. Checking the map I see I am about four hours away from Nookville. That's a great name for a tiny, secluded, safe place to reside. I find it ironic that the family chose a place with that name to get away all those years ago. I should be in Nookville well before lunchtime. The drive is nice --- relaxing really. Traffic varies. Sometimes it's busy and sometimes it seems like only a few cars are on the road. The last hour the traffic has really thinned out and my anticipation grows. I'm getting excited to see my friends. It's a pretty drive. Nature can really be wonderful. It can be both beautiful and breathtaking and it can be mean and ugly. Up ahead I see a family of partridge crossing the road. They aren't the smartest birds but they are almost off to the side. I could easily miss them but I just turn towards them and run over them --- a mother with five babies. I hear the thud and crunch as my tires crush them. I look back in my rear view and see I got four of the babies. I missed the mother and one baby. Shit! I could go back and finish the job but decide they aren't worth it. I watch the birds in my mirror. Talk about stupid birds. They just stand there waiting for the next car. I don't even think the mother realizes what happened to her babies. I smirk thinking about the stupid birds. Then I think of my girls. Never knew what hit them --- survival of the fittest right? That's nature. Adapt, evolve, and survive. I keep playing the bird crush over and over in my mind. I look for more animals but they aren't cooperating. And then I see the sign ahead --- You Are Now Entering Nookville, and below it says, A Neighbourhood Watch Community --- population 9,999. I smile. It's not my first Neighbourhood Watch Community. I wonder who will be the 1,000th baby so they can change the sign? Maybe it has already happened, and they just haven't changed the sign yet. I find the local high school easy. I want it just for future reference in case things don't go as planned. I am hoping to wrap this up on Sunday or Monday. Now it's time to find their house. I remember where it is. You see I have been here a few times the last twenty years. Just to check up on my girls. I remember the first time I came. I was going to collect her and when I finally found her I saw she had two daughters. They were about three years old at the time. I thought Ah --- that's so nice of her --- two little girls and her. What a nice family she has. So I decided to wait. Like I tell you I'm very patient --- and determined. So I decided to wait for the girls to get older before collecting. The idea appealed to me. And so that is how I decided to arrive at this very moment. It's been a lot of years but now the fruit is ripe. Time to pick my fruit and enjoy it. I'm just so excited. I have to be very careful if I am to be successful. Collecting three girls at once --- well --- that is a first even for me. I have a good plan though and the first thing I need to do is observe from a safe distance. I need to discover their routines. Everyone has routines. We are all creatures of habit. I will need to see what their daily habits are and then hone my plan. I've already planned some scenarios. I don't think I can get all three at once. That would be tough. I like to surprise. So I think I will get the daughter's first --- the two of them and then target the mother shortly after. It will all have to be done quite quickly --- the quicker the better. This is exciting.

I find the street and up ahead is their house. I stop and park and just watch. I see two cars in the driveway. I assume they are their cars. One is a silver coloured Chevrolet Impala. It looks fairly new and in good shape. The other is a sleek, black Nissan SUV type. I wonder if Marianne still has the same job as last time I was here? She was selling real estate a couple of years ago. I have visited her often--- she didn't know I was visiting her --- about every three years or so. So I would see the girls as they were growing up. I think the girls are about eighteen now? If not they are darn close. I don't want to park here too long. It's a residential area and lots of older houses here. They are nice as far as old houses go. Nice looking neighbourhood. I notice the trees and grass. It's a quiet street so I don't want to cause anyone to be suspicious. I only stay about two minutes. I didn't see anyone except a few younger kids playing up ahead about sixty yards or so. They are playing catch on the sidewalk --- three kids --- two boys and one girl. America's National Sport --- good ole baseball. Seeing them playing on a Saturday morning makes me think back to when I was a kid going outside to play. I get a bit nostalgic thinking about it. Playing catch but especially all those road hockey games we had. They were good times. I wish I was there again but then I remember where I am and why I am here. I start the van up and decide to go for a bit of lunch and then come back to observe. I need to remain inconspicuous. I head to the local coffee shop. Shit! No drive-thru! How the hell can they have no drive-thru? It's the twenty-first century for Christ's sake! I decide to go in and notice the cameras right away. They don't have cameras in the parking lot though. I have my cap on and pull my hood up to cover my face from the cameras. I am also wearing my shades. I don't' want any cameras that might identify a stranger in town just a day or two before three of their residents go missing. I have my thermos and get a coffee and a whole-wheat carrot muffin. It's a big muffin and it looks real good. I can tell right away they bake their own. I order it using just a regular accent. I almost decided I would use a French accent but then realized that would really stand out as unusual in such a little town. I get my muffin and drink and head back to the van. I decide to eat and drink on the run. I go back to the van and take a bite of the muffin. Really delicious and I think I should stop here again. I take a sip of the coffee. Now that's good fucking coffee. I mean it has to be the best freaking coffee I've ever had in my life. Or is it just because I'm so excited that it tastes so bloody good? I eat and drive back to Marianne's street. I do a drive by and notice the car is no longer in the driveway.

"Shit!" I mutter under my breath as my eyes narrow. "Where the fuck did they go?"

They couldn't have gone far so I drive aimlessly looking for them. As I'm driving I am thinking I have to be careful Marianne doesn't see me. Even though it's been twenty years since she's seen me last she still might recognize me. I am a bit heavier now but I am still in good shape. I think I probably weighed about 150 pounds back when I was 16 years old and now I am a good 193 pounds. I am also about 3 inches taller. Still I have to be careful in case she recognizes me. That would be a really big problem. Her two daughters --- I feel confident I could walk right up to them and they wouldn't have any idea who I was. I wonder if Marianne told her daughter's about me? Probably not but I bet Marianne has kept her daughters close to her vest and is very protective of them. After twenty minutes of scouring town I finally see their car. I park far enough away to observe. This town has free public parking on the street. That's good cause I don't even have to leave the vehicle. Their Impala is in a mid-sized parking lot and I'm parked about two hundred feet away. That should be far enough away. I've finished my muffin. I finished it pretty quickly and I'm just taking sips from my thermos. They must be in one of four buildings --- a drug mart, a variety store, a dollar store, or some kind of Martial Arts Centre. I don't know if it's all three of them here or just one or two of them? I wait and watch a few people coming in and out of the various buildings. After thirty minutes I see the two teens coming out of the Martial Arts Centre and I am pretty sure it's the daughters. I watch closely and I am right --- it's them. They walk to the Impala laughing and one of them takes the FOB out of her purse and clicks the FOB and the lights flash on the car for an instance. I pull forward a few yards to get a better look and man --- they are looking real good --- real sweet. They don't get in right away. They seem to be waiting for someone. Must be Marianne I am guessing. They put their purses in the car and then start fooling around in the parking lot. They each practice some spinning heel kicks and I can tell they are pretty good at it. Their form and techniques is good.

"Well --- well --- well. So the girls are into Martial Arts. That definitely makes things more interesting." I mumble to myself, "That is good to know."

The two girls wave to someone but I can't see who it is yet? Is it Marianne? Is she training in the Martial Arts too? Then I see whom it is walking towards them.

"What the fuck? This can't be happening? No fucking way! No bloody way! What the fuck!"

I am in shock. I subconsciously lean my body closer to the windshield for a better look not believing my eyes.

"No way." I am in total shock. "What are the odds --- a billion to one?"

I shake my head but it is true. This is just too weird. I smile almost exactly like when Kyle won the lottery all those years ago. There, standing not one hundred and fifty feet in front of me are not only my two girls but also that bitch Tabitha. How the hell did this even happen? This is just so unexpected. I start laughing at my good luck. God – it's good to be me.

I'm staring at all three girls, as I'm lost in a world of utter joy. If only Kyle were here to see this. He'd be going nuts to see her again. Tabitha is older than the girls so I wonder how the hell do they know each other? I have no idea but I am just so happy. I mean I was happy before but this --- well --- talk about a bonus for the taking. I'm in a state of euphoria. I watch the three girls from afar as they talk and giggle in the parking lot totally oblivious that my eyes are upon them. I roll the window down hoping I am close enough to hear them. Then I realize something. Tabitha knows this van --- and me. I suddenly duck down as I try to hide. I definitely don't want her to see me like this. She would think I am stalking her and I am sure she would call the police. I am immediately rearranging my plans to include her. Dare I try to collect four girls on one outing? Do I even have room for four girls in my van? It would be a tight squeeze for the drive home. Fuck --- that would make me the king of the Universe if I could pull that off. What an incredible feather in my hat that would be. It would also be one incredible good time for me. I couldn't imagine a more fulfilling time. I watch as the girls talk for a few minutes longer and then they give each other a hug and go to their cars. I notice Tabitha gets into a white Mazda 3 hatchback. I decide to follow her but from a safe distance. I just hope when she leaves the parking lot she turns the other way and doesn't pass this van. The girls get in their cars and leave the parking lot. Both cars turn the other way away from me. That's good! I start my van and am careful following them. At the first light the girls turn right and I see them sticking their hands out the window waving to Tabitha. Tabitha sticks her arm as well to wave good-bye. I can't hear them but I can tell they are yelling at each other. See ya soon I imagine them saying. They have no idea just how true that is going to be but not quite what they had in mind. I laugh at the thought. Tabitha drives straight through the light and I follow her. The lights about to change but I make it and she is far enough ahead that I feel safe. A few minutes later I see Tabitha has her turn signal on and she turns right into an apartment complex parking lot. I stop far enough to be out of sight but I can still see where she parks. I want to know where she is going. I watch her get out of the car. She really is quite stunning. Even from this distance I can tell she is not your ordinary girl --- nothing ordinary about her. I'm getting hard just thinking about her. She walks to one of the units and then I see a door opening and a young man comes out to meet her. He is smiling and she runs to give him a big hug. My face furrows and my eyes narrow as I watch closely what is happening right in front of me.

"So that bitch has a boyfriend or some guy she is living with. It sure doesn't look like she is visiting. What a fucking cheating bitch. It didn't take her long after Kyle to find a guy. She must be a slut. That slut!"

I don't even realize I am talking to myself at first. I shake my head. *This bitch is just asking for it. I'm no fan of Kyle but I find myself taking this personally.*

Then I remember she mentioned to Kyle that she had an older brother. Could this be the older brother? I watched very closely to see how they react to each other. Is it brotherly or are they going to kiss? She kisses him on the cheek --- I think? It was pretty near the lips though. I don't give a shit. I want this bitch as part of the package deal.

I watch her go inside with her boyfriend. I decide he must be a boyfriend. Okay --- time to drive back to Marianne's place and get into my surveillance mode. I hadn't even seen Marianne yet and she is the prime target. I want her because she is the one the got away. I drive down their street and I see their cars in the driveway. I park at my spot again and I see a lady coming out to the car. It's her! Marianne! I watch her like a cat watches a mouse. She opens the car door and gets something then runs back in the house. I watch her go up the four or five steps. Yea, she still has one fine ass. I shiver thinking about it. It brings back such good memories. I smile as my breathing increases. Then I realize I don't want to be parked on a residential street --- too noticeable. Some neighbour might call me in. So I start the van and drive off for the night. Time to find a place to get some supper and bed down for the night. I'm going to have another night in the van and another night to plan for an extra guest at the farm. I have to be careful getting supper. Now there are two people that would recognize me in town. Tabitha and Marianne and if anyone of them recognizes me that would be a real monkey wrench. I have to be invisible.

I decide on a sub to go. I am eating way too many subs lately. I get a bowl of soup to go too! I drive out of town and find a little back road that is probably never used. I find a nice little hiding place and park. I am covered with foliage. This will do for the night. I won't have to worry about any cop knocking on my window in the middle of the night checking me out. I eat in the driver's seat and am thinking about tomorrow. I decide tomorrow will be the day. I start to plan for the extra girl --- Tabitha --- but then start thinking about Kyle's meeting with Tabitha. There was a problem there. It wasn't that long ago and if Tabitha were to suddenly go missing people might be able to connect her to Kyle and start investigating. I start to wonder how much did Tabitha tell that Amy girl or anyone else? Is there a whole circle of friends that were told about me --- or rather Kyle? Does Amy have my licence plate number on a piece of paper somewhere? Did Tabitha tell anyone my last name? Kyle is such an idiot for using his real name. In the end I decide that no --- I can't collect Tabitha right now. Stick to the original plan. Three girls are plenty complicated and Tabitha might just be too hot right now. I decide no Tabitha --- this time. I'll save her for another time. When things cool down and people forget. I know her last name. I should be able to find her again. Yes --- I'd better wait two or three years. And who knows? Maybe by that time she will have a kid --- a daughter. I hope not. I don't want to wait too long. I sigh and am slightly depressed. Tabitha would have been a great addition to my collection. So tomorrow is the day and I finalize my plan. I play it over and over again in my head. Try for the morning and if it goes without a hitch I should be on the road late morning or afternoon. I go to bed early with visions of sugar girls dancing in my head. Everything is ready. I hope the girls are.

I slept pretty good, considering the big day. I wake up early --- and excited. I finish the quarter of sub I had left over from last night. I check my coffee as I sip from the thermos. It is barely lukewarm but I sip it anyway. I check the time --- 6:43 A.M., it's probably much too early and the girls won't be up this early. Then I wonder --- do they go to church? I don't know? I panic just because I don't want them to be around lots of people. Are they going to stay in today or will they go out? Are they going to get together with friends --- boyfriends? I start to doubt my plans and I begin to think I should take more time to discover their routines. I'll play it by ear and hope that they go out by themselves --- like yesterday. I mean I can go into the house and take them but that increases the risk factor exponentially. A phone inside to 9-1-1 --- neighbours watching --- don't get careless. I've been doing this a long time and have been very successful. Stick to a plan. Don't get greedy Lucas I tell myself.

I stay hidden until 8:00 A.M. and then drive to town to get a refill for my coffee. I get a bagel with the coffee. I'm the only customer. I decide to eat later --- just too nervous. I take a tour down their street and as I suspected the two cars are still there and the neighbourhood seems abandoned of life.

Steven R. General

I just drive by trying to see if I can catch a glimpse to see if they are up. I see nothing but shades. I'm betting they don't even wake up till 10:00 A.M. This is going to be a hit and miss approach. That's okay --- I have all day. In fact, I have all the time in the world to kill. I'd just rather it be sooner than later. This is what I refer to as the "Cat and the Mouse Game." I think about my Jasper's back at the barn catching their mice. I smile at the irony of it all. I keep driving and decide to see if anything is open besides the coffee shop before 9:00 A.M. but decide to stay in my van. I just drive around the town like a tourist sight-seeing. What a boring place. If you like small towns this would be fine. Then I laugh because I live in the country, which is even more remote. At least here you would have neighbours within spitting distance. It doesn't take that long to see pretty much everything there is to see. I head back to Marianne's place and I suddenly see one of the girls step out on the porch to pick up the morning paper. They're up or at least she is and she is dressed --- not in her pyjamas. My heart races upon seeing her. I am hoping they are both up. Twins are usually like that. They do everything together including getting up. I pull over for just a second and I am thinking that they are probably going to have some breakfast first before going out. I'm wrong. Suddenly both girls are on the porch and so is Marianne. My heart is going a hundred miles per hour seeing all three of them together --- like the Three Musketeers. They go down the steps --- laughing and then the girls get in the Mazda but Marianne gets in the Nissan. They are all going out somewhere. Shit! I can't follow both vehicles. Where the hell are they going? Both cars back out and start coming my way. I duck down as they drive by. I watch them in the side mirror and then start the van and turn it around so I can follow them. Marianne is following her daughters --- that's what it looks like. Several minutes later both cars pull into a restaurant. They're going for breakfast. I smile. The family that plays together stays together comes into my mind. I park just far enough away that I can see them get out and walk together into the restaurant. I decide I can't collect them here like this. Not all at once. I remember the girls were coming out of the MMA center and were doing kicks in the parking lot. I need to wait for a better opportunity. I wait.

They must be really gabbing in there as they take an eternity. Who takes an hour and a half for breakfast? I'm getting frustrated. Finally I perk up as I see them leaving. They hug and get in their cars and leave but they don't leave together this time. The Mazda goes one way and the Nissan goes another way. I follow the teens. Where are they going now? They stop at the same plaza they were at yesterday. Are they going back in the MMA center? No, they go into the local Variety store. I don't think any other stores are even open yet? They go in the variety store and I pull in beside their car so my van is blocking the view from the variety store clerk. I have my cap and hood on and look up. No cameras. Perfect. I power my windows down just a bit and lock the doors. Then I wait impatiently. GOD I wish they would hurry up before someone else pulls in the parking lot. I don't have to wait long. Here they come. As they pass by my van I try to slide my arm down through the top of my window to open the door. I made sure my arm wouldn't fit through. They see me.

"Hi --- I've locked my keys in the van," I say acting exasperated at my situation. "I realized as soon as I closed the door but too late. What a dummy I am? Both girls look at me.

"Don't you have an extra set of keys Mister?" The one twin asks me. I shake my head no.

"Pretty stupid huh? I guess my mind was somewhere else. Say --- you girls have nice slender arms. Do you think you could try and slide your arm down and grab the knob or the handle and unlock it for me? I bet that would work."

"Well --- we're supposed to be somewhere."

"Pleeeze," I plead. "I would so appreciate it. I could give you ten dollars." I reached for my wallet.

"No --- that's okay. Keep your money. I'll try." One of the twins said.

Then both twins came to the window and one twin tried to squeeze her arm down but it wasn't easy. The other twin was standing beside her giving instructions.

"You almost got it Stephanie. Just a bit further and to the left."

Suddenly they felt a prick on their necks at the same time.

"Hey," they both said at the same time.

Both teens turn around --- their hands on the back of their necks. I caught them an instant later as they fell. That's the good thing about this method. Out like a light in seconds. I opened my cargo van door and quickly put the girls inside the van. Then I picked up the two purses that had fallen on the parking lot and put them in the van. I closed the door with a resounding thud. I take a quick glance and the parking lot is deserted. I'm sure no one saw. I open the front driver's door and quickly climb to the back where the two girls lay. I got my zip locks and fastened them to the girl's ankles and wrists. I bound the girl's wrists behind them. I put a gag on them and unhitched the latch and lifted the bed. I put both girls in the separate bunks and closed the lid. I rush to the driver's seat and start the van and drive out of the parking lot. The whole thing probably took no more that a minute. Now I have to find out where Marianne is?

I drive to Marianne's house but her Nissan isn't there. I search the town and then minutes later I find her van parked at the grocery store. Seems hardly anybody shopped in this town at this time of day except her. Her car is the lone vehicle in the lot. I parked the van beside her Nissan --- just like I did a short time ago with the girls. I wait but it seems like forever. And then she is walking out with her groceries in hand. I hide behind the van like a cat --- watching everything. She used the FOB and unlocks her car and puts the groceries in the back seat. She turns and opens the front door to get in. She never made it. I grab her from behind and at the same time stuck the needle in the back of her neck. Her eyes turn --- trying and see me and in that instant I whisper,

"Hi Marianne --- remember me?" I smile.

And then there was nothing but blackness for her.

CHAPTER 26

I catch Marianne before she collapses to the pavement and with my other hand open the cargo door and put her in. I fetch her purse off the ground and put it in the van. She takes care of herself. She must run or something. She definitely is in great shape. Trim and toned --- just like her daughters. I easily lift her into the van and shut the door. I turn to look around and I am alone. I get in the van and climb to the back and quickly put the zip ties and gag on her --- just like her daughters. I unhitch the latch and lift the bed and put Marianne in the compartment. I start driving away --- shaking I am so excited. I can barely contain myself. I drive just outside of town to the exact spot I had parked for the previous night. I quickly go through each purse and pull out their cell phones. I remove the batteries and put everything in an RFID pouch. I open the compartments and stare down at my girls. I'm so happy. I search each girl for anything that might be a communication device or give away our location. I also check to see if they have anything in their pockets that could be used as a weapon against me or to get out. They are bound and drugged. I know what I'm doing. I put the purses into the separate compartments with them. I spend less than a minute on each girl. Satisfied --- I lower the lid and make sure the latch is secure. The girls get air through the air vents but I had never taken three girls before. It was a tight squeeze. I scurry to the driver's seat and start the van and am soon on my way. I turn on the radio but not loud. It's going to be a beautiful day. The weather sucks --- cloudy and looks like rain but it I don't care. I sip from my thermos and finally dug into the bag that had my bagel. It tastes so good and I am ravenous.

It would be a long drive. No stopping for overnights on this special trip back --- just a quick stop to get the gas cans and put gas in the van when needed. And to travel the speed limit and obey all traffic laws. The drug dosage should keep the girls under until just before our arrival at the "Palace of Pain," some fourteen hours away. I'll make sure the girls stay medicated. It's a long time but they should be okay. Wouldn't want to get home and find a spoiled package. No --- I'll check their vitals on the way. I checked the clock. It's noon hour exactly. High noon and I was high on thrill and excitement. I would have to be careful. I'll have to watch for cops making certain I travel the speed limit and drive carefully. I have my gun if I need it. No smell of drugs or alcohol in the van. I should be fine. About an hour into the drive I go over some bridges. There is no traffic so I stop and reach over for the RFID pouch. I stand on the bridge and look to the water below. The water looks deep? I wipe any fingerprints off just in case and I empty the batteries and cell phones into the dark water. I shake the pouch making sure it is completely empty. I look around and I am alone. I get back into the van and resume my trip. The electronic footprints are gone forever --- just like the girls.

The drive seems longer than usual. Probably because I am psyched about what lays ahead for the girls when I get them to the farm. The twins will know they are probably together because they were together when I collected them. But Marianne will have no idea I have her daughters in my possession. When the time is right I will let her know. I can't wait. I have never been this excited before. I make a quick stop for coffee and to take a piss. Later I fill up the van from the gas cans. This might be the time when a cop stops to check if I'm okay while I stand at the side of the road filling up my van. I had better be on the lookout. I start to wonder if it might be better to just fill up at a gas station but decide no --- they have security cameras these days. I check on the girls at every stop to make sure they are still breathing and not in distress. I've read a lot of medical journals so I feel I know what I'm doing. The anticipation is killing me. I imagine in my head the scenarios I will have at the Palace of Pain over and over again. It's like Christmas in the summer.

The hours pass and soon I'm in familiar territory. It won't be long now. I've seen several cops on the trip. Some by the side of the road --- some at the coffee shops --- and some just drive by me. No idea of the precious cargo I carry. That keeps me awake when they are so close yet have no idea what they just passed. I smile when they are no longer in sight.

I'm on my back road now. Haven't seen any vehicles the last thirty minutes. My headlights shining into the pitch black darkness of the night. I'm minutes away. I start to think of my cats. It hasn't been that long --- a shorter trip than I thought it might be. The Jaspers will be happy to see me. I forget about the cats. I think about me unloading the girls and taking them downstairs. My Palace of Pain has been around for a long, long time. And if I have anything to say about it there is so many more to come.

There's my driveway and my mailbox. I almost by-pass the mailbox --- I'm just so anxious to see my prizes again. I stop though and take out the mail. I don't even look at it but drive up the driveway, stop and get out to unlock the gate. It hasn't rained lately. I know that because the driveway is completely dry --- even the low areas. I lock the gate behind me --- just in case. As I pull up to the back of the farmhouse it looks eerie --- even to me. The area is completely void of light except for the headlights as I head towards those back steps. I should call them the Steps of Doom or some other silly title. The motion detector I recently replaced senses my arrival and floods the area with light. I smile. I back the van up to the steps. I walk between the seats and lift the bed to check on my girls. I slide the top pieces back. I see all three of them as I have each girl completely separated from each other. They are still --- sleeping. They look so alive as I watch their chests rise and fall as they breath. I slide the lids closed again and lower the bed. I exit the rear of the van. Then I hear the Jaspers and see them running to the top of the stairs. Yes --- they miss the farmhouse just like me. I go up the steps and unlock the door and let them in first. I turn all the necessary lights on and quickly check the place to make sure everything is okay.

I then hurry out to the van. I open the back door and climb up and lift the bed and slide one of the daughter's compartments open. I don't know which daughter it is? They are identical and I don't know them well enough to tell them apart --- yet. I am going to get to know them very good though. She is still unconscious. I lift her out and carry her to the back of the van and sit down with her in my arms. I use my right hand to gently comb the hair from her sweet face so I can see her better in the light. I haven't been this close to them ever. This is my first real chance to examine her. She is beautiful. I then slide out of the van --- my feet touching the ground and I fling her over my shoulder fireman carry style. She isn't very heavy. I am guessing she is around 120 pounds. Up the steps we go and then through the living room and down the steps to the basement. I open the secret entrances with ease. I'm very good at this now. I've had lots of practice. I carry her through the corridor and place her in the second room and gently place her on her back on the table. I cut her zip ties and examine her wrists and ankles. They are slightly marked from the twist ties but not very much. I leave her clothes on --- for now. I fasten her down --- wrist and ankles. I take a quick glance at her. I can't stop smiling. My breathing increases not from the physical exercise of carrying her but just from my excitement. I don't look long. I have others that need to find their proper places. I hurry back to the van and do the same with the second daughter. I look at her face and she is the spitting image of daughter number one. GOD life is good. I carry her downstairs and enter the first secret room. I gently place her on the table --- fully dressed --- remove the ties and secure her ankles and wrists. I stare at her --- trying to remember everything about her --- and her sister. Who is the older one and by how much? I'm actually drooling at what I don't know about them. They are strangers but I feel like I know them. I go back and forth between the two rooms --- staring at each beauty for a few seconds. This is way better than Christmas. I remember I have my real prize still waiting for me in the van --- the one that somehow got away. I head back out to the van --- almost in a trot --- my breathing so heavy I feel like I have run a marathon. The Jaspers are meowing as I pass them each time. They try to follow me but refuse to go outside again.

Don't worry boys --- soon we will all feed and be merry. I go to the back of the van and look around. All is quiet at the Palace. Total blackness reigns just off the rays of the spotlight shining down. The parking lot reminds me of a prison scene in some movie with the security lights shining down on the compound. I turn back to the van and stand looking at the bed. I want this moment to last. I climb into the van and lift up the bed and slide the compartment open. There she is --- my greatest treasure. I still recognize her from all those years ago when I began my journey. She is older but she still looks great. She has the same hairstyle --- well --- almost --- just a bit longer. I lift her up and carry her to the back of the van and do the same thing I did with her two daughters. I have her in a sitting position as I prop her up. I use my fingers to move the hair away that is partially covering her face. She looks exquisite not from sheer beauty but because she makes me feel young again. I hug her while she is sitting on my lap, which feels good to me. It feels good. I kiss her ever so softly and whisper.

"I love you Marianne." Then I add, "Almost. We are connected you and I. We will always be connected. Till the end of time."

I sigh and caress her cheek. It's soft and she smells good to me. I imagine that is how she smelled to me all those years ago. I slide off the van and sling her over my shoulder and up the steps we go. I go slower now --- not because I am tired but because I want to remember --- to savour all of this. I take her downstairs but I put her on the sofa in the downstairs room. I decide she can keep her clothes on --- for now. I get my favourite wire and fasten it to the ring on the wall and then fasten the other piece to her left ankle. I then lay her down on her back and lean over her. I stop and smell her again. I love her smell. I then remember I have some things to do. I have to go back out to the van and get my luggage and lock it up. Then I have to feed those damn cats. They are making a racket as they have followed me downstairs. I run up the stairs and the cats follow me. I go outside again to the van. The cats are pissed at me --- I can tell. I grab the three purses. I almost forgot about them. I have to keep my wits about me. I make sure the bed is secure and latched. I gather the purses and the luggage and lock the van up. I don't usually lock my vehicles here on the property but I lock the van for now. I will need to clean them later --- and check for any evidence left behind. I go back in the house and put the purses on the kitchen table. I decide I'd better feed the cats as they are bugging me like crazy. I get the cat food and water bowl. I put the three water bowls down first. The cats look but aren't interested in water. I fill up the three bowls and open up some wet cat food to mix in with the dry. The three cats are rubbing up against my legs --- waiting for their food. I place the bowls on the floor and instantly they are at their bowls munching away. I decide to get out the cream and give them a bonus treat. It is after all a very special occasion worthy of a celebration.

I go back downstairs to check on Marianne first. She is still sleeping and I can tell she has moved slightly --- she's on her side now. A quick check of the area --- just in case to make sure there is nothing she can use against me or to escape. I then go into the back two rooms and check on the girls. They are both sleeping peacefully. I touch their warmth. The fun is going to have to wait. I want them awake the first time.

I turn the lights off so that when they wake up for the first time in their new surroundings they will see nothing but darkness. The darkness makes it is much more scary. I lock the rooms up and go back to check on my Marianne. I touch her again ever so softly on the cheek. She is nice and warm. I run my index finger slowly across her full lips. They are full and beautiful.

CHAPTER 27

I then go up the stairs and turn the light off. I'm tired from the long day and am beginning to get a terrible headache --- a migraine so I take a few pills. The migraine must be from the many hours of driving I guess. I get them sometimes --- the migraines I mean. I go in the kitchen and the cats are at their cream bowls lapping away and purring a mile a minute. I open the fridge to see what I have to eat. I grab the bread I put in there so it would last longer and make a cheese sandwich. I open a can of Chicken noodle soup and put it in the microwave. I get a glass of orange juice and take it to the kitchen table. I want to go through the girl's purses while I snack. You can tell a lot from a girl's purse. It's a treasure trove of information and secrets. I start with the one I know is Marianne's purse. It's a white purse with some shiny chains on it. I'm no purse expert so I have no idea how much it might cost but it looks like a nice purse. It seems both casual and elegant at the same time. I examine the purse --- even smelling it. I begin emptying the contents on the kitchen table. Man --- this thing holds a lot of stuff. I sift through it putting the interesting stuff to the left and the junk stuff --- like deodorant, feminine hygiene products, beauty products, etc. to the right. I pile the more interesting stuff like wallet and identification pieces in front of me. There are even a couple of bills and two letters in the purse. I put them front of me. I'm eating my sandwiches and soup as I examine each and every piece. I think of that movie when the alien was studying the belongings of his captures and I begin to laugh. This is a part I enjoy. Going through a woman's things. I examine her driver's licence. I see her address and height and weight --- colour of eyes. I notice she has a birthday coming up real soon. Well --- happy birthday Marianne. You're never going to celebrate it though. I'll be deciding when I take you based on how things go and how I feel. She was carrying her passport with her? I have to wonder why she would do that? I check through her credit cards. She has a lot of them. I see her vehicle registration and ownership with the DMV. She has a gym membership card. That might explain why her body is in such good shape. I quickly scan through her stuff. I notice she has a can of pepper spray. Too bad she won't get to use it on me. The two letters are next and I open them up. They aren't sealed. One is from a lawyer. It is a letter about child support for the two twins. In a nutshell it states that all obligations for child support are over --- except tuition costs for college. It does state there is a number of years back pay still owing by the father. It lists his name as John Smythe. *So they have a deadbeat dad who didn't pay his child support.* The other letter is from what I am guessing is a friend of Marianne. It is talking about surprising the twins with a family trip to London, England. So they were planning a surprise vacation for the twins. How nice of them --- the trip that is never going to happen. Well --- perhaps that lady who wrote the letter will have to go with someone else. My leg begins bouncing up and down as I am finding out so much about my girls. I go through the information way too fast. I decide I will look at it all in depth later. For now I will just take the quick tour. I put everything back in Marianne's purse and push it to the other side of the table. I focus on one of the twin's purses and empty the contents on the kitchen table. This one holds a lot of stuff also. I notice the purses are really quite heavy. They seem to have everything in them but the kitchen sink. I quickly go through her belongings and check the driver's licence. This one is Samantha's purse. I look closely at the picture doing my best to memorize it. I notice she just had her birthday this month. I notice they are older than I thought. I don't spend as much time on this purse. I notice lots of make-up, eye shadow, and feminine hygiene stuff and pepper spray. So Marianne is making sure her daughters are protected. Now it all makes more sense, the MMA training, and pepper spray. I wonder if they are trained with guns --- or if they have one? I haven't seen any signs of firearms and I check for knives. Sometimes knives can be disguised as something else. I did check their clothing and I'm sure they have nothing on them --- except their clothes. I put all Samantha's belongings back in her purse and then move on to Stephanie's purse. It is similar to her sister's purse but slightly different. Guess they need to be able to distinguish who owns what purse. Stephanie's purse is almost an exact twin of her sister's purse. She has some breath mints and gum in her purse. Other than that they are identical. I shake the pepper spray can and can tell it is full. Never discharged. I look up at the clock on the wall in the kitchen. It is a rooster clock --- red and green with a bit of yellow --- the colour of hay. What else would you expect in a farmhouse? It's getting close to the time. I put all the contents back into her purse and stand up to stretch. It's been a long day and I've been awake a long time. I'm tired and need to sleep. I struggle to keep my eyes open. The snack has made me extra sleepy. The twins should be waking up soon so I decide to go downstairs and check on them. I figure Marianne is about half an hour away from recovering from the drugs. Once the drugs start to wear off the effects wear off quite quickly --- within four to five minutes before returning back to normal --- before muscle control is fully functional. I get a bag and grab four water bottles. I'm thirsty too! I can already guess the young twins reaction when they wake up. It is Marianne's reaction I am looking forward to the most --- that fabulous moment when she first realizes just who I am. Bet she never thought she would see me again. I have lots of surprises for the girls. I'm a lucky guy --- them --- not so much. I walk to the door and open it and turn the light on. I go down the stairs slowly but only take two steps when I realize I don't have my mask on. Shit! I go back upstairs and open the cupboard in the living room corner. I pull out one of my many masks. Yes, this black half mask will do just fine. I put it on and check it out in the bathroom mirror. It's perfectly scary and menacing. I grab the bag of water bottles as I start to feel a twinge in my loins and it is a good feeling. I stop half way down the stairs to peek at Marianne who is still unconscious on the couch. I put the water down where she can't reach it. I want to make sure she is unconscious --- just in case she is faking it. I walk over to check and touch her. I gently blow on her closed eyelids and nothing. Her breathing is normal. I then head towards my teens that are resting in the back rooms. As I approach the oil tank I take another quick look at Marianne and close the tank behind me. I walk the short corridor and open the door where it is dark --- and silent. I turn on the light. Instantly I peek in and see the girl --- I don't know which twin it is on the table? She is awake and struggling with the restraints. She sees me and starts to scream. Walking over to her I just stop to look at her. She's a real fighter --- just like her mom. She's going crazy on the table and staring at me. She's definitely afraid. I love that look --- the look of fear. We haven't even started yet and already she's in terror. She should be. I talk to her.

"You can struggle all you want. It won't do you one bit of good. And you can yell and scream all you want. There is no one to hear you." She sees the bottom part of my mask smile.

"Why am I here? How did I get here? What's going on? Who are you? Let me go! Let me go now! They'll be people looking for me! Let me go!" She gritted her teeth as she continued to yell and snarl at me. Then she added, "Where's my sister?" *Yep --- she's a fighter.*

"I suggest you save your strength. It will do no good to yell at me but yell if you want. I will answer all your questions but I'm a little busy right now. Are you comfortable? Would you like a drink of water?" I take out the water bottle and hold it to her lips but she is fighting me --- and the water bottle. "That's okay --- you can drink later but you will drink. You will do everything that I ask you to do."

"Never!!!" She growls back at me.

"I'll be back in a minute. Are you Stephanie or Samantha?" I wait for an answer but she won't answer me. I study her face as I try to remember her driver's licence photo. Her eyes are like daggers. I love it.

"Okay, you don't have to tell me now but you are going to talk to me --- believe me. Or you will be punished. You won't like my punishment. None of them do."

I walk past her and into the next corridor to the next room. I come to the door and slowly open it, and then close it shut. I turn on the lights and instantly I see the other twin twisting and turning her head around trying see just where she is. She sees me for the first time and starts to scream --- just like her twin sister. I've closed the door so the sister can't hear her screams. The place is completely soundproofed. They are the perfect rooms for my games. I slowly walk in --- my eyes fixated on her. She stares back at me with that same look of total fear.

"You stay away from me! Don't come any closer! Stay back!" I stop just for the amusement.

"Why hello. Are you Stephanie or Samantha?" I ask in a friendly tone. She doesn't answer.

"Where am I and where is my sister?" She demands to know. This one is slightly quieter but I still see that fire in her eyes. She struggles with the restraints.

"You won't be able to get out of the restraints. They are made especially for this purpose --- to restrain people. You are my special guest. Are you comfortable? Is there anything I can get for you?" My smile is more of a smirk.

"You untie me and let me go!" She demands.

"Sorry --- but I can't do that. The games haven't begun yet."

She stares at me and looks about the room --- trying to figure out what all the stuff is on the wall and on the tables. I know she has no idea on what they are for.

"Where's my sister?" She demands.

"I left your sister. I just took you. Your sister is probably looking for you. Your mom is looking for you too I imagine."

"You know my mom?" She asks with fear in her voice.

"Oh --- we met --- once --- a very long --- time ago." I can sense my smile grow even bigger. I believe my smile probably looks quite sinister now. I've practiced in the mirror --- for the benefit of my girls.

Her eyes get big and her breathing gets even louder. "You're him --- aren't you?"

"So you know about me huh? I wondered how much your mom told you? You've been out for a long time. You are probably thirsty. Would you like a drink of water?"

She too refuses the drink. *What is it with all this mistrust anyway? What is the world coming too?*

"Okay --- you're suspicious." I take the water bottle and take a drink myself so it doesn't touch my lips --- to show her it isn't drugged. I offer the bottle to her lips and this time she accepts it. She struggles to lift her head and sips from the bottle all the time her eyes looking up at me with hate --- pure hate.

"That's enough for now. I have to leave you for a few minutes but I will leave the light on. I won't be long."

"So --- what's your name?" I turn back as I am leaving and I wait but she doesn't answer.

"You are going to tell me. I promise you that you will tell me and answer any questions I ask."

I leave the room and walk to the previous room where twin number one is. She sees me come back and starts yelling again. This one likes to talk.

"Let me go! You won't get away with this! Where is my sister? Unstrap me right now."

"Your sister is fine. I didn't take her. She is probably looking for you right now. I'm sure the police are looking for you too!"

I try to reassure her. I like to play mind games --- then later take it all away.

"Do you want that drink of water now. I bet you're thirsty."

I take a short swig from another bottle so it doesn't touch my lips. I offer it to her lips.

"It's not drugged."

She refuses a drink the second time.

"I'll be back in a minute. Don't go anywhere now." I laugh when I say it.

"I'll leave the light on --- in case you're afraid of the dark."

I'm giddy and funny tonight but the pills aren't helping my migraine so much. I go back to the main downstairs room where Marianne is resting. I walk in and she has stirred but isn't awake yet. I sit down at the table and wait --- and watch her recover. The timing couldn't be more perfect. Within five minutes her eyes are open and she looks around confused and dazed trying to figure out where she is and what happened? Finally she begins to recover enough to sit up and she seems more alert. I have remained quiet and still. I am partially in the shadows so I am pretty sure she hasn't noticed me. I decide to talk.

"You're awake sleepy head. It's about time you woke up."

She turns to try and find the voice. I emerge from the shadows. She sees my mask and starts screaming. I'm still fairly certain she doesn't know who I am. She's just terrified to be here.

"You can scream if you want --- no one will hear you. We are quite alone and away from any other ears."

"Who are you and why am I hear?" She stands up and for the first time notices the shackle on her left ankle. Suddenly there is more fear flooding her face.

"Why Marianne --- you don't recognize me. And we were so close at one time. I'm disappointed."

I get up and slowly walk out of the shadow and into the light. Even with my mask on she isn't sure who I am. I'm sure her mind must be going a mile a minute. *It couldn't be HIM --- it just couldn't be HIM. That was too long ago --- I imagine her thinking.*

I slowly lift my mask off --- like it is a game of hide and go seek in slow motion. When the mask is off I take my hand and run it through my hair.

"It's me Marianne --- your old friend Kyle." I whisper the name to her across the semi-darkness. After all --- that's the name she knows me by. She gasps and then faints --- right down to the floor with a resounding thud. *Well --- I expected a reaction but I didn't expect this. This so much fun! I'm enraptured just thinking of what is to come.* A quick check and she is breathing. I rush to the first room where the loud twin is and gag her --- her protesting all the time. Then I cover her up with a hospital type cream green blanket. Then I scurry to the next room with twin number two and do the same thing. I gag her and cover her with another cream green coloured blanket. Then I wheel twin number two into twin room number one. They can't see each other --- or even talk. I put the two twins almost side by side. Then I rush back out to the main downstairs and Marianne is still passed out. Must have been quite the shock. I zip tie her just in case and unshackle the ankle bracelet. I gag and pick up Marianne and carry her into room number one. I put her on the third table that I have placed to the left of daughter number one and daughter number two. I do it as quickly as I can and cut the zip ties and put the restraints on her wrists and ankles. She's ready but she's still unconscious. I go in the drawer and break out some smelling salts. I waft it over her nostrils and she reacts --- jerking away and avoiding the putrid smell. She's awake and can see she is now in a different room --- shackled to the table and gagged. Her eyes are filled to the brim with terror. I put my lips down to her ear and whisper.

"Welcome back Marianne. I didn't forget about you but it seems you forgot about me. It's so good to see you after all these years." I'm in heaven.

She muffles and is trying to speak through her gag. I take the gag off. She doesn't even talk for a second but just stares at me like a deer about to meet its maker.

"Why?" Her eyes search for an answer. "Why would you come back? You like young girls --- not girls my age? Why am I here? I didn't tell any-one about you."

"Yes --- and I really should thank you for that. You could have told the police. They would have had a very good description and might have even caught me. You could have saved all those other girls through the years but you didn't. I really should just let you go as a thank you." All my smiling was starting to tire out the muscles in my face. "And by the way --- I like girls your age too."

"You should let me go Kyle. That would be a very smart thing for you to do. If you think about it you owe me that much." Her eyes were looking at me with the faintest of hope.

"But if I let you go we can't have our party. You were after all the only one to ever get away from me. I admire you --- digging your way out like that. It couldn't have been easy. You have what I call gumption. I'm really quite impressed."

She just stared at me --- her bosom going up and down as she breathed heavily.

"Besides --- family get-togethers are so much fun --- don't you agree?" She stared at me in a deafening silence after that remark.

I walk over to the closest table. She watches my every step and I slowly, ever so slowly slid the green sheet away starting at the feet.

Marianne started screaming when she saw her daughter's shoes and the daughter screamed as best she could through her gag.

"I believe you two know each other."

"No Kyle --- no --- please --- let her go. It isn't right. Are you all right? Has he hurt you honey?" Marianne is asking daughter number one. I call her number one only because I am not sure of their names yet. They will tell me though --- trust me --- they are going to be talking and telling me lots of stuff.

"Stay with me Marianne." My eyes meet hers and I flash my teeth at her. I walk over to the other table with the light green blanket lay. Marianne starts screaming again.

"NO! --- NO! --- GOD --- have mercy! NO! -- Please NO!"

I ever so slowly slide off green sheet number two.

"Drum roll please. Ta-da! And I believe you know this young girl too! They are the spitting image of you Marianne when --- you know --- you were at that young tender age. When you first had the privilege of meeting me."

All three girls scream --- two through their gags and one without when they see each other --- strapped to the sacrificing tables in the Palace of Pain. With the two twins trying to talk and Marianne crying to both her daughters it was a miss mash of sounds. Marianne blubbering and trying to sooth her daughters --- telling them they are going to get out of this --- that they'll be okay. I don't tell them I'm the bearer of bad news. I just want to listen. Ah --- what the hell. I'll take off the twin's gags and let them talk to mommy. They are probably missing each other. Hey --- I can be a nice guy --- sometimes. I'm a firm believer in the importance of family. I can be a sarcastic bastard.

CHAPTER 28

I've never heard so much wailing and crying and blubbering in my whole life. I've collected two girls at a time but only the one time and it was different. One of them was pretty much unconscious most of the time. She kept fainting. Darwin's Law --- survival of the fittest meant I just had to kill her first. And I couldn't do it slow like I like. No, she kept passing out so finally when she woke up I was just so pissed off at her lack of endurance I just killed her outright. Slit her throat and watched her gurgle. I freed her hands so I could watch her clutch her throat --- both hands covered in her own blood. Her eyes were wide open as she felt her life leaving her. I could actually see life leaving her through those changing eyes. Most girls think it can't happen to them. Well --- I got news for you --- it can. She was screaming a bit but the cut was deep so her vocal cords --- and the mass amount of blood loss didn't help her. She gulped and gurgled but her struggle was quick. She bled out really quite fast. And now I have three girls at once. By GOD they are making such a fuss. You'd think their beloved puppy just died or something for fuck sake. I pull up a chair and sit and watch and listen. Just like I was at the movies. All that was missing was the popcorn. The next few hours and days are going to be filled to the brim with fun times. And I am going to enjoy every second of it. These girls are fighters and that makes it all so much the better. I like that. They are all breathing even more deeply now. After ten minutes of them talking I am get tired of all this. All they are doing is repeating the same thing over and over and asking me questions. Why am I doing this? What right have you? You'd better let us go right now! Think about what you are doing? Hell --- I've been thinking about it for a couple of decades. They are even pleading and trying to make a deal with me. Do I look like Monty Hall? It's a rhetorical question. Fuck no!

Finally I've had enough of this bullshit. I am getting bored --- and tired. I didn't get to sleep all day like they did and they are bugging my headache. I stand up and stretch --- all the while they are blabbing.

"Quiet!" I yell out. I'm not really mad. I'm just sick of it all. "Shut the fuck up! --- Now!" There is silence as they all stare at me. "That's better."

I look at each girl giving them my serious don't fuck with me look. "How long you are here depends on my wants and needs --- and the level of cooperation I receive from each of you. Now I have a question to one of the daughter slaves." I walk over to the first slave daughter to the left of Marianne and lean down to her face --- looking at her. She attempts to pull away. I smile. "Tell me your name? Are you Stephanie or Samantha?" She doesn't answer. "Ah --- the first defiance after the rules were read. A punishment is in order."

I walk over to a long skinny table near the slave's feet and remove a light blue covering on a tray. I pick up the tray and walk back to the girl who refused to answer. I hold the tray high so they can't see what's on it. I lower the tray as their eyes widen when they see its contents. The tray has one of my surgical kits with shiny, stainless steel surgical cutting instruments. Top quality. I don't cut corners.

"That's Stephanie! That's Stephanie! That's Stephanie! Please don't cut her. She doesn't understand. No please! Cut me instead! She doesn't understand yet! Please!"

I look at Marianne and am impressed. "That's very noble of you to sacrifice yourself to the cutting for your daughter."

"My name is Stephanie! My name is Stephanie! Sorry --- I didn't mean to not answer. I just didn't understand. Don't cut mom --- please!"

I turn to Marianne. "You ask that I won't cut Stephanie so I won't. And Stephanie has asked that I don't cut you so I won't cut you either. However, Stephanie needs some sort of punishment. I know --- I pick up the tray and take it over to the other girl --- the other twin. I put the tray down and say in a low tone, "Stephanie needs to be punished so I will punish her sister for what Stephanie has done? My back is facing Marianne and Stephanie as I pick up a scalpel and hold it up examining it --- the gleam of the lights reflecting the room like a mirror. I lower the knife slowly and hear all three girls screaming for me to stop. I stop what I am about to do and turn back to face Marianne and Stephanie. I look at Stephanie.

"Do you want me to cut your sister for your wrong doing Stephanie?"

"No! No! Please don't!" She is sobbing now. The girl with the attitude is sobbing and I haven't even started.

"So you promise to cooperate fully now Stephanie?"

"Yes --- just don't hurt her. Don't hurt any of us. I will cooperate." Her eyes are already bloodshot and full of tears.

"All right then, I will show some mercy this time but remember this because I am liable not to show such mercy in the future should you disobey. Do you understand Stephanie?"

I walk around to the outside so now I am facing all the girls. I lean down to the twin and stroke her hair. She is breathing so hard I think she could possibly pass out.

"Take it easy girl. I won't hurt you --- if you cooperate. What's your name?"

"My name is Samantha." Her eyes focused on mine and in fear.

"Glad to meet you Samantha. You must be the smart one. You answered right away." I stroke her hair --- it's so soft. I lean down further and smell her --- I take a big whiff of her fragrance and inhale it in. "Now tell me Samantha --- who is the older twin? You or Stephanie?"

"Stephanie is older."

"My oh my --- you are a fast learner Samantha. You answered my questions right away. I like that. And how much older is Stephanie than you?"

"She is eighteen minutes older than me."

"A whole eighteen minutes older than you." I smile. "You know Samantha I have one more question for you. Are you and your sister virgins? I'm just wondering."

216

I turn to look at Marianne and her head is struggling to lift off the table for a better view. She too it seems is waiting for the answer to my question.

"Yes --- we are virgins," her eyes questioning me in the now silent room, except for the breathing.

"Just like the old days when a girl would save herself for marriage huh?" My eyes find Marianne. "Marianne --- They are just like you were when we met all those years ago --- remember ---you were a virgin too! You see girls --- your mom gave me her virginity all those years ago but she did it before she was married. It is so hard to find a decent virgin these days." I sigh. "I can respect that. Oh --- I just thought of something. Perhaps you girls are lesbians and don't even like guys? Are you a lesbian Samantha? Do you prefer the girls?"

"I'm not a lesbian," Samantha answered. Her eyes narrowed in response.

"I'm glad you're not a lesbian." I look over to Stephanie. "And what about you Stephanie? Are you a lesbian?"

"No --- I'm not a lesbian either."

I walked over to the girls and pushed their tables almost together.

I began walking around all three tables. I stopped at Samantha's table near her feet. I removed her running shoes and removed her socks. She has absolutely fabulous feet. The bottoms of her feet looked so soft. I put my nose down and inhaled the smell as I looked at her. She stared back at me with a "What are you doing look?" I then reached for my tray and picked up the scissors. All three started squealing when they saw that.

"Hey --- relax. Geez! I'm not going to cut her."

"Leave my daughter alone! You promised me Kyle!"

"Well --- actually I promised I wouldn't cut her but then I started thinking. I took your virginity back in that forest and I have two virgins here right in front of me. So I thought what a great opportunity for you know --- a family moment --- the deflowering of the virgins. I'm a very good lay --- or so I've been told. You remember Marianne? I do. I'm a great teacher of the art. I'm going to give you girls all night to think about it. The real fun will begin tomorrow." *I'm so witty.*

I pull the sheets over the girls right up to their necks. I tuck the sheets in just like a father might tuck his family in at bedtime.

"I'm going up to sleep now. I suggest you sleep too! Tomorrow is a big day. I will allow you a shower and washroom break --- separately of course. And then some breakfast. And then well --- your daughters will be virgins no more. Like I said, if you are nice to me --- I will be nice to you."

I walk away and shut the light off. Before I leave the room and close the door to total darkness I stand in the light of the door behind me. I say one more thing,

"Sleep tight girls. Sweet dreams now."

I close the door and make sure it is secure. I go upstairs to the kitchen and look at the clock. Damn --- it's late. I step out onto the porch and take a deep breath of fresh night air. Life is good. I go to bed and I am asleep like a baby in no time. I'm exhausted. Damn I wish I had some Viagra left. I might need a barrel of it over the next couple of days.

CHAPTER 29

In the darkness of the room the girls are crying. Marianne talks to her daughters trying to come up with some strategy and plan.

"That man is a monster mom. I would rather die than let that animal touch me tomorrow," Stephanie gritted in the darkness.

"I hate him too mom. We need to do something," Samantha whispered.

"I know --- he is a sick monster but we must stay on his good side. I have seen what he can do and believe me there is no way I want you to feel his sadistic side. He won't just kill you --- he will make you suffer unbearably for a very long time. We need to plan ahead and be prepared should an opportunity arise. He mentioned tomorrow we would have a shower and washroom break. It sounds like he is only going to take us one at a time so he can control us but we must be ready. I am so glad I insisted you take those Martial Arts classes. We have been studying the Martial Arts for years and that will be our advantage. He probably doesn't know that we are capable of defending ourselves. Study our surroundings and look for anything that could be used as a weapon or tool for escape. I don't mean to scare you and I wish I didn't have to tell you this but he is not letting us go. He wants to use us and then will dispose of us when he is done. We must keep our spirits up and be creative. I am sure he has done this for a long time and is probably very good at controlling his captives. Those knives on the tray are very sharp and could be used as both a weapon or to cut free and escape. The problem is how do we get our hands on them?"

"Mom --- I'm completely helpless. I can barely move my arms and legs. These restraints are very tight. I think our best chance is when he takes us to the washroom to kick him in the head or groin." Stephanie whispered. It seems all the girls were whispering for fear he might be listening.

"What if he puts shackles on us when go out? We won't be able to kick him or punch him then. Although we might be able to get a good choke hold on him to render him unconscious." Samantha added.

"Yes --- that's good --- keep thinking. We also need to think what happens after. Say we knock him out. We need to restrain him quickly before he wakes up and if we are restrained we probably need to find a way to get out of our restraints --- a key, a hacksaw or something. When I was in the other room I noticed lots of tools on a bench --- and there are some stairs there that lead upstairs."

"We never saw this other room. When we woke up we were just strapped to these tables. There must be more rooms downstairs." Samantha confessed.

"That's good Samantha. You see we all know bits of information that could help us and save our lives. Did you notice anything in that other room Samantha?" Marianne was hoping there was something that could help them.

"I saw lots of strange things hanging on the walls and on the tables. I don't know what they were but they were not for anything nice. It looked like a dungeon --- although I've never seen one. There was a steel cage in the room --- big enough to hold several people or animals. I saw a couple of machine things in there too but I don't know what they do? They looked kind of medical --- like for a hospital or something? I saw a couple of power tools --- and there were drains on the floor. I saw three doors. Two at one end and one at the other end that leads here --- the other two doors I don't know where they go?" Samantha was excited and her whispering was getting slightly louder.

"That's good Samantha. The room I was in had a couch, table and some chairs. I checked and from what I could tell all the furniture is bolted or nailed to the floor. I couldn't even pick up a chair. There was also a large steel ring secured to the wall and I was attached to it by some kind of chain --- or rather wire --- an ankle shackle was clamped on me. I was sleeping on the couch when I first woke up and noticed the ankle shackle attached to me. I mentioned the stairs. This is important. I think that is the way out to the main floor of the house or building and would be the way to escape." Marianne was getting excited because now they had some hope --- faint hope but hope none the less.

"Is he alone mom? Is he working alone? Did you see or hear anyone else while you were in that room?" Stephanie chimed into the darkness of the room.

"I didn't see or hear anyone else. I believe he is working alone. We have to be aware of every little thing because it might be important. He'll be back down in a few hours or sooner so we have to always be prepared to act. I think the element of surprise is our best advantage. He doesn't know we all have years of Martial Arts training but that will only help us if we get the chance to use it."

The girls whispered for another couple of hours before they decided they better sleep so they were ready for tomorrow or whatever would come their way.

"No way he is taking my virginity mom!" Stephanie suddenly blurted out after ten minutes of silence.

"STAY ALIVE! That is the first thing. I know how you feel but remember to work as a team and to stay alive. We don't want him mad at us --- believe me when I say that. Now try to go to sleep. Good night luvs!"

"Good night mom," both girls said it at the same time.

"Try to sleep girls. Tomorrow is a big day. We're going to need all our strength. Remember to keep a cool head."

I woke up a few hours later. I jumped out of bed like it was the best day of my life. I wanted to go and say hi to my girls. I noticed I was still dressed in the same clothes. I must have been was so tired and excited that I didn't even take time to change. My headache was gone. I got dressed and hurried downstairs. I pretty much passed the main floor and went directly downstairs to see how my guests were doing. I moved the oil tank and turned on the lights in the corridor and opened the door to the first room. I turned the light on in the room and noticed all three girls were awake and looking at me. They must have heard me in the corridor.

"Why good-morning girls. I hope you slept well." I waited for a response but there was only silence. "When I speak you answer. Do you need more punishment?"

All three girls then replied reluctantly, "Good-morning."

"Well --- that's better. See --- that wasn't so difficult was it?" I pull the sheets off the girls.

"I have to go to the bathroom." Stephanie suddenly demanded.

"You'll have to wait Stephanie. I want to put coffee and tea on for you girls --- and myself."

"But I have to go really bad. It's been a long time and I have to go --- right now!"

I looked at her. She was gritting her teeth. She was up to something. It was easy to see on her face no matter how much she tried to disguise it. "Well --- if you really have to go now --- go ahead --- go." I smiled.

"Well --- untie me so I can go to the washroom."

"No --- you can go right now --- where you lay. Would you like me to take your pants off for you Stephanie? So you can go. Is it number one or number two? Do you need to piss or take a shit?" I walked over and picked up the scissors.

"NO --- I'll wait."

"Very well --- whatever you say Stephanie. Now does anyone want a tea --- or a coffee --- or a juice?" They all chose juice. "Okay --- I'll be right back with the juice."

Stephanie was in shock. She didn't expect that response from him. *He said he would let us shower and use the washroom for crying out loud.* Samantha spoke first.

"Seriously --- he expects us to shit on the table where we lay?"

"I think he might take us to the washroom soon. He was displaying his control over you Stephanie. You were pretty much demanding to be taken to the washroom. It is difficult but remember to use manners with him. I think that is what he expects. Hang in there and remember what we discussed last night."

Within five minutes he was back with the juice and an apple for each. He had straws for the juice and held each juice in turn so the slaves could drink. He held the apple for them to take a bit but they all refused.

"Okay, so you are probably wondering what is on for today. I will have a real breakfast for the three of you after the washroom shower break. As I mentioned each of you have gained this privilege but each will be escorted separately --- for your own safety --- and mine. And then I am having sex with all of you. You'll be nice and fresh and clean. And incidentally I saw the two of you practicing your Martial Arts kicks in front of that studio in town --- so I know you know Martial Arts --- just in case you were planning something." I stared at the twins and saw their surprise. "Didn't think I knew that did you?" I couldn't stop smiling. I love surprises. There was utter silence from all the girls. "Were you thinking of a surprise for me during the washroom escort? Well --- here's another surprise --- I have been practicing Martial Arts for years --- all the disciplines including Brazilian *Jiu-jitsu*. I find it comes in very handy at times --- don't you?" The girls didn't answer. "That was very smart of you Marianne to get your daughters to train in the Martial Arts."

"Well --- they're just beginners really." Marianne tried to say convincingly.

"Oh --- just beginners are they? They didn't look like beginners to me. And so I checked and discovered they have participated in some tournaments." Again I heard nothing but crickets in the room.

"I have a question for you Stephanie. That girl you and Samantha met in front of the Martial Arts Centre --- what was her name?"

"What girl?" She rolled her eyes at me. She really has a problem rolling her eyes but I'll fix that.

"The red-head that was with you at the car --- out front." I waited. *I could see her thinking what should she say?*

"Oh --- that girl --- I think you mean Melanie?"

"Oh --- so her name was Melanie?"

"I believe that's who you mean."

"Uh --- huh." I stared at her and felt my face turning red at the lie. I walked around and stopped and leaned down to look directly in her eyes. She stared back in defiance --- and in fear. "You are lying to me. Now you are going to be severely punished Stephanie."

"Her name is Tabitha --- I think that is who you mean --- not Melanie." Samantha was trying to rescue her sister.

I turned to look at Samantha and smiled. "Yes --- that's better. Thank you Samantha. I'm glad you tell the truth. And what is this Tabitha's last name Samantha?"

"Her last name is Cahill. Her name is Tabitha Cahill."

I shake my head in approval. "And that man she is living with --- is that her man?"

"No, she's living with her brother for the time being. Why do you ask about her? Are you interested in her?"

"I don't know her and I'm not interested in her. I just saw the three of you together and at first wondered if she was perhaps your older sister. I didn't know who she was so I checked. Good thing she wasn't your sister or I would have needed another table --- wouldn't I?" I lied about not knowing Tabitha's name.

"I was wondering when we might have our washroom break?" Marianne asked.

"Yes --- I imagine you need to use the washroom. Soon but first I need a punishment for Stephanie for her lie. That is disrespectful Stephanie. I don't like liars. Hmm --- what should I do? Your lovely sister did kind of bail you out but I can't let that go -- the not telling me the truth without a punishment." I waited for her response.

"I didn't mean to tell a lie --- I was mistaken. Melanie is another girl."

"Oh Stephanie --- every time you open your mouth you just get trapped deeper and deeper. You just lied again to me. You know whom I meant. I now know what your punishment shall be --- although it is hardly a real punishment. You'll be first after breakfast. I'll have to think of a second punishment for the second lie you told me."

I walked to the tray and picked up the scissors and went back to Stephanie. I looked at Stephanie's eyes that suddenly seemed as big as saucers. I smiled. I moved to her splayed legs and began removing her shoes. I bent down and smelled her cute feet --- white socks and all. The socks had little flowers on them. Very becoming for the deflowering of a virgin.

The room was loud with shouting from all three girls but I expected that --- and I welcomed it. Stephanie was really struggling as I cut her pants slowly, ever so slowly.

"Hey --- you should take it easy Stephanie --- I might cut you by accident. We wouldn't want that now would we?"

She had great legs --- like her sister. So smooth and muscular but slim as well --- such soft blonde hairs on her legs. She and her sister would look great in heels. In no time I had her panties off. Ah --- they were almost the same as her sisters --- how cute. Just a slightly different shade of pinkish white and she had butterflies on her panties. I smiled and I could see a real fire in her eyes. I leaned forward to her face and whispered,

"Fight me --- I love it when they fight me. Don't worry --- you're going to be first after your morning shower."

S oon all three girls were without clothes.

"First, I promised you all a washroom and shower break before breakfast. So we will do that now. I know Stephanie complained that she really needed to go to the washroom but I see in her eyes she is still quite angry --- and she did lie to me so she will go last. I will take Samantha first. She has been the most cooperative and respectful. I will take each of you separately to the washroom. You will have fifteen minutes and I will give you your privacy. I will be outside the door waiting with a timer. I will tell you when your fifteen minutes is up and if you are late I will punish one of you. Even though I said I wouldn't cut or bruise you know that there are many other ways I can cause great pain. So far you haven't experienced that. They can be really quite --- gruesome. The washroom is well stocked with anything you may need. There is nothing in there that could be used as a weapon though. You will walk to the washroom in front of me --- naked. After you have finished there are three white, fleeced bathrobes that you may wear on the walk back to this room. Just a second --- I need to get something first."

I walk over to one of the stainless steel cabinets and take out a key and unlock the cabinet. I reach up and remove a handgun. I make sure it is clearly visible to the girls. I can tell instantly they are nervous. The exact reaction I wanted.

"Try not to worry. This is a Glock 17 Generation 4 gun. It's loaded with hollow point bullets. They are better at stopping a threat. The bullet spreads out upon impact and exits the body taking a sizable piece of flesh and bone with it." *Well --- that certainly worked well as an attitude adjustment. What is the saying? "Look at their faces --- Priceless!"* "We aren't going to have any trouble though are we girls?"

Marianne answered for her daughters as all eyes are upon the gun. "No Master --- no trouble at all."

"Good! Then lets begin."

I walk over to Samantha and pull on her right wrist restraint and unfasten the buckle. Her one wrist is free.

"Samantha --- free your other wrist and then your legs and sit up. Listen carefully for my instructions."

Samantha frees her left wrist and then rubs her hands over her wrists to soothe them. Then she bends forward and unbuckles the leg restraints. She uses her hands to massage her ankles where the restraints were. She looks at me --- obviously afraid.

"Good job Samantha. Now swing your legs to your left and get off the table and stand by the table." She does as she is instructed. "Good --- now walk to the door over there," I point with the gun, "and open the door. There will be a short corridor leading to another exit. Go. I will be a short distance behind." I turn to the others and smile. "We'll be back in about fifteen minutes."

As Samantha walks by her mom they exchange looks. Samantha is the perfect good girl. She does only what is asked --- no more and no less. When we get to the end of the corridor I tell her to "Just push" and the wall opens. We step out and are at the oil tank. She sees the entrance is disguised.

"Turn right and then turn right again at the corner. Walk towards the yellow light. That is where the washroom is." She walks but keeps turning her head to look back. "Keep your eyes straight ahead Samantha." I can't help but watch her beautiful ass wiggle as she walks in front of me. I notice I am getting aroused.

We come to a light brown door that is already open for her.

"Go in the washroom Samantha. You may close the door --- it doesn't lock. Your fifteen minutes starts now. Make good use of it."

She watches me as I sit down in a chair that I place a few feet from the entrance, all the time keeping the Glock in my hand. She goes in and closes the door.

Back at the room the two girls are talking. Marianne tells Stephanie, "Stephanie --- there is no way he is letting us go. He is planning to kill us. Sorry to scare you but you need to know."

"I figured that out mom. He is planning on having sex with us first. We have to try and do something and do it now."

"Yes --- I know. We need to be careful but this shower and breakfast time may be our best chance to do something. We need to do it fast. I worry that after he is finished with us what he will do to us. He tried to murder me all those years ago and I have no doubt that is what he has planned for us."

Once inside Samantha instantly is searching the room. There are no windows and really no way to escape. She quickly searches the cabinet for anything she might use for a weapon or for her escape. Her mind is racing. Two minutes later there is a knock on the door.

"Thirteen minutes left Samantha. Just letting you know."

She turns to look at the door. She hops in the shower and has a very quick, nervous shower. She dries off and pees but is really too nervous to use the washroom. She finds a new white bathrobe and puts it on. There are three new hairbrushes still in the package on the counter. She opens one and brushes her wet hair and suddenly she jumps when she hears another knock on the door.

"Five minutes left Samantha."

"Okay Master." She calls back. *Shit! There is nothing here that is of any use. Damn! Maybe the hairbrush but that is about it.* She knocks on the door and calls out. "I'm done --- I'm opening the door and coming out --- okay?"

"Come out then Samantha."

She opens the door and sees him standing there --- the gun still in his hand.

"You're early. You still have three minutes left. Do you want to use them?"

"No thank you. I'm done. I would really like to stretch my legs. I have been --- we have been restrained for a lot of hours. Would it be all right for me to just walk around a bit and stretch? *Please say yes --- I want to look in this room and see if there is anything here I can use?*

"No --- maybe later at breakfast. The others are waiting. Walk back and I will follow."

As she walks back she tries to memorize everything she sees along the way for future reference. *You never know when something might be useful.* She retraces her steps trying to walk slower without it being noticeable but all too soon they are at the oil tank. Her mind is racing. There seems to be nothing she can do. It seems in an instant they are back in the room. As soon as she enters, her sister --- the one with the big mouth speaks. Both mother and sister release a big sigh of relief.

"Any trouble Sis?"

"Silence! I did not give you permission to speak slave!"

Instantly Stephanie is silent as she lays on the table. Her eyes turn away and she gulps. "Sorry Master," is all she says in a tiny whisper.

I try to get my calm back. There is silence in the room and there is a definite tension that can be felt. Samantha has been waiting patiently but when I look I see a worried look on her face.

"I'm okay --- don't worry." I take a big breath.

"Samantha --- climb on the table and fasten you ankle restraints first and then your right wrist restraint. I will secure the last one. You may keep the bathrobe on."

She does as she is told but needs reminding to make sure the restraints are tight enough. She thinks, *Shit! I was hoping I could make the restraints somewhat loose. Must find a way to escape.* She tightens them --- reluctantly.

I tell her to put her left hand up where the last restraint is waiting. When she does I move forward and secure the last restraint. I check her restraints to make sure they are secure. They are.

"Good --- one down and two to go." I walk over to Marianne and put the gun down off to the side. I can see all eyes are upon me. "Remember I said that all of you will walk to the washroom naked --- myself included." I admire her body. She takes good care of herself. There aren't many almost forty years olds with a body as sexy as that. "You're next Marianne."

"Permission to speak."

"Granted."

"Could my daughter Stephanie go first? She really needs to go and I can wait."

I look over at Stephanie. She is looking at me.

"No --- you're next and she will be last --- if she goes at all. I haven't decided yet. I'll do the same with you Marianne. I will release the left wrist restraint and you use that hand to unbuckle the right wrist and then your two ankle restraints." With the gun in one hand I free her left wrist by pulling on the restraint. Then I step back as she slowly frees her other limbs. She too is rubbing her wrists and ankles where the restraint was. "Swing your feet out to the right and sit up and wait." She does as instructed. "Stand up and wait Marianne." She stands and waits. I stare and admire her hourglass figure. She is more voluptuous than her daughters. Her breasts have grown bigger. Her daughters look spectacular too but they are athletic whereas Marianne looks like a divine feminine figure. "Walk to the door and follow my instructions exactly."

She turns to look at her daughters and they at her --- then starts walking. Marianne is walking and notices he is walking about six or seven feet behind with the gun. At the oil tank she notices it is a hidden entrance. She had no idea even though she is now entering the same room she woke up in all those hours ago. She sees the workbench off to her left and tries to memorize what is on it without being obvious.

"Keep walking and turn right at the corner and head for the yellow light. That is where the washroom is."

"Yes Master," is her only reply.

She looks at the stairs and wonders where they lead? Are they the steps to possible freedom? She then sees the couch she woke up on and notices the ring on the wall. *Where is the wire he used?* She turns right and keeps walking towards the yellow light. Her eyes are looking left and right searching for anything that might give her hope --- and a chance. Then they are at the doorway.

I watch her ass walking in front of me. What a spectacular ass. It jiggles just right each time she steps. She has a great body. Her legs look quite powerful. She looks magnificent walking in front of me. I'm definitely aroused --- and dripping. She has had quite the effect on me.

"Stop --- here is the washroom. You may go in and you will have fifteen minutes. You may close the door --- it doesn't lock. There is a white bathrobe for you after you are showered. Your time starts now."

She turns and notices my erection. She stares at it --- and then stares into my eyes.

"Don't worry Marianne --- I'm not going to fuck you just yet."

She goes in and closes the door. Instantly she is looking --- searching but the bathroom is quite spartan. She opens each nook and cranny but nothing. She sighs --- she is desperate. She hears a knock on the door and his voice.

"You have thirteen minutes left."

She takes a quick pee but no bathroom break for her. She hasn't eaten in hours anyway. She turns the shower on so it warms up and showers and shampoos quickly. It feels good but she can't stop thinking about how to escape and save her daughters. She steps out of the shower onto the mat and grabs the fluffy towel and dries herself. She puts on a bathrobe from the cupboard. She grabs another towel and rubs and dries her hair. *Not even a hair dryer is supplied.* She opens a package with the hairbrush and brushes her hair --- her eyes still searching the room for something --- anything. Then she hears a knock on the door.

"Two minutes Marianne. Don't be late."

"Yes Master." *Shit! Now what? This isn't turning out so good.*

A minute later she opens the door and he is standing there --- gun in his hand. He's smiling at her --- staring at her. He still has his erection. She walks out --- faced flushed and he backs up. She turns left and begins walking.

"Why do you have the towel on your head? You don't need the towel Marianne. Get rid of it."

"Sorry Master." She takes the towel off her head and drops it to the floor and keeps walking slowly.

He bends down to pick it up. In an instant she turns, pivots and she begins the delivery of a magnificent but powerful left shin kick right to his jaw. He reacts and fires the gun. A loud blast echoes in every room of the house, including the room the girls are in.

Stephanie and Samantha look at each other in fear. Then they turn to the doorway that is still partially open.

"MOM! MOM! MOM! MOM!" They scream out in unison. They strain to see out the door but obviously can't.

"MOM! MOM! Can you hear me? Are you all right? MOM!" Samantha screams out. They hear nothing.

"That bastard killed Mom Samantha screams." They are beside themselves with grief. They struggle violently but can barely move.

"Oh MOM!" Stephanie is bawling. Samantha is screaming.

Then they hear a noise and turn to look at the doorway.

"It's him --- he's come to kill us," Stephanie screams out.

CHAPTER 31

Suddenly Marianne bursts into the room with the gun in her hand. "MOM --- you're alive --- what happened? Are you all right? We thought he killed you. Where is he? Did you shoot him? Is he dead?" Stephanie gasps out between her near hyperventilating breaths.

"I'm all right." She runs forward and undoes Stephanie's one wrist strap. "Quick --- free yourself and then quickly free you Sister. Find the zip ties. I think I remember he kept them in that drawer over there. Then bring them to me."

Stephanie began freeing herself quickly but then they both yelled out, "No Mom --- don't leave us --- stay here," but she was gone. "MOM! MOM!"

Marianne ran back to the spot where Lucas lay on the ground completely knocked out. She was fortunate she didn't get shot when the gun went off. After he fell she delivered several hard head stomps with her heel. He was bloody and he was out cold. She held the gun to his head --- ready to fire --- thinking about firing but she didn't. Her daughters meanwhile were now free and rushed out of the room to find Mom and see what happened. They stood there --- Samantha in the bathrobe and Stephanie still naked. They saw Mom and rushed over to her. They also saw him --- out cold on the floor. They hugged each other but then Mom spoke.

"Okay girls --- first we need to tie him up and make sure he can't hurt us. Did you find the plastic zip ties?"

Samantha answered," Yea, we brought the whole bag out but why don't you just shoot him Mom?"

"Shoot him Mom! Kill that bastard!" Stephanie added with eyes filled with disdain. "Or I can shoot him if you want?"

"No darling. I didn't shoot him. I kicked him in the head. I thought about shooting him. Believe me I thought about it. Take a few zip ties and tie his wrists behind his back good." The girls did as their Mother told them. His hands were securely restrained behind his back.

"Okay --- let's drag him over to the couch. We can find that wire restraint he used on me and put it around his neck and then zip tie his ankles together. Then call for help."

They moved him to the couch. Then Marianne rummaged the workbench and found the wire and ankle restraint. She brought it over and secured it to the wall and the restraint to his neck. The girls hadn't put the ties on his ankles yet.

Steph, you run back to the washroom and get yourself a bathrobe. Sam, you go back to the table room and get our shoes. We're going to need them when we leave."

While the girls were gone Marianne stared down at the man and fantasized what she would like to do him. Both girls returned at the same time to witness Kyle lying semi-conscious on the floor face down, his legs spread wide open. Marianne, in bare feet was standing on his family jewels. Her powerful, beautiful calf muscles flexing as she raised up on her pretty toes. She twisted slowly and cruelly on them as they ground into the floor under her full weight. They were trapped and there was nowhere for them to go --- except down. They were getting flatter and flatter with each merciless twist. *He deserved it. It was payback time.*

"Mom," Samantha breathed out. Samantha and Stephanie's eyes were wide open.

"Oh, sorry girls. I just want to punish him."

Just then the girls returned to see their mom standing near the man --- staring down at him. She was still daydreaming.

"Mom --- you okay?" Stephanie asked. "Your mind seems to be somewhere else?"

Marianne came out of her trance like state when she heard her daughters. "Huh? Oh --- you're back girls. Yea --- I'm okay. Um --- let's secure the zip tie to his ankles before he wakes up. Then find out where those stairs lead? We have to call the police and get the hell out of here."

"We should just kill him mom. Shoot him for what he did to you --- for what he's done to us. He's an animal. He doesn't deserve to live." Samantha looked at her mom.

"No darling. We have to think of the other girls he's killed. And I am sure there are others. We have to think of their families. And he needs to face them --- and the police for what he has done. Maybe he will tell the families where their loved ones are buried? We have to think about that. They would want to know that."

Mom looked at her daughters with sad eyes. She couldn't tell them. She didn't want them to ever know the great secret she hid in her heart. That this man, this evil man lying on the floor was in fact their father. Her daughters were the only good things about that terrible day two decades ago when he raped and tortured her and left her for dead. That when she found out she was pregnant with his children her first thought was to commit suicide but she couldn't. Then she thought about having an abortion but couldn't. How she thought about giving them up for adoption but she couldn't do that either. Especially after holding them for the first time --- and seeing those two little faces looking up at her. She would keep them for her own. And she would never tell them who their real father was. They were her kids and she would protect them forever. When they were lying on the table she almost yelled it out --- hoping that maybe that would stop him but she realized even that probably wouldn't stop him. He probably wouldn't believe her anyway. No, she would take this secret to her grave. It was heavy on her heart but her girls must always believe that the man John Smythe that she was married to for only a few short years was their father. Dark secrets --- we all have them lurking in our shadows and they can burden us through the years.

"It's time to leave!" Marianne called to her daughters. They checked his zip-tied ankles and wrists before they left.

Up the stairs they went, all the while not knowing what to expect. He lived alone --- or so it seemed. They found the phone and tried to call but couldn't. The phone required some kind of code or password to call out. They raided the fridge and grabbed some water and fruit to go --- and some chocolate bars. They saw their purses on the kitchen table and gathered their purses. They peered about their surroundings nervously. This was a house of death. They noticed the time --- it was afternoon --- they hurried outside. They saw three vehicles. They found the key in one of the vehicles --- a pickup truck. They started it up not knowing where they were going. They followed the driveway and came to a locked gate. Shit!

"Just slam through!" Samantha tried to convince her Mom.

"There's two extra key on the key chain. I'll try that first. Keep an eye out." Marianne got out of the car carrying the gun and one of the keys fit. She unlocked the gate and drove to the end of the driveway. In both directions there were no signs of neighbours that they could see. They just noticed all the No Trespassing signs. "Which way girls --- left or right?"

"Who cares? Just drive and get out of here," Stephanie answered.

Within a mile they came to another farmhouse, this one visible from the road. They saw two kids playing out the front and a man and lady there. Marianne told her daughters, "Let's hope they have a phone."

The three girls sat at the kitchen table --- Marianne had the gun by her side. She wasn't ready to give it up yet. The kids were told to play outside. The lady and man sat inside with Marianne, Stephanie, and Samantha at the table. They were drinking tea and the couple made soup and sandwiches --- which might seem strange but the three were starving. The police arrived about forty-five minutes later and knocked on the door and the man got up to let them in. The police came in and listened to their story. These things just don't happen in their county --- or that's what they thought. Each girl was taken into a different room and several police officers listened.

The lead officer spoke over the walkie-talkie. "Men --- go to the house and surround it. I've been informed the man is inside and restrained with zip ties downstairs. There may be others so be extremely careful. We aren't quite sure what we are dealing with here beyond a kidnapper and rapist. The F.B.I. is sending agents as well. I also want two police cruisers blocking the road both ways a mile in each direction."

The neighbours told the officers who the man was and what little they knew about him even though he had lived there a number or years.

The lead officer called into headquarters. "Check the data base and send me everything you have on a Kyle Krycanta. He has at least one car, a 2015 Ford F-150 pickup truck --- licence number DDT 669."

"You say he is restrained downstairs --- is that correct." The lead officer asked Marianne.

"When we left him he was restrained with zip ties and some kind of shackle thing that he used on me. He should be in the basement."

"I'll need a description --- the schematics of the interior of the house and anything else you can help us with. Do you need to go to the hospital? I can get a medical team here before you go?"

"I think we are okay but a medical team is a good idea.

A call came over the radio; "This is Officer Lewis --- requesting a medical team immediately. Sending you the location now. Get a medical helicopter here ASAP."

"Roger that." The voice on the other end replied.

"Now tell us everything you know about this guy --- what he did --- when --- how long you have known him. When did all this happen?" Then he yelled out to another officer, "Get me a couple of female officers in here now. Burns and Schell --- tell them I want them to come here." He then turned back to Marianne and said, "You'll probably talk and feel better talking to female officers."

Two female officers entered the room and were introduced. The male officers left the room.

Marianne took a deep breath and sigh and then said, "Let's see --- where should I begin? Well --- it started a long time ago --- twenty years ago in fact …"

CHAPTER 32

A convoy of police cars and S.W.A.T. vehicles drove down the long drive-way to the farmhouse. Three police cars parked at the entrance. The police quickly had the house surrounded. There seemed to be two entrances to the house --- a front door and a back door. Officers in full gear set up quickly --- bunkering down with guns and scopes scanning the house for any movement. The attack was coordinated over the police radio.

"Get ready --- when I say we move we all go in. Suspect may be downstairs but take no chances." Officer Sandstorm was in charge of the team. They all watched the house with guns zeroed and waited for the signal.

When the signal was given the Officers advanced to the doors and then gunfire erupted. They stopped and dropped trying to protect themselves. Then a barrage of gunfire was returned to the house. Windows smashed as bullets flew at every wall and window in the house. After thirty seconds the gunfire stopped.

"He's got some kind of automatic assault rifle. He's firing on us. Take cover --- repeat --- take cover."

"Anyone hit --- anybody down? Report." Came over radio.

"Team One --- no one hit, Team Two --- no one hit, Team Three --- we're okay here Sir, Team Four --- two down Sir. Chuck is in the grass --- can't get to him. Can't tell if he is alive --- he's not moving and isn't responding to our calls. Mike was hit too but he's okay. Hit in the shoulder area. Sir --- the bullets pierced the vest. Repeat --- suspect has armour piercing shells."

"Shit! We need to get Mike. We can't leave him there. He needs help." Officer Sandstorm grabbed the megaphone and yelled, "You in the house. This is the Police. You are completely surrounded. Drop all weapons and come out of the house with your hands raised."

Nothing --- no response.

"This is your last chance. If you don't come out we are going to release the teargas."

"Fuck You!" A male voice responded from inside. "You aren't taking me alive. "I'll kill any cop who comes close. I'll kill every one of you fucking bastards. Come and get me pigs."

A few seconds later tear gas canisters were shot through the windows and gas fumes spewed in the interior of the house. Coughing sounds could be heard from inside --- and then a few seconds later one loud gunshot. All the officers outside heard it and slumped further down for extra cover. A few seconds later fire erupted in the house from several flashpoints. The place was rigged and booby-trapped with explosives and fireballs and explosions were suddenly everywhere.

"Call for fire-trucks --- we've got a hell of a fire going here," Sandstrom ordered the call Officer.

Team Four ran in during the chaos and recovered Officer Mike. He was alive but not looking good. Both Officer Mike and Chuck were rushed to the hospital in the back of a cruiser. No waiting for an ambulance.

There were huge explosions every few seconds from the house. Suddenly the van ignited and exploded --- not from the proximity to the house but from a timed remote. That sent Officers to withdraw back further away from the vehicles. Suddenly the car exploded sending officers even further back for safety.

"Stay away from the barn and vehicles men. The place looks like it's booby-trapped --- be careful."

In no time the entire house was a blazing inferno. Flames shot high and smoke filled the sky darkening it. A black plume of deep charcoal clouds billowed above the flames.

As Officers stood by helpless except to watch, Officer Green stood beside Sandstrom. "Well --- there goes that guy --- and anyone else who was in the house Sir."

"Yea --- fuck --- and most of the evidence. I can feel the heat all the way over here. Man, that's hot. There must be chemicals or oxygen tanks or something in there --- to burn like that."

When the F.B.I arrived they could do nothing but stand by and watch the house burn. There was nothing else to do for now --- except watch it burn --- and wait.

Fire trucks showed up an hour after the alarm was sent in. That's the response time when you live in the country. When it was safe they fought the fire for hours --- going back to the closest pond on the farm and using that water to continue fighting the fire.

The F.B.I Agent in charge, Agent Miller was talking with Officer Sandstrom.

"The fire team is going to be fighting this fire for hours. It's a big one. It will be several hours before we can go in. No one is going to survive this one. I have called for a special forensic team and they will be here shortly. It's going to take a long time before we can go in --- depending on the structure and after burn."

Sandstrom was chewing gum. He was always chewing gum. It was his trademark. "Yea --- it's going to be one long night --- that's for sure."

They both stared at the fire --- watching it slowly devour the house. "I've been briefed about the three girls --- I've got agents interviewing them now and we are coordinating with your officers --- sharing our information. It's likely from what I'm hearing this guy has been doing this for years --- perhaps decades. I've sent agents out to check the area for anything suspicious. We've already found a large incinerator about a quarter mile back from here."

Sandstrom turned to Miller. "An incinerator huh? I didn't notice any farm animals."

"We've checked and are still checking but our information is that this farm hasn't had any livestock on it for a few decades. We are trying to track down when the incinerator was purchased and by who."

A call came for Agent Miller. "Sir --- we found something."

"What'd you find Watson?"

"We have what looks like a fairly fresh grave here back near one of the outbuildings. We've marked it off and are going to check it after checking the area for evidence."

"Okay Watson --- keep me informed --- over."

"Roger that Sir."

"Fuck!" Was all Sandstrom could say after hearing about the incinerator and the grave.

"I have teams checking the farm but it's a big farm. It's two hundred plus acres I believe. That's a lot of real estate to check. I've also ordered some special equipment and a team to check for anything buried on the farm. It can check what's under the ground without digging."

Sandstrom was numb. He'd been around but in all his years had never seen anything like this. "You know Agent Miller --- I got a feeling about this place --- and it isn't good."

"Me too!"

Then they both continued watching the flames. Darkness was fast approaching. It was going to be one hell of a long night.

By mornings dawn the fire had burnt much of what was left to burn --- or so it seemed. Water was still being doused across the charred building and smoke was still rising --- this time more of a white smoke. It would still be a few hours before they could go in. The embers were still hot and the place would have to be checked for structural integrity --- not that much was left standing.

Miller and Sandstrom were sipping a morning coffee that was delivered and eating some kind of sandwich. It was supposed to be a breakfast sandwich. It wasn't very good but it was warm at least.

Miller spoke between a sip. "That grave turned out empty."

"That's good. But then why is there a grave? Maybe he moved the body? Or he planned to bury the three Wynne's there."

"Yea --- that would be my guess. We're still looking out there. The forensic teams can go in the house and start sifting through the rubble in a few hours."

"Probably not going to find much --- after a fire like that." Sandstrom added.

"Oh --- we'll find things. We always do. The team is pretty good and you'd be surprised what we might find. It's interesting work but it's also scary work."

"Scary?" Sandstrom looked at Miller.

"If there are kids. That's the worst."

"GOD --- don't think I'd want that job. My job can be tough enough."

Miller looked at Sandstrom. He understood what he meant.

A few hours later the Fire Marshall and team gave the okay. It was safe to enter the building. You just had to be careful. The upper and main level floors were completely gutted. There was no roof. It was first to go. The walls were pretty much gone except for some stone structure that looked starched and cooked from the flames.

The forensic team went in first. There was about twelve of them. Sandford watched them go in.

"They're going to be a few hours," Miller spoke sipping his coffee. Sandstrom nodded back.

"I'm going to send the Swat and some team members home. I don't think we're going to find anyone --- alive that is."

Miller nodded to Sandstrom. "You feel like taking a drive. Like I said, we got a few hours. We could go and check out the farm --- see how the other Agents are doing --- if they found anything?"

"Yea --- sounds good."

They did the rounds but nothing to report so far. It was early though. Miller when he saw the ponds wanted them drained and checked. He wanted the river area checked as well and the forest areas. It was a big job. A couple of hours later the two were driving back to the farmhouse when a call came for Miller.

"Miller here."

"Sir --- this is Agent Dryfuss --- we think you should see this."

"You find something Dryfuss?"

"Oh yea, finding lots of stuff but Sir --- you really should see this."

"Well be right there."

Sandstrom looked at Miller. He wanted to see too!

"Yea --- you can come. We just can't touch anything and we have to be careful where we step." Sandstrom nodded. "I'd better get us some boots. It's going to be messy down there. They got the boots and walked to the house and went down some makeshift stairs. The old stairs were gone. Agent Dryfuss was there to meet them.

"This is Sandstrom Dryfuss --- Dryfuss this is Sandstrom." They exchanged a brief nice to meet you greet. Dryfuss was wearing his usual gloves for the job. "So --- what'd ya find Dryfuss?"

"Better if you see for yourself Sir. Walk where I walk. It's good the Wynne ladies told us about this oil tank and secret hidden entrance. It would have been very difficult to find without their help."

The walked over to the old oil tank which was pulled away from the wall and walked to the first room --- with the three tables in it.

"Holy shit! Sandford stared. Miller was quiet.

"There are a few rooms Sir --- follow me. Don't go over there." He pointed to another exit. We found out they're booby-trapped?"

Miller asked Dryfuss, "How come this place isn't burnt down? It looks like it was hardly touched by the fire."

"At some time this whole area was fireproofed. It's basically all stone. Follow me Sir."

They walked through another short hallway and came to another room that was filled with lots of hanging tools. They weren't your regular hanging tools but to an expert it was easy to see they were made for another purpose --- torture.

"Holy Fuck!" Miller uttered staring around the room. Now it was his turn to be shocked. Sandstrom just looked in disbelief.

"There's more Sir --- follow me."

At the end of the room was another hallway. Dryfuss pointed to a marked off area and said, "Don't go down there --- another booby-trap."

They entered a third room and it was some sort of storage room --- filled with canisters and barrels and bags --- lots of --- stuff.

"Is this what I think it is Dryfuss?"

"Yes Sir --- lye, ether, taxidermy stuff and more. The guy must have had a background in chemistry? And some of the drums are full of blood. I suspect human blood but we will need to run tests."

"Good GOD! What's this machine?"

Dryfuss answered, "That Sir is a blood pumping machine --- it drains blood from the body."

"Holy Shit! Fuck me! Sandstrom gasped out.

Dryfuss turned to both men. "One more room --- you had better brace yourself Sir. Follow me."

Dryfuss turned to Sandstrom, "You may not want to see whatever is in here Sandstrom."

"No --- I want to see. I need to see."

They followed Dryfuss and swung a black door open. Inside were two agents snapping pictures.

"HOLY FUCK! NO GOD DAMN WAY!" Sandstrom yelled out. His face turned white.

Miller just looked in shock.

"There are fifteen of them Sir. They are all stuffed --- they've been taxidermied."

"Unfucking believable!" Miller swallowed.

"They all have name cards in front of them Sir. Like they were posed as an exhibit in a museum."

Inside, sitting in chairs, like they were at some kind of sick tea party were fifteen girls --- dressed nicely and sort of looking like they were still alive.

Dryfuss spoke, "Pretty twisted Sir --- even in my experience. These first four look old --- like they've been here a long time. The others are newer. Some I can recognize from our search list. Sir --- this one here --- do you recognize her --- the name?"

Both men looked and their jaws dropped.

Dryfuss said what both Agent Miller and Officer Sandstrom already knew. "That one there is that Police Officer that went missing last October. They found her abandoned van at the mall parking lot with her kid inside."

"Shit --- Officer Bello --- yea --- I remember. They found the son in the car but he was all right. Man --- this is going to be tough for a lot of people. This guy was one sick bastard."

"Over here Sir you'll see three empty chairs. The chairs already have name cards ready for the next intended victims."

Agent Miller and Officer Sandstrom saw the names on the cards, Marianne, Stephanie, and Samantha Wynne.

"They were extremely fortunate they didn't end up here Sir," Agent Dryfuss added.

Sandstrom suddenly cried out, "I have to leave this room --- I can't breath --- I have to leave --- now."

"Okay Sandstrom. You'll be okay. I'll walk you out."

As they walked out and were finally outside the house it was easy to see Sandstrom was still having a hard time. He wasn't used to seeing first hand something like this. Miller sat him down and sat beside him.

"Easy Sandstrom --- we'll contact the families and police force. We'll take care of the publicity. It's what we do." Sandstrom just nodded.

Another Agent approached Miller. "Sir --- we found a body. We are pretty sure it's him. He's burnt bad --- not much left of him. Looks like he shot himself in the face before the fire took hold. He has no teeth. We have forensics working on it and will let you know in a few days what we find."

Miller nodded. "Thank you Agent Watt."

"I'm going to have a medic check you over Sandstrom. You don't look so good. You look pretty pale."

Sandstrom just nodded as he stared back at the house.

A few days later, forensics confirmed the body in the house died of a gunshot wound to the face --- a 12-gauge shotgun blast to the mouth, before being consumed by the fire. There wasn't much to work with and identifying the corpse would be tough but not impossible. They also found a lot of firearms --- some burnt up and some in fireproof safes --- along with gas masks --- grenades --- night vision goggles and other military stuff.

The family was contacted --- the three sisters. They were called in by the F.B.I. and met with three agents in a recording room.

"Hello --- thanks for coming. I wish we were meeting under different circumstances. I'm Agent Miller of the F.B.I. and this is Agent Taylor of the F.B.I. This is Officer Harris of the police force." They shook hands. Harris was there more as a courtesy.

"Thank you. I am Sandra, this is Kera, and this is Kristen." They all sat down.

"Thank you for coming. I know this is a difficult time for everyone but we need to ask you some questions."

"Yes, we understand. We want to help as much as we can." Sandra answers.

"Thank you. When was the last time you talked or had contact with Kyle?" Officer Williams was asking the questions.

The girls looked at each somewhat bewildered. "For me --- it's been a long time --- a year and a half I guess?" Sandra wasn't sure.

Kera answered, "By phone --- maybe a year ago Christmas?"

Kristine added, "Long time for me too --- last summer --- June I think --- by phone."

"So none of you have had any real contact with Kyle for a while? Nothing recent?"

"No --- we haven't been close for a lot of years. Kyle changed --- especially after our parents died. His brother is much closer to us. Kyle changed though." Sandra was looking at her sisters who were nodding in agreement.

"His brother?"

"Yes, his brother. We tried contacting him but haven't heard back yet."

"Kyle has a brother --- older or younger?"

"Older --- by about twenty-five minutes."

The Officers stared at the sisters dumbfounded.

"Kyle and Luc are twins --- identical twins. They were close until they were about --- um --- fifteen or so I believe --- then Kyle starting changing. Luc was way more friendly and easier to get along with. Kyle won the lottery years ago and bought the farm. After that he changed even more."

The three officers looked at each other --- shocked.

"You didn't know Kyle was a twin? That he had a twin brother?" Kera asked.

"No ma'am, we did not --- and identical you say? Now that is interesting. Luc? Is that short for Lucas?"

"Yea --- we tried contacting Lucas but we haven't seen or heard from him in maybe two weeks?" All the sisters nodded. "That's not usual. He usually talks to us at least once a week. We are all worried about him."

"So it was Kyle that owns the farmhouse?"

"Yea." The three sisters answered together.

The three officers stared at each other in silence. They were confused. Which twin was responsible for the kidnapping and murders? Marianne had said it was Kyle but the sisters said Lucas had disappeared? And Kyle owned the farm. Maybe it was both of the brothers?

When the police found out Kyle was a twin the investigation went in an entirely different direction. They could not find the brother Lucas. He was missing and nowhere to be found.

Agent Miller spoke to his team a few days later.

"There is some new information on the suspect Kyle Krycanta. We know he had an identical twin brother --- one Lucas Krycanta who is still missing. Now this Kyle may have killed the brother? He may not have? And maybe the brother just took off somewhere to get away on vacation? Or maybe the two were working together? We believe the body we found at the farmhouse was Kyle? We're still waiting for D.N.A. findings. The suspect's bank accounts and financial holdings were emptied out a few weeks ago. We are tracing where the money might have gone but so far nothing. The money trail seems to have vanished. The amount was substantial --- millions of dollars. We know that. We are working on an exact figure. In the meantime we are going to issue a warrant for Lucas --- or Kyle --- until we can figure out what the hell happened? We found a very disturbing diary in a chest in the restraint room. I'm going to read some of it to you right now.

Diary:

To all you girls out there – you have no idea how close many of you have come – like Gail and so many other girls - close without even knowing – without even being aware that "WE" were there – "WE" are out there – watching you --- patiently waiting for our time together – You have no idea Evil Never Dies

Lucas

"I noticed the diary used the WE phrase several times Sir. Sounds like this Kyle and Lucas might have been working together?" One of the agents added.

"We just don't know at this time if they were? We have a lot of questions and no answers so get working men. We need answers." Agent Miller responded.

CHAPTER 33

It was exactly three weeks later at the farm that the F.B.I. discovered something else. They were finding bodies --- lots of bodies --- in the ponds --- in the forest --- in the fields. So far seventy-three bodies and there was a certainty there would be many more. They were really just beginning to dig and there was a lot of acreage still to be searched. A few of the bodies were old and had been buried for a long time. There were a lot of Jane Does. Analysis confirmed they were all female except nine were male. There was still more work to be done. The incinerator was a tough one. The forensic scientists were struggling to find any traces of identifiable D.N.A. of any kind. There were no bones or teeth present. That had to mean the incinerator was cleaned out --- that they were removed. Anyone who met that end was burnt to a fine white ash and all evidence wiped out as if they never existed. And the authorities believed there were certainly more victims that met their end off the farm.

Agent Miller and a few members of his team were called once again to what was now referred to as "The Taxidermy Room." Not the best name for a crime scene but it certainly fit. Agent Miller and three on his team were led into the room. The bodies had been removed. They had discovered that those first four women in the room were actually Patricia Garrick, Sally Garrick, Elizabeth Garrick, and Rose Garrick. They knew the names from the place cards but now they knew who they were from examining very old records. The records indicated they lived a long time ago --- from the early 1800's. The F.B.I. hadn't yet been able to identify all the girls. There were still five whose identities were unknown --- except for their names on the place cards.

"Agent Miller Sir," the other agent then nodded to the others, "Watch this."

He walked to the back wall, feeling it when suddenly a back portion of the wall slid to the side and behind it was what looked like a tunnel. He flicked a light switch and the long tunnel illuminated looking like a path leading to a cavern of hell.

"Are you ready for a long walk, Sir? It will take about ten minutes. I have flashlights just in case the lights were to go out."

The tunnel was about six feet high and forty-four inches wide. The tunnel was mainly level and had only a few slight bends in it.

"Where does this lead Agent Brook?"

"Well Sir --- we are about to find out. I travelled down to the door and then called you."

"Well --- I'll be damned. Talk about a house of horrors filled with surprises." Miller said as they entered the tunnel.

"Yes Sir --- and I think there may even be more secrets that this house keeps hidden away. I haven't ever come across a house like this Sir."

It was cold in the tunnel and the air was damp --- almost dank. The air seemed unhealthy for a set of breathing lungs. He felt the sides of the tunnel. Not the best place for anyone who had claustrophobic tendencies. It was freezing and smooth to his touch. Finally after a ten-minute walk they came to a door like piece of wood that seemed to be on a forty-five degree slant. Agent Brook swung the door open and then daylight shone in. The old door was full of dust and dirt as it opened --- like it hadn't been used in decades --- maybe longer? There was sunlight surrounded by forest and what was definitely a clearing with a poorly constructed road leading through the forest. The road was bushy and obviously not well travelled. It was more a horse trail than a mud, gravel road.

"What the hell? There's a kind of parking lot and a road?"

"Find out who owns this property and where this road leads to? And check the road for any recent traffic --- tire marks --- footprints --- anything."

"Yes Sir. We will do that today." Agent Brook replied as he wrote it down. They surveyed the immediate area and discovered a set of footprints. They stared at a short trail of footprints that seemed to disappear.

Agent Brook said it first. "Do you think it was him Sir?" Miller looked at Brook.

I don't know but this is certainly one of the most perplexing cases we have ever had on file.

"And the man in the house that was shot in the mouth with the shotgun --- the one that was burnt to death? Do you think it was Kyle? Or do you think it was Lucas? Lucas is still missing as well."

"I don't know Brook. We're checking the D.N.A. and what was left of the body now but he was a twin, meaning the D.N.A. would be inconclusive regardless. I won't be totally convinced until we find both brothers --- both bodies --- dead or alive.

Agent Miller and the two agents that accompanied him stared down the bushy road --- and wondered? Who built that tunnel and for what purpose? How long ago was it built? When was the last time that tunnel was used? And especially where is that other brother? They were lot of unanswered questions and answers were not easy to come by.

It was raining during Kyle's funeral. There wasn't much left of a body in the coffin. It was a real crappy day as a misty rain soaked anyone attending. There were only a few people there. Sisters Sandra, Kera, and Kristen stood shivering under black umbrellas as they stared at the dirt and listened to the pastor but not really hearing his words. The three sisters were crying --- not so much for Kyle but for all the women that their brother was responsible for murdering. They still couldn't believe it was true. There were two undercover agents at the funeral as well. They were dressed in black but stood out like an unknown man in a sandbox with a bunch of kids on a Saturday morning. And there was the unmarked police van just off in the distance taking pictures of all attending the funeral --- just in case the other brother showed up. And then it was over. The pastor shook their hands and offered his condolences and then hurried off to his vehicle. The three girls stared at the tombstone. Sara spoke first.

"What the hell kind of tombstone is that? I've never seen anything like it. I mean what does it mean?"

Kristen looked at her sisters. "I have no idea but it is sure weird. We certainly had a weird, crazy brother. We didn't know him at all?" Then she asked, "Sara, did you put those flowers on top of the tombstone?"

Sara's answer was to the point. "No --- I didn't send those flowers --- I thought one of you did?"

All three sisters looked at each other and shook their head no.

There was the silence of the mist and then Sara whispered as she stared at the flowers, "Well, if none of us sent the flowers, then who did?"

The three sisters stared trancelike at the writing on the tombstone before Kristen spoke softly --- almost as if she was whispering only to herself. "Maybe it's a code --- or a riddle --- a message from the grave? It doesn't make any sense but we all know Kyle and Lucas were extremely intelligent. They were really quite brilliant. Maybe it's a message for us?"

The two sisters turned to look at Kristen and then turned back to stare at the tombstone again. All three gazed at the tombstone for five more minutes in silence --- oblivious to the fact the mist had changed to rain. Finally Sandra spoke ---

"I'm worried about Lucas. It is as if he just disappeared. Even the police can't find him. I wonder if he's dead?" There was a long pause and then, "To hell with this. Let's get the hell out of here. First I want to take a picture of this tombstone though."

She pulled out her cell phone and then snapped three pictures of the tombstone. The other two sisters snapped pictures as well. Then they left --- trying as best they could to stay semi-dry under their umbrellas. They got in the car and then slowly drove out of the cemetery grounds past the gate.

Two F.B.I. agents walked forward to get closer to the tombstone. They stared at it --- their eyes blinking as the raindrops tattered their eyes that were straining to see. They stared at it but were as puzzled as the sisters. They heard the sisters talking earlier.

"Have you ever seen or heard of a tombstone like this before?" the one agent asked the other.

"No --- pretty fucking weird if you ask me. Take some pictures for our coding experts to look at. We'll have to talk with the company that made the tombstone. Maybe they know something? It all looks like mumbo-jumbo to me. I bet you it means something though --- some kind of hidden message from the grave. Bloody weird though. Spooky."

"Yea spooky! Why the hell would a guy leave a tombstone like that?"

They took more pictures --- lots of pictures and stared at the tombstone for a long time but try as they might it made no sense to them. They walked back to their vehicles and got inside and turned to stare at the grave and tombstone one last time before they slowly drove off as the rain started to pour down.

Ninety-three days later at a special medical clinic in an unnamed town in South America a man sat in a chair with a doctor and nurse in front of him. The man's face was covered in bandages.

The doctor was speaking to the man in broken English with a heavy unknown accent. It seemed to be of a mixed descent.

"I am going to carefully remove the bandages now. Remember that I told you your face is still going to have much swelling and bruising. After I remove the bandages I am going to wipe your face with an ointment and then apply special cream to speed up and help with the healing process. Then you will be able to see your new face for the first time. Remember it is going to heal and get much better. It is important to allow only a tiny bit of direct sunlight on your face. It is still delicate and the skin needs to avoid direct sunlight for a time. After --- in three weeks or so when your face has healed and you are ready we can take pictures for your new identification pieces. Are you ready to see your new face? Remember your face will not look so good now but later it will be much better."

"Yes --- doctor. I am ready and anxious to see what I look like. Remove the bandages please."

The doctor began cutting and peeling away the face coverings. It seemed to take forever as he carefully peeled away the layers upon layers of bandages like he was meticulously peeling an onion. The doctor then began wiping the man's face with a cool, damp soft cloth that smelled slightly of mint --- or so the man thought.

The doctor every few seconds would mumble; "Aha" or "Hmmm" or "Good --- Very good."

The nurse generally kept silent but watched closely. She was holding the stainless steel tray for the good doctor to either put the face bandages on or pick up the medical wipes. Finally the doctor said to the man,

"Excellent --- your new face turned out very good."

He pulled a chair in front of the man and sat down and moved very close. The doctor studied his work and finally told the nurse, "The mirror. Hand it to him." The man held out his hand for the mirror. The nurse handed the man the mirror and the man raised it up to look at his new face for the first time. He stared at his face with steely grey eyes checking each new and different feature of his face. There was some bruising and swelling but it looked pretty good considering. Try as he might he couldn't recognize his own face. It was as if he was looking at a stranger. The grey eyes stared back at him. The man nodded his head up and down in approval.

"This is much better than I expected doctor. Terrific!" The man smiled as he continued moving the mirror around while examining his face. His new face mesmerized him as he studied it from every angle.

"Well Sir --- you get what you pay for and you came to the right person. Your fingerprints will be the same --- and your voice the same. You can change your voice though with practice and as you mentioned previously you believe the police don't have your fingerprints. Remember we can wipe them out --- for an extra fee --- as we talked about. Your D.N.A.

is the same as well as your dental records. We can change your dental footprint as well --- for a small fee of course."

"For the moment this should suffice doctor. I'll let you know about the other stuff."

"I need you to stay here as we discussed --- just to make sure everything is perfect but the facial surgery looks very successful." The grey eyes nodded and smiled yet again. "After that you can go where you want to --- with your new passport, driver's licence, etc. There will be no problems I am sure. The new I.D. will be ready three days after the final pictures are taken when the bruising is gone."

"Great Doctor --- that's great. I'm going on a little vacation time --- far away but after that I have some people --- friends --- that I want to stop by and say hi to. Three beautiful ladies are waiting for my unexpected visit. Um --- correction --- make that four beautiful ladies that I want to see one last time. Yes --- I can't forget about the redhead. They are going to be very surprised to see me again. I can't wait to show them my new face and talk about old times. They're going to be very surprised and shocked." The grey eyes studied the reflection in the mirror and they seemed to smile back at him in eerie silence. "I actually owe them something --- but I have a couple of stops to make first. Life is going to be good again." The man smiled.

It's a beautiful Sunday morning. It's early --- six A.M. and the trail is ready for the run. The trail is always ready for you – waiting like a good friend. Amanda Noones is eighteen years old and ready to run. She stretches out --- flexing and warming up and then starts her run. The teenager runs here often --- usually on Sunday mornings. It's the perfect place for running for her. Secluded --- private --- with just the right amount of hills. Amanda sometimes puts her earphones on to listen to her favourite music --- which includes Taylor Swift. She loves Taylor. This time she doesn't put her music on. She begins to run --- slowly at first --- it is part of the warm-up. She welcomes the fresh, clean air in her lungs and the sounds of nature that surrounds her. The birds are singing their morning songs and the spring flowers are already out. Amanda just wishes her friend Lynne was here running with her. Usually Lynne comes out to run on Sunday mornings with Amanda but this morning Lynne must have slept in. Amanda knows her run. Two miles in and then two miles back. She varies her speeds to keep her heartbeat up. She's in great shape. There are benches strategically placed at set distances for visitors on the trails. There are several benches where the trail entrance meets the parking lot. Amanda runs watchful of the twisted roots and rocks along the path. She knows them all as she has run the trail numerous times for the last three years. Near her turnaround point there is a hill that the locals call "Heart Attack Hill." She runs to the top --- her heart pounding and is thankful when she reaches the top. She decides to continue and walks down the hill --- cooling off as she descends. She hasn't been this far before. It opens to a gorgeous meadow with a long walkway leading to a wooden bridge that crosses the meadow. Walking half way across the meadow --- her hands on her hips taking deep breaths she fills her lungs with the needed air. She bends over slightly --- her arms dangling. She shakes her arms out --- straightens up and takes a moment to enjoy the wonderful scenery. She thinks to herself how lovely it is as she sees the morning mist rising slowly from the pond water and the reeds. She hears the frogs --- the many frogs croaking as they too enjoy the warmth of the first morning sun. Suddenly a strange feeling comes over her.

"I wish Lynne was with me," she utters under her breath as her eyes search her surroundings.

She doesn't know why but she has this strange feeling she's being watched. The feeling is definitely there. She looks all around expecting to see someone --- or something. She doesn't. Quickly turning back she starts running again --- running back to the car. She runs to the top of the hill --- seemingly faster this time. She turns to look back but sees nothing but forest --- and the trail. She trots down the hill watching her step and at the bottom begins to run the trail back to her car. Amanda keeps a good pace --- faster than usual. She runs almost all the way --- her heart beating fast but she doesn't have that tired feeling like usual. Must be the adrenalin. Finally as the minutes pass Amanda sees the parking lot ahead and her car and she starts to feel better --- to feel safe. She enters the parking lot and stops in front of her car and takes out her phone. She scans the forest she just left to make sure she is still alone. She is.

"Finally I'm back in an area that has cell service." She lets out a big sigh of relief. There is no cell signal when running the trail. She calls Mom. It's still early but Mom should be up. The phone rings and on the third ring Mom answers. Amanda smiles.

"Hi Amanda. Did you and Lynne have a good run? You certainly left early. I have such a dedicated daughter."

"Hi Mom. Lynne didn't come this time. I guess she slept in so I went running by myself."

"What!!! Amanda --- you know I don't want you out there running by yourself. It's so secluded out there. Don't ever do that again --- promise me."

"Okay Mom --- I promise I won't do it again."

She knew her Mom was probably right. She looked around the parking lot as she spoke. The lot was basically empty just as when she arrived --- except for one other vehicle that was now parked there. There were several different trails for people to enjoy --- and it was a Sunday --- a fantastic day so it could be expected people would show up to use the trails.

"Well all right then --- never again though. Are you heading home now Darling?"

"Yes Mom. I'll be there in about forty-five minutes."

"Okay --- good --- and remember to drive safe. No texting while driving now."

Amanda rolled her eyes. "Yea --- I know Mom --- I know. You know I don't do that."

"Okay --- good. I'm making my world famous low fat smoothies Amanda. I'll have one waiting for you when you get home."

Amanda couldn't stop smiling. She could really go for one of her Mom's smoothies.

"You're the best Mom. I'll see you shortly. I love you Mom."

"I love you too Darling." There was a bit of a pause. "Amanda?"

"Yea Mom?"

"What's all that noise I hear in the background? It seems to be getting louder as we speak."

Amanda looked up to the trees. "It's crows Mom. There are lots and lots of crows here at the parking lot. They just showed up. It's very strange. That's what you're hearing."

And then the crows were quiet. "I'm gonna leave now Mom. See ya soon. Luv ya."

"I love you too Hun."

Just as Amanda was about to get into her car she heard a dog barking. She turned to look and coming out of one of the other trails was a man --- and he had a little puppy dog on a leash. The man saw Amanda and smiled and the puppy saw her too and began barking and pulling on the leash --- trying to run over to say hi to the girl. Amanda couldn't help but smile when she saw the little puppy.

"Aw --- what a cute little puppy." Amanda cooed as the puppy strained the leash to come over and say hello. "He's so cute!" The puppy pulled the stranger over.

"Yea --- a regular cutie pie." The stranger smiled back at her.

"How old is he?" Amanda asked.

"Only six weeks old. It's a she and I guess it's her birthday --- exactly six weeks old today."

"Wow --- she's so tiny and only six weeks old. That's young." She knelt down and stroked the little puppy.

"Yea, but that's the best age --- when they're young. I like them when they're young. They're so --- cute and innocent." The stranger smiled at his comment. "I'm glad I stopped here. I'm just on my way out west --- to visit an old friend --- and her two daughters. Come to think of it --- they are probably right around your age."

She looked up at the man and smiled back. "Would it be okay to pick her up? Do you mind?" Amanda's eyes got big looking at the little puppy. She was focussed on the puppy.

"Be my guest. I don't mind at all. She likes to be picked up."

"What's her name? Oh --- you're such a cutie." Amanda purred as she picked the little puppy up and held it up to her cheek. The puppy began licking her cheek over and over like one might lick an ice cream cone on a hot day.

The man laughed. "Well, well, well --- looks like she's really taken a shine to you. She likes you." The man smiled. He could smell the girl's hair as he moved slightly closer. "At first I named the puppy "Mutt" because she is really just a Mutt but then I named her Lucas. I've had trouble naming her."

"Lucas? But isn't that a boy's name?" Amanda looked at the stranger as her eyebrows furrowed down. "That's silly. She needs a girl's name," Amanda cooed.

"Ya know --- I think you're right. She does need a girl's name. Any suggestions? What would you name her? I'm interested."

"Oh --- I don't know? How about Lucy --- or Suzie --- or something? But not a boy's name."

"Hmmm --- okay --- I like Lucy --- Lucy it is --- and it's kind of close to Lucas." The man smiled. He enjoyed watching Amanda play with the puppy.

Amanda smiled back. She lifted the puppy to the sky and said, "You just got a new name little girl. From now on your name is Lucy. I can't believe how cute she is. I love puppies."

A few seconds later Amanda's phone rang. It was Lynn calling her. The puppy stared at the phone as it rang and rang. Suddenly the puppy began barking at the phone. The phone was also on vibration and it moved slowly across the asphalt of the parking lot at each ring. When the phone would stop ringing --- it would stop moving. Then the phone rang again and twitched as it inched across the parking lot. The little puppy barked and barked at it --- charging at the phone --- then stopping inches away. The puppy was playing with the phone. This was fun. There was no one to answer the phone and so after a few rings it went directly to voice mail.

"Hello --- hello --- Amanda --- are you there? Pick up Amanda. Aahhhhhh!!!!! Sorry but I must have slept in. I had the alarm set? Geez! Do you still want to go for a run on the trails? We could still go? It looks like a great morning out there. Give me a call when you get this message. I'll be waiting. Luv ya!"

When the phone went silent for the final time the little puppy went over to sniff the phone and then sat down beside the phone. The little puppy tilted her tiny head trying to figure out what just happened? The puppy looked around the parking lot for someone --- someone to come and play with her --- someone to help her. The puppy didn't like being tied up to the front of Amanda's car and being left alone. The puppy tried to escape --- pulling on the leash --- tugging on that leash --- growling at the leash but after a minute she gave up. There was no escape for her. The puppy looked around again and then looked up when she heard the crows start calling. The crows were looking down at her from the trees --- jumping from branch to branch --- hopping lower and lower as they descended the trees --- getting ever closer and closer to her. Their eyes were upon her. The young puppy became afraid so she crawled under the car and lay down on the cold, damp pavement --- trying to hide --- waiting and hoping for someone to come and free her. She sighed. She rested her tiny little chin on her baby front paws and she suddenly began to shiver and tremble in fear. Her cute little puppy dog eyes were suddenly sad and afraid as they looked around the parking lot and she was thinking where did everyone go? Won't someone please help me? Please?

ABOUT THE AUTHOR

Steve General is First Nation and graduated with two degrees from the University of Guelph and Laurentian University. His background is in psychology and education. He has an interest in abnormal and criminal psychology. His main field of study has been in education but recently has taken to writing. Growing up he wrote poetry and music and played guitar. He also wrote short stories and as a young teen made tapes with his siblings which included travelling across space and meeting aliens, being in war zones, and prison type scenarios to name but a few.

Other interests include protecting people and animal rights, climate change and saving Earth. He has lived in the remote north of Canada but prefers places with a Starbucks, where he has done much of his writing.

He currently resides in Ontario, Canada.

He may be contacted on twitter @authorsrgen
   Or via e-mail @blueauthor.15@gmail.com

www.ingramcontent.com/pod-product-compliance
Lightning Source LLC
Chambersburg PA
CBHW070859180626
46817CB00003B/842